WHEN THE SOUL MENDS

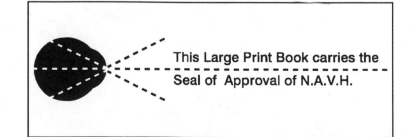

This Large Print Book carries the
Seal of Approval of N.A.V.H.

SISTERS OF THE QUILT, BOOK 3

WHEN THE SOUL MENDS

CINDY WOODSMALL

THORNDIKE PRESS
A part of Gale, Cengage Learning

GALE
CENGAGE Learning™

Detroit • New York • San Francisco • New Haven, Conn • Waterville, Maine • London

LIBRARY OF CONGRESS CATALOGING-IN-PUBLICATION DATA

Woodsmall, Cindy.
  When the soul mends / by Cindy Woodsmall.
    p. cm. — (Thorndike Press large print Christian fiction)
  (Sisters of the quilt : bk. 3)
  ISBN-13: 978-1-4104-1218-8 (alk. paper)
  ISBN-10: 1-4104-1218-0 (alk. paper)
    1. Amish women—Fiction. 2. Amish—Fiction. 3. Large type
  books. I. Title.
  PS3623.O678W477 2009
  813'.6—dc22   2008049615

Published in 2009 by arrangement with WaterBrook Press, a division of Random House, Inc.

To my husband

I could fill a thousand books
with words of love
and still not have shared
but a small portion
of who you are to me.

SISTERS OF THE QUILT SERIES
MAIN CHARACTERS FROM
BOOKS 1 AND 2:
WHEN THE HEART CRIES AND
WHEN THE MORNING COMES

Hannah Lapp — age twenty, Old Order Amish. Two and a half years ago, at seventeen, she left her family home in Owl's Perch, Pennsylvania, in disgrace, and she established a new life in Winding Creek, Ohio, with her shunned aunt Zabeth. She had been secretly engaged to Paul Waddell for several months.

Zeb and Ruth Lapp — Hannah's Old Order Amish parents. In addition to Hannah, they have six other children: Luke, age twenty-four; Levi, age twenty-two; Sarah, age eighteen; Esther, age fourteen; Samuel, age nine; Rebecca, age six.

Luke Lapp — Old Order Amish. He is Hannah's eldest brother and one-time close friend, but he struggled to believe the truth about his sister's tragedy. He is married to Mary Yoder.

Mary Yoder Lapp — age twenty, Old Order Amish. Mary is Hannah's best friend and

7

is married to Hannah's brother Luke. Mary's parents are Becky and John Yoder, and she has nine brothers.

Sarah Lapp — Old Order Amish. She is a troubled person and generated rumors about her sister Hannah that contributed to Hannah's disgrace.

Zabeth Bender — Hannah's aunt who took her in and helped her navigate the Englischer world until she passed away the summer after Hannah turned twenty.

Martin Palmer — turning twenty-nine as the book opens. He's an Englischer raised by Zabeth Bender after his mother died. He and Hannah became friends and a support for each other soon after she arrived in Ohio. He's fallen in love with her and has asked her to marry him.

Faye Palmer — Martin's thirty-five-year-old sister and a drug addict. She ran off, leaving her children, Kevin and Lissa, with Martin and Hannah.

Kevin Palmer — Martin's seven-year-old nephew.

Lissa Palmer — Martin's six-year-old niece.

Paul Waddell — age twenty-four, a Plain Mennonite. As a college senior, he dreamed of marrying Hannah and using his social-work degree to help families.

Then he discovered his fiancée's secret.

Katie [Gram] Waddell — Paul's Plain Mennonite grandmother. She lives a mile from the Lapp home and had Hannah working as a helper until her attack. Paul lived at Gram's during his summer breaks.

Dorcas Miller — age twenty-four, a Plain Mennonite. She is friends with Paul and his family and attended the same Plain Mennonite high school as Paul.

Carol — Paul's older sister and a friend of Dorcas's. Carol's husband is William, and they have two young sons and a baby girl.

Matthew Esh — age twenty-four, Old Order Amish, and a loyal friend to Hannah. He had been in love with Elle Leggett. His parents are Naomi and Raymond Esh, and he has two brothers: David, age fifteen, who died in a fire a few days prior to the start of this book, and Peter, age thirteen.

Elle Leggett — age twenty-five, not confirmed into the Amish church. She was born to Englischer parents, but Elle's mother died, and her father abandoned her when she was a child. Abigail and Hezekiah (Kiah) Zook — a childless, Old Order Amish couple — took her in and raised her Plain.

Dr. Jeffrey Lehman — an older gentleman who is Hannah's mentor and friend. He runs the Amish birthing center where Hannah works.

CHAPTER 1

Hannah's car faded into the distance of the paved horizon. The cold concrete chilling Martin's bare feet and the lukewarm cup of coffee in his hand confirmed that this was no way to begin a Saturday morning. Watching the place where Hannah's vehicle had disappeared, Kevin and Lissa slowly stopped waving. For the first time since Hannah had landed in Ohio — two and a half years ago and not yet eighteen — she was on her way back to her Pennsylvania home and the Old Order Amish family she'd left behind. Maybe he should have insisted on going with her.

Lissa tugged at the hem of his T-shirt. "She packed a lot of stuff."

His niece's big brown eyes reflected fears she didn't know how to voice at five years old. Martin tried to catch Kevin's eye to see how he was doing, but he stared at the ground. Hannah really hadn't packed very much, but this had to feel like a replay of when their mother ran off months ago. When Faye had packed a lot of things into her car, she dropped Kevin and Lissa off with Hannah while Martin was at work, and never returned.

Martin suppressed a sigh, tossed the brown liquid from his cup onto the green grass, and held out his hand to Lissa. "She'll be back, guys."

Lissa slid her hand into his. "Promise?"

"Yes. Absolutely." Martin gave her hand a gentle squeeze. "Her sister called to say that a good friend of Hannah's had an accident and is in the hospital. She'll probably be back in time for her classes on Monday. Wednesday at the latest."

Kevin shoved his hands deep into his pockets. "I didn't know she had a sister."

Martin shrugged, unwilling to say too much about Hannah's past. "She hasn't been to see her family or friends in Pennsylvania for years." With the coffee cup dangling from his fingers, he put his hand on Kevin's shoulder. "Now they need her for a bit." He headed for the house, leading the children.

Earlier this morning, while Hannah called possible hospitals her friend might have been taken to, Martin found an Ohio-

12

Pennsylvania map. Once she knew the name and address of the hospital, they studied the map together while he highlighted the route she'd need to take. He didn't know which caused her the most nervousness: her injured friend, having to see her family again, or driving in unfamiliar territory, but right now he wished he'd pushed a little harder to go with her.

He thought about the gifts he and Hannah had exchanged last night. He'd given her an honorary mother's ring and had slid it onto the ring finger of her left hand. She hadn't agreed yet to marry him, saying his proposal a few weeks back had been brazen and romance-free, which it had. But when he took her to Hawaii over Christmas, he'd find the most romantic way possible to propose.

A smile he couldn't stop seemed to spread across the morning.

Martin opened the front door. "How about some Cracklin' Pops cereal and cartoons?"

The muscles across Hannah's shoulders ached. With the toll roads and service plazas of the Ohio and Pennsylvania Turnpikes behind her, she pulled into the parking lot of the hospital and found a space for her car.

Her frazzled nerves complained, but she was here now — whatever *here* held in store. Trying desperately to remember who she'd become over the last couple of years, not who she'd once been, she stopped at the information desk and waited for the woman to end her phone conversation.

Her sister Sarah had managed to get hold of her phone number and had called last night to tell her about Matthew being hurt in a fire. Hannah promised to come — a pledge she now regretted. In some ways it'd been a lifetime since she'd last faced her Amish community, yet the quaking of her insides said it'd been only yesterday.

The gray-haired woman hung up the phone. "Can I help you?"

"Yes, I need the room numbers for Matthew and David Esh."

The woman typed on the keyboard and studied the screen. She frowned and typed in more info. "We have a Matthew Esh, but there's not a David Esh listed." She jotted down the room number on a small piece of paper. "It's possible he's already been released or perhaps was taken to a different hospital."

"Maybe so. I'll ask Matthew." Hannah

14

took the paper from her. "Thank you."

She went to the elevator, trying to mentally prepare to face Matthew's visitors — people she knew, people she was related to, those who'd accused her of wrongdoing before they washed their hands of her. Nonetheless, she'd come home.

Here. Not home. She corrected herself and felt a morsel of comfort in the thought. These people didn't own her and had no power to control her, not anymore. She stepped off the elevator and headed toward Matthew's room. Odd, but the place appeared empty of any Amish. She gave a sideways glance into the waiting room as she passed it. There were no Plain folk in there either.

Stopping outside the room, Hannah said a silent prayer.

Ready or not, she pressed the palms of her hands against the door and eased it open.

A man lay in the bed, but she couldn't see his face for the bandages across his eyes. He turned his head toward the door.

"Hello?" His voice echoed through the room.

"Matthew?"

His forehead wrinkled above the bandages, and he clenched his jaw. "Just go

15

home . . . or wherever it is you're livin' these days. I got no more use for you."

She froze. If this is what awaited her from Matthew, one of her few friends, what would the community be like? But maybe the man wasn't Matthew. His body was larger, shoulders thicker and rounded with muscle. His voice was raspy and deeper than she remembered. And Matthew would have visitors, wouldn't he?

"Matthew?"

He shifted in the bed, angling his head.

"It . . . it's Hannah."

Only the soft buzzing sound of electronics could be heard as she waited for his response. Wondering a thousand things — whether the eye damage was permanent, why he didn't have a marriage beard, and where everyone was — she moved closer to the bed.

Finally he reached his hand toward her. "Hannah Lapp, at last back from the unknown world."

Ignoring his unsettling tone, she put her fingers around his outstretched hand and squeezed. "How are you?"

The stiltedness of their words said that a lot more than two and a half years had passed between them.

He shrugged and then winced, reminding

her of the pain he must be in. "I've lost David . . . and every part of my business. How
do ya expect me to be?"

David is dead?

The news twisted her insides, making her
fight to respond. "I'm so sorry, Matthew."

He eased his hand away from hers. "I'm
grateful you came all this way, but I'm too
tired to talk right now."

"Sure. I understand. Where is everyone?"

The door swooshed open, and a nurse
walked in. "I'm sorry, miss. He's not to have
visitors." She held up a laminated, printed
sign that said No Visitors Allowed. "It'd
slipped off his door."

That explained why he didn't have friends
or relatives here, but he didn't appear to be
in bad enough shape for a doctor to give
that order. Hannah studied the nurse, but
she just shook her head without saying
more. The only reason he wouldn't be *al-*
lowed to have visitors was because he'd
requested that of the staff. And clearly he
didn't want to make an exception for her.

"Okay." She slid her hand into his once
more, wishing she could at least know more
about the condition of his eyes. But he
seemed in no mood for questions. "I'll come
back when you're feeling better."

"There's no sense in that. I'm goin' home

17

tomorrow. But . . . David's funeral is Monday." His voice cracked, and he took a ragged breath. "If you're still here, we could meet up afterward while *Mamm* and everyone is distracted with the gatherin' at the house."

The words Matthew didn't say weighed heavily. He didn't want her going into the community to see anyone. He wanted to meet her alone, in secret.

Unable to respond, she grappled with the space separating them. She'd expected distance from her *Daed* and Mamm, the church leaders, and even Gram, but she hadn't for one second thought Matthew would sidestep her. He'd understood, even disobeyed the bishop to help her. Built the coffin for her baby, dug the grave, and said the prayer. Taken her to the train station, bought her a ticket, and stayed with her until time for the train to depart the next day. Did he now regret that he'd stuck by her?

Unwilling to push for a specific plan, Hannah gave his hand a final squeeze before pulling away. "Sure. I . . . I'll catch up with you then."

Desperate to clear her mind, Hannah hurried out of the hospital and into her car. She pulled out of the hospital parking lot

18

and drove — to where, she didn't know. Old feelings of loneliness washed over her, but she kept driving, as if she could outrun the sting.

By the time her emotions began to settle, she had no idea where she was. Glancing in the rearview mirror, she pulled her car onto the shoulder of the road. Fields of yet-uncut hay seemed to go on forever as cars whizzed past. Unsure of the county or town she was in, she grabbed the map off the seat beside her and searched for her location. Nothing looked familiar. Realizing the stupid thing was upside down, she flipped it around.

At this moment all she wanted was to be at home with Martin, but the next few days had to be walked through first. She'd given Sarah her word. Even as that thought crossed her mind, she wondered if there was morc to it. If maybe some deeply hidden part of her wanted to be here. Desperate to hear Martin's voice, to feel like she did when with him, she took her cell phone out of her purse.

"Hey, sweetheart, where are you?"

A sense of belonging washed over her the moment she heard his voice. "I was hoping you could tell me."

He laughed. "Are you serious?"

"Yeah, sort of."

"Do you know the name of the road you're on?"

"No. All I know is I want to be there, not here." In spite of her effort to sound upbeat, she came across as pathetic and didn't want to imagine what Martin must be thinking about now.

"Look at the directions I printed out, and tell me what point you got to before you became lost."

"I turned left out of your driveway."

His low chuckle was reassuring. "Very cute."

Determined to show Martin she could handle this, she studied the map. "Yeah, you've told me that before, only then you could see me." She angled the map sideways. "Wait. I got it. I know where I am." She pressed her fingertip against the map and followed the line before realizing she was wrong. "Lost without you."

"Metaphorically, I love the sound of that, but you should have let me take you there. You've never driven anywhere outside a twenty-five mile radius of Winding Creek."

"You're not helping."

"It's a little hard to help from here with no" — he mockingly cleared his throat — "POB to work from."

She heard the familiar beeps of his laptop

starting up. "POB . . . ah, engineering lingo."

"Yep. Point of beginning. I'm logging onto Google maps right now and will try the satellite visual. Tell me about your surroundings."

"Oh yeah, that's a great plan. I'm surrounded by cow pastures and no houses. Found the right spot yet? There's a Holstein watching me."

"On Google maps, no. The right spot for you? Yes, it's right here in Ohio with us."

She heard the rustle of fabric. "Did you go back to bed after I left?"

"I ate breakfast and watched cartoons with Lissa and Kevin. But then Laura arrived, so I let the nanny do her job while I took a nice long nap, until you became a damsel in distress. The Mary Jane to my Peter Parker."

"What? Damsel in distress," she muttered. "So what does that make you when you don't know the difference between a skillet and a pot?"

"A typical male who just happens to be . . ." He paused. "Come on, work with me here, phone girl. Who just happens to be . . ."

"Charming and intelligent." She mimicked his clearing of the throat. "According to him."

21

He laughed. A loud crash echoed through her cell. Lissa screamed, and Hannah's breath caught.

A bang, as if his door had been shoved open and hit the wall, filtered through the receiver. "Uncle Martin, Laura said you better come see this. Lissa might need stitches."

"Phone girl, I'll need to call you back in a few. Okay?"

The next sound she heard was the complete silence of a cell-phone disconnection. Wondering what she was doing here rather than being there to help Martin, she closed her phone. At sixty-two, Laura was a skilled nanny, but Hannah wanted to be the one with him going through whatever the day brought.

Looking at the map one last time, she thought about calling Dr. Lehman. He was more than just her boss, and he regularly visited relatives in Lancaster, some forty miles southeast of here, so he might be able to help her. But rather than chance disturbing him, she decided to continue driving until she found a landmark she recognized. She pulled back onto the road. After a solid hour and many times of turning around, she found the road that led to Owl's Perch. Martin hadn't called her back, and she hadn't been able to reach him. His voice mail picked up immediately, which meant his phone was turned off. Whatever was going on, she bet his Saturday was tough, nanny's help or not.

The oddest sensation slid up her back as she drove alongside the Susquehanna River. She'd been in this very spot three years ago, heading for Hershey Medical Center because Luke and Mary had been taken there by helicopter after their accident. She remembered the days that followed, months of hiding her rape from everyone but her parents and hoping against hope that she wouldn't lose Paul.

"Brilliant, Hannah, you were afraid of losing a jerk." She mumbled the words, then turned the radio up louder, trying to drown out the whispers of resentment against him. The familiar territory had to be the reason for the fresh edge of offense that cut against her insides. In all the time she'd known Paul, he'd lived on a college campus not far from here, except for the summers, when he stayed with his Gram. She'd only seen this area twice before, once on the way to the hospital to see Luke and Mary and again about two weeks later on the way back home, but in each instance she'd been keenly aware that she was in Paul's stomping grounds. At the time she felt connected to him, hopeful they could overcome the obstacles that stood between them and getting married.

Silly, childish dreams.

Needing a stronger diversion than worship songs, she pushed the radio button, jumping through the stations until she found a familiar song by Rascal Flatts, "I'm Moving On." She cranked up the sound full blast and sang along, assuring her anxieties that she would survive the oddity of being here as well as the misery of not being with Lissa throughout whatever ordeal she faced.

The waters of the Susquehanna weren't brown and frothy this time. The river looked crystal clear as the afternoon sun rode across the ripples. In less than an hour she'd be in Owl's Perch, and as badly as she wanted to arrive, she didn't want to face her father. What was she going to say to him?

A dozen songs later, that question was still on her mind as she drove into her parents' driveway. Her mouth dry and palms sweaty, she got out of her car. The cool September breeze played with her dress and loose strands of her pinned-up hair, but there wasn't anyone in sight, and the wood doors on the house were shut. Without any sounds of voices or movement coming through the screened windows, she was pretty confident

24

no one was home. She knocked loudly anyway. It was rare for everyone to be gone if it wasn't a church day.

When no one answered, she made a complete circle, taking in the old place, its chicken coop, barns, lean-to, and smokehouse. A sense of nostalgia reverberated through her as she absorbed the homestead where she'd been born and her mother before her. The tops of the huge oaks rustled. She walked to the hand pump, pushed and pulled the handle until water poured forth, and filled a tin cup. Taking a sip of the cool water, Hannah sensed an odd connectedness to her ancestors. A great-grandfather on her mother's side had dug this well, and springs that fed it had been sustaining her family for generations.

The quiet peacefulness moved through her, making her realize how much she'd once cherished parts of the Plain life. She hadn't expected this, and for the first time in a long time, she wished she understood herself better. Spotting the garden, she walked up the small hill to the edge of it. The last of the corn had been harvested weeks ago, and now all that remained were the cut-off brown stalks. The pea plants had been pulled up for the season. The cold-weather plants — broccoli, cauliflower, and cabbage — were thriving. She'd loved gardening from the first time her Daed had placed seeds in the palms of her hands and helped her plant them. Daed and she had come to the garden every day, watching, weeding, and watering. In the end those seeds produced enough food for her family to eat well all year long. Suddenly missing who her Daed and she had once been, her eyes misted. How much easier it would be to sort through her feelings if she understood the magnitude of emotions that came out of nowhere and took her to places she didn't know existed. Perhaps in that one thing, she and Sarah weren't so very different. Her sister seemed to respond immediately to the emotions that marched through her, and Hannah stood against them, but either way they left a mark.

Her mind returned to the strange conversation she'd had with Sarah — the jumbled words and thoughts that circled with no destination. She needed to find out what was going on with her. Deciding to go see Luke and Mary for answers, she went to her car. She backed out of the driveway and headed down the familiar dirt road she used to walk regularly when going to Gram's. The hairs on her arms stood on end as the paved road turned into a gravel one, the one where the attack had taken place. She locked her car doors and turned the music up to blaring, trying not to think about it. A few minutes later she pulled into Luke's driveway.

Getting out of the car, she noticed that his shop didn't appear to be open. The windows, blinds, and doors were closed. It seemed like he'd have the place open on a Saturday. She knocked loudly before trying the door.

When it opened, she stepped inside. The shadowy place didn't look anything like a usable shop. It looked like a storage room for buggy parts, not leather goods. Waiting at the foot of the stairs that led to the second-floor apartment, Hannah called, "Luke? Mary?"

The door at the top of the steps creaked open, and a half-dressed young man stepped out. "They don't live here. Never have. We rent the place."

He might be Amish, but she couldn't tell for sure since he only had on a sleeveless T-shirt and pants.

He descended a few steps.

Hannah backed up. "I'm sorry for interrupting you."

"No interruption at all."

Luke and Mary never lived in the home

above the harness shop, both of which were built by the community just for them? Unwilling to ask any questions, Hannah went to her car.

Opening the door to the vehicle, she spotted Katie Waddell's white clapboard home amid fenced pasturelands. The once-worn footpath from here to Gram's was thick with grass. Hannah closed the door to her car. Maybe it was time to push beyond her fears. She headed for the old farmhouse. Except for a few fences that needed mending, the place looked good. Her heart pounded something fierce as she crossed Gram's screened porch to the back door.

"Look at me, Hannah." As if catapulted back in time, she could hear Paul's voice and feel the soft rumble of his words against her soul. *"I've been aching to talk to you before I return to college. There are some things I just can't write in a letter."*

She shuddered, trying to dismiss the memory and ignore the feelings that washed over her as she knocked on the door. No one answered. She peered through the gape in the curtains that hung over the glass part of the door and knocked louder. After several minutes she gave up, left the porch, and moved to the side yard, thinking Gram might be in the garden. But one look at the garden said no one had been in it for quite a while. Paul's old rattletrap of a truck sat under a pavilion near the garden, the hood up and the engine dangling above by a thick chain.

Eeriness crawled over her skin as if she were trapped in one of those *Twilight Zone* episodes Martin had told her about. Whatever was going on, life seemed to have changed for everyone else as much as it had for her. She headed for her car. It was time to find the hotel near Harrisburg where Martin had made reservations for her and settle in for the night. She could have stayed at a hotel closer to her community, but according to Martin, the one he'd chosen was nicer: very safe, with breakfast included, and a business center in case she needed Internet access. Unfortunately she'd be stuck there all day tomorrow since it was a church day. Visits by estranged Amish may not be tolerated any day, but especially on a Sunday. And Matthew had made it clear she needed to wait until after the funeral to be seen by the community as a whole and by his family in particular. If that's how strongly Matthew felt, her father would magnify that sentiment a thousandfold.

Regardless of what it took, she'd get through the next few days with her dignity intact. They'd trampled her spirit once. She'd not give them another chance.

CHAPTER 2

Hannah.

Paul woke with a start.

The nighttime breeze rustled through the sheers of the half-open window. He turned the alarm clock toward him. Three a.m. Regardless of the time, it wasn't likely he'd go back to sleep.

He pushed her "Past and Future" quilt off him.

"Past and Future." Paul stood and began folding the quilt. Even in the dim glow of street lamps, he could see the handiwork of the Amish girl who'd promised to marry him. Last Tuesday he'd found her — seen her, rather — in front of an upscale Ohio home in the embrace of her husband.

It was time to get this thing off his bed and out of his apartment. Mary had given it to him after Hannah left, saying it had more of Hannah in it than anything else. It was supposed to keep him warm until she returned and they wed. He wasn't sure what to do with it just yet, but it wasn't staying here.

Dark gave way to light as he sat with a coffee cup and a stack of his clients' files on the table in front of him. Reading and taking notes on Andrew Brown's family, he continued to map out the issues each family member dealt with to see if he could find a common thread, a connected problem he was missing. He'd head for work, then go to Gram's and mend a few fences before nightfall, but right now these moments without interruption belonged to him.

The shrill ring of his phone ended his private study time, and he knew Monday had begun.

He rose from the table and lifted the receiver. "Paul Waddell."

"Paul, it's me, Luke. I hate to call you so early in the morning. Should have thought to contact you sooner, but it's been crazy around here."

"What's going on?"

"I'm sure you've heard by now, but I thought I'd call anyway."

"I've been in the mountains all weekend, camped out with friends."

"E and L shops burned to the ground Friday."

Paul's thoughts jumped to each person in the Lapp and Esh families. "I'm really sorry. Is everyone okay?"

"No." Luke paused. "David died." His voice wavered. "And Matthew was injured. Aside from needing therapy and some scarring on his back and shoulders, Matthew will be fine." Luke's words came out quiet and slow. "David's funeral is this afternoon, one o'clock, at our Old Order cemetery."

Funeral. Hating what this meant for Matthew and his family, Paul couldn't manage to respond.

"Things haven't work out between Elle and Matthew, and . . . well . . . I think it'd do him good for as many friends as can to be there."

"Absolutely, I'll be there."

"Good. I knew I could depend on you. But, uh, look, I should warn you." Luke took a heavy breath and talked even slower. "Sarah found the paper you brought to the house with Hannah's phone number and address. She called her and asked her to come home. We haven't seen anything of her yet, but Sarah swears she promised to come for a few days and was supposed to be here two days ago. Sarah came up missing early Saturday morning, and when we figured out she'd hired a driver to take her into Harrisburg, we all went there looking for her. We found her at the train station, determined to wait for Hannah."

Paul appreciated the sentiments behind Luke's explanation, knowing his friend was trying to prepare him for bumping into Hannah. "Well, if she does come, it'll be a good time for your community and family to make peace with her before any more time passes. I'll see you this afternoon, and if you need anything, just call."

Paul drove to work, second-guessing himself as to whether he should take the day off or not. He pulled into his parking space and headed for his office. Throughout the morning he tried to hear every word his clients spoke, but he found the clock jumping in time and he'd taken no notes during the sessions. It wasn't so much knowing Hannah was supposed to come back as feeling concern for how her family would react to her. She bore few traits of having been raised Plain. That was obvious the moment he saw her last week — wearing a short-sleeved, thin cotton dress with no pleats while laughing and kissing a man.

Feeling like a second-rate counselor, he checked the clock. "Andrew, our time is up for today, but if you can allow extra time next week, I'd like to go back over some of this."

"My wife likes what she's seeing in me. I do too. Even m-my son seems better."

Andrew's stumbling over the word *my* reminded Paul they had quite a bit of road to cover before healing included the father-and-son relationship.

Paul rose. "I'd like to see your wife and children again as soon as it fits their schedule."

Andrew followed his cue and stood. "You're a lot of help, Paul. I haven't lost it with the kids for over a month."

He walked Andrew out of his office and down the carpeted stairway. They stopped at the receptionist's desk, which sat in the large open area of the old foyer, dining room, and living room combo — all of which were furnished in home-style comfort for clients of the Better Path. The office space and mission was an old homestead, and everything in it was designed to retain the homey feel.

"Halley, would you put Andrew on the books for the same time next week, and he won't be charged for this week."

"Really?" Andrew looked surprised.

Although guilt shadowed Paul, he couldn't tell Andrew why he wasn't charging him.

It'd taken too long to build a rapport with the man to undermine his confidence with a confession of not hearing all he had said today. "Take care, Andrew, and I'll see you next week." He turned back to Halley. "Did you reach my appointments for this afternoon and reschedule?"

"Yes. And Dorcas called."

Paul nodded. "Did she say what she needed?"

"No, but she asked you to call her before you leave today."

"Okay, thanks." Paul went back up the stairs and into his office. It'd feel good to talk with Dorcas, to try to connect with reality over any lingering dreams of Hannah's returning to him.

He lifted the phone and dialed the Miller home.

"Hello." Dorcas sounded tired.

"Good morning. What's up?"

"Paul." The excitement in her tone was undeniable, and he smiled.

"Did you doubt I'd call back?"

"I wasn't sure how long it'd take you to get the message and then find the time. I wanted to remind you of Evelyn's birthday today. Everyone's meeting here for dinner. Your parents are arriving around five. I'd hoped you could be here by seven."

He'd totally forgotten about her sister's birthday celebration tonight. "Did you hear about the fire in Owl's Perch?"

"Yeah, I heard. My mother's cousin Jeanie called. That's so awful."

"I'm going to the funeral, and I want to stay around here today in case there's anything I can do for Matthew. Sorry."

"Oh." She sounded disappointed. "I should have thought of that. Of course you're going."

On a whim Paul came up with a plan she would like. "Since I'm pulling weekend duty at the clinic, I'm off tomorrow. I need to get some fences mended at Gram's. Care to spend the day there with me?"

"You're serious?"

"Sure, why not?"

"Well . . . no reason. You've just barely shown any interest in . . . well, you know, and your invitation is just surprising, that's all."

He paused, willing himself to open up to her. "I've been thinking about things this morning, and maybe I'd held on to the idea of Hannah's coming back because I didn't want to admit defeat more than I actually wanted her back."

"That makes sense."

"I guess I should've figured this out way

before now."

"Do you think she'll return for the funeral?"

"Maybe, but I'm sure you'll feel better when you hear that she's married."

"She's married?"

"Yes, I found out when I went to Ohio last week."

"I'm really sorry."

Confident she wasn't all that sorry, he imagined she was probably relieved and quickly becoming hopeful. Paul placed his latest notes on Andrew into the appropriate file. "That's nice of you, but it's water under the bridge and long gone. Do you want to come to Gram's tomorrow?"

"Absolutely."

He slid the file into the cabinet and locked it. "I'll come get you in the morning, and we'll go out for breakfast first."

"Oh, Paul, that sounds wonderful."

"Good. I need to run. The funeral starts in an hour."

"I'll see you tomorrow. Okay?"

"Sure thing. Bye." Paul hung up the phone, feeling more on track with his life than he had in years. Why had it taken seeing Hannah married and happy before he could connect with his own life?

He grabbed his suit jacket and headed for

his car. Driving toward the cemetery, Paul was thinking about the Esh and Lapp families, wondering what, if anything, he could do to make this time easier. He'd sure like to help get the shop back in working condition — if they would accept his help. The community itself felt nothing but distrust for Paul, as if maybe it was his fault Hannah had been pregnant and had run away. Thankfully, Luke and Matthew didn't feel that way, but whether Paul would be allowed to pitch in and help rebuild was another matter.

Speculating whether Hannah would actually come home for this or not, he trailed behind the long line of horses and buggies as they slowly wound their way to the cemetery. Thoughts of the last two years with Dorcas floated through his mind. Maybe he hadn't been waiting for Hannah to return. She'd been seventeen years old and six months pregnant when he left her standing there crying after him. Maybe guilt had more to do with his waiting all this time.

The stark black buggies set against a nearby field with large rolls of golden, baled hay looked picturesque, but the reality of life, anyone's life, never seemed to match the peaceful image of a quick glimpse. He parked his car near a group of horses and carriages in a dirt and gravel area across the street from the burial spot. Those who'd come to pay their respects quietly made their way to the site.

Unlike most Amish funerals, all parts of the ritual would be conducted with a closed casket because of the fire. Their heritage kept them from having a photo to set up on a table near the casket like *Englischers* might.

Hanging back with the other non-Amish neighbors, Paul spotted Matthew near the grave as men prepared to lower the casket into the ground using ropes. Matthew was the only Amish man here without a jacket on. It had to be due to the burns on his back. Since Paul had come to assure Matthew he had people who cared, he stepped around the crowd, including Hannah's parents and younger siblings, and went to Matthew and offered his hand. "I'm really sorry."

Matthew didn't even look up as he shook Paul's hand. "*Ya.* It's a miserable thing."

Luke caught Paul's eye and gave a nod, and Paul returned it. Mary stood beside him, leaning heavily into her husband.

He reached to clasp Matthew's shoulder, but Matthew pulled away. "Second-degree burns leave the nerves exposed. It's more pain than I can tolerate most days."

Wishing for the right words, Paul nodded. "I should have thought . . . Matthew, when you're well enough and begin clearing the debris and rebuilding, I want to help."

Staring at the freshly dug hole, Matthew sighed. "Hannah came to see me Saturday." He gave a stiff shrug. "I wasn't sure what I thought of her returning — still not. But I'm sure I came across unwelcoming and —"

An Amish man spoke loudly. "Dear ones, let's bow in silence."

The weight of today settled over Paul as he closed his eyes. The gentle winds across his face and the warmth of the sun made the day one that should be enjoyed. Instead the focus was on loss.

Death seemed like such an odd thing. One did not have to die or know anyone who'd died to experience it. Death came without pallbearers or grave sites. The death of a dream, hope, and even love. He hadn't re-alized love could die. One day breathing. One day in poor health. One day dead. Never to be resurrected.

But it didn't have to be that way, not for every family that became ill. What had hap-pened to Hannah and him had been hor-rible, but the death of a family — one that had taken a vow before God — that's where he wanted to stop death. Like with Andrew's family and . . .

Another image of Dorcas filled his mind, making him long to connect with life. It was too precious and too short not to spend it on love and family. Life beckoned to be lived. Love called to be embraced. And he intended to do both.

When the preacher said *amen,* another Amish man stepped forward and began reading a hymn while the pallbearers slowly placed dirt on the coffin. Paul looked through the crowd, praying for the families that were represented. Movement off to the left caught his eye. He glanced in that direction, just beyond the trees and near the shoulder of the road where a few cars had parked.

Hannah.

She was wearing a dark green dress and leaning against a gold Honda a hundred feet away. She removed the sunglasses from her face. An air of control and poise surrounded her like an aura. He thought she was right not to come too close, to handle this quietly and with no fanfare. Yet she was present for Matthew's sake . . . and maybe her own. Even if her people could recognize her, they wouldn't see her where she stood, not unless —

"Hannah!" Sarah's scream pierced the formality.

Her father grabbed her arm. "Hush."

Every eye turned to where Sarah was looking and saw Hannah. Mary gasped and started to head for her, but Luke put his arm around her and whispered something.

Sarah broke free of her father's grip and took off running. "Hannah!"

Zeb Lapp followed her, unable to keep up with her all-out sprint.

Hannah dipped her chin and rubbed her forehead. Paul hated this. He wanted to step out and go to her, to give her at least one person as a shield against the murmurs and stares. Someone to be a friend. But he'd only make things worse for her if he did.

He understood anew why she'd given up and left once she lost hope in their relationship. The reason she hadn't returned — until her sister made contact, needing her — stared hard at him, and he got it. There simply was no winning inside Owl's Perch for Hannah Lapp.

CHAPTER 3

Every person Hannah had known growing up turned to stare at her.

Her Daed was still a good thirty feet away when he finally caught Sarah's arm. "Stop this. Now."

But she flailed her free hand and kept heading for Hannah. "You came! I knew you'd keep your promise!"

Her Daed lost his grip, and she took off again. He took long strides toward Hannah, and when his gaze met hers, she felt like an unruly child. "Well, do something."

Hannah read his lips and his expression more than heard his words. She nodded and closed the gap between them. Sarah grabbed her, almost knocking her over. Unexpected warmth flooded Hannah. No one could have made her believe the feelings she had for her sister right now. Sarah had caused such harm to Hannah's life in the past. And yet the tie to her younger sister was undeniable.

The hug lasted a good minute before Hannah removed her sister's arms. "You have to go back now, Sarah. We'll have all the time you need later."

She glanced at the funeral and back to Hannah. An expression crossed her face as if she'd forgotten where she was and why. She looked at her palms and began scrubbing a thumb against the palm of her other hand.

Hannah slid her hands into Sarah's, stopping her sister's odd gesture. She squeezed her sister's hands and nodded toward the cemetery. "Go on."

Sarah looked a bit calmer.

Daed arrived, out of breath and definitely out of patience, if he'd had any to begin with. He paused, his face red. His eyes narrowed, and he skimmed her from head to toe.

"What were you thinking?" Her father whispered the words. "Gone for more than two years and arrive just in time to interrupt a community funeral. And look at you." He pointed at her hair and then her dress. "You didn't remain Plain."

Wondering if she looked that different or if she simply wasn't what he'd expected, she shook her head. She wasn't Plain, but she was his daughter.

He pointed to her car. "Go on to the house, and Sarah will meet you there later."

Hannah looked across the crowd that stared at her with heads grouped in pairs, whispering. Refusing to allow powerlessness to engulf her, she lifted her chin, squared her shoulders, and slid her sunglasses on. Before closing her car door, she heard the preacher speaking loudly, beginning the service again. Hannah drove away.

Of all the possible times to cause a scene, a funeral had to be the worst. She never should have come.

Doing as her father told her, she pulled into the driveway of the Lapp homestead. When she'd talked to Martin yesterday, he'd told her that Lissa had climbed his five-tier glass shelves, and it broke with her on it. She received four stitches in her left leg on Saturday. Lissa couldn't be in better hands than Martin's, but that didn't keep Hannah from wishing she'd stayed with them.

She got out of the car and headed toward the bench that sat on a knoll behind the Lapp home. It favored the one at her aunt Zabeth's cabin, the one where she and Zabeth used to sit at the beginning and ending of each day as oft as the weather permitted.

Drawing a deep breath, she took in every familiar aroma she'd grown up with. The smells changed with the seasons, but September's fragrance brought a flood of memories — summer's heat breaking, the last of the garden's produce, and the aroma of freshly cut hay. Her childhood had been as idyllic as allowed any human on this planet. It wasn't until she hit her teen years and began wanting things that weren't Old Order Amish that life under her father's roof became bumpy.

She let her mind wander, and it filled with a dozen hayrides, take-a-pet-to-school days, and summertime produce and lemonade stands. Memories of laughter ringing across the fields as she played with her siblings eased in and out of her thoughts. In the midst of them all, a vision of Paul crept in, and before she could stop it, she heard his voice as clearly as the day he asked her to marry him.

"Hannah, you are all my thoughts and hopes . . . There's no one for me but you . . ."

A shudder ran through her, and she slid her fingers over the diamond and ruby ring Martin had placed on her finger before she left.

47

The sounds of a horse and buggy approaching interrupted her thoughts, and she stood. There wasn't a male in the buggy, just Mamm and Sarah. Before Mamm pulled the buggy to a stop, Sarah jumped off, ran to Hannah, grabbed her hand, and pulled her toward the barn. "We gotta talk."

Hannah tugged back, stopping Sarah from leading her anywhere. "Yes, I know. That's what I'm here for, but I need to see Mamm first."

Her mother pulled the buggy to a stop beside Hannah and sat there, staring. Feeling as if she'd just stepped out of a Victoria's Secret ad, she reminded herself how modest her below-the-knee, dark green cotton dress was. Her favorite dresses were made of mostly polyester with enough spandex to make them fit and flow in a way that wasn't appreciated among the Amish. She'd chosen her dress today carefully, knowing how ingrained the views toward clothing were.

Her mother's brown eyes locked on hers. "Hannah?"

The doubt in her voice said she had changed in more ways than just her clothing.

She swallowed hard, unsure how to break the ice between them. "Hi, Mamm."

Mamm set the brake, gathered her skirts,

and climbed out of the buggy. She stood in front of Hannah, saying nothing. Her mouth opened a few times as tears welled in her eyes.

Hannah slid her arms around her and hugged her. "I'm fine, Mamm. I told you that in the letters."

Her mother engulfed her, her body shaking as she sobbed. "Oh, child, how could you stay gone so very, very long?" She took a step back and stared into Hannah's eyes. "I've missed you."

Hannah knew nothing to say. If her parents had tossed any understanding or affection her way before she boarded that train, she might have stayed. But now she couldn't receive an unspoken apology without question.

"How did you see me that night, put balm on the gashes in my hands, and dry my tears, yet decide later that I hadn't been attacked after all?" Her insides quaked as she dared to speak her mind. In Zabeth's home, openness had been cherished more than restraint, and Hannah longed for that with her Mamm.

Her mother's eyes grew wide with disbelief, and Hannah knew she'd just burned the bridge Mamm had wanted to cross.

Hannah slid one hand into the side pocket

of her dress, wishing she could talk to Zabeth about all that was going on. "How did you get my number?"

Sarah clutched Hannah's arm firmer. "Paul brought it to the house last week."

Paul knew how to reach me? The slap in the face stung a bit even now, and she wouldn't mind being able to return the favor. A wallop of one. He knew how to reach her, which really wasn't the point — not any longer. What did she care? Years ago he could've returned her call the night she stayed at the hotel, waiting until time to go to the train station, and yet he didn't.

Hannah focused on her sister, thinking maybe she was mistaken. "He brought my address and phone number to the house?" She searched Mamm's eyes for understanding. "Here?"

Mamm nodded. "He's made a bit of peace with your Daed. I think he and Luke are friends. Matthew too."

Disbelief rang in her ears, making her lightheaded.

For the first time ever she realized the man played games. He had to. It was the only thing that explained his behavior. He didn't return her calls or try in any way to make peace with her, and yet he'd become friends with Matthew and Luke, and he'd brought information about Hannah's life to her Daed.

Of all the nerve . . .

Mamm shooed a fly away. "I talked to him once myself. He . . . he doesn't seem to be such a bad guy after all."

"Oh good grief!" Hannah took a step back. Paul had them totally bamboozled. "You know what? Let's not talk about Paul."

Sarah started clearing her throat in long, weird sounds while rubbing her right thumb across the palm of her left hand again. Hannah remembered the odd sounds as an old habit of her sister's when she was tense. The palm-rubbing thing was newer.

Mamm looked bewildered. "But, Hann —" Her mother shook her head. "You're impossible to understand. What's wrong with me thinking he's okay? Isn't that what you wanted?"

She thrust her hands, palms up, toward her mother. "I wanted that when it might have mattered, and there's no way you would have ever given him a chance if I'd stayed, but now you do?" She sighed. "And I'm the one who's impossible to understand?"

Sarah began rocking back and forth on her heels. "The male cats eat the mama cats' babies." The words pushed out through labored breathing. "And fires destroy truth that's not even there." She put her thumb on her middle finger and turned them, as if doing the motion for the itsy, bitsy spider song. She sang the words. "The tongue sets on fire the course of life."

Chills climbed up Hannah's back and through her scalp. What was wrong with her sister?

Mamm clapped her hands. "Stop it, Sarah."

Her sister stopped moving her hands. Her eyes darted back and forth. "You can't hate each other." She moaned.

Hannah reeled under the shock of her sister's words. She didn't hate Mamm, not even close, but her mother had stood silent as the men decided Hannah was a liar and guilty of sexual sin.

Sarah's lips were turning blue as she continued breathing fast and heavy.

Hannah put her arm around her. "Mamm, get a lunch bag and bring it here." She forced a smile. "Sarah, look at me."

This breathing issue was new, wasn't it? Sarah turned her head, avoiding her gaze.

Mamm stepped forward. "What's going on?"

Hannah placed her fingers on Sarah's jugular, taking a quick assessment of her heart rate. "She's hyperventilating, best I can tell. Get a lunch bag, please." Hannah took Sarah's cheeks into her hands. "Sarah, look at me. I want you to imagine being in a field of flowers. Remember that game?" Hannah did. When they were kids, she spent as much time trying to calm Sarah down as she spent doing chores.

Mamm came out the door with the lunch sack. Hannah took it, shook it open, scrunched the top part, and put it over Sarah's mouth.

She tried to claw it away.

Hannah resisted. "None of that. You called me to help, and you're going to let me help, right?" She covered Sarah's mouth with the edge of the bag. "Imagine that we're lying in the field, counting all the different types of wildflowers: black-eyed Susans, morning glories, daisies, forget-me-nots . . ." She prattled on like when they were younger.

But this was different. Sarah was different. Worse. Whatever was going on, it wasn't a bad case of nerves or a meanspirited sister or even jealousy, as she'd thought for years.

Sarah's breathing eased.

"That's my little sister." She lowered the bag, but she intended to keep it with her.

Sarah's fists were clinging to the sleeves of Hannah's dress. "Where's the baby?"

Hannah blinked. "What?"

"You . . . you gave birth. Where is the baby?"

Hannah looked to Mamm.

Mamm's face paled. "After you left, Sarah began looking for things. We didn't know what she was searching for." Tears streaked down her face. "I . . . I guess the baby's been it all along." Mamm wiped her face with her apron, closed her eyes for a moment, and then began again. "Sometimes she has burns on her hands that no one can explain. The day after the Bylers' barn burned, I found charred clothing in the trash."

The oddness of being in some alternate world pushed against Hannah, making her feel like she was stuck inside a dream. Was it possible her sister was guilty of setting fires? Hannah moved to the steps of the porch. Nausea came in waves.

Did her mother understand that if Sarah was guilty of setting fire to Matthew's business, she was guilty of manslaughter in the eyes of the law? And belonging to an Amish community that was willing to protect its own from the courts would not stop the legal system.

Hannah studied her sister. Sarah clearly had times of acting normal, like now as she stood there looking ordinary and . . . and perfectly sane. But was she? The questions about where Hannah's baby was and the odd little sayings and songs had ended abruptly, leaving her to appear like any other Amish girl.

Hannah swallowed. "Sarah, you wanted us to talk. We can go for a ride in my car or use the horse and buggy."

Sarah shook her head, her fingers trembling. "Daed might not like it if we go off together."

Their Daed might not like it? Sarah was an adult! Irritation swelled again, forcing her to stockpile it. Under Zabeth's tenderness and support, she had forgotten how infuriating life with Zeb Lapp could be.

Mamm looked to the door, and Hannah waited to be invited inside, but the invitation didn't come — probably a verdict passed down from her father. Hannah gestured for Sarah to sit next to her on the porch steps, unsure what to think, let alone what to do next.

Doubts as to whether her mother and she could ever recover the closeness they'd once shared pressed in on her. Hannah rubbed Sarah's back, reassuring her through physical touch of things that couldn't be promised in words. In the Englischer world,

55

words flowed quick and cheap, saying things that shouldn't be said, telling things that shouldn't be shared. But here, words were too rare and perceived fate accepted without a fight. How many Englischers ran for help and medicines, spewing the ills of their life to anyone who'd listen? And here, how many Amish stood stalwart in silence, reaching out to no doctor and telling no professional of the pain they bore?

Wasn't there any balance in the world?

Determined to weigh each word, Hannah began. "Mamm, Sarah's changed a good bit since I left, don't you think?"

Her mother gave a nod.

"I think she needs to see someone professional."

"No." Her mother studied Sarah, who sat quietly as if she'd withdrawn into a world they couldn't enter. "All she needed was to see you."

"Mamm, what just happened was not someone who only needed time with her big sister."

"But she's such a clear thinker some of the time, as if . . ." She paused.

Grief for Mamm settled over Hannah. Having a willful, difficult husband was one thing, but watching helplessly as her children's lives slipped from her arms into chaos was too much for any woman.

Needing to talk with Sarah without adding to the heartache Mamm was dealing with, Hannah took Sarah by the hand. "We'll be back in a bit, okay?"

"I'll fix us . . . Do you drink coffee?"

"I do."

A faint smile crossed her mother's face. "I'll set a pot on the stove."

Hannah and Sarah walked across the road to the dock. Sarah removed her shoes and stockings and sat on the edge of the pier, dangling her toes in the water.

Having given up the traditional black stockings long ago, Hannah slid out of her shoes and sat next to her sister. Bream swam near their feet, looking for morsels of bread. "Samuel could catch five or six fish with one scoop of the net today, ya?"

Sarah swooshed her foot through the water quickly, scattering the fish. "Ya."

"And we could spend hours cleaning his fine catch of the day to produce half an ounce of meat per fish."

Sarah giggled. "Our aim was noble though, to prove he could provide a meal for the family."

"Is that what we proved? All this time I thought our aim was to keep him out of our hair that morning while you and I worked the blackberry patch without his" — Hannah cleared her throat — "help."

They shared a laugh, and Sarah wrapped her arm through Hannah's. "I'm not crazy."

"Me either," she offered.

Sarah laid her head against Hannah's shoulder. "I feel crazy sometimes."

Hannah kissed the top of her head through her prayer *Kapp*. "Me too."

She squeezed tight. "You won't leave me again, will you?"

Hannah leaned her cheek against the top of Sarah's head. "What's going on? I mean really and truly, all the dirt, no secrets."

"Like we used to do . . . before going to Gram's became more important to you than being with me?"

Taken aback that her sister knew when she began pulling away from the family, Hannah lifted Sarah's chin and gazed into her eyes. "Yeah, like we used to."

"If I tell you everything, will you take me to see your baby?"

"Talk to me, Sarah."

"Jacob's seeing Lizzy Miller these days," Sarah began, and Hannah let the conversation meander wherever Sarah wished.

If Hannah was hoping for some encouraging news, she didn't get it as her sister made perfect sense some of the time but then talked in circles about Hannah's baby, the fire, and how things were different with everyone since she left. As her sister talked, it became clear she had issues that went way beyond Hannah's scope of understanding of the human psyche. She'd veer off into nonsense, and Hannah couldn't figure out how to bring her back around to reality. She wasn't even able to give a straight answer to what she meant about starting the fires.

"Sarah, everyone needs help at times. I received a lot of mine from counselors at the Rape Crisis Center. I think you might find help by going to a different kind of counselor. Maybe he or she will know about medications that can clear your thoughts a bit."

"I'd like that."

"Good. Come on." Hannah walked back to the house with her. As they crossed the road that separated the house from the pasture with the pond, Mamm came onto the porch, holding a tray with a coffeepot, cups, and cream and sugar.

They came to a stop at the foot of the concrete steps. The awkwardness between Hannah and her mother seemed to stand sentry, keeping them from each other. "I need to take a rain check on the coffee. I really have to go, but I'd like you to consider letting Sarah see someone."

The dishes clanked and rattled as Mamm set the tray down on the top of a wooden keg they used as an end table. "It's not up to me. You know that."

"I know, but you have an influence, Mamm. Use it with all the power you can muster."

Her mother pursed her lips, looking displeased that Hannah would be so bold. Hannah gave Sarah a hug. "You stay close to home, and we'll talk again soon. Okay?"

Sarah held on, making Hannah forcibly remove her arms from around her. Mamm grasped Sarah's hands and pulled her into a hug. The two stood side by side as Hannah went to her car.

"Hannah," her mother called.

She turned. Her mother walked to her and stared into her eyes. "I . . . I'm sorry for not standing by you, for not coming to you after your Daed refused to let you come home."

And in that moment, Hannah saw traces of the long journey of regret written on Mamm's face.

Mamm shuddered. "Even when your Daed and me got word of what had happened and came to the funeral, I stood mute, so lost inside my own grief and so shaken by the rumors that I didn't even embrace you."

There were things Mamm wasn't saying, like the fact that she'd started to come to Hannah that day by the grave site, and Daed had stopped her. But Mamm wouldn't lay blame. She'd only confess her part and leave the rest alone. Hannah longed for forgiveness toward her mother to sweep through her, but it didn't. The Amish way was to forgive, or at least confess forgiveness, but she couldn't.

Wondering if her years of hiding out in Ohio had more to do with her own inability to forgive than anything else, Hannah hugged her mother. "Let's handle Sarah with as few regrets as possible. Okay?" She stepped back, looking at her mother.

Mamm nodded. "Ya."

Hannah got into her car and pulled out of the driveway. Her mind ran in a thousand directions without finding solutions to any of the issues at hand. It'd take more than a name of a therapist to convince her family it was absolutely necessary that Sarah see a counselor and get on medication.

Her Daed seemed to barely tolerate Hannah's being here, even at a distance. What would he or the church leaders be like when she asked them to handle things more like the Englischers did?

CHAPTER 4

Matthew weaved through the crowd of church folks and relatives in his Mamm's kitchen and walked outside. People stood in small groups on the front porch, talking in muted tones and eating. All eyes moved to him, and he nodded and spoke briefly before going into the barn. He bridled his horse and mounted it without a saddle. If he stayed at the house one more minute, he might lose his will to live.

The sadness in his mother's eyes was too much, and he'd already grown weary of trying to comfort her. He aimed the horse west and let it amble along. The brokenness and guilt made him unsure if he'd ever get out from under it. He'd worked so hard and had nothing to show for it. Nothing but debt from money received and promises made for a product he could no longer make. But that didn't compare to the Grand Canyon–size ache inside him for David. If he'd spent more time with his brother, he might have some sense of peace. Instead, he'd stayed too busy to really listen when David tried talking to him.

And Elle.

Whatever patience David needed, Matthew had probably used it on Elle.

Elle. Born an Englischer. Raised half her life in an Amish home. Left two years ago, promising to return, join the church, and marry him.

He'd loved her. Believed in her. Worse, he still longed for her. He had to be the biggest fool ever born.

Her father's request for her to come away from the Amish community that had raised her and to live with him in Baltimore for six months had ended long, long ago, and yet she continued living there. Her reasons were numerous — helping her dad in his bakery, attending photography school, keeping her part of the contracts she'd signed with a studio — and her promises of returning and joining the faith continuous. When he'd written to her, releasing her from the promise to marry him, she'd returned, complaining about his lack of faithfulness to give her time.

What bothered him the most was that he didn't really know how he felt about Elle.

He wanted to be free of her while he longed to hold her.

From the crossroad he saw a woman kneeling beside David's grave. He pulled the horse to a stop, taking in the scenery. Feeling some odd connection to life for the first time since this had happened, he wanted a closer look. He guided the horse along the edge of the paved road until he came to the grass and dirt entryway. Dismounting, he winced in pain. He led the horse to a hitching post and wrapped the reins around it before heading to the grave site.

Kathryn.

She ran her hands over the fresh dirt as tears splashed onto the ground. Matthew's eyes clouded for a moment. He'd seen her a dozen times at his house since the fire, helping Mamm dress and serving meals to his Daed and Peter, but never once did he think how she must be feeling. Until this moment all of David's comments about talking with Kathryn and admiring her hadn't clicked. But whatever the two had going, it probably hadn't been romance, especially since David had been only sixteen. She was older and seeing someone from her own community, a man he'd met for the first time earlier today. Yet that seemed to do nothing to dull the pain he was witnessing.

"Kathryn."

She gasped and stood to her feet. "Matthew." Her lips quivered as she wiped at tears that didn't slow. "I'm sorry."

He shook his head. "No need to be sorry. I envy the tears."

She scoffed. "And I the lack of them." Without any sign of the tears stopping, she looked at the grave, and a soft moan escaped her. "He had so many dreams and desires. It's so unfair."

Surprised that she didn't say what everyone else was saying — that God knew best — Matthew found comfort in her words. "A fallen planet is no easy place to live."

"Ya, but heaven is." She drew a deep breath. "We talked a few weeks back. I know he told you he was unsure about remaining Amish, but I showed him scriptures of what it takes to be saved, and he prayed with me. He accepted the forgiveness Christ paid for and chose to believe God's Word above all circumstances; he just wasn't so sure he'd join the Amish church."

Although her words would be considered heresy by many, they poured salve on his aching soul. Most of his fellow Amish who'd joined the faith spent their lives trying to live as pure as possible, hoping salvation would be theirs at the end of the journey but always unsure. He understood their belief, agreed with it for the most part. It seemed some sects of Englischers wanted to believe one prayer did it all; after that they could do things their own way until death took over. Kathryn's confession of confident salvation through a simple prayer would stir quite a hornet's nest if news of it reached certain church leaders, but it brought waves of peace to him.

Tears worked their way down his face, the first ones since he'd lost his brother. Odd as it seemed, they brought a sense of relief. "I didn't know . . . thank you."

"I shouldn't be thanked. I can't do spit." Kathryn mimicked a country accent. "How many times have you had to retrain me on how to file your work orders? But God — He can make donkeys talk."

Matthew chuckled, and more tears fell.

Kathryn took another useless swipe at her cheeks. "I reminded you of my work skills and made you cry." She giggled through her tears. "No?"

He wiped his face, thankful for the release only crying could bring. "Ya, that's it."

The laughter and talk stopped, and they just stood there, staring at the grave.

"You can rebuild, Matthew." She whispered the words. "I overheard you telling your Daed that you can't or won't, but you can."

A car engine turned off, and they looked to the road several hundred feet away. Elle got out of the car. She waved, clearly wanting to talk. Matthew motioned that he'd be there in a minute.

Kathryn turned from Elle and swiped her apron over her face. "I'll go on back now and leave you two to talk."

Matthew looked around the edges of the field for Kathryn's buggy. "How'd you get here?"

She smoothed her apron back into place. "Walked."

"That's quite a walk. You must've been pretty desperate for time alone."

Kathryn cleared her throat and offered a wobbly grin. "Just me?"

He smiled. "At least I rode a horse. Here, take her. I'll either walk or catch a ride with Elle."

"Ride bareback? In this? Clearly, being raised without the benefit of sisters did nothing for your understanding of the restraints of the female Amish garb."

"You can straddle it or ride sidesaddle. It's a gentle horse, so you won't have a problem."

Looking a bit skeptical, she nodded. "If you say so."

"It was good of your Daed and Joseph to come today. It was quite a ways for them."

"Only a little over two hours by driver."

"Have they already gone home?"

"Daed has. Joseph is staying with the Bylers, hoping I'll be more in a mood for visiting before a driver takes him home tomorrow."

"Go on back and spend some time with him, Kathryn. Mamm has plenty of other help for tonight and tomorrow."

Elle waited by her car as he walked with Kathryn to the hitching post. He laced his fingers together and offered his hands as a step onto the bareback horse. As he stooped to help her, the pain across his back and shoulders was almost unbearable. She slid her foot into his hands and positioned herself on the back of the horse as if she were sitting on a sidesaddle.

Matthew passed her the reins. "Thank you, Kathryn. I needed this."

"Ya, me too." She took the leads. "I'll continue to pray God's best for you and Elle."

"Thanks." He slapped the horse's rump and ambled to Elle's car, hoping his movements looked natural rather than stiff and painful.

Elle angled her head. "How are you?"

"Better." He leaned against the car. "What's on your mind, Elle?"

"I wanted to offer my deepest sympathy. I just don't have any words to share . . ."

"I understand what you mean, and I'll pass that along to the family. But you didn't ignore my demand for space in order to share your condolences. So I'll ask again, what's on your mind?"

"The same thing that's been on my mind since before the fire: us. I don't want to lose you. Tell me I'm not alone in that."

He stared at the ground and shook his head. "I'm not sure what I feel, Elle, but I can't do this, not anymore."

"I know. Me either. But . . ."

Matthew lifted his gaze. "But what?"

"Maybe you should give us another chance, consider this as a good time for you and me to start over. It might help if you got out of Owl's Perch. There are so many things you could make a living at with your talent."

"Outside of Owl's Perch or outside of the Amish faith?"

"Please don't get angry again. I can't take it. Just hear me out."

The strength that had entered him a few minutes ago faded. "I'm listening."

"I've thought for a long time that it'd do you some real good to get away from here, just for a while. The business had you so consumed . . . changed who you were, but now you can take a break. I think you'd like Baltimore, and it might open up new ideas that'd help you find a different career."

Matthew folded his arms across his chest, wondering if she actually believed the load of manure she'd just dumped at his feet. "I should just give up here and go to Baltimore. Is that what you came here, today of all days, to say?"

She moved in closer. "Matthew, I've not handled us right. I know that, and I couldn't be any sorrier." Dipping her head, she whispered, "You can't imagine the remorse I carry. But I love you, Matthew. I can't get free of that."

He gazed at his brother's simple tombstone, totally unsure of what he wanted to do from here. The idea of getting away held stronger temptation than he'd felt in a lot of years. "This is not the time."

She nodded. "You're right. I know you are. It's just that this is what I came to talk to you about before the fire. I had to come back again and let you know that just because the business is gone doesn't mean your life is too. It's a huge, fascinating world in Baltimore — just entering the city is exciting and will bring encouragement into your life. I needed to share that hope with you."

Hope? Confusion is more like it.

She reached out and cradled his cheek in the palm of her hand. "I'll go now, but you'll call me in a few days, please?" She tilted her head, appealing for a favorable decision.

The warmth of her hand brought up emotions he wished didn't exist, not for Elle. He remained silent, willing himself not to respond to her. Part of him wanted to grab her and kiss her until the awful pain of what life had done to him eased, but that wasn't the answer either.

He nodded.

Finally she pulled her hand away and went to her car. The notion of going to Baltimore echoed through him like the lustful desires of his youth, and he wished she hadn't come by. Not today.

CHAPTER 5

With her cell phone to her ear, Hannah paced the floor of her hotel room. "I know, Martin, and I'm sorry. Your yelling at me isn't going to change anything."

She'd tried to explain her need to stay in Owl's Perch for at least three more days, maybe a week, but he wasn't in much of a reasoning mood.

"I'm not yelling," he snapped. Then silence. Then he sighed. "Hannah, sweetheart." His voice was calmer, and she knew he was trying. "It's ridiculous that these people get another chance to damage your life. After investing nearly two full years in nursing school, will you even be allowed to graduate if you're not here for class by Wednesday night?"

"I don't know. The mandatory attendance rules have a little give, but I'm afraid to ask. Whatever the answer, it changes nothing concerning my plans, and I don't need the anxiety of knowing I'm ruining my chance at graduation by staying here. Sarah needs my help, and I'm going to do what I can."

"It's not that I care about the degree or your being a nursing school graduate. You know I don't. But you've worked so hard for it. Why can't someone else do this?"

"Because it's not a course anyone in the Amish community will pursue for her if I don't. And whether she's innocent of setting the fires or not, you can't think I'm going to leave her in the community's hands. Although I'm not sure what Daed will agree to even if I get a counselor lined up."

"You can't save the world. Doesn't any of this seem uncomfortably familiar to you? You went out on a limb for Faye, and we ended up with two children to raise, a stack of bills for therapists, and she is nowhere to be found. Come on, this isn't your battle."

Hannah wanted to protest his laying the blame solely at her feet for their becoming guardians over Kevin and Lissa, but she'd taxed him over a need-help issue with his own sister, and he'd done it her way. At her insistence they'd gone through a lot to try to get his sister off drugs, only to have her run off and abandon her kids. Until today he hadn't voiced any blame.

"I can't leave. Not yet. I won't drag this

out one minute longer than necessary."

"Great. Just great."

She closed her eyes, feeling that awful sense of powerlessness take a seat on her chest. Since meeting Zabeth, it hadn't been a part of her life. "Martin, please don't do this. You can't imagine how hard this is."

"Then come home."

She took slow, deep breaths, trying to free herself of that claustrophobic feeling. "I will, but I need to find help for Sarah and try to figure out if she started the fires or not."

"Just how the . . ." He stopped short. "How do you expect to do that?"

"I have no idea. I was hoping you'd help me figure it out."

"Sorry, I'm not caught up on my *CSI* episodes."

"It's not like you to act like this. I basically have no support here."

When he didn't respond, she let the silence hang.

"Yeah, okay," he whispered. "I hear you. Kevin's whining nonstop about when you're going to return. I really think he's scared you're not coming back."

"Assure him I'm only gone because of family issues and I'm coming home as quickly as I can."

"And Lissa misses you way more than I

expected. The stitches in her leg really bother her, especially at night, and she won't let the nanny get near her once it's bedtime. I guess because she doesn't know Laura well enough yet. I've paced the floors with Lissa on my hip for two nights."

"That's because you're a good man, albeit spoiled and testy from time to time."

He didn't laugh, which was even more unusual than his present disposition. "Was spoiled." He sighed. "Before children took over my bachelor pad. Right now I'd pay anything to buy myself a little sleep and an evening out with just the two of us."

"Mmm. You can buy almost anything, that's true, but are you aware you can't buy my love but it's yours anyway?"

Martin chuckled. "Yeah?"

"Yep."

"I guess I am being a bit whiny and demanding."

"Just a bit?"

"Well, I can't be charming all the time."

"You're telling me."

He laughed. "Man, I miss you."

She refused to remind him it'd only been since Saturday. It'd clearly been a rough couple of days. "I know. I'll get some help for Sarah squared away and be back as quickly as I can manage. Okay?"

"Yeah, I understand, but I don't like it."

"I got that part, loud and clear. Let me talk to Lissa and Kevin."

"Sure, hang on."

Lissa's and Kevin's precious voices did more to ease the tightness across her chest than anything else, and by the time she finished talking to them, she felt more like herself. After disconnecting the call, she went to the business center of the hotel, got on a computer, and started searching for psychiatrists and psychologists who catered to the Plain community. Although it soon became clear this was not an easy task, investigating whether Sarah was guilty of starting the fires would be worse. The community would have no desire to let anyone ask questions or snoop around, and they'd stonewalled her years ago. If she could just figure a way around their avoidance of her, then maybe she could find some answers.

After another miserable night without sleep, Martin sat behind his desk at work, suppressing a yawn as he shifted the set of blueprints in front of him. Thankfully he'd talked Hannah into letting him hire a nanny a few weeks before the family emergency whisked her out of state. Still, he hadn't realized how much Kevin and Lissa depended on Hannah like a mother. At only twenty years old, she tended to be more nurturing than most of the women his own age.

Remorse settled over him as he spot-checked the curb grades. He'd been really hard on her yesterday and had wanted to call her back several times throughout the night, but it would have been even more selfish to wake her. In all the time he'd known her, he'd never been that difficult. Felt like being that way, yes. Given in to it, no. Dating an Amish girl wasn't easy. She just had this take-the-high-road way about her, a way he didn't get but found equally frustrating and intriguing. When she looked at him with those gentle brown eyes that always held a trace of absolute stubbornness, he did his best to keep a respectful tone. Hannah Lapp Lawson — daughter of the Old Order Amish, niece to his surrogate mom, Zabeth, and a fledgling crusader of women's health — needed his support, not his griping.

The fledgling-crusader part concerned him.

A tap on his door made him look up. Amy stood in the hallway, leaning against the doorframe with her head inside his office. "Hey, lunch plans. Noon. Three engineers, two landscape arcs. We're going to Sperati's. You joining us?"

"Depends. You're not planning on dumping that fried onion thing and its sauce in my lap again, are you?"

She snapped her fingers. "Now you've foiled my plan."

Martin tapped the set of plans in front of him. "Have you come up with a landscaping plan for River Mill yet?"

"I'll have the landscape plan done for River Mill before you have the engineering plan done for Headwaters."

Martin yawned. "No doubt. Give an old man a break, will you?"

She pointed a pencil at him. "Don't start that nonsense. I'm older than you."

"Yeah, by what, a year, maybe two? It's the eight-and-a-half-year difference between Hannah and me, with the add-on of children, that's taxing my ever-thin patience."

She shifted, straightening the gray tailored jacket of her pantsuit. "Patience is a decision, one I'd love to see you make." She pulled her lips in, trying to hide her smile over the teasing jab.

He leaned back in his chair. As professionals who'd worked together since he was a college co-op — earning money and experience while still in school — and she a second-year landscape architect for the

78

same engineering firm, they knew each other decently well. Years later, when the opportunity to buy the business fell into his lap, he was already familiar with the business's clients and procedures. "Hannah wishes that too."

Amy pointed to the stack of books on his desk. "You ready for your engineering exams next month?"

"I hope so, but I hadn't planned on becoming a parent to two kids a few months before the state exams."

"Yeah, I bet. If finding a sitter is a prob, I'll make myself available the day of the exam. Other than that, you're on your own." She stood upright. "Noon. Sperati's. Doug's driving if you want to ride with us. Otherwise, we'll see you there."

Amy's heels clicked against the tiled floors, leaving him to wrestle with his guilt again.

Zabeth wouldn't be pleased with him right now, and if she were still alive, she'd tell him so. But Martin never thought that the needs of Hannah's family might come into the picture. When Zabeth left her family, all ties were permanently severed. She'd been shunned, and that ended it, unless she had chosen to give up her love of music — playing or listening — which she hadn't.

Clearly, after two and a half years of silence, the voices of Hannah's past had begun to speak. It wasn't what he'd expected, but he would have to adjust.

CHAPTER 6

Uneasy about the day ahead, Hannah rolled the grocery cart toward her car. Her best use of the day would be to return to Owl's Perch and see Luke. Figuring her Daed wouldn't help her, she knew the next best option was her brother. But she'd not spoken to him or Mary, leaving her unsure of her welcome. Nonetheless, he was the oldest Lapp son, and if he were on her side, it'd help . . . maybe.

She lifted the hatch to the trunk of her car and set two bags of groceries and a bag of ice into the large cooler she'd brought from Ohio. Then she placed the bag containing nonrefrigerated items on the floor of the trunk. Since she didn't want to eat out and she couldn't cook at the hotel, this was the best plan. Yogurt, cereal, milk, fruit, vegetables, and some sandwich items would hold her until she returned to Martin.

She didn't share his love of dining out,

even if money wasn't an issue, which it was for her. If she would allow him to put money into her account, she could have plenty of cash at her disposal, but she liked herself better when she lived inside her own budget, meager as it was. Closing the trunk, she retrieved the car keys from her dress pocket. As she pulled out of the parking lot, she heard a loud pop as the car ran over something. A quick glance in the rearview mirror let her know she'd just shattered some type of glass bottle. She thought about stopping and checking the tire, but it seemed fine.

It struck her again how different the landscape looked as she drove in from the east side. Driving this particular route hadn't been part of her experiences while growing up here, but she was getting a feel for the layout of the area. She turned onto the paved street that ran in front of Gram's house and tried to visualize how it connected to the road her parents lived on. The roads ran parallel, with Gram's ample farm as well as Lapp and other properties, between the two, but where was the road that connected the two?

A shudder ran through her. The dirt road behind Gram's place was where the attack had taken place. She flipped the radio up

82

loudly and hit the Lock button on her car. When she spotted Gram checking her mailbox, Hannah thought about stopping. Of all the people who'd rather not see her, Gram had to be way up on the list. Still, the desire to see her, to explain her side of the ugly rumors took over Hannah's insecurity, and she looked at the carport, which sat more than a thousand feet from the road. A quick glance said no one was home but Gram, and Hannah found herself slowing down and turning into the driveway.

With her cane steadying her, Gram turned to catch a glimpse of whoever had pulled in behind her. She tipped her head to the side, her brows knit.

The sight melted Hannah's heart. She turned off the engine and got out of the car. Suddenly caught off guard by not knowing what to call her, Hannah removed her sunglasses. "Hi."

"Hannah?"

She nodded. "Can I visit with you a minute?"

"Oh, Hannah, come here." She motioned for her, and Hannah closed the distance. Gram wrapped her free arm around her and held her. "You never should have stayed gone this long. Never." The raspy voice made her grateful she'd stopped.

It was a good minute before Gram released her. "How are you?" She took a step back. "Let me look at you."

Hannah posed, gesturing with her arms out. They both laughed.

"You look well. A little fancy for my taste, but well." She motioned toward the house. "Ride me on up the lane, and let's have a cup of hot tea and talk."

Since it was still early morning midweek, Hannah felt safe to enjoy a visit without being concerned that Paul might show up.

Gram eased into the car, pulling the cane in after her. "This is very nice."

"I bartered for it, sort of."

"That sounds like you. How'd you manage to barter for a vehicle?"

Hannah explained about landing in Ohio and Martin needing someone to drive Zabeth, leaving out as much personal information as possible. They moved into the house and talked while sipping on tea. Gram didn't mention Paul; for that Hannah was grateful. She kept the topics neutral, things like Hannah's schooling and work. In spite of her reason for stopping by, Hannah couldn't make herself talk about the rape or pregnancy.

Gram set her teacup in a saucer. "So, are you home because of the trouble at the Esh place, or is that just a coincidence?"

"I'm here because of that, yes."

"And how's Sarah these days?"

"I . . . I'm not sure I should . . ."

"As tight-lipped as ever, Hannah?" Gram lifted the flowered teapot, offering to refill her cup.

The words stung. She'd kept so many secrets in the past. "I have plenty, thank you."

She set the pot on the table. "Your sister just fell apart after you left. Came here looking for the baby. Paul and I arrived home from Sunday school one time and found her sitting in the middle of the guest room with baby clothes strewn all around her. Paul talked to her as best he could, tried a couple of times to help, but your Daed wouldn't have it."

"As outlandish as it may be, I hope to change his mind on that topic." Hannah rose. "It was really good to see you, but I need to go."

Gram stood, leaning heavily on her cane as she grabbed a piece of paper off the counter. She held it out toward Hannah. "You pass me your address and start writing to me, at least twice a year. And you call me Gram. None of this avoiding using my name or wavering on what to call me."

Surprised Gram had picked up on her evasion, she smiled. "Gram, it was really good to see you."

Hannah wrote down her address and cell number before leaving. She went out the back door and across the screened porch. Grateful to have spent some time with Gram, she realized she had a friend in the elderly woman, which surprised Hannah a lot. She cranked the car and put it in reverse.

Thud-ump. Thud-ump.

She paused and then continued backing the car down the long asphalt driveway. The thumping noise grew louder and faster as she picked up speed. Stopping the car a couple of hundred feet from the house, she glanced around inside the vehicle and saw nothing that might cause a bumping sound. She pulled the lever to the trunk, set the emergency brake, and got out. Everything in the trunk looked secure. She closed the hatch and walked around the outside of the car. When she spotted the flat tire, it took restraint not to kick it.

She knew absolutely nothing about changing a tire.

Paul listened as Dorcas told him the latest goings-on at their home church. He went to church with Gram more Sundays than he made it to Maryland to attend with his family and Dorcas. But that needed to change.

"So, old man Mast was standing near the back door of the church when Norene came running inside, terrified of a yellow jacket, and plowed right into him, knocking him off his feet."

"Hopefully he didn't get on to her too badly." Paul slowed the car and turned into Gram's driveway. "Norene has allergic reactions . . ."

Hannah.

She was stooped by the right front tire, removing lug nuts. A plastic bag of what appeared to be groceries as well as a cooler were sitting on the ground near the open trunk of her vehicle. He glanced at Dorcas, whose eyes were fixed on him. He nodded up ahead. "That's Hannah."

She looked, her lips turning white within seconds. "Talk about getting plowed under."

Paul shook his head. "Don't let this rattle you. I'll pull you up to the house, and I'll go see her."

"Paul, no."

"It has to be done. You know it does." Paul drove onto the grass to pass Hannah's car, which sat in the middle of the narrow driveway. She glanced up, but he could see little expression around her large sunglasses.

After pulling up to the house, he got out of the car, went around, and opened Dorcas's door. He escorted her into the house, came back out, and walked down the driveway.

Hannah glanced up. "I'm fine, but thanks." She pushed down hard on the lugnut wrench. It didn't appear to budge.

He stepped up to her, expecting her to back away so he could remove the lug nut for her, but she didn't move.

"I said I was fine. You've done plenty. Trust me." The words came out through gritted teeth as she exerted effort against the lug nut. It loosened, and she lost her balance. Sprawling her hands against the pavement, she righted herself and put the wrench on another bolt.

"Hannah, I'm so sorry."

"I know." She nodded. "You have no idea how completely I know that you're sorry." She loosened the last lug nut and dusted off her hands.

In spite of her unjust assessment, Paul refused to defend any part of his reaction that day. "I . . . I realized you were telling the truth, and I came back . . . but you had just boarded the train, and no one knew where to."

She removed the lug wrench and tossed it on the ground. "Don't. Okay? Just don't." Straining, she tried to remove the tire. "You want to lie to everyone else, yourself included, go ahead. What do I care?" She fell onto her backside when the wheel came off, got her feet under her, and leaned the tire against the car. "You don't want to have this conversation with me." Shifting the spare tire onto the hub, she tried to get the holes to line up so it'd go on.

"Maybe not, but I'm here anyway."

"Oh yeah, you're here. I happen to be *in* Gram's driveway. Excuse me if I don't faint at the effort you put forth to see me."

"There's not much point in my trying to tell you anything if you're not going to believe a word I say."

Giving up on aligning the spare with the hub, she set the tire on the ground. "Exactly."

"Can you at least let me help you get the spare on your car?"

"You can trust that I'll leave the car and walk for the rest of my life first."

"Well, forsaking things and walking off seem to come naturally, so that's not a real shocker."

She knelt in front of the hub and took the spare tire in hand again. "I learned it from the best." After finally getting it in place, she pulled a lug nut out of her dress pocket.

"Paul." Dorcas's friendly voice called from the front door of Gram's.

"Yeah, Dorcas?"

"I need your help, please."

"Sure thing. Be right there."

Hannah's face glistened with sweat, and her dress was covered in smudges of road soot. Paul couldn't imagine Dorcas ever being so stubborn about anything. "See, some people know how to ask for help when they need it."

Hannah slowly rose to her feet. "Well, if she's putting her life in your hands, she needs to be able to easily ask people for help."

"It must be nice deciding I'm the only one at fault here, Hannah. Reminds me a lot of your dad, which is sad if you think about it." He turned and headed for the house.

"Yeah, that's it, Paul. I get like this because I'm like my Daed. This has nothing to do with the fact I'm justified!"

Without responding, he went inside.

Dorcas stood near the door, looking pale and stressed.

"What do you need?"

She handed him a jar of mayonnaise.

He opened the lid. "I need some time

alone." He went upstairs to his room. How had the conversation with Hannah ended with his being mean? Disbelief settled over him, making him sorry he'd succumbed to her anger. She had a right to hate him. In spite of her mammoth secret, she'd been a traumatized seventeen-year-old girl, and he held no blame against her.

Besides, she had plenty of reason not to believe anything he said. If he'd been thinking straight, he'd have explained about the missing money from their joint savings account. He moved to the window and stared at the dirt road behind Gram's, the road Hannah had walked to come see him every chance she got during the summers. Even her reason for being on that road was his fault. Hating what'd just taken place between them, he leaned against the window frame. "God, forgive me."

Seeing her today and knowing all that had caused her to leave more than two years ago, he realized why he had waited for her to return.

He owed her.

And he had been willing to pay any price she needed because of his hand in creating the devastation of her life. But the love he had for her had grown thin and useless over the years as she had changed from the girl he fell in love with to someone he barely recognized. She'd hidden too much, and he'd left her when he should have stayed, but here they were, years later, needing to find forgiveness for themselves and with each other.

Hannah tossed the flat tire and jack into the trunk, followed by the cooler and bag of groceries. Unable to stop trembling, she climbed behind the steering wheel, hoping the stupid spare wouldn't fly off its hub as she backed out of the driveway.

Just let me get out of here.

Her "sunny" temperament probably had Paul turning somersaults that he had moved on. She choked back tears. She'd never dreamed of acting like a maniac, of raking cutting words across him like a hay mower.

Reaching the main road, she jerked the car into first gear, tears blinding her vision. After years of hoping to never have to face him again, it'd been worse than she'd ever imagined. Much worse.

What was he doing off work at this time anyway? Except for summertime or Thanksgiving, he'd never managed to come to Gram's midweek before, but today, well, he just had to show up.

"Arrrrrrrgh." She slammed her head

against the headrest, feeling like a complete idiot.

Worse, she'd really let him have it, and she was more angry now than before. Tons more. A whole lifetime more.

"Jerk." She pressed the accelerator to the floor. Needing time to calm herself, she wound her way through a few back roads. Soon enough she was passing the Lapp house, but she kept going. The dirt road. She eased off the gas as the fence-lined road with mostly trees on one side and pastures on the other seemed to draw her. Walking this road had been her connection to Paul, her hope for a future with him. When hidden by the lay of the land on the deserted dirt road behind Gram's property, she stopped the car and turned it off.

Her heart burned from racing, not just from her encounter with Paul, but from where she was. Hannah drew a deep breath and got out of her car.

This was where her nightmare began. Closing her eyes, she felt tears sting. There seemed to be no getting free of it. Until she returned to Owl's Perch, she'd been sure all her work at the rape center, facing the past and helping others, falling in love again, and going to nursing school meant that the aftermath of the attack was behind her, not *in* her, stagnant and toxic.

"What just happened at Gram's, Father? I thought I trusted You . . . had put all the disappointment and anger into Your hands." Even as she said the prayer, anger tumbled around inside her. If the anger unleashed at Paul wasn't bad enough, she reeled, feeling trapped.

But she couldn't just drive away. Sarah needed help, and Hannah intended to see that she got it, because it was clear that Sarah was as trapped inside her mental imbalance as Hannah had been inside her circumstances. No one deserved to be abandoned to either of those. No one.

The man's voice echoed inside her head . . . *"Can you tell me how to get to Duncannon?"*

Hannah doubled her fists. "God will turn for good what was meant for evil, and I will come out better in life because of the attack. Better! Do you hear me?" She made a complete circle, yelling at her surroundings.

She gazed up at the crystal blue sky, feeling traces of hope that only God could give.

CHAPTER 7

With Mary beside him, Luke guided the horse and buggy down the dirt road he'd seen Hannah driving on just a few minutes ago. When he saw her pass the Lapp house, he figured she might be headed to the apartment where he and Mary were supposed to be living, the place the community had built for them while they were mending from their accident.

When he spotted her car, it was parked on the dirt road itself, not in the driveway of his building. Hannah was leaning against the front of it with her back to him. Why was she here, on this road of all places?

He brought the buggy to a stop, and she turned, catching a glimpse of him before standing and heading his way. The closer she came, the more he realized that she barely resembled her former self. It wasn't just that she'd become a woman and wore the clothes and hairstyle of the Englischers, but he couldn't put his finger on what else made her so different.

"Hi." She stared up at him while playing with the sunglasses in her hand.

"Look at you. All grown up. When I saw you at the train station, a white sheet had more color and shook less in the wind than you."

She smiled. "Yeah, but I survived . . ." She slid her glasses into a side pocket and pressed her hands down the front of a very dirty dress. "And then life got better."

Feeling as ill at ease as he did when he was a teen trying to hide his emotions, Luke couldn't take his eyes off her.

"Luke." Mary elongated his name.

"Oh ya, sorry." He jumped down and helped his very expectant wife down too.

Mary stumbled as her feet hit the ground, and Luke steadied her. She watched Hannah, staring at her much like Luke was. Hannah's eyes went to Mary's stomach, and a slow smile crossed her face. Mary closed the distance between them, and the two women fell into an embrace.

As he watched his wife tremble, he realized she'd never truly shared with him just how badly or how often she'd missed her closest friend.

When they took a step back, Mary looked

unsure and awkward again. Luke pointed at Hannah's hair and clothing. "I saw a glimpse of you at the funeral, but . . . you're not living Plain?"

She shook her head. "No."

"At the train station you had on Plain clothing."

"Of course. All I had in the way of identification was a photoless ID. The only way that's accepted is if the Amish clothing accompanies it. Did you think I'd been living Plain all this time?"

"I'd hoped."

It seemed the volume of unwelcome discomfort between them could've filled every silo in Owl's Perch. Clearly his sister was now an outsider.

Mary smiled. "I hope ya own nicer and cleaner dresses than this one, or being fancy needs a new name."

Hannah swiped her hands over her stained dress. "I had a flat tire."

She'd done what? Luke studied the car. "You know how to change a flat tire?"

"No, but I figured it out . . . hopefully. If I didn't, I'll know it when the tire comes off."

Mary nudged him. "Leave her alone already and give her a hug. I know you want to."

He stared at his sister, wondering if she

97

was as different on the inside as she looked on the outside. He moved like he'd been thrown from a horse a few days ago, all stiff and uncomfortable, but he embraced her. "I suppose there are worse things than living as an Englischer, although I'm not sure what they are." He squeezed her tighter. "I've missed you so much. Don't you ever leave here again without telling us how to reach you." He released her. "Ya?"

She nodded. "Wait here."

Hannah came back with a business card. "This has my cell number on it and my work number. You call, I'll answer."

Mary held out her hand for the card. "It'll be less likely to get lost if I keep it."

"Hey." Luke laughed and grumbled.

Hannah passed him a card too. "Take this, and we'll see if you can keep up with it."

"Thanks." He read the card. "So you work for this Dr. Lehman?"

Hannah nodded. "You would be hard pressed to find a better man anywhere than Dr. Lehman."

"Paul said your last name is now Lawson." Luke glanced up from the card. "Seems nothing about you is the same."

"Zabeth helped me change —"

"Zabeth?" Mary interrupted, flipping the card over as if looking for answers.

98

Hannah's eyes reflected sadness, but she offered a smile. "Daed's twin sister, one he never spoke of. She lived shunned for close to three decades, and . . . I stayed with her until she died in May. She helped me change my last name when I arrived."

"Changed it?" Feeling offended, Luke fought to suppress it. Neither man nor woman should change their God-given name because it suited them. "Were you that ashamed of being Amish?"

"Luke," Mary scolded him, shock filling her eyes.

Hannah tilted her chin, staring him in the eye. "That had nothing to do with my decision, but I had several reasons. Mostly I had to let go and start over. Will you hold that against me?"

Luke held his tongue in check, wrestling to see this from her perspective.

"Look, I don't want to argue or defend myself. What's done is done, and Sarah called me home."

Especially because she was here for the first time in years, Luke didn't want to quarrel either. "I'm pretty sure Daed thinks you're married."

"It doesn't much matter what he thinks or how he feels on this topic. I'm not married now, but I will be soon enough."

Luke removed his hat and scratched his head, wondering where all the lines of right and wrong were in this. "Except if he learns you're not married, he'll try to persuade you to come under his roof and join the faith. When that doesn't happen, he'll blame himself, making Mamm's life harder."

Mary slid her hand around his arm. "Then maybe it'd be best if we don't say anything."

He fidgeted with his hat, watching his sister. Finally he nodded. "Probably so. For now."

It was a few moments before the awkwardness faded a bit and Hannah gestured at Mary's abdomen. "I see your childhood dreams continue to come true."

Mary's cheeks flushed with pink. "It must be for all the world to see these days, no matter how large and pleated the dress."

Hannah nodded. "When is the baby due?"

"November, right before Thanksgiving." Mary rubbed her stomach. "I've been so excited that I wanted to put an ad in *The Budget*."

The horse nudged Mary, knocking her forward. Hannah steadied her before the animal whinnied loudly, making Mary jump and Hannah and Luke laugh. Hannah pulled a set of keys from her dress pocket and pressed a button on the keyless remote. The trunk opened. She grabbed a bag of baby carrots and opened them.

Luke rubbed the horse's neck. "Do you always carry horse snacks with you?"

Hannah placed a carrot on the palm of her hand. "I bought some groceries so I wouldn't need to eat out so much while here."

"You're staying all week?" Luke asked.

She shook her head. "No, I need to find answers for Sarah and get back to Ohio. Not only do I have a family that needs me, but every day I'm here I lessen my chances of graduating from nursing school come December, and someone else has to take my clinical rotations. If I miss class on Wednesday and Thursday, I'm likely to give up all chance."

"Clinical rotation?" Mary asked.

"It's a lot like doing apprentice work, only in a hospital."

Mary's brows crinkled. "You do that separate from working for Dr. Lehman?"

"Yeah, each requires time every other weekend, and then I work for Dr. Lehman during the week, around my school schedule."

Mary glanced at Luke, her greenish blue eyes mirroring a bit of hurt. "And you have a family? No wonder you ain't been back. You left yourself no room for missing us."

Luke shifted. "What exactly do you want for Sarah?"

"I . . . I think she needs professional help, Luke."

He didn't respond.

Hannah gazed into his eyes. "You have to see the problems too. Not wanting them to exist doesn't keep them from being real, and it doesn't help Sarah."

"I'm not sure what you think you can get done while you're here, but Daed is not going to agree to Sarah seeing someone. Paul mentioned that to Daed not long after you left, and I wouldn't recommend repeating the idea."

Mary touched his arm, gazing up at him. "If Sarah's setting the fires, we don't have a choice but to try to get her some help." She looked to Hannah. "The family is trying to keep her from running off, but your parents are exhausted from the effort."

Luke put on his hat. "I really don't think Sarah's setting the fires. I got no proof. Just hunches. Sarah's got problems, but it's not like her to hurt someone."

Hannah's forehead creased. "Well, she did plenty of damage to my life, and she meant it too. But whether that was just a sister thing, I don't know." She gazed down the road toward the Lapp home. "I guess it's time for me to talk to Daed. I have to see him anyway before I leave. I might as well stick my neck out all the way while it's on the chopping block."

"I'll stand beside you, if you think it's the right thing to do," Luke offered.

"It'd be great if you and Mary could be at the house, but let me talk to him alone first. If I know Daed, my chances of winning this debate are best if he doesn't think I'm trying to get people on my side and turn them against him."

Luke notched his hat tighter on his head. "Sound thinking."

He was sure Mary would like a few minutes to talk with Hannah alone, but he couldn't suggest she ride with Hannah to the house. If Daed saw his daughter-in-law riding with his wayward daughter, the bishop would be on Luke's doorstep soon enough, with frowns and words of correction for both Mary and him.

"You know, I need to mosey on up to my old harness shop and try to collect rent." Luke climbed into the buggy. "Mary, why don't you stay here, and I'll be back in a bit."

His wife smiled at him. "Sure."

Hannah held out her hand for Mary. With their heads almost touching, the two began talking as if time had stolen too little to really matter.

CHAPTER 8

The sound of a car in the driveway made Sarah drop what she was doing and head for the back door. The plate clanging against the floor meant little to her.

"Sarah," Mamm scolded above the noise of the wringer washer, "you can't let go of everything because you had a new thought."

She paused, turning to look at the twirling metal plate and scattered scrambled eggs. "Sorry."

That was the right word. She was sure of it. It seemed to her that words carried enough weight to change anything, if she could just find the right ones. Without returning to help clean up the mess, she barreled out the back door.

Hannah opened the driver's side door while fidgeting with a cord of some type. She placed a small silver thing in her dress pocket and then got out. "Hey, Sarah, how's your morning going?"

105

Sarah got right in front of her sister. "You gotta take me to see your baby, then maybe we can all go to Ohio together. I know the babe's a toddler now, but . . ."

"Sarah, I explained all of that yesterday when we were on the dock. Remember? The baby died. Didn't others tell you this already?"

"It's not true. The baby is alive. We just haven't found where they took . . ."

"Her," Hannah finished the sentence. "I had a girl who was born too premature to live. It's fairly common with teen pregnancies."

"No!" Sarah screamed the word. "No. No. No. No!"

"What's going on?" Daed came out of the barn yelling. His eyes moved from Sarah to Hannah. "Hannah." He gave a nod.

"Hi, Daed."

Sarah wanted to scratch their eyes out. They behaved so orderly, so stoic, when there was no way that's how they felt. Why couldn't someone in this family say what they were feeling? Why did they hide so much, even Hannah's own child? Well, clearly it was up to her to show the truth.

Hannah wiped the palms of her hands down her dress. "I came to talk . . ."

Daed nodded. "It's much past time. We

have a lot to talk about."

"I spoke with Sarah yesterday, and she'd like some help."

"So that's what you want to talk about?" Daed paused, staring at his eldest daughter. "You lied to me coming and going. Then you're gone for years only to come back to meddle in things that are none of yours. I think your visit has lasted long enough, don't you?"

"Daed, I . . . I was seventeen, and by our own traditions it was my free time to find a mate."

"The *rumschpringe* is to be used to find an Amish mate, and you know it!"

"I understand that's every Amish parent's hope, but those years are for young people to step outside of parental authority and find their own path. Did you not do much the same during your teen years?"

"You're too much like Zabeth."

"I found her and lived with her until she died. Did you know that?"

"I figured as much. And seeing you now, I can't say it did anything positive to help guide you. From the time you were a little bitty thing, you were too much like her. I was blindsided by trusting you to be who you appeared to be, a dutiful girl who wouldn't lie to me. I got no use for a liar."

Ready to yank her own hair out, Sarah watched as Luke and Mary pulled into the driveway and drove the horse and buggy up to the far side of the carriage house. He barely glanced at Daed, and she bet he had no power to improve things between Hannah and Daed.

She couldn't let Hannah leave.

Flames danced in her head.

Fire.

The thought soothed her rumpled nerves, and Sarah took several steps backward without either Hannah or Daed noticing. She slipped off to the shed, found her stash of matches, and grabbed her push scooter.

With the matches in her pocket, Sarah rode the scooter, propelling it with her foot, as fast as she could to Katie Waddell's.

The fires brought Hannah, and fire will keep her.

Burned wood and ash crunched under Matthew's feet, making him cringe at the memory of what'd taken place right here. Maybe Elle was right; maybe getting away from Owl's Perch was a good idea, a better one than he wanted to admit. What had living Amish gained him so far?

Loneliness and ashes.

She'd said she loved him. He longed to

believe that, needed it now more than ever. The half-burned beams were good for nothing but being knocked down. Over two years of hard work gone. It made him sick. The only thing that seemed to bring a trace of hope to life was Elle's invitation to come to Baltimore. Everything else felt as empty and lifeless as this building.

"Matthew." Kathryn's voice called to him from the direction of his house.

How could he rebuild the place that killed his brother?

"Matthew?" Kathryn clapped her hands, drawing him from his thoughts. She stood at the edge of the burned-out place. "You okay?"

"I'm fine. Did ya need somethin'?"

"Your mother asked me to have you come in. She'd like to apply the salve to your back while she's up for a bit."

Matthew lifted a charred buggy wheel. "Elle's asked me to go to Baltimore and stay for a while."

"A few days there while you're healing isn't such a bad idea, I guess. You can't do much here until you heal more, and the newness of Baltimore might lift your spirits and give you a different perspective."

Her voice had the first bit of edge to it he'd ever heard, and he looked up.

She held his gaze. "What?"

"You don't like the idea."

"I have concerns. You'll answer to the bishop about this for sure."

Matthew nodded. "He won't learn of it until I'm gone."

"I don't know what you'll tell your Mamm or Daed — or even your brother, for that matter — that will keep from adding fear and stress to them."

He tossed the ruined wheel onto the ash-covered ground. "It's my life, not theirs."

"Your pain is talking, not Matthew."

He kicked a half-burned leg of a work-bench, causing it to fall. "The pain has been burned into me until we're one."

"For now. But it's your choice whether the pain grows stronger than you or whether you grow stronger than it. And I happen to think making choices that hurt those we love will cause the ache inside a person to grow stronger and the true soul to grow weaker."

She just didn't get it. It wasn't her brother that had died, or her back that burned and hurt constantly, or her business that had burned down, or her love that beckoned her away. "That sounds an awful lot like flowery words from someone who doesn't know and can't possibly understand."

"I didn't lose a business. That part's true, but I did lose a brother." Pain flickered across her face, and she paused. "Abram drowned, and" — she closed her eyes for a moment — "I go on."

For the first time Matthew realized who Kathryn was — Elmer Glick's daughter. When Matthew was about twelve years old, Elmer Glick had lost a son in a drowning. That son was Kathryn's brother, which meant, according to rumors that had flooded in from Snow Shoe some eighty-five miles away, Kathryn had come close to drowning too.

Sick of pain and death, Matthew motioned toward the house. "I better go in and see Mamm."

CHAPTER 9

The fires brought her, and fire will keep her.

The words tapped a rhythm inside Sarah's brain. She left her scooter near the side of the road and climbed over the cattle gate at the back of Mrs. Waddell's property. A Holstein bull grazed in the adjoining pasture, so she ran full speed across the field. If he saw her and had a mind to, he might come right through that fence that needed mending.

The fires brought her, and fire will keep her.

She opened the gate that led to Mrs. Waddell's yard and went straight to the barn. Looking around the place, she spotted a can of gasoline. Isn't gas what people said caused the fire in the attic of Matthew's shop?

She spread the liquid over some bales of hay, realizing how beautiful the powerful stuff was. Fascinated, she poured it across the dirt floor as she walked out of the barn.

Covering her shoes and the ground with the golden fluid, she found beauty in the swirling little pools as rainbows of colors floated and shifted around. She set the nearly empty can beside her.

"Mrs. Waddell," she called. "Mrs. Waddell." When she didn't come to the back door, Sarah called again.

Paul came out the back door.

"Fire brought her, and fire will keep her. Ya?" She pulled the box of kitchen matches out of her pocket.

He ran toward her. "Sarah, what are you doing?"

She put the head of a match to the side of the box. "I told you she'd come back, but she's going to leave again if I don't do something. We can't let that happen."

"Sarah, no." Paul stopped. "Your shoes and the hem of your dress are soaked in gasoline. Don't strike that match."

"I want Hannah to stay and help me find her baby."

"Sarah, give me the matches." He stepped closer.

She ran the match down the side of the box, and a few sparks zipped around, but it didn't light. "Don't come any closer."

"Okay, okay. Tell me what you want."

"Hannah to stay."

A girl came out the back door. "What's going on?"

"Dorcas, you remember Sarah. She's going to give me the matches and come inside so we can talk."

Dorcas came closer. "Hi, Sarah. Wh-why don't you come on inside? We'll visit."

Sarah lifted the box and match at her threateningly. "I want Hannah!"

Paul stepped forward, but Sarah knew what he was thinking. She held the match against the side of the box, ready to light it.

"Okay." Paul stopped cold. "Dorcas, bring me the cordless and the phone number Hannah left for Gram."

"A phone number?"

"I saw it lying on Gram's table. I'm hoping it's to her cell and that she has it with her."

Dorcas ran inside.

"Sarah, move the match away from the box, and I'll call."

Sarah did as he asked, cradling the match in the palm of her hand while pulling out more matches. Dorcas brought him the phone and paper.

Paul took the items from her. "Dorcas, I want you to go inside. If she so much as causes a spark, the fumes will explode, and the gas can will ignite too." He punched numbers on the phone, how many Sarah wasn't sure. "I want you safe. Please."

Dorcas nodded and went inside.

"Hannah, this is Paul. Sarah's at Gram's barn, and she'd like you to come here. It'd be best if you wasted no time, please." Paul paused and then disconnected the call.

"What'd she say?"

"She said okay."

"Nothing else?"

"No, but I'm sure she'll be here shortly. May I have the matches now?"

Sarah shook her head. "Not yet."

Hannah closed the phone, wondering how to handle this. All her hopes of what she might accomplish by staying calm and respectful with her Daed mocked her. Clearly, getting him to agree with her on anything would take more than politeness.

He gestured toward her phone. "Can't go anywhere without being attached to that thing? The whole churchgoing world spends more money on fancy gadgets in a month than they offer to God in a year."

"That can be true of some, I'm sure." She slid her phone into her pocket, chafing at the constant negativity that flowed from her father. "Daed, that was Paul. Sarah's at Mrs. Waddell's."

He startled, looking about the place. "Ruth!" He headed for the house. Luke and Mary came out of the carriage house.

Hannah heard the gas-powered wringer washer turn off.

"Ruth!" Her father yelled again.

Her mother ran outside and paused when she saw Hannah. A look of pleasure graced her face. "Good morning."

"Hi, Mamm."

Daed waved his hand through the air. "Isn't Sarah inside? You're keeping a watch on her, right?"

Terror filled Mamm's eyes. "The last I saw her, she was with you. Has she gone missing?"

Daed opened his mouth, but Hannah interrupted him. "No, she's at Gram's with Paul. I need to go."

"I'm going with you," Daed said.

Mamm wiped her hands on her apron. "Should I come too?"

Daed headed for the car. "You stay here and watch the children."

Her father climbed into the passenger's seat and closed the door.

Hannah turned the key, starting the engine. "You didn't want her to see whatever it is we'll see, did you?"

He shook his head. "It's too hard on her."

She backed out of the driveway and headed for the paved road that led to Gram's. "Harder on her than waiting at home?"

He stared out the window. "Your ways of questioning every decision a man makes is wrong."

Resolved that she'd never really connect with her father, Hannah shifted gears. "And you're right just because you have title of being head?"

"You're talking women's feminism stuff. It's an abomination, and you know it!"

"More than you seeing me minutes after the rape and later deciding I'd lied?"

Her father crossed his arms over his chest and sulked. That worked just fine for her. She carried plenty of wrongs in what'd happened, but she wouldn't bear his share simply because he held the position of head of the household.

She stepped on the accelerator, allowing her father to ride in silence. She pulled into Gram's driveway and up to the house and stopped the car. Running across the yard and to the barn, Hannah wondered what her sister was up to.

Paul came into view but not Sarah.

Hannah slowed. "Where is she?"

He nodded in the direction of the barn.

With a gas can at Sarah's feet and her skirt hem wet, it didn't take Hannah long to put it all together. Having no idea what to say to her sister at this moment, she looked at Paul. Daed came up behind her, breathing hard from hurrying across the yard.

"Those are matches in her hands." Paul spoke softly. "If I can get close enough, I'll tackle her and take them, but at this distance she could cause a spark while I'm running toward her. It's the fumes of gasoline that are explosive. If she lights a match —"

"No soft voices!" Sarah yelled. "I hate all the murmuring that goes on behind my back! It's everywhere I go — even in the house."

Paul turned his attention to Sarah. "Okay, we won't whisper. Can we move in closer so we can talk without yelling?"

"A little."

The three of them eased forward.

"Stop right there."

Hannah took a few more steps. "Sarah, what's all this about?"

"I want to know what you did with the baby."

"I explained all that. Can't you believe me?" Hannah inched forward. "The night after being accused of wrongdoing in front of Daed and the church leaders, I gave birth too early, and the baby died. I'm not lying."

Daed removed his hat. "Are you saying it's my fault you went into labor that night?"

Sarah's pale face made her dark eyes stand out even more. "No! The baby isn't dead! It isn't!"

Paul took a few steps forward. "Sarah, everyone here knows what happened. What will it take for you to believe us?"

"You only know what she said, and so does Daed."

Hannah stepped closer. "The baby died in my arms. She lived long enough for me to name her, fighting for a breath her lungs weren't mature enough to take. I cried until I thought I'd go crazy. But then the tears had to stop, and I had to find what was left of me and move forward."

Paul inched toward Sarah again. "What do you need from us, Sarah?"

Sarah pressed four matches against the striking surface. "Then it's my fault!"

He stepped in front of Hannah. "Why is it your fault?"

She stepped to the side of Paul, removing him as her shield. "I'm not sure you want to go down that volatile path. Not now."

"We need to diffuse this so we can get the matches."

"I realize that, but . . ."

"Maybe she knows things we don't. I think she should tell us why it's her fault."

"You're opening Pandora's box." Hannah ground out the words.

Ignoring her comment, he moved forward again. Sarah raised the matches and box. "No closer."

"Did you set E and L on fire?" Daed asked.

Sarah squared her shoulders. "I did."

Her father moaned as he slumped.

Paul pointed to the gas can. "Did you use matches or gasoline?"

" 'The tongue is a fire, a world of evil . . . and sets on fire the course of life.' It doesn't need matches or gasoline."

Somewhat taken aback that Paul had managed to target the issue, Hannah thought maybe his other question had more merit than she'd given him credit for. "Why is the death of . . . my baby your fault?"

"What's her name?" Sarah asked.

"What?"

"The baby. You said you named her."

Except for the letter she'd written to Paul while on the train to Ohio, Hannah had told no one her infant's name, and she wasn't sharing it now with Daed standing here. She shook her head. "It doesn't matter."

Sarah screamed, like a child throwing a

120

tantrum, as she joggled the matches against the strike plate.

Paul held out his hand, calming her. "Rachel."

Sarah sank to the ground and began to rock back and forth. Paul knelt in front of her, and she held the box of matches out to him. Staring into his eyes without blinking, Sarah whispered, "Help me."

Paul took the matches and put them on the ground behind him, and then he clasped Sarah's hands in his and whispered something that made tears roll down her cheeks.

Hannah glanced to her Daed, who was walking off toward home.

Paul stood and helped Sarah up. He then walked her to the back door, where Dorcas stood watching Paul's every move.

When Dorcas eyed Hannah, a thousand negative emotions roiled through Hannah, but she couldn't voice her thoughts. Paul had once told her that Dorcas attended every family function and that she practically lived at his parents' place half the time. She had positioned herself to be Paul's girl before Hannah ever left Owl's Perch. Hannah had no proof and yet no doubt that was what had happened. Still, she needed to keep this visit to its point and talk to Paul about Sarah, so she stepped forward and held out her hand. "Hannah Lawson."

Dorcas looked to Paul before shaking her hand. "Dorcas Miller."

Paul turned to Sarah, staring into her eyes. "I need to talk to Hannah, just while you get a shower and change clothes. Can you do that?"

Sarah nodded. "Okay."

Paul motioned into the house. "Dorcas, Sarah needs a change of clothing. Can you find her something and stay with her while she showers? I'll be right out here, well within earshot if you need me."

"Sure." Dorcas flashed a condescending look Hannah's way before the two disappeared into the house.

Indignation at Dorcas growled, but Hannah ignored it. Suddenly the great outdoors didn't seem large enough to hold the awkwardness between Paul and her.

He slid his hands into his pockets. "What happened today with Sarah has been brewing for a long, long time. I'm sorry it happened, but I think it's good you were here, and I think we just witnessed the worst of it."

The only comforting thought Hannah could find at the moment was gratefulness that Martin wasn't here to see just how dysfunctional her family was. "Sarah needs to be checked into the mental health ward of a hospital. How do I go about doing that?"

"That would be a huge mistake, Hannah."

"Could you do me a favor and not use my name like we're friends?"

Paul nodded. "Look, regardless of how you feel about me, the clinic I work at is a wonderful facility and can help her, but a hospital is a mistake for a lot of reasons. The coldness of an institution will push her closer to the edge, and they'll start pumping meds in her left and right."

"Push her closer? Were you out here today?"

Paul studied her. "Are sarcasm and anger your only ways of communicating nowadays?"

To you? Yes.

He stood calm and reserved, obviously waiting for her to give an answer he was willing to work with.

After his help with Sarah just now, she should probably apologize for her tone. Bitterly opposed to that idea, she gave a nod. "Noted." She drew a breath and willed herself to find her nice voice.

Paul shifted. "Look, I shouldn't have said that about your dad and you earlier. And you have every right to be angry with me."

"Contrary to how I sound, I'm really not interested in venting my anger. All I want to do is help Sarah and get out of here, but you had no right to pass my number to anyone without asking me first."

"Your dad sent word through Luke that they wanted to locate you and had received a letter when your aunt died that gave him an idea where you were. Since I knew how to take that bit of piecemeal info and find you for them, I did."

She blinked. "My Daed?"

Paul nodded. "I was surprised too. Look, I was wrong to leave that night without hearing you out. I'm asking you to forgive me."

She shrugged. "Until arriving back here, I thought I had. But now it seems none of the prayers covered actually having to see you."

"I did come back for you."

"Don't." She held up her hand. "*If* you came back, you came back too late."

They stood in Gram's yard looking at each other as if they were strangers — no, it was worse. She saw a man she'd once thought was worthy of her giving up everything just to be with him. There was no telling what he was thinking, but if love was blind, what was happening between them now was more like a piece-by-piece dissection under a high-powered magnifying glass.

He pulled out his billfold and passed her a business card. "I have a counseling license and work at the Better Path. It offers an array of helps for people."

"You're a counselor?" She narrowed her eyes, trying not to gape at him. "This is the more suitable career that your church agrees with? You delved further into psychology, and they agreed with it more than social work?" The last time she'd tried to make contact with Paul, some young woman, maybe even Dorcas, told her that he had to make a career change to please the church leaders. The disbelief in her voice mocked his choice of a profession, and she didn't even try to cover it.

Paul shook his head — a slow, resigned type of shake — as if she were too much of a pain to deal with. "You know, I really am trying —" He stopped short when her phone rang.

She pulled it out of her dress pocket. The caller ID said it was Martin. Ignoring Paul, she pushed the green icon. "Hello."

"Hey, sweetheart, I thought of the solution to all our problems. Have you figured it out yet?"

Warmth and comfort slid up Hannah's

spine, and she held the phone tighter. "Not a clue."

"We shouldn't have ever had sisters."

A burst of laughter broke through her current misery, and a tear trickled down her face. The tenderness in his voice made her ache to tell him the horrors of her day, of her own misbehavior of lashing out at Paul . . . of wanting to lash out even more.

She saw a half smile break through Paul's reserve before he grabbed the gas can and moved it into the barn, giving her privacy.

She walked to the knoll, gazing out over the peaceful fields. "I've been so wrong today. You wouldn't even recognize me. I've ripped people apart, and the thing is . . . I had no idea that kind of anger and bitterness lurked inside me."

"Phone girl, give yourself some room here. It's okay to lose it a few times with people who said they loved you and then didn't even throw you a life preserver when you were drowning."

Another tear slid down her cheek. She drew a deep breath. "Thank you."

"I'm really sorry for the other night."

"I know, but this isn't a good time to talk, so I'll call you later, okay?"

"Sure. No beating up on yourself, and we'll talk soon."

"Bye." She closed the phone. Walking to the barn area, seeing Paul, being here — it seemed impossible to process it with any sense of reality. "I . . . I'm off the phone."

With a pitchfork in hand, he tossed the gasoline-soaked hay into a huge metal bin. He glanced up. The lack of condemnation, disappointment, or anger on his face was disconcerting. Was he the jerk who'd abandoned her, taken her portion of their money, and refused to return her call — or not?

He gathered more hay on the tines and pitched it into the bin. "I didn't mean to break a confidence by sharing the baby's name."

Wishing she knew what to believe about this man in front of her, she did her best to temper her answer. "I guess I should have just told her when she asked. I tend to be a little stubborn about things at times."

Paul didn't nod or sneer or even crack some smart remark.

"That's your cue to say, 'You think?' "

He rested the tines of the pitchfork in the ground. "The phone call seems to have helped you find a little perspective on today."

"Yeah." She squeezed the phone in the palm of her hand. "Martin." She slid her phone into her pocket and ran her fingers over the ring he'd given her. "The first time I met him," she laughed, "it was *after* a rather ugly argument."

"So you argued with him and then met him?"

"Yeah. But the argument wasn't my fault."

Suppressing a smile, he answered, "Uh, yes, I . . . I'm sure it wasn't."

She blinked, staring at him before a whispery laugh escaped her, and he joined her. Silence followed, a welcome kind of truce of some sort. "So now what?"

"You listen to more reasons why the Better Path is the best place for Sarah?"

"Let's skip that for now and assume my opinion is outnumbered by you and Sarah, then what?"

"You take her there and get her forms filled out. I'll follow in my car and do what needs to be done to get a psychiatrist on site. Maybe not today, but some psychological testing will need to be done by tomorrow afternoon and a step-by-step plan developed. The place has full-time, short-term care. She'll be sedated at bedtime, her room locked, and she'll be monitored so she can't do any more slipping out during the night."

"What if she's guilty of starting the fires, of killing David?" Hannah's words barely came out in a whisper as she forced herself to ask about her worst fears.

"Normally that's not something I, or any other psychologist, would tackle, but since it's important to the safety of everyone in the community as well as to her being at peace, I'll work on finding some answers while she's under supervision."

Wondering what the cost would be, Hannah nodded. Regardless of all else, she'd stumbled on a beginning place for Sarah.

CHAPTER 10

Hannah stood at the window inside Dr. Stone's office, waiting for her to return from taking Sarah to her room for the night. Before leaving the Better Path over two hours ago, Paul had managed to reach the doctor and get her to come in to see Sarah today rather than tomorrow. For that, Hannah was grateful.

Her father's stubbornness seemed no better now than two and a half years ago. Still, she'd need his approval regardless of what Dr. Stone recommended. Sarah required her family and community, a place to live, and someone to provide for her when she was released from this place — all of which meant doing what it took to keep Sarah in the good graces of their Daed.

The receptionist had left about thirty minutes ago, and except for Hannah, the main-house segment of the Better Path was completely empty. A nurse, Dr. Stone, and

Sarah were in the patient facility out back, which looked like it'd once been a *Daadi Haus* for an Amish home. The place was probably older than Dr. Lehman's birthing center, but it was nicer with its hardwood floors, refurbished interior, and homey décor. Dr. Lehman's clinics were sparse, functional, and had ancient linoleum floors. She hadn't really thought about it before now, but the windows at her clinic were covered with unopened, aluminum mini-blinds to give a constant sense of privacy to the women inside. But here the windows were adorned with opened plantation blinds and lacy valances.

The Tuscarora Mountain stood in the distance with huge oaks spread across the land before it, reminding her of how much she'd once loved the beauty of Owl's Perch. But it no longer felt like home, in spite of the bittersweet longing that had crept up on her once in a while during this trip. Mostly what had flooded her was deep anger. Hoping to temper her reactions from here on, she watched as Paul pulled into the driveway behind the clinic and headed for the *guest* housing, as they referred to it.

Dr. Stone came out of the small house and met Paul, as if they'd timed his arrival back at the clinic with her leaving Sarah in the nurse's care. Meticulously dressed with matching nails and perfectly sculpted short brown hair, the forty-something doctor passed a file to Paul while talking. Trying not to chafe at the absurdity of this situation, Hannah kept a vigil. Paul glanced up to the window where she stood before returning his focus to Dr. Stone and walking with her toward the clinic. Their muffled voices filled the air as they entered the building and came up the stairs to where Hannah waited.

Dr. Stone motioned for Hannah to take a seat as she walked to the front of her desk and leaned against it. "Sarah has decided to stay with us over the next few weeks. It took awhile to help her see the need, but after eighteen it's best if the patient chooses to stay. Otherwise we could need the courts to intervene. If you'll bring her some clothes and any personal items she wants, you can spend a little time with her tonight, but after that we prefer no visitors for at least a week." She tapped the desk with her long, fake nails. "I still have a lot of patients to see at my full-time clinic, so I need to leave now, but Paul is prepared to fill you in on anything you'd like to know."

Not comfortable with the doctor asking Paul to explain what was going on with her sister, Hannah decided to be more direct. "What's wrong with her?"

"She seems to have four overlapping issues. None alone is too serious, and even the four are certainly manageable with help, but she's gone a long time with no intervention."

"We just didn't realize her issues were this serious."

The doctor nodded. "Family members tend to accept the odd behaviors of their own as part of who the person is, and the peculiarities can often increase slowly over years." She glanced briefly to Paul. "I understand you've been gone the last two and a half years."

"I have."

"With no contact?"

Suddenly feeling like her life was on trial, Hannah answered, "I didn't leave a way to be contacted, and I wrote very few notes, which were generic in content. Has that added to Sarah's issues?"

"She does have symptoms of adjustment separation anxiety disorder among other things."

"Was that a yes or a no to my question?"

"It was neither. It's possible your absence contributed to her condition. It's possible it didn't." Dr. Stone pulled a sheet of paper out from a stack on her desk. "She's requested to have Paul as her regular therapist."

"No." Hannah stared straight at him. "Absolutely not."

The doctor frowned. "Is there a reason why you feel he's not a good fit to work with Sarah? He is a Plain Mennonite, which gives him an advantage in understanding her."

Hannah had plenty of reasons for her opinion. In spite of his good showing at Gram's, she simply didn't trust him. Maybe he was who he said and acted like he was, but she had a solid basis for thinking otherwise. "But he's known her for a while. He's friends with our brother and has dealt with our Daed. Doesn't that disqualify him or something?"

Dr. Stone leaned forward. "So you think he's too emotionally involved to hear her without bias?"

Hannah swallowed, trying to maintain some semblance of professionalism. "Look, you're basing this request on what Sarah wants. Earlier today she *wanted* to set fire to herself. Maybe you're mistaken to put so much stock in her opinion."

The doctor gave an indifferent nod and passed the paper to her. "This is a list of our counselors. It's a short list, but each name has a bio. Only Paul works here full-time. The others come in a few times a week or less, so if you decide not to use Paul, you will need to understand the limitations you're placing on Sarah's counseling sessions. You can discuss this with your family and let Paul know. Whether he's her counselor or not, it's very important to her that she feels she can return home when her time here is over." She pointed to Paul. "Which means you will need to talk with her family while you're getting her personal items from home." She glanced at her watch. "I prefer that Paul be present for that conversation for many reasons I don't have time to explain. When you return with her things, I hope you have good news for her. If not, let Paul coach you on the best phrases to use so we can avoid wording things in a way that will upset her."

Hannah glanced at Paul. Daed had to approve this plan for Sarah's sake, but Hannah couldn't even manage to agree with Paul on anything. So how were they going to pull this off?

"Do you have a list of ways we can reach you if need be?"

Hannah pulled the last two business cards she had with her out of her pocket and passed one to Dr. Stone and one to Paul.

She nodded. "Good." She tapped her watch. "Well, I need to go. Paul, we'll have a conference call tomorrow at ten. I think we discussed all other aspects while on the phone earlier. Anything I've forgotten?"

Paul shook his head. "We covered it. I know how to reach you if a need comes up."

Dr. Stone looked at Hannah. "Regardless of who is chosen as the therapist, Paul will be the coordinator for all issues concerning Sarah for the intensity of the next month. After that he can step down and pass the responsibility to someone else." Dr. Stone held out her hand to Hannah. "I'm sure we'll talk again in a few weeks."

The doctor left.

Paul tilted the file in her direction. "We need to discuss a few things on our way to see your Daed."

Despite wanting to object and to drive herself, she simply nodded. This was unbelievable. Aggravating. Annoying. And . . . maybe the only way she'd get out of here and back to Martin before she ruined her chance of graduating from nursing school on time.

"You ready?"

She'd never be ready for this next venture, but it had to be done anyway. "Yeah."

Paul headed for his vehicle, and she went

for hers.

"Han . . . um, Ms. Lawson, we need to ride together. The fewer vehicles in your Daed's driveway, the less frustrated he'll be, and we need to talk on the way to prep for the visit there."

She'd told him not to refer to her as if they were friends, but calling her Ms. Lawson wasn't the answer either.

"Then I'll drive."

He frowned.

"Problem?"

"No, I guess not . . . except I saw your effort to bolt that tire on this morning and . . ."

Caught off guard by his remark, she laughed. Her eyes met his, and for the second time something besides stress glimmered between them — and she was grateful. "Oh, shut up and get in the car, Waddell."

He shrugged. "I'm really hungry and tired. I don't want to get stuck without a spare."

She opened her car door. "I have groceries in the trunk of my car." They both got in, and Hannah turned the key. "So you won't die of starvation if we get stranded."

"So if we get stranded together, what would I die from?"

Hannah chuckled, remembering how well they used to quip their way through things. "I won't incriminate myself."

Paul laughed and opened the file. "Here's the deal . . ."

After pulling into her parents' driveway, Hannah turned off the car.

Paul slid the file between the seat and the console. "It'd probably be best if we left our cell phones in the car."

She'd disagree, except if their goal was to appease her father, Paul happened to be right. She plunked her phone into the console before getting out. Knowing she'd need to remain outside the house, she didn't go to the door closest to them but headed for the front porch. Without questioning her, Paul followed. She knocked and waited.

Her father opened the door.

"Hi, Daed. Sarah's doing much better this evening, and we came to talk with you about where she is and what can be done for her."

Her Daed nodded before he turned back toward the living room. "Luke, get a few kitchen chairs and bring them to the front porch. You need to join us. Ruth, ask Mary to take Esther, Rebecca, and Samuel to see the kittens in the barn until we call them." He then stepped out and motioned Hannah to the porch swing.

From things Mamm and Luke had said, it sounded like her Daed and Paul had met, but clarifying that could cause ill will from her father. And they'd clearly seen each other earlier today; still a proper introduction seemed necessary. "Daed, this is Paul Waddell. Paul, this is my Daed, Zeb Lapp."

Paul held out his hand, and Daed shook it. "Mr. Lapp."

Without speaking or offering any friendliness, her father took a seat next to Hannah, which took her by surprise. Luke came outside carrying two chairs, and Mamm was behind him.

As Mamm walked to her, Hannah stood. Her mother hugged her right there in front of her Daed. "Are you hungry?"

She should be. It was almost dinnertime, and she hadn't eaten since early morning, but she wasn't. *"Denki, Ich bin ganz gut."*

Saying "Thanks, I am fine" in her native tongue felt a little strange. Outside of working with Amish women in labor, she never used the language anymore. Zabeth rarely spoke it, and Hannah followed suit. Dressing like an Englischer seemed to cause everyone to avoid using Pennsylvania Dutch with her, even Mary.

Mamm gently cupped Hannah's face in

139

her hands. *"Liewi . . ."* Her eyes misted, but she was unable to say more than *dear.*

"I love you too, Mamm."

Her mother sobbed and pulled her close. Daed sat in silence, watching them. Shaking, Mamm pulled away and took a seat in a nearby chair. Hannah sat next to her father. He reached over and patted her hand. Was he offering some type of apology? Or was he simply saying thank you for bringing some peace to Mamm?

Paul leaned forward. "Mr. Lapp, have you had time to share today's events with your wife and Luke, or should I begin our conversation by recapping?"

"I told them enough. Move on with what needs to be said."

Paul remained unruffled in spite of her father's sharp tone. "Sure, no problem. What happened today with Sarah may seem extreme and was probably very upsetting, but I believe her behavior was a cry for help more than a true indication of instability."

Luke placed his forearms on his knees and stared at Paul. "You can help her?"

"Sarah is a good candidate for receiving help. We don't have the lab results back, so we can't be sure yet if some hormone imbalance or physical ailment is adding to her issues, but regardless of that, the physicians

140

and counselors at the Better Path can help her. She's checked herself into the clinic and wants to stay for a few weeks, but she needs to know that she can come home to live and that no one will be angry with her for getting help."

Fully aware that Paul was avoiding saying *he* could help her, Hannah looked at her father. "Daed, Sarah needs more help than we can give her."

He stared at the porch floor, arms folded across his chest. "We? There is no 'we.' You left and intend to leave again."

All hints of the restoration that'd taken place between her and her Daed only moments earlier disappeared. Ten things popped into her mind at once, all sarcastic, albeit true, pictures of why she wasn't a part of the "we," but she held her tongue.

Daed pushed his straw hat back a bit on his head. "I thought when she had time with you, she'd snap out of this stupor of hers. I've been wondering if she's just trying to gain attention, and Paul just confirmed it. I won't have my daughter mixing with the Englischers while those doctors dive into psychology trash and try to get an upper hand over God in her thoughts."

Hannah wanted to stand up and scream, but she determined to speak softly. "That's not what he meant when he said a cry for help. Her reaction today was similar to a reflex. If something is coming at you, you flinch. It's an automatic reflex. That's what this cry for help is like." She looked to Paul. "Is that accurate enough?"

He nodded. "Yes, but if we let Sarah continue down this path, her reflexes, so to speak, will take over more and more of her life, and her chances of regaining control will lessen."

Daed waved his hand as if shooing them away. "This is ridiculous. God knows what He's doing."

Hannah nodded. "Yes, but *He's* letting you see Sarah's need. He has put people near you with answers and help for her. I know you're leery and rightly so. Far too many people follow the trends rather than think things through, but if you ignore what you saw today, it'll only get worse. That can cost Sarah her future."

"She has no more of a future than you did after the unmentionable."

His final words hung in the air. Indignation pulsed through Hannah, burning her skin. She choked back the words that begged to be released.

Paul's eyes stayed on her before he cleared his throat. "Mr. Lapp, Sarah's prognosis —"

"Ah." Hannah interrupted Paul and faced her father. "So, Daed, you're the one who gets to decide who does and doesn't have a future. See, now I get it. If I'd just known that, why, I could have given up years ago." She smacked the palm of her hand against her forehead. "Silly me." She stood, tossing a half-apologetic glance to Mamm for speaking out against Daed. "I bitterly object to you, in your finite mind, deciding I was used up and washed up, and I won't let you decide it for Sarah either." She walked to the edge of the porch steps and paused before looking at her father again. "Your sister understood that love reaches out against all the odds and against all reasonable hope. I learned so much about freedom and hope and faith. Why can't you understand that people and circumstances aren't bound to what you can see in them today? If they were, there would be no need for faith." Hannah descended the steps.

The sounds of hoofbeats interrupted the conversation. Matthew Esh brought the horse and buggy to a stop.

He dipped his head in a nod to the group in general. "Hello."

Everyone except Hannah spoke to him. Unsure whether he wanted her to speak, she waited. His eyes moved to Paul, and she figured he'd like to comment on the oddity of his being at the Lapp place.

Matthew then looked at her. "I came by, hoping we could go for a ride and talk a bit."

Without a moment's hesitation, Hannah hurried closer and stopped when she was near the horse. Matthew studied her. "Well, I haveta say, like the last time we were right here like this, your getup again leaves a bit to be desired."

She didn't need to look at her dress. It was a mess of stains. She smiled. "Are ya saying I'm not dressed well enough to be standing beside your horse?" She lowered her head, hoping to make her voice sound deep. "If the brand-new horseshoe fits, Hannah Lapp . . ."

They both laughed, which meant he remembered them sharing that bit of conversation. Matthew looked the part of a man now. His eyes carried wisdom, and his frame was that of a man who did a lot of physical work for a living.

"Hannah," Luke called.

She turned.

"Sarah can live with us when she gets out. I'll work with Paul and do what I can to help her."

She glanced at Paul. Luke's words were

144

most welcome, except the part about Paul. "There are other counselors at the clinic."

"Ya, but no one is going to understand being Old Order Amish as much as a Plain Mennonite. It'll help Sarah to have a less worldly viewpoint, won't it?" Luke looked from Hannah to Paul.

Paul remained silent on the subject, but she sensed defeat.

She tried to invoke a professional tone as she shared her feelings. "I'd much rather she worked with someone else."

Her father stood and leaned against the porch railing. "I agree with Luke. If Sarah's to get this so-called help, then at the very least, let her work with someone less in the world than the rest of them."

Mamm nodded.

"We need to talk." Matthew's words were muted and clearly meant just for her.

Hannah turned and studied him for a moment.

He set the brake and leaned toward her. "I know things you don't. Let's ride, and we'll talk."

Hannah pulled her car keys out of her pocket and walked back to the porch. "Mamm, will you get all the items Sarah needs to stay at the Better Path for a few weeks?"

Her mother nodded. Since they trusted Paul so much, he could finish explaining the procedure concerning Sarah and then take her clothes back to her.

She pushed the keyless remote, unlocking her car door. After hurrying to the car and grabbing her phone, she tossed the keys to Paul. Well, they almost made it to him. "In case you need to go."

He grabbed them off the concrete floor of the porch. "I'll head back to the Better Path soon."

Matthew released the brake. "I'll drop her off there when we're finished talking."

That was a long way by horse and buggy, so she figured Matthew must have a good bit he wanted to talk about. She went to the passenger's side of the buggy and climbed in.

Paul got behind the wheel of Hannah's car, unable to fit his legs inside the vehicle until he figured out how to move the seat. With the seat positioned right, he backed onto the main road. Sarah was finally getting the help she needed. It wouldn't be happening if Hannah hadn't come home. She and her Daed didn't get along, but she wielded more power over him than she knew. If Paul had his guesses, that alone caused Zeb to fight her tooth and nail.

Lion-heart.

He'd dubbed her that several years ago because she'd carried the nobility, strength, and fearlessness of a lion. The name had fit more than calling her a sweetheart. It wasn't as if she was void of sweetness, although he'd not witnessed much of it today. To his way of thinking, any sweetness she'd held on to was less her guiding force than the determination that ruled her heart. But he wasn't sure the name Lion-heart fit anymore.

She was more like a sentinel, with cutting words in place of a sword. Under all her anger there seemed to be pure determination. She had some issues to work through, but he hoped she wouldn't let the need to forgive defeat her. Surely after overcoming all she had, she'd find her way to forgiving everyone who needed it.

His cell phone rang. He grabbed it, opened it, and pushed the green icon, barely glancing from the road. "Paul Waddell."

No one spoke, and he tried again. "Paul Waddell."

"Uh, yeah, I heard you the first time," a man snapped. "And you have Hannah's phone because . . ."

Paul removed the phone from his ear and

gazed at it as if it had an answer to the man's question. "While working with Hannah's family to make some arrangements for Sarah, we must have gotten our phones mixed up."

"Where's Hannah?" The edge of anger in the man's voice gave way to a bit of concern.

"She's . . ." Wondering whether to tell him she was with Matthew or not, Paul hedged. "Not here."

Silence hung, but the man's frustrations were plenty loud.

Needing to shift gears, Paul moved the phone to his other ear. "Martin, right?"

"Yes."

"I'll tell her you called when I exchange phones with her."

"Yeah, thanks."

To the man's credit, he didn't inundate Paul with questions. For that he was grateful, because the last thing he wanted was to cause trouble for Hannah, although she seemed well capable of standing up for herself.

CHAPTER 11

Matthew brought the horse and buggy to a stop outside the Better Path. The sun had slid below the horizon long ago, and they'd talked for hours as the horse ambled along. She'd always thought Matthew had an inner compass that most people lacked, and she saw it now, even as grief tormented him and confusion summoned him to leave Owl's Perch for a spell.

But his firm stance about Paul's innocence in the situation, including the missing money, had been shocking . . . and very hard to believe. Still, it was Matthew doing the talking, and she loved him as much as she did Luke and had always trusted his judgment without question. Unfortunately that worked against her as he defended Paul's overreaction the night he realized she was pregnant.

The electric lights inside the Better Path contrasted starkly with the Amish homes they'd passed along the way, with the dim glow of the kerosene lamps shining through the windows. The clinic sat nestled in the center of an Old Order Amish fortress, more populated than Owl's Perch. Before returning from Winding Creek, she'd not seen or at least not noticed this clinic that stood outside of Owl's Perch.

Matthew set the brake and leaned in. "I'm glad we got to talk."

Hannah nodded, although he'd said many things she was less than glad to hear. "You should make those appointments like that hospital doctor told you to. Your back needs to be debrided several more times and . . ."

He shook his head. "I'm fine. I got the salve Mamm can put on my back, and if any signs of infection begin, I'll see a doctor."

"That's a very stubborn way to deal with this. You'll have more scars, and it won't heal as quickly."

"You're awful pushy, aren't ya?" He grasped the leads tighter. "I'm fine. Trust me."

Resigned, she nodded. "You have my address and phone number, so you call or write anytime you have a mind to."

"I'll do that. And you go easy on Paul. In the tragedy that happened to you, he's a victim too."

Not at all sure she believed that, Hannah kissed his cheek. "Take care, and don't be afraid to get away and see life from a different perspective. I think it'll only be good for you."

"Ya really think so?"

"I think it'd be a mistake not to go, Matthew. Challenge your faith. Challenge your thoughts about Elle. Don't let fear stop you."

He straightened his hat. "Then I'll take your advice and get out for a spell."

Hannah climbed down. "Good night."

He pulled away and left her staring at the Better Path with his words of faith in Paul still ringing in her ears. Not wanting to face him and admit she might have been too harsh, she slowly climbed the steps. Through the screen door, she could see him in the kitchen, standing in front of the stove. The aroma of sautéed mushrooms, bell peppers, and bacon wafted through the night air. She eased the squeaky door open, and he glanced her way.

Neither spoke as she made her way into the kitchen and leaned against a counter.

"You hungry?" Paul cracked an egg against a bowl and dumped its contents in with half a dozen others and then wiped his hands on the kitchen towel that was draped across one shoulder.

Her stomach had stopped growling hours ago, but the dull hunger remained. "I'm okay."

His blue eyes glanced at her, reflecting a look that said he was doubtful, but he said nothing.

Nervous at being the slightest bit vulnerable with him, she had to admit to herself that she'd rather die in her wrongness than have any part of her real self exposed to him ever again. That sentiment probably caused her to be unjust beyond reason to him . . . or at least beyond what Matthew said was reasonable.

With a bit of a hop, she took a seat on the counter. "Matthew said you really did come looking for me, and he explained a lot of things, and . . . maybe I've been a little unfair in my prejudices against your working with Sarah."

Paul beat the eggs briskly with a fork. "The fact that I came back for you afterward hardly exonerates me. I should have heard you out that night. I should have believed in you." He stopped and held her gaze. "I wish there were words beyond *I'm sorry*."

She knew that feeling intimately, had felt it to her soul concerning Rachel and trying to keep secrets. For the second time she wondered if it was possible that part of the reason she'd left had nothing to do with the injustice heaped on her. Had she left because she couldn't face how poorly she'd handled things?

Still pondering that question, she was beginning to think he hadn't received her phone message before she boarded that train because he'd been out that night searching for her. And then she left him no way to contact her. Why she'd handled things as she had would take some figuring out, but her personal inner workings weren't Paul's fault. They'd both mishandled things, to say the very least.

"Nevertheless," she whispered.

All of Paul's movements stopped.

Hannah's heart seemed to hiccup under the weight of his subdued shock. "You know, I think I'm hungry after all."

"Good." A slight grin tugged at the corner of his lips. He gestured toward the bowls of various ingredients. "What do you like in your omelet?"

"A little of everything you have there, but go light on the bell peppers."

"You got it."

"Matthew said you didn't take the money. Any idea what happened to it?"

Paul dumped the eggs into the hot skillet. "Not fully."

She heard it in his voice; she'd hit a wall. "And not anything you want to talk about."

Adding ingredients to the eggs, he shook his head. "The money wasn't important, okay? I'd planned on replacing your portion when the opportunity —"

"No," Hannah interrupted, sounding flat-out mean. She drew a breath and measured her words. "I was just . . . curious. Am I so weak in your eyes that I can't cope with knowing what you know?"

His movements stopped. "No, of course not. I . . . I just . . ."

Whatever the rest of his sentence was, Hannah was sure he wasn't going to say it. "Who took our money?"

Paul folded one side of the omelet onto the other. "Not long after you were attacked, a young Amish woman, or someone wearing Amish clothing, went into the bank. She had the bankbook and pretended to be you. I didn't know the money was missing until after you left."

"I thought I'd lost the bankbook, but you think the guy who attacked me got hold of it and put someone up to emptying that account?"

"That scenario matches up with the evidence." He slid an omelet onto a plate and passed it and a fork to her. Without asking, he poured her a glass of orange juice and set it next to her. She remained on the countertop, and when his omelet was done, he leaned against the counter near the stove.

"The doctor gave Sarah a mild sedative when she arrived, and the nurse says she's been dozing off and on the last few hours. I took her the clothes your mom packed, and she asked if you'd come see her when you arrived. She seemed upset that you were out with Matthew, thought you'd be angry with her again. Care to share why?"

Hannah drew a long, ragged breath. "This isn't going to be easy, is it?"

"You mean my being Sarah's counselor?"

Hannah stabbed another bite of eggs. "Yeah."

"It could be worse." Paul shrugged. "You could be my therapist."

His jesting tugged at her, making her want to smile. She pushed a piece of the omelet around on her plate, stalling. "The rumor about the midnight ride in my nightgown, remember the one?"

He nodded.

"Sarah exaggerated it without realizing the person I'd gone for a ride with was Matthew. When he found out those few minutes had turned into a vicious rumor, he only held his tongue because I asked him to. No one doubts anything Matthew says, so if he'd told the community the truth, she would be in really big trouble." She took another bite of food.

"It's not human nature to ask someone to keep a secret rather than set the record straight. Why didn't you let Matthew say his piece?"

"The damage for me was done, and it was only one of several rumors, so clearing that one thing up only held the power to ruin Matthew and Elle, a relationship that began budding shortly after we went for that ride." Hannah took a sip of her juice. "I can't explain it, but Matthew is like a brother. Neither one of us realized how that ride might look." She slid off the counter, wondering how Paul could so easily have believed all those lies about her and left her. She wouldn't ask, whether from fear or some other reason, she didn't know — didn't care to try to figure it out.

Hannah took another drink and set the cup on the counter. "So you think Sarah's afraid of the truth being revealed?"

"Absolutely. I think she should get this off her conscience by telling the truth, not this week and maybe not next, but soon."

"You can't be serious."

"Facing our fears, skeletons, and mistakes is paramount in finding ourselves — in living with ourselves. Once it's done, that fear will be laid to rest, and she'll be stronger for having dealt with it and have more peace because she's not carrying the weight of that fear every day and night."

Hannah put her plate in the sink, thinking how well this new vocation suited him. His career as a counselor should make her uncomfortable, as if he were analyzing her, but he truly seemed to use his schooling only to assess things, like she did with her nursing skills. He wasn't supershrink analyzing, and he certainly wasn't judging.

Assessing. That's what he was carefully doing. It was a skill Dr. Lehman had taught her, even in the emotional realm as she counseled Amish women about their health concerns. She'd expected Paul to peer down at those he counseled, as if he held some secret powers over them, but that's not what he was about, and she found that disturbing for reasons she refused to think on.

"I'd like to see Sarah now."

He set his plate in the sink. "I have to tell you something first."

"About Sarah?"

"No, not at all. Martin called." He reached

157

into his pocket and pulled out a cell phone. "You and the clinic have matching cells."

"What?" Hannah jerked the phone from her dress pocket. "You didn't answer my phone, did you?"

"I thought it was the one I signed out from the clinic."

She'd intended to tell Martin all about today, but there hadn't been time. Hannah sighed. "It's not your fault." She exchanged phones with Paul. "Sarah?"

"Right this way." He motioned to a back door and then stopped, allowing her to go first. They walked in silence across the yard and up the narrow concrete sidewalk.

She took a deep breath of the cool air. It carried the aroma of her childhood — freshly mowed hayfields, livestock, and a hint of honeysuckle.

Paul reached for the doorknob and then paused. "She's been very calm since arriving, but I suspect she'll get upset and try to convince you she can't survive if you return to Ohio. Stay calm and firm in your resolve that you have to go home. It won't help her at all if you give in to her self-image of being weak. She needs help, not babying."

"And for that stance on your part, I'm very grateful. Martin will be too."

"Glad I can help." Paul opened the door.

From a door to the right, Sarah ran out into the hallway and flung herself against Hannah and clung to her. "You're here! You'll stay, right? You'll stay in Owl's Perch and come visit me every day. We can see each other all the time without Daed around."

Hannah hugged her sister. "No, Sarah, I can't stay, but we can write to each other. You can call me when the staff here says you can." She pulled away, looking her sister in the eye. "I have a very busy life in Ohio, and I have to go back."

"But you'll come visit regularly, right?"

Hannah glanced at Paul. She hadn't thought ahead enough to consider what she'd do about visits. "My schedule won't allow much room until after the first of the year."

"But . . ." Sarah's eyes held panic. "You're leaving me?"

"We can talk by phone regularly." Hannah looked to Paul, silently pleading for some support.

"Sarah, she's separate from you. Remember?" He put one hand on Sarah's wrist and motioned for Hannah to step back. "You have the strength to stand on your own without her and without your thoughts tormenting you. We're going to spend time proving that, and you'll find peace and continue to get stronger while she's gone."

Sarah sobbed. "Don't go."

"Rita," Paul called, "would you help Sarah back to her room, please?" A woman in scrubs came into the hallway almost immediately. "Sarah, I need to talk to Hannah for just a minute, and then she'll come tell you good night before leaving."

Reaching for Hannah, Sarah was guided out of the hallway by Rita.

Paul turned his back to the door Sarah had just gone through. "I have an idea that might help her, but I'm not sure how you'll feel about it."

"And one Lapp daughter's hysteria is all you can handle at a time." As soon as the words left her mouth, she realized her sarcastic side was showing again. When had it become a natural part of her?

"I've never seen you hysterical. Justifiable anger is not the same."

She preferred sarcasm over being patronized. "Your idea?"

"When you left, Mary gave me the 'Past and Future' quilt. Sarah didn't like that it came to me, but I kept it anyway." He shrugged. "Since you designed it and sewed a lot of it with cloth from Sarah's and your childhoods, she might find that comforting

160

for a while. I have it in my car."

"How many years did it take you to learn to make a conversation so generic? And why did Mary pass the quilt to you?"

"Generic?"

"You use odd wording, which causes a lack of clarity in what you mean — which is your point, I'm sure. 'Comforting for a while . . .' Does that mean you're returning it to me? If you're going to say something, make it clear."

"Noted."

She stared at him. Giving him that one-word response earlier hadn't bothered her at all; receiving it annoyed her. "And you didn't answer about the quilt."

"Mary gave it to me when I was dealing with the shock of your being gone."

"Gave it?"

"Yes."

"And it's in your car?"

"Yes."

"That's it? That's all the explanation I get?"

"I'm hopeful you'll take what I've said and not keep probing for answers." Paul's shoulders were square and his stance unmovable, in spite of the mildness in his words. It was a part of him that she remembered well — respectful noncooperation — and no one ever seemed as good at it as Paul Waddell.

She laughed softly. "I guess you've earned a break. The quilt can be a visual reminder that I'll always be a part of her future just as I was a part of her past."

"Perfectly worded. You tell Sarah while I go after it."

CHAPTER 12

Martin lay on his bed with the remote control in his hand, flipping television stations at an annoying rate, even to himself. The large red numerals on the digital clock glared the fact that it was past midnight. And he hadn't heard from Hannah yet.

Paul Waddell.

Disgust rolled through him. Surely this brief encounter — whatever it was — wouldn't resurrect any old feelings she'd once had for him. It'd taken way too long for Hannah to find peace and for her heart to be free of Paul. When she had begun showing an interest in Martin, he'd made her wait until her twentieth birthday before they went on their first date — mostly because the idea of being past his mid-twenties and dating a teenager crossed a moral line that U.S. laws didn't cover.

Now he was at home with his niece and nephew and their part-time nanny while

Hannah was somewhere in Owl's Perch with Paul Waddell's cell phone in her pocket. He should have gone with her.

Tempted to call again, he jolted when the phone beside him rang. The caller ID indicated it was Hannah. "Hey."

"Hi. Did I wake you?"

"No, I've been waiting to hear from you."

"Yeah, I'm sure. I'd be upset if the tables were turned, but dealing with him was unavoidable."

The fact that she gave credence to his feelings and didn't try to brush off the incident as nothing diluted his concerns. "You okay?"

"I will be when I'm back with you and the children . . . tomorrow."

"Tomorrow?"

"Yeah. That's sort of why what's-his-name had my phone by accident. It was my fault, but the good news is Sarah's at a mental health facility and I'm leaving for Ohio in the morning. I'd be tempted to leave even at this hour, but I had a flat today, and I'm not traveling at night on a spare."

"A flat?"

"By itself, it may have been the easiest part of my day after I arrived in Owl's Perch. I just want out of here."

Grateful for the sincerity of her tone, he felt more like himself again. "I want you to take the car in tomorrow morning and have a new set of tires put on before you head home."

"It only needs one."

"If it got one flat, they must all need replacing. Just use the credit card, and I'll take care of the bill."

"I'll get one new tire and pay for it myself, but I appreciate your generosity."

He resisted the desire to challenge her reasoning, figuring she didn't need him to debate with her at the end of a rough day. Besides, she'd still do it her way, and he'd end up feeling like the bad guy for trying to take care of her. He'd come up with an excuse to use her car one day next week and have the tires replaced; she'd never know.

Martin changed the subject. "You'll be glad to know it's a teachers' workday tomorrow, so Kevin and Lissa will be off all day."

She cleared her throat, and he wondered if she was crying. "That sounds like heaven."

"You *have* had a rough go of it if you think those two are paradise," he teased.

"But you always manage to be a good uncle anyway." He heard her yawn. "I'm at the hotel and bushed. I'll see you tomorrow. Okay?"

"Sleep well, phone girl."

"Good night."

Golden rays of the new day's sun streaked through the cloud-covered morning as Hannah pulled into Mary's driveway. She hadn't planned on coming by this morning, but she couldn't leave Owl's Perch without more time with her friend. She had even dreamed about her last night. However she had managed to squelch her feelings for Mary in order to begin life anew in Ohio, they'd resurfaced with a tenacious desire.

As Hannah got out of her car, she spotted Mary on her knees in the garden.

Hannah chuckled. *Potato-harvesting time.*

Wishing she'd worn something more appropriate for working a garden, she shielded her eyes from the sunlight and walked toward her. "Are you praying for some help while you're down there?"

Mary jumped and then laughed. "Well, look at you . . . all cleaned up."

Her words were kind, as they'd been yesterday, but something in her eyes said Hannah was a stranger. On the road yesterday she'd seemed very open, and they'd talked with ease, but the topic had stayed on Sarah and all that had taken place concerning her since Hannah had left. But standing here now, Hannah felt a wall, a thick one — one she wanted removed if it was possible.

"Kann Ich helfe?" Hoping that reverting to Pennsylvania Dutch would make a difference, Hannah offered to help.

"Bischt du zu draus in da Welt?"

Hannah should have known she looked "too out in the world," too worldly, for Mary to be comfortable with her — driving a car, wearing jewelry, attending college, having buttons run the length of her pale yellow skirt.

Hannah covered her heart. *"Ich bin net zu draus in da Welt."* She tapped her fingers over her heart, trying to reassure Mary that she wasn't too out in the world. "Not here, Mary."

Still on her knees, Mary studied her, clearly torn between this different-looking Hannah and the friend she'd once loved dearly.

Mary patted the soil beside her. *"Kumm. Loss uns blaudere bis unsrer Hatzer verbinne."* Come. Let's talk until our hearts unite.

Hannah knelt. She lifted Mary's hand and pressed it against her cheek. "Denki."

Mary's brows knit, and she hugged Hannah tight. *"Mei liewi, liewi* Hannah." *My dear, dear Hannah.*

Those words seemed to cause the wall between them to completely fall. If it hadn't, Hannah knew it could, if they put a little effort into it. Why had she let her fears and maybe even her ego cause her to hide her whereabouts so completely? Before she left today, she'd make sure Mary knew how very sorry she was for doing such a selfish thing.

At the head of the rectangular table, Martin went down the workload list in great minutia with his project managers. The weekly event often threatened to cause death by boredom, but the process was necessary.

"Doug, how long until the foundation on SWG is ready to be poured?"

"Depends on when the surveyors get the staking done."

Martin turned to Alex.

Alex shrugged. "We can have that done Thursday, but Kirk's requested a walkabout with you and Amy before he signs off on the plans."

Martin nodded. "What's a good time for us to do that, Amy?"

"Christmas."

The men chuckled. Amy's presence always added a bit of flavor to the dull workload process. Everyone in the room and their significant others were headed to Hawaii over Christmas. His employees and Amy worked really hard throughout the year, arriving early, leaving late, and helping this company be a leader in its field. "Anything just a tad sooner, like this afternoon or tomorrow?"

"Sure, either one really, but, uh . . ." She flopped the pen around on the stack of papers in front of her. "How rough is the terrain on this site?"

Doug tapped his middle finger on the table over and over again. "Jeans and a flannel shirt, definitely. And boots, without heels."

"That rules Amy out," Alex said. "Now if she could wear those black leather pants and those spike heel boots . . ."

"The thorns would rip my leather pants. But thanks, Alex."

Martin had no idea if she really owned leather pants, but he doubted it. As the only female at these weekly meetings, she took a good bit of teasing.

"Amy?" Martin asked, trying to veer the conversation back to its point.

She folded her hands. "I'll wear old jeans tomorrow, but if I break a nail, I want an extra day in Hawaii."

Alex whistled and pointed out the plate-glass window.

Hannah.

Martin's heart rate increased, and he suppressed the goofy grin that threatened to cover his face. She stood just outside her vehicle, a blue green dress following her hourglass figure as she repinned her mounds of curly hair back into a clasp. It was a vain effort some days, but she didn't wear it down in public.

"Easy, Alex. She's taken."

Alex looked from Hannah to Martin. "Are we looking at 'phone girl'?"

Martin had forgotten that Alex hadn't met Hannah. Amy hadn't either, but the others in the room had come to a few of the band gatherings throughout the year. Martin nodded. "Hannah Lawson is her real name, and if she comes in, try to act refined."

Alex shook his head. "Is she legal? I mean she looks young . . . for someone your age."

Doug scrunched a piece of paper and tossed it across the table. "Cut the nonsense. You're looking at the mother of his future children."

Ignoring the stabs at humor, Martin rose. "Doug, take over for me."

Martin left the room and hurried down the corridor, heading for the closest exit. He went out the side door and started talking as he walked toward her. "Wow, you

170

drove to Ohio and my office in the same week."

She met him halfway on the sidewalk, a smile highlighting her rosy cheeks and flawless complexion. "A woman of endless talents."

She slid her arms around his shoulders, and he wrapped her in his arms. Her body trembled. "Hey, you okay?"

"Sure."

But he wasn't convinced, and with Hannah he might not ever know.

He held her tighter, grateful she was home. "Have you been to see Kevin and Lissa already?"

She put a bit of space between them and gazed up at him. "No, I came here first."

"Really? I'm impressed." He cradled her face in his hands, wanting to kiss her. "If we weren't being watched . . ." He nodded toward the window.

She tilted her head. "You care what they think about kissing me?"

"No, but I figured you did."

"Ah, always the perfect gentleman."

Man, how he tried — not just because of who she was in all her Old Order Amish innocence, but also because of how much younger she was. Her age was the only reason he hadn't pushed her harder to agree to marry him. But he was sure she'd say yes when he asked again as they shared a romantic alfresco meal at sunset on the beach in Hawaii.

Her smile wobbled, and something he'd seen before, but never could define, reflected in her eyes as she took a ragged breath. "How about if I pick up a few groceries — maybe fresh fruit, a loaf of deli bread, and a rotisserie chicken — and you take off early? All four of us can go to the cabin before I have to leave for class tonight."

"The cabin?" He laughed and shook his head. His million-dollar home with her own private cottage out back did nothing for the girl, but the scant cabin she'd lived in until the needs of Kevin and Lissa made it convenient for him to get her out of there held her heart ransom. "Wouldn't having a picnic here at the office be easier?"

She poked out her bottom lip, mocking a pout. Since she hadn't requested this in a long time, surely he could stand one night of it. "Whatever makes you happy, phone girl."

She tilted her chin in that way that said her will was set, her resolve complete. But why was this appearing now?

"You." She placed her hands over his.

"You and Kevin and Lissa make me happy."

Her uncharacteristic declaration meant more to him than she could possibly understand as a twenty-year-old. He'd navigated living single for too long. Dates were easy to come by, but finding someone who made life more than it was without that person wasn't as effortless. By the time Hannah entered his life, he'd begun to fear it would never happen for him.

Unable to resist, he slowly kissed her cheek several times, breathing in the aroma of everything that made him connect to life in a way that work and financial success couldn't match. He eased his lips across her warm, soft skin until he found her lips. "I love you, Hannah."

CHAPTER 13

Matthew lit a kerosene lantern and carried it with him as he descended the stairway to the ground floor of his home. The rooster crowed loudly, even though the first rays of light weren't yet visible. Thunder rumbled in the distance as the sound of a gentle rain against the windows kept rhythm with the grandfather clock in the hallway. He set the lantern on the coffee table and laced his black boots.

Muted sound and movement in the dark kitchen caught his attention. Once he finished the last knot, he grabbed the lamp and headed toward the sound.

When the lantern cast its glow across the room, Kathryn's attention turned from the stove. "Hey, I didn't wake you, did I?"

He shook his head and set the lantern on the table. "What are you doin' up?"

"Same as you, I suppose. Can't sleep." She wiped her hands on a dishtowel and laid it across her shoulder. "What is it about death that disrupts everything to do with life — hunger, sleep, clear thought?"

Matthew eased into a chair. Kathryn wrapped a potholder around the handle of the coffeepot that sat on the eye of the gas stove. She lifted the pot, silently asking if he wanted a cup. He shook his head, uninterested in food or drink.

She poured herself a cup, dumped some sugar and milk into it, and took a seat across from him. "It'll get easier, Matthew. You have to trust in that, even as these days carry enough pain and guilt to make you believe otherwise."

It was nice to sit in a quiet room with someone who understood. She'd been the only person to acknowledge his sense of guilt. If she hadn't, he might not have understood the thing that seemed to cover him with blame so thick he thought he'd suffocate.

Unable to tolerate the back of the chair touching him, Matthew propped his forearms on the table. "I saw Hannah night before last. She said to tell ya hello."

Kathryn smiled. "I remember seeing her at the annual school sales when we were kids, but I bet I haven't seen her in six or so years. How is she?"

"Different."

"Aren't we all." It wasn't a question, and Kathryn was right. She wrapped her hands around the coffee mug. "We dress and live the same basic way as our ancestors, and yet the changes and temptations that war inside us must rival that of the Englischers."

The softness of her voice, her hope laced inside truth caused Matthew to feel something beyond his confusion for a moment. "But I always thought our sense of community and devotion to the simple life gave us the strength to resist the temptation to doubt or give up."

"And now you're not sure it does?"

Matthew ran his hands across the well-worn oak table his great-grandfather had built. "Can I ask you a question?"

She gazed into his eyes, and he noticed for the first time the golden radiance to her brown eyes. "Always."

Feeling welcome to be himself and to share the tormenting thoughts that ripped at him, he was grateful she'd agreed to stay on for a while. "What happened that day on the pond, and how did ya cope?"

Slowly her hands crossed the table, and she slid them over his, assuring him she'd answer in a few moments. After a bit she withdrew her hands and rose from her chair.

In spite of his declining coffee a few minutes ago, she poured him a cup.

After setting it in front of him, she took a seat and placed the pot on a folded dishtowel on the table. "Abram and me and Daed had been at the pond since before sunrise, catching fish and singing loudly because the harvest was over and we were in the mood to play. Daed was sitting on the dock, and me and Abram were in a dinghy in the middle of our acre pond." She paused, turning the mug around and around as if lost in the memory. "Abram was being silly, rocking the boat while I screamed like a girl."

Matthew laughed softly. "Females tend to do that . . . sound like a girl."

"They both thought it was funny." A smile edged her lips. "The water sparkled, and their laughter echoed. And then everything changed. Green, murky water surrounded me. The boat had tipped, dumping out both of us. I didn't even know which way was up until I saw Abram's feet kicking near the surface of the water. I swam that way, feeling like my lungs would burst before I reached the top. I came to the surface coughing and struggling to get air. He was screaming for me to help him. Daed was on the dock, peeling out of his shoes and screaming for me to swim for the dock." She paused. "I headed for Abram, and Daed screamed my name, pointing his finger at me. He said, 'You obey me this instant!' And I did. He dove into the water, but by the time he got to Abram, he'd gone under, and Daed couldn't find him until it was too late." She lifted her gaze and stared into Matthew's eyes. "While I was making my way to the dock and Daed was swimming out to him, Abram called to me over and over again. There I was, a twelve-year-old girl, flailing in the water, trying desperately to get to the dock so my Daed wouldn't be mad at me." She rubbed the temples of her head as if it hurt. "I hated myself for a long time, wishing . . ." She took a sip of her coffee, looking lost in pain.

"You know why your Daed wouldn't let you go after him, don't ya?"

She wiped a tear and nodded. "I do now, but I didn't for a long time. I just remember crawling in my Daed's lap every day for months, crying until I couldn't cry any longer. He just held me, assuring me Abram was in heaven, happy and safe, but it was years before I understood that my parents would have buried both of us had I disobeyed." She drew a deep breath. "I think they thought I was traumatized enough without telling me I would have died too. But it seems that in the end all that matters is finding a way to survive the grief and trusting in the goodness of life beyond the pain." She clasped her hands together, staring at them. "You did your best to save David. You were a good and kind brother. What else could be done?"

Matthew nodded, but he still hadn't found the answer to the question that haunted him — how to find *his* way out of the dark hole that surrounded him.

Maybe no one could answer that, but it seemed it was time to go to Baltimore and see if it held any peace or distractions for him. "I'd appreciate if you could stay here helping Mamm while I'm in Baltimore for a few days, a week at most."

"I . . . I can . . ."

"But?"

"My Daed's been asking me to come back home since before the fire. I could stay for a week, but he's right; my family is there. When the Bylers' barn burned, I came here to help them because they're our cousins. And . . . Joseph's patience with me being here is growing thin."

He barely gave a nod.

Her fingers touched the back of his hands. He looked up. "Go. Find some peace and strength. I'll stay until you get back."

"I figure I just need a few days."

CHAPTER 14

Hannah laid the quilt to the side and wriggled her hands into a pair of medical gloves. In spite of the clinic having electricity, only kerosene lamps were used until time for delivery. It gave the place a homey feel the women appreciated. *"Es wunderbaar Bobbeli iss glei do."* Making small talk in soothing tones was important to moms in labor, so Hannah encouraged Lois that her wonderful baby was almost here.

Sweat trickled down Lois's thirty-something face as she moaned through another round of labor pains. *"Net glei genunk!"*

"Ya." Hannah moved to the foot of the birthing bed. Lois was right — not soon enough. It was her fifth child, and labor had begun nearly sixteen hours ago. According to her chart, Lois always had slow, methodical labors. She'd been in labor for several days with her first child.

While Hannah waited for the contraction to ease so she could perform a pelvic exam, Snickers meowed from somewhere outside.

The lines across Lois's face relaxed as the last of the pain subsided. "If that cat's up a tree again, it'd be awfully entertaining to see you go after it . . . like you did before."

The memory made her laugh. "Lois, that has to be the most legendary Tuesday quilting to date — Amish women poking fun at me while I climbed a tree to rescue a cat. But it's too cold and too dark out there this time."

Lois went almost limp against the pillow, relaxing. "I remember you climbing that tree, hanging that cat over the outstretched sheet us women were holding out. Then when you released it, it plunged through the air, screeching, claws out." She started laughing. "Mercy, Hannah, in one way or another you've been a blessing since you started working here."

"Denki." Hannah raised one eyebrow, dishing back some of the teasing Lois was giving. "Take a deep breath and hold it. I just want to see if it's time to call Dr. Lehman."

"Surely it is."

Hannah checked Lois's cervix and nodded. "I think so." She removed the gloves, washed her hands, and went to the phone.

Although labor had been a long ordeal, interrupting Hannah's Sunday with Martin, she and Lois had made good use of their time, even working on Lois's half-done log cabin star quilt. The pattern was Lois's favorite, and so far she'd made one for each of her children — only this time she was months behind in finishing it. If Lois wasn't so set against getting an epidural for pain, she'd probably have the baby in her arms by now. An epidural often relaxed a woman, and the contractions were able to do their job faster.

Hannah had been here part of yesterday and all night, which meant after Lois gave birth in the next hour or two, she'd have to sleep, then study, and then attend Monday night classes before getting home close to midnight.

The hayfields disappeared from sight as the view turned into asphalt, glass, and steel.

Baltimore.

As they drove toward the city at sixty miles per hour, Matthew watched the scenery, hoping the gloominess that'd taken over his mind and heart would lift. Haze covered the sprawling skyline of buildings, warehouses, and factories with their large stacks filling the sky. Billboards lined the side of the freeway, advertising phones, trucks, gyms — call now, buy now, things and more things. They crossed a huge concrete-and-steel bridge into an area of high-rise buildings butting against stretches of multilane roads. Not particularly feeling the excitement Elle said he would, he turned to face his driver.

"Been here before, have ya, Nate?"

"A few times. My wife loves the National Aquarium, though we haven't been in a while. If you get a chance to go, they might have the sea otters — well, I think they're otters, or maybe they're sea lions — that are outside for everyone to see. Though that may only happen in the summer. Either way, I think you'll enjoy visiting there if you have a chance."

The massive structures did look a little interesting. Nate maneuvered the vehicle this way and that as the minutes rolled on and the view changed again. Long brick buildings with doors and windows that were similar to a home's lined the street. Surely he wasn't looking at some type of house.

"Row houses," Nate said, as if he'd read Matthew's mind.

On second look some had a hint of homeyness to them with curtains in the windows and flowers in window boxes. Others had paint peeling around the trim. As they continued down the street, they passed a section of brick buildings where the lower windows and doorways were sealed with cinder blocks while the upper windows looked like a fire had consumed the insides of the buildings. Across the street three middle-aged women sat on the steps of one house, talking. Parked cars lined the street, leaving two lanes for traffic between them. A young woman in a tight, short dress and a snug leather jacket paraded down the street in high-heeled, shiny boots while pushing a stroller.

Nate pulled up to a curb. "This is it." He put the truck in Park and set the brake.

Matthew stepped out of the vehicle, seeing a few well-placed trees amid concrete and brick everything. The three-story brick place with fancy molding along the cornice looked more like a sardine inside a can — packed in tightly — than a home.

Nate opened the lockbox in the bed of his truck. "You're gonna stick out a bit here unless you get rid of the hat and suspenders."

"More than that girl we passed awhile back?"

Nate pulled out the sacks with Matthew's

clothes. "You'll see women dressed in a lot more and a lot less before your week's up."

Elle bounded out the door and down the steps. "You're here and right on time too."

Matthew nodded. "We're here. That's true enough."

She tilted her head. "Can I have a hug?"

"An easy one." He put his arms around her and hugged her, glad his skin wasn't near as sore to touch as it had been. As he took a step back, a tall man wearing a black suit and a fitted hat covering only the crown of his head passed by.

"Nate thought I'd stick out."

Elle glanced at the man. "Nah, if it exists in the world, there will be traces of it here."

Her comments seemed odd, considering things she'd said about needing to wear certain Englischer clothes during her time here, but he didn't want to question or challenge her on it right now.

The half-dressed woman pushing the stroller came toward them.

Elle tugged on Matthew's shirt. "After the shock wears off, you'll find it easy to enjoy."

Nate passed Matthew the two large paper bags carrying his clothes. "I need to go. Told Kathryn I'd be back to pick her up by two."

Matthew shifted the full bags, wondering if he'd brought too many clothes. "Where's she needing ya to take her?"

"My place. With your phone not in working order, the missis invited her to use ours. Kathryn said she needed to use a phone and desk for business of some type. She said the Bylers' phone shanty is too limiting."

Matthew gave a nod. The phone lines in his shop were destroyed. Without the status of operating a business, the bishop wasn't going to approve having a phone shanty put in. But he didn't know what possible business Kathryn could be up to.

Matthew put the sacks on the sidewalk and paid Nate. "Monday morning at eleven. I'll meet ya right here —"

"Actually . . . ," Elle interrupted, "why don't you just call him when you're ready to leave? I have a phone. He has one. It's easier, and I was hoping you might stay longer than just four or five days."

"Longer?" Matthew studied her, wondering just what she was hoping for. "But I told Kath—"

"Okay." She snapped the word, and her violet-colored eyes spit anger, reminding him how little patience she had with any other female being in his life. "You can leave Monday, but why don't you call Nate to confirm rather than put it as a definite?"

"That works too." Matthew slid the rest

of his cash into his pant pocket, hoping it'd last him. But as he stood there, he began to unravel a few things about who he and Elle were together — a couple who'd never really had a chance to form an easygoing, enjoyable friendship. His time in Baltimore would help with that.

Nate closed the lockbox. "That's fine. I'll wait until I hear from you to make plans. Enjoy your time here." He waved as he climbed into his vehicle.

Elle grabbed one of the sacks. "Come on. I have your room all ready."

Looking at the tall, narrow, brick building, Matthew had to admit that the trip had already lessened the intensity of his grief. Maybe Elle was right — getting away might help.

They entered through the front door and walked up two flights of stairs before Elle stepped into a bedroom.

She set his bag of clothes on the bed. "This is yours for as long as you want it. When you're ready, I have lunch made. I need to return to the bakery in an hour, but I was hoping you'd come with me, maybe help out since I have to work anyway. You could give our commercial ovens a try or run the counter. Dad said I could have off early tomorrow, so I'll take you to the Inner

Harbor and show you a view of the Chesapeake Bay and a hint of Baltimore's nightlife. It'll be fun."

Lace curtains covered the window, a whirling fan with multiple lights hung from the ceiling, and a huge radio with even larger speakers sat on a white dresser. Feeling curiosity stir, Matthew placed the other sack of clothes on the bed. "Sounds like an interesting few days, Elle. I'm looking forward to it."

She smiled in a way he hadn't seen in more than two years and kissed his cheek. "Thanks."

CHAPTER 15

Darkness covered the neighborhood as Hannah pulled into Martin's driveway at seven thirty. The question-and-answer time during today's Tuesday quilting ran late, and then paperwork concerning recent births had to be filed before she left. On her way across the lawn, she smelled smoke. She sniffed the air — no, she smelled burned food.

The back door flung open, and a blur of Martin holding a smoldering cookie sheet flashed before her just as he hurled the smoking things in her direction. She screamed and jumped back. Shock registered on his face as their eyes met.

He broke into uproarious laughter. "Hannah, sweetheart, I'm so sorry." With the pan in hand, he stepped outside and walked to her, still laughing. "But it's what you get for not being here to prevent this."

Kevin and Lissa stood in the doorway,

watching. Hannah tried to keep a straight face, but it was hopeless. "I don't know what's funnier, burned cookies sailing through the air at me or you in pink oven mitts with a fringed towel tucked in your jeans."

He dropped the pan, jerked the pink things off, and threw them on the ground. "What pink mitts?"

"Too late. I know what I saw, Martin."

"And whose fault is it that my home, a.k.a. the bachelor pad, has pink oven mittens?"

"Yours. You bought them. I thought you'd done it for me, but obviously I stand corrected." She picked up a burned round thing from the grass. "What was this before you got hold of it?"

"Chocolate-chip cookie dough," Lissa yelled out the back door. Kevin folded his arms over his chest, obviously not happy about the burned cookies.

Hannah bit her bottom lip, thoroughly soaking in the man in front of her. His eyes reflected amusement, and there was a bit of white flour in his thick, dark hair.

He came within inches of her. "Hi."

"Hi." She pulled the towel loose from his jeans. "Need some help?"

"Always." He kissed her cheek while his

face reflected desire for a real kiss.

"What's going on?"

He rolled his eyes. "Kevin needs six dozen homemade cookies for tomorrow."

"Six dozen? Tomorrow?"

He nodded.

She put the towel around his neck and pulled him closer. "Why didn't we know this before tonight?"

"I plead the Fifth."

"Why am I not surprised?" She brushed her lips against his.

Lissa banged on the glass of the open storm door. "Hannah, come see what Uncle Martin did."

She narrowed her eyes at him before entering the house. The counters were covered in dirty dishes, and the sink had remnants of burned cookies. "My kitchen!" She clamped her hands over her mouth.

Martin laughed. "You can have it."

Kevin huffed loudly. "I'll never have those cookies, and everyone will . . ."

Martin held out his hand in stop-sign fashion. "Relax, Kevin. I'll get this done." Martin looked to Hannah. "I will."

Lissa frowned at Kevin. "I believe you, Uncle Martin."

Kevin turned and walked out of the room, mumbling, "I'll believe it when I see it."

Lissa followed him, wagging her finger and complaining at him.

Martin shoved one hand into his jean pocket. "He's a bit sensitive right now. If this doesn't get done, in his eyes it'll be like screaming to the whole school that he doesn't have a mother."

"Ah, would you like some help?"

He gestured at the counters and sink. "Think I need it?" His face became serious. "Some days what Faye's done to those kids makes me so . . ."

Hannah placed her fingers over his lips. "They have you, and we both know that's saying more than Kevin and Lissa can possibly understand right now."

Martin kissed her fingers. "And you."

"And me." She glanced at the stove. "Hey, 450 degrees?"

"I was hoping to get the cookies done faster that way."

"And how's that working for you?"

"Sarcasm. You know, I wouldn't have coached you to hone that skill had I known you'd use it on me. We need to make a fresh pot of coffee and get the kids in bed . . . please." He elongated the last word, letting her know he was more than ready for a break from his niece and nephew.

"While you read to them, I'll clean the

kitchen. After we tuck them in for the night, we'll get a fresh start. Okay?"

"That seems like a lot of work for a man who only wants some time with his girl."

She grabbed the coffee decanter. "Regular or decaf?"

"Regular and lots of it."

With a long wooden peel in hand, Matthew removed two loaves of bread from the commercial oven. He set them to the side and pulled out a few more. After ten days in Baltimore, grappling through the fog of grief had left him more apathetic than renewed. Still, that was more welcome than the intense pain of loss.

Twinges of guilt pricked him each time he remembered that he'd not kept his word to Kathryn about returning within a few days. He'd called and left a message with Nate, asking him to tell her he was staying longer.

Her voice circled inside his head. *You can rebuild . . .*

But rebuilding seemed wrong. Why should he get to restore his life when David's was over? Matthew swallowed hard, unable to answer that question.

The bell on the front door of the bakery rang, letting him know the first customers of the day had arrived. What irked him was when he did feel something other than apathy, it tended to be loneliness, and yet he was right here with Elle. It wouldn't be fair to think she could remove any of his grief and confusion, but he'd expected to feel a closeness of some sort.

Elle seemed content enough here. They'd attended a huge Englischer church on Sunday. It'd been . . . interesting and overwhelming, and he was glad that while on that extended buggy ride, Hannah had told him about the many differences in the Englischer world.

Elle's father, Sid, came into the kitchen through the swinging door. "Hey, Matthew, why don't you slip out of that apron and handle the customers while I take over back here?"

Removing the apron, Matthew went to the customer counter with the glass displays filled with baked goods. Sid had made a dozen statements about how much customers were responding to his presence in the bakery. Although he thought it possible Elle wasn't aware, he wasn't fooled. Sid wanted him at the bakery, not because he needed his help, but because his Amish clothing and accent appealed to customers.

Matthew waited on customers and ran the register. Sid kept the baked goods coming until it was time to shut off the ovens and clean up the kitchen. The place was quiet during the afternoon lull when the bell on the front door rang.

Elle breezed in, all smiles as she slid out of her jacket. "Sorry, the photo shoot took longer than we expected."

Sid came out of the kitchen and looked at Matthew. "You won."

Matthew nodded. "Yep."

Elle huffed. "Won what?"

Sid wiped a wet cloth across the counter. "He said you'd be here around two. I said closer to four. You're always late. We just bet as to how late. You're not nearly as late as usual since Matthew's around."

Elle slid the apron strap over her head. "Are you betting, Matthew?"

"Won a loaf of stale bread to feed to the ducks and the right to leave thirty minutes early."

"Well done." Elle kissed his cheek.

"Think so? It seems a bit stiff for a man who's not actually employed by your father."

She giggled. "I guess I didn't think about it like that."

Sid passed the wet cloth to Elle, a teasing gleam in his eye. "But you have to stay late to make up for the time you've missed."

She stuck her tongue out at him. "Be nice, Dad. We have company."

He moved to a table and sat down. "Matthew, I know you didn't like it when Elle left Owl's Perch, and I probably should've handled that better, but I think you should consider moving in with us. We got plenty of room and plenty of work."

Matthew pulled out a chair from a nearby table, turned it around, and straddled it. "Why me?"

Sid frowned. "What?"

"Why me? There are plenty of people needing jobs."

"Because it'd make Elle happy."

Nodding her head, she smiled broadly, making Matthew wonder if she was in on this with her dad or just an innocent bystander.

Either way, they both knew he was a baptized member of the faith, so this request meant they were asking him to leave the faith, didn't it? He laid his arms across the chair's back. "What made ya want me to come here rather than Elle comin' to Owl's Perch and joinin' the faith as she agreed?"

"Well, I've thought your joining us here was a good idea for over a year, and when your shop burned down, I thought maybe you'd be open to the idea of coming here."

The man made it sound like he'd offered this while considering Matthew's feelings or best interests, but he doubted if Sid was anyone's friend. The man was nice enough outwardly, but from Matthew's perspective every bit of niceness was wrapped around a selfish motive. He seemed to only know the fine art of using people. He'd bailed on his daughter, leaving her to be raised by an Amish family that had befriended her mother before she passed. Never once did he make contact or pay the Zooks anything for childcare. Then he showed up when he needed Elle's help with the bakery, and now —

"You want me to move in?"

Sid nodded. "Sure. I'd love it."

"And if I remove all signs of being Amish, would ya love it then?"

Elle wheeled to face him, shock written across her features. "Matthew."

Matthew shrugged. "It's a fair question."

Sid strummed his fingers on the table, looking as if he'd expected this conversation. "This is a good business, and I'm willing to bring you into it because Elle loves you. You can live rent free and have all the time you want with my daughter. But for this arrangement, wearing your Amish garb is little to ask of you."

"Dad, you're assuming I'll stay here. I invited Matthew so we could have some time together, but I might move back and become Amish."

Sid rose. "You've been saying that for over two years, Elle. Face it, you like it here more than you like the Plain life, but the decision is yours."

She scowled at her dad before she held her hand out for Matthew's. "We're leaving for the afternoon, okay?"

"You guys have fun."

Matthew rose and helped Elle on with her jacket before sliding into his own. As they stepped onto the sidewalk, the afternoon sun against their backs helped take the edge off the cool nip in the air.

She slid her hand into his. "I'm sorry about that. He learned a few months back how much better the Amish bakeries do. I guess he thinks we should try to use that pull if we can. He'd have me wearing the Amish clothing if I would, but I won't. If I wore the dress now after being established as not Amish, it'd come across as fake and offensive to our customers."

Matthew wasn't impressed with her stance. She had known how her father felt, his reasoning and motives, when she invited him here. He freed his hand and slid it into his jacket pocket.

She grabbed his arm, stopping him from walking, and stared into his eyes. "I . . . I wanted to give you as much time here as I could before we talked, but if you don't like it here and want us to return to Owl's Perch, I'm ready to join the faith and make that commitment."

It seemed he should feel excited, but he did at least sense a break in the fog of confusion.

"Matthew?"

He gazed into the eyes that used to mean hope and a future. Pulling away, he started walking again. She quietly strolled beside him. He'd come here wanting something he thought might still exist, love for Elle. But the longer he stayed, the more he knew that whether she was here or in Owl's Perch, whether Englischer or Old Order Amish, he had no desire to marry her anymore.

Tired of looking for distractions and a way to ease his pain, Matthew felt something click into place. Odd as it seemed, he almost sensed that he *heard* something click into place. Maybe he hadn't really been waiting for Elle to return but only thought he was. Maybe that was the distraction God had used or allowed, but in reality he was waiting for something else.

Someone else.

Elle tugged on his arm. "Hey, let's go to the Inner Harbor tonight."

He gazed down at the most flawless beauty he'd ever seen, fully aware that he wanted more than what she could give him. "Elle, we need to talk."

CHAPTER 16

Mary shoved a clothespin over the edges of the last wet towel before bending to grab the empty laundry basket. A pain caught in her side, stealing much more than just her breath. Cold fear ran through her as she released the basket and waited for the pain to subside. Comparing her due date to today's date, Mary tried to think clearly. According to the midwife, she was due the week before Thanksgiving. It was only the eighth of October.

What have I done?

The doctor's warning not to conceive a child this soon after her injuries from the horse-and-buggy accident rang inside her head. Although she was at risk, he'd said the baby would be fine, hadn't he?

Mary leaned against the clothesline pole. How could she be this stubborn?

Thoughts of sharing this burden with Hannah released a bit of her anxiety. She'd cut ties with the doctor because he'd wanted to control her life. The midwife . . . well, no one wanted to say it aloud, but the woman was a gossip. Mary couldn't confide anything in her. But she trusted Hannah completely. Besides, if anyone could understand what she'd done and why, Hannah could. Easing herself upright, she searched the place for her husband. Not seeing any sign of him, she made her way to the phone shanty. With Hannah's business card in hand, Mary dialed her cell.

"Hannah Lawson. Please leave a message."

"Th-this is Mary. I . . . I need to talk to you as soon as you can." Mary started to hang up but changed her mind. She stole another glance across the yard to make sure she was alone. "I'm scared, Hannah." Feeling an awful pain down her right side, she hung up the phone. Maybe she should call the midwife. She thought about visiting her surgeon, the one who'd seen her through the physical traumas of the horse-and-buggy accident, but he'd be furious when he realized she'd ignored his instructions. Besides, he always seemed to hold back more information than he actually shared, as if her life was his to understand and make decisions for.

Suddenly all her desire to get Luke to the altar paled as the reality of what she'd done closed in around her. Surely Hannah would have answers for her and could get them through this with both her and the baby safe and Luke none the wiser. Surely. How could she have been so brazen in her decision while hiding secrets and convincing herself she was choosing to trust God over doctors?

This wasn't the first time she'd doubted her actions, but now it was impossible to convince herself the baby and she would be fine. Knowing nothing else to do, she headed for the house. After opening the window nearest the phone shanty, she lay on the couch, waiting for Hannah to call.

Closing her eyes, she counted the beats of the clock, the only noise inside her Mammi Annie's home.

The phone rang, and she pushed herself upright, trying to hurry and be cautious at the same time. Just as she rounded the outside corner of the house, she saw Luke grab the phone.

He motioned for Mary and shifted over, offering her the small bench seat inside the phone shanty. "Last I talked to Paul, Sarah was doing much better, but I talked to Mamm this morning, and she said that

Daed was planning to take the church leaders to the Better Path to try to meet with Sarah today. I'll find out from Paul how it went when he comes by here later." Luke talked on, making anxiety ripple through Mary.

There was a time when Hannah knew Mary's hopes and dreams without words needing to be spoken, but were they still that bonded? Surely Hannah wouldn't ask Luke any questions about why Mary had called earlier. She rubbed her stomach, trying to assure herself all was well. About the time she feared she might just scream and jerk the phone from him, he finally passed it to her.

Hoping her voice didn't give anything away to her husband, Mary lifted the phone to her ear. "Hi, Hannah."

"Mary, are you okay?"

"Sure, I'm fine. How are you?" Figuring Hannah thought she was nuts, Mary ached for her husband to go on about his day and let her have a few minutes alone. Of course, that wouldn't be near enough to explain what was going on, but it'd give her a moment to get advice concerning the pain in her right side.

God, please don't let my sin hurt our baby.

"Mary, what's going on? You're scaring me."

"I . . . I bet it's been busy since you returned to Ohio, ya?"

Hannah hesitated. "It's been busy, yes." Her voice was a mixture of softness and worry. "Is Luke still there?"

"Yes, he is. Did you want to talk to him again?"

"No, just give him a hug for me. Mary," Hannah spoke softly, "if you're having any sort of trouble, you need to call the midwife. Do you hear me?"

"Yes. It was good to hear from you. Bye." Mary hung up the phone, feeling like a ball of anxiety, but at least Hannah had understood her unspoken words.

Inside his office at the Better Path, Paul read over two weeks of notes on Sarah. He'd worked with her intensely, and even though they had quite a journey ahead of them, her future held promise. That was the good news. The bad news was that the lines in Sarah's mind that separated reality from thoughts, dreams, or feelings did more than just blur. They controlled her actions and motivations. When Sarah had learned of her sister's trauma and the death of her baby, she emotionally experienced the trauma as if it'd happened to her. And she carried a lot of guilt for the trouble she'd caused Hannah. The medications Dr. Stone prescribed for her helped, but she had quite a ways to go.

Using Hannah's business card as a reference, he'd e-mailed a status report to her at the end of each week, not sharing anything confidential, but letting her know Sarah was doing well and continuing to improve. Hannah sent back three words: "Received it, thanks." He'd covered similar info with Luke and Mary in person, and he looked forward to seeing them again this evening. With Sarah moving in with them soon, a discussion at their place would help Sarah adjust back to her world more easily.

"Paul." Halley's voice came through the intercom.

"Yes."

"Zeb Lapp is here to see you."

He could have bet money this day was coming. "Send him up." He put Sarah's file away and went to the landing just outside his door to greet Zeb.

"Mr. Lapp." Paul motioned to his office, followed the man inside, and closed the door. "What can I do for you today?"

"I want to see Sarah."

Paul took a seat at his desk. "I'd like to

put that on hold for a little longer. She's feeling less confused right now and is making progress. Unfortunately, how we feel about our relatives, even ones we love dearly, can cause a lot of confusing emotions."

"We aren't interested in confusing her. Just the opposite. We want to ask her to shed some light on a few things. It should help her."

"Is Ruth with you?"

"No."

"Who are the 'we' you referred to?"

"She's my daughter, and this really isn't any of your business."

Paul rose and went to the far window. In a buggy sat three stiff Amish men dressed in black. He returned to his seat. "As I said, in the two weeks Sarah has been here, she's shown a lot of improvement, but she's not ready for any visitors. My professional opinion is that it is not a good idea for you and the church leaders to meet with her anytime soon unless you allow an outside moderator to be present."

"We will meet with her today, without anyone else in the room. They've put everything aside to come here, and you will let me see her."

So the men in the buggy were the church

leaders. "Mr. Lapp, I apologize for the inconvenience, but this is about what's best for Sarah. I'll not budge on the issue as long as she's staying here." The meeting with her Daed and the church leaders seemed inevitable, but he needed time to talk with Sarah and prepare her. "If there's nothing else . . ."

"And she's set to be released when?"

"Well, originally we thought maybe by tomorrow, but that currently doesn't appear to be in her best interests." Not since Zeb and the church leaders were planning on questioning her.

"As her father, can't I have her released early?"

Paul shook his head. "No. She's an adult, and the decision is hers."

"Then let me talk to her."

"I'm sorry. That isn't a good idea for today. I don't think she's ready just yet."

Zeb stood. "I came here in good faith, wanting to meet with my daughter before she was released to start any more fires, and this is the stand you take?"

"We all want what's best for Sarah, but I'm concerned that being asked questions like this will undermine her new sense of having control over her life. Perhaps you could mull over my concerns and we could talk again."

Zeb stood. "We'll be back." He turned and walked out without saying anything else.

Not yet sure how to handle this, Paul checked his watch, gathered his schedules and time sheets, and headed for the board meeting that had begun five minutes ago. If he wanted Sarah's time extended, it'd take some amazing powers of persuasion. Since the Better Path rarely had people who required the kind of watchfulness Sarah did, the staff wanted her released. Although occasionally Rita needed to stay overnight when dealing with patients, this longer-term stint with Sarah had been hard on Rita's family. Ethics and rules didn't allow men to stay with female patients, so Paul couldn't take over for her, and there was no one else trained or available.

Without knocking, Paul walked into the meeting and took a seat.

Bob pushed a paper across the table. "Paul, here's the agenda for today. We didn't start without you, in hopes you had some ideas concerning the —"

A beep came from the intercom. "Paul, there's a call for you from Hannah Lawson on line three. I told her you were in a meeting, but she's insistent that you take the call anyway."

Paul gathered the papers into a pile and

left them on the table. "Not a problem, Halley. I'll take it in my office. Thanks." He stood. "I'm sure it won't be a long call, but I need to take it."

Bob leaned back in his chair. "Okay."

Paul went to his office and closed the door. "Paul speaking."

"Listen, I just got off the phone with Luke. Daed is on his way with the church leaders to meet with Sarah. Do not let that meeting take place."

"I didn't. He's already come and gone. When you called, I was in a meeting with the board to see if Sarah's stay can be lengthened so I can keep her environment controlled while I figure out how best to deal with this."

The line remained quiet.

"Ms. Lawson?"

"I really appreciate . . . and you . . . should call me Hannah."

"Sarah's safe, Hannah."

There was another pause before she cleared her throat. "I hate to ask, and you're doing plenty already, but I . . . I need a favor. If I knew someone else to ask, I would."

"Go ahead."

"Mary called my cell and left a message. She sounded really upset, but when I called

211

her back, she acted nonchalant. Luke was there, and I get the feeling that whatever she called about, she didn't want him to know." She clicked her tongue. "I know how this sounds, and it's not a trait of my entire community to hide things from their spouse or . . . fiancé."

"I'm not anyone's judge, and I wasn't thinking that."

"It's just that if something isn't going well with the pregnancy, she wouldn't want to alarm Luke, and she's not one to trust Englischer doctors any more than most of the community, and . . ."

"Yeah, I've come to realize over the last few weeks that's quite an issue around here." Paul checked his watch. "I'm supposed to see them tonight about Sarah. I'll go on by their house when I get off the phone and check on Mary."

"Then you won't be able to get an extension for Sarah."

"I'll handle it."

"I'm coming in tomorrow. I intend to face Daed *and* the church leaders and put an end to this meeting they want with Sarah. I should be there by lunchtime, but if Mary is having any tightening across her stomach or any other odd symptoms, she needs to call the midwife immediately."

"I'll make sure to get a few minutes with just her and relay your message. If I think she's trying to ignore any symptoms, I'll call the midwife myself."

She was silent again, and he waited.

"If you talk to her and she needs me sooner . . ."

"I'll call and let you know. Anything else?"

"Any news about the investigation concerning the fires?"

"Not yet. I really don't think we'll hear anything for a few more weeks." Paul opened the drawer and grabbed Sarah's file. "While you're here . . . I mean, since you're coming in anyway, there are a few things we — you and Luke and me — need to cover about Sarah."

"Oh . . . yeah, sure, that'll be fine. Bye."

"Bye." Paul lowered the receiver from his ear.

"Paul, wait."

She'd finally said his first name. And without choking on it too. He put the phone to his ear again. "Yes."

"Thank you."

"Anytime, Hannah."

CHAPTER 17

Hannah ended the conversation with Paul, feeling nauseated at the surly to-do list staring at her. She didn't want to walk down the hall to tell Dr. Lehman that she needed more time off to deal with another family issue. Worse, she'd need to leave Kevin and Lissa again and tell Martin she was returning to Owl's Perch. They were supposed to celebrate Martin's birthday tomorrow night. But the thing she had most hoped to avoid — facing Daed and the church leaders again — loomed before her.

The quiet peacefulness of her surroundings inside the Amish birthing center had become a part of who she was. It was one of the beloved places in her new life. The respect she'd gained through her work and school caused her to no longer feel like the shaky, incompetent girl who'd landed in Winding Creek two and a half years ago. But this return to Owl's Perch to deal with her Daed and the church leaders had her nerves taut. Needing a bit of fatherly support, Hannah headed down the hallway to find Dr. Lehman. Over the years she'd grown close to her benefactor. She talked to him about everything, and he'd become like the dad she wished she'd had.

Grabbing the lab reports from her in-box as she passed by the mail center, she noted the empty waiting room before tapping on his door.

"Come on in, Hannah."

She opened the door. "How do you do that?"

He laughed. "If you don't know by now, I shouldn't tell you." His gray hair glistened under the electric lights, and his abundant wrinkles creased with each word spoken. "You have a style all your own, even how you tap on a door." He leaned back in his chair. "Did you get the birthing reports logged already?"

"Almost, but . . . I need time off again to go back to Pennsylvania."

He laid down his pen. "Issues in Owl's Perch?"

"Yes, I'll be back in time for my classes Monday night and will work here long hours next week to make up for everything."

He gestured toward the overstuffed chair

in front of his desk. "We haven't really talked since you returned. How'd things go when you went home?"

She took a seat, glad for the friendship they shared. "Not great. I lost my temper too often, but Sarah's in a safe place to begin getting well."

"In your shoes I'm sure I'd have lost it with them too."

"I . . . I gave the most grief to Paul."

"Ah, well, we won't analyze why you targeted the somewhat innocent bystander." Dr. Lehman clasped his hands together on the desk in front of him. "Where is Sarah?"

"A place a bit similar to this, only it's set up for counseling instead of birthing babies. It's called the Better Path."

He rocked back in the office chair, looking both relaxed and deep in thought. "I think you're absolutely right to reconnect with your family. That was my hope back when I helped you find your aunt and made a way for you to stay in Ohio. Take whatever time you need, but you should let the Tuesday quilters know what's going on."

"I'm sure this will be the last time I'll need to leave unexpectedly."

"Maybe. It'll be best if you tell them your unpredictability with being here is rooted in the needs of your Amish family. So during

Tuesday's quilting you'll cover this, okay?"

She stood. "Okay."

Hannah sat in the carpool line, waiting to drop Kevin off at school. Martin wasn't overly pleased with her returning to Owl's Perch, but after a small explosion, he had helped her pack. To make things easier this go-around, she asked to take Lissa with her. Martin didn't hesitate, saying Kevin was effortless enough for the nanny and him to deal with while Hannah was gone, but Lissa wasn't. Since she was only in kindergarten, she could get away with missing a day or two of school, and Hannah would be home by Monday night for her nursing classes.

While a teacher's aide helped Kevin get out, Hannah went around the car. The aide moved on to open the car door for the next vehicle in line. Hannah knelt in front of him, straightening his shirt. "I'll be back in a few days, so you keep Uncle Martin from staying up too late at night and eating too much junk food." She ruffled his hair. "Okay?"

"Aw, Hannah, it's Friday. Staying up too late, potato chips, and SpongeBob make the weekend fun."

Clearly his uncle had discussed this with him. She kissed Kevin's cheek. "A man weekend, huh?"

"Yeah." He put his little arms around her neck and hugged her. "Lissa ruined it last time, but I didn't say nothing to her about it."

"You're a good big brother." She winked at him and hurried back around to the driver's side. He waited on the sidewalk until she was behind the wheel, and then he waved and went into the school.

With Lissa prattling endlessly for hours about cartoons, friends at school, and the differences between the Amish and Englischer homes, Hannah drove to Owl's Perch. Her mind ran in a dozen directions, but she'd at least decided to see Mary first and deal with Sarah second. Hannah slowed the car as she came to the four-way stop near the Better Path. Why was her Daed's horse and buggy parked under a shade tree behind the building?

She cut into the driveway and put the car in Park. "Come on, sweetie." She unbuckled Lissa and carried her inside the home-turned-clinic. The receptionist glanced up from her computer. "Ms. Lawson, right?"

"Yes." Hannah set Lissa's feet on the floor, and the little girl headed straight for a group of toys in the corner near the desk. "I saw a horse and buggy out back. Do you know who's here?"

"Sarah's father and a couple of other men. They're in a meeting . . ." She pointed to a closed door.

Hannah took off.

"Wait, Ms. Lawson."

Hannah pointed at Lissa. "You make sure she stays near you." Without waiting for the woman to respond, she opened the door. Sarah sat at the table with Paul, a stranger, her Daed, the bishop, one preacher, and the deacon. Hannah's chest constricted. Why on earth had she trusted Paul?

"What's going on?"

Her father frowned. "Has it become your place to question every man?"

"Has it become your place to interrogate every daughter?"

Paul rose from his seat and walked to her. "Let's step outside, please."

She barely glanced his way. "Daed, surely you're not blind enough to allow this type of meeting again."

Paul tapped her shoulder. "Come on, let's step outside and talk."

Ignoring him, she stared straight into the eyes of the bishop. He wasn't nearly as intimidating as she'd remembered. "And I see no reason why Sarah's health is the church's business."

Paul wrapped his hand around her bicep. "Roger, put all conversations on hold until I return, please." He pulled her out of the room, closing the door behind them.

She jerked against his grip. "Let go of me."

He released her and held his hands up as if proving he'd done so.

She pointed her finger at him. "You gave me your word you wouldn't let this happen."

"Hannah, I'm there with her, ready to defend or end the meeting or whatever else is needed. Roger, an arson investigator, is in there with the results of what started the fires. Sarah was doing great. Let us finish."

"You're an idiot if you think you'll understand the undercurrent of what's being said or implied. I . . . I went through something similar, and it took me a year to get over those few hours."

"I'm really sorry that happened, but what's taking place today isn't about you."

A small, warm hand slid into Hannah's, and she looked down to see a large set of dark brown eyes staring up at her. Fear creased Lissa's features, and Hannah forced a smile.

She knelt in front of her, brushing wisps of hair from her face. "It's okay, Lissa. Just a little spat between adults."

Lissa frowned up at Paul. "You're not supposed to be mean when somebody comes to visit you."

At least she had her loyalties in place. In this little girl's eyes, regardless of Hannah's outburst, she couldn't possibly be wrong. Still, Hannah was being a horrible role model.

"I apologize." Paul tipped his head as if bowing to her wishes. "I'll be more careful. Halley, why don't you show Lissa the new colt in the neighbor's pasture?"

Halley rose and walked around her desk, held out her hand for Lissa's, and waited. Lissa watched Hannah intently.

She winked. "It's okay. I'll be right here when you get back. Go ahead."

Lissa released Hannah's hand and took Halley's.

They were barely out the front door when Hannah turned back to Paul. "This is just another time of Daed not doing his daughters right. And you said you wouldn't allow that meeting."

"The meeting was inevitable. When Roger had the arson report ready this morning and Sarah appeared able to cope with all of this after I talked to her about it, plans changed. This meeting is better taking place in a controlled environment."

"I expected you to hold your ground and not allow this, though I'm not sure why."

"Hannah," — he rubbed his forehead — "I've done nothing wrong. Over the last two weeks, between counseling sessions and medication, Sarah has begun to realize the difference between what she actually did and what she dreamed of doing. Your Daed has been calm and careful with his words, surprisingly remaining on Sarah's side the whole time. But when Sarah is released, she will still move in with Luke and Mary for a while. I can help Sarah and maybe, on some level, even your Daed, but I can't make you trust me, and I can't have you undermining Sarah's progress."

Part of her saw the truth in his eyes, despite all her doubt and anger, and told her she was unjustly accusing Paul. Again. She plunked onto the couch and buried her head in her hands, trying to gather some composure. She heard Paul walk off, but her embarrassment for acting like a maniac didn't ease. At least the meeting could continue with him in there and be over all the quicker so she could see Mary and get out of Owl's Perch, the land of perpetual emotional overload.

The sound of ice against glass caught her attention, and she looked up.

"Here, this might help." Paul held a glass of water out to her.

She took it from him, sipped on the cool liquid, and set the glass on the end table.

Paul shifted. "The arson investigation confirmed that Sarah's innocent."

She looked up. "What? Are . . . are you absolutely positive?"

The lines across Paul's face eased into a familiar smile. "Yes. Roger is the father of a good friend of mine and has been an arson investigator for well over two decades. Since an insurance company isn't involved, he did the investigation as a favor. Even though the Bylers' barn burned quite awhile ago, Roger discovered the possible source to be cigarette butts. Then he poked around, asking questions until a few guilt-ridden teens confessed they'd been smoking in the loft just hours before the barn burned to the ground. He said that investigating the source of the fire for Matthew's shop was pretty quick and easy. Someone had stored gasoline in a leaky can in the attic and then left a lit kerosene lamp nearby. His conversations with David's family verified that David had put the gasoline up there earlier that day to keep it away from some children who'd come in with customers placing orders. Then he lit a kerosene lamp in the attic to search for something and must have forgotten to blow it out. A few hours later the explosion occurred."

"Paul . . ." He'd done a great job, but she couldn't make herself voice that. "I shouldn't have come in so angry and accusing. It's just when it comes to . . . well, it's easy to assume the worst."

"I understand."

"Don't you ever lose your temper?"

Paul sat on the oak coffee table in front of her. "Once." He interlaced his fingers and propped his elbows on his knees. "It cost me everything."

Unable to look him in the eye, she wanted to speak, to say something gracious and understanding, but nothing came to her.

He passed her the glass of water. "Look, about the meeting, with the tension between you and your Daed, I think it'd be best for Sarah if you let me handle this."

"Okay." She took a sip of water. "Every time I see you, I act like an uncontrolled idiot."

"Not long after you left, Luke and I agreed you'd return successful . . . and have quite an attitude for those of us who'd been wrong." He shrugged, a smile tugging at his lips. "We just didn't think you'd take years to return or have a husband when you did."

Hannah set the glass on the table, staring at him.

A husband?

A door jerked open, and her father stepped out. "Roger won't let anyone even speak to Sarah until you return."

Paul glanced that way. "I'll be there in just a minute." He angled his back to the door where her father stood. "I was able to talk with Mary for a minute last night. Privacy with you seemed paramount to her, and she asked if you'd come get her today as early as possible. If you need a place to talk, you're welcome to bring her here. No one in her community will think it odd for you two to be here since Sarah will be moving in with them when she leaves." He motioned to the landing. "Upstairs, first door to your left is an unused office. It has a couple of extra couches and stuff. Just put the Do Not Disturb sign on the doorknob, and no one will even knock. I'd better get back to the meeting."

Mute, she sank back onto the couch.

He thought she was married? She moaned, knowing she should have thought about this before now.

CHAPTER 18

Matthew paid Nate and climbed out of the truck. The white clapboard home with green shutters was a welcome sight. The aroma of burned wood drifted through the air, making him cringe. At least this time he knew why it'd been stealing his desire to rebuild.

The familiar sound of wet fabric being snapped in the air caused him to walk around the corner of the house. The morning sun glistened against Kathryn's white prayer Kapp, her light brown hair evident under it. Her tanned arms stretched to hang out the day's laundry, and awe at the woman in front of him caught him by surprise. She didn't even notice him, and yet her presence inside him was undeniable.

From the get-go, his relationship with Kathryn had been different from what he had with Elle. It was built on things they had in common, on workdays, and the kindness in her heart to offer him true friendship. He wondered just how much Joseph meant to her and if he had any chance of winning her over. Paying her to stay and help his family while he went off with a girl he'd once asked to marry him had probably been the stupidest thing he'd done since he'd met Elle Leggett.

Kathryn grabbed the wooden basket and fiddled with clothespins inside it while walking.

"Hi," Matthew said, causing her to stop right before she ran into him.

The seriousness across her face wasn't the welcome he'd hoped for, but what could he expect from her?

She gave a nod and redirected her route.

He stepped in front of her. "I don't even get a hello?"

"Did you enjoy your extra time in Baltimore? I hope so, because it caused me to break my word."

"I . . . I'm sorry. Whatever problems it caused, I'll straighten them out."

Kathryn passed him the laundry basket before reaching under her apron and pulling out a letter. "It's my resignation."

He shook his head. "I'll not take that."

She placed it in the basket and walked off. "It's done whether you read it or not."

"Kathryn, wait." He jogged that way and

stood in front of her while she plowed on. "Just hear me out. I spent days in a fog, so confused I didn't care about keeping my word to return."

"You had no right to simply call and leave a message that you weren't returning on time."

"Kathryn," — Matthew grabbed the letter and dropped the basket onto the ground — "give me another chance. I'm here to stay, to rebuild. I made decisions while there, good ones."

She shielded her eyes from the sunlight and stared at him. "Elle is behind you in this plan of rebuilding?"

Matthew shrugged. "I finished endin' things with her. We don't even make good friends. How could we make a good marriage?" He shifted, using his body to shield her from the sun. "She may or may not ever join the faith. I wish her well, but whatever she chooses, I'm glad it's over — in spite of the promise I once gave her."

Kathryn propped her hands on her hips, staring at him. "If you ever tell me one thing and then do another, I'll . . ."

Curious, Matthew taunted, "You'll what?"

The smile across her face said she'd moved from frustration to teasing. "I'll tell your Mamm."

Matthew chuckled and flexed his muscle. "And what's she going to do about it?"

She laughed. "Daed wants me home and . . . and Joseph."

At twenty-two she was certainly old enough not to do as her father wanted, but she wouldn't. "Don't you think your Daed will give ya more time if I talk to him?"

She crossed her arms, looking like she might be giving weight to his question.

Still holding the letter, Matthew grabbed the laundry basket. "I guess the first question I should have asked is, are you willing to stay?"

Even if it causes problems with you and Joseph?

But he wouldn't voice that last part. Why invite trouble?

She looked to where the shops had stood. Burned framing and caved-in roofs. "Getting a chance to see E and L come back to life? Ya, I'm willing to let *you* talk to my Daed about that."

Matthew chuckled. "He is a reasonable man, right?"

"No doubt."

"So what is his push to get ya back home lately?"

"I'm not sure, except maybe Joseph is putting pressure on him. My Daed has said from the beginning that he didn't want me staying here so long that I might be tempted to put down roots in a community this far from home."

"I guess I can understand that."

"I'd rather find a way to juggle both, being here to help with E and L when needed and going home for a few days or so whenever I'm not needed. It's expensive hiring a driver to take me the two hours to home and then drive back. But there's no kind of job at home for me that comes close to the kind of satisfaction I get out of running your office."

"I'll talk with your Daed."

"I went through the files while you were gone. Lots of the papers were partially burned, but I was able to figure out who'd done the ordering. I placed a bunch of calls and have a large stack of orders for you."

"Ya figured out who made the orders from what was left of the forms?"

"That, and I remembered some of the orders, and the caller ID on the phone still worked, even after the fire. I was able to retrieve over thirty numbers and call people back to take their orders again."

"And what if I'd not chosen to rebuild?"

"Then I'd have passed the orders on to a place in Indiana. We can't leave people stranded. It's just not right. And speaking of not right, you owe me no promises, ever, but if you give your word, you'd better keep it."

"Or you'll tell Mamm."

Amusement danced across her face. "You got a better threat?"

"Yeah, but I'm not tellin' what it is."

She laughed and took the letter from him and ripped it in two before shoving it into her hidden pocket. Seriousness replaced her smile. "I'm sorry for the added grief you must feel, but I've had concerns about your happiness with Elle."

"But you said you were praying for us."

"Praying the best for you two. Before vows, it's not a given that what's best is marriage."

Her words circled through his mind, and Matthew was hopeful that maybe Joseph wasn't the right man for Kathryn either.

Matthew grabbed the basket, and they walked toward the house. "We have work to do and loss to cope with, but any sadness over things not working out with Elle took place long ago."

From across the kitchen table, Hannah gazed into Mary's eyes, wishing they were alone. With no way to know what was on her mind and no way of finding out until they went somewhere private, Hannah only knew the same thing she came here knowing — Mary had a secret, and she was scared. Mammi Annie sat in the living room, keeping a vigilant ear for every word spoken.

Hannah sipped her coffee. She'd finally been allowed inside someone's home, and this was how the welcome played out? The rocking chair in the corner of the room creaked as Lissa swayed it back and forth while munching on a sandwich. The clock ticked on. It amazed Hannah how the sounds stood out in an Amish home. With no electric buzz from automatic washers, dryers, or dishwashers and certainly no televisions, radios, or entertainment centers, each home carried a peacefulness that Hannah loved — in spite of the stoic restraints that had to be navigated. But at nearly three in the afternoon, they needed to do something.

"We could go for a ride, but I get the feeling whatever is going on, we can't talk with a little one in the car." Her muted tones were quieter than the old timepiece ticking in the living room. Hannah wasn't going to chance Lissa hearing something she could repeat to Sarah. Between Sarah's emotional issues about babies and her ability to share things she shouldn't, it could stir up a lot of trouble for Mary.

Mary's half smile quivered, making dozens of tiny dimples in her chin. "We have to do something."

The only thing Hannah knew to do was return to the Better Path. Although a bit unsure what they could do with Lissa while they talked openly, it appeared to be their best chance of communicating. Since Mammi Annie was listening, they couldn't even whisper without the possibility of being heard.

If Mammi Annie were a little friendlier, Hannah might consider leaving Lissa with her while Mary and she went for a walk. But she had concerns about what Mammie Annie might ask and how Lissa might answer. Whatever tattered reputation Hannah had within Owl's Perch, she needed to guard it for Sarah's and Mary's sake.

"Come on. It's time we went to the Better Path. You need to talk to Paul about Sarah's release, right?"

Mary glanced into the living room and rose. Hannah lifted Lissa into her arms, and the three left the Yoder place. As they drove down the narrow, paved roads, Mary kept rubbing her stomach.

"Does it hurt?" Hannah asked.

"No. I had a few sharp pains hit yesterday. That's when I called you. Then they went away."

"What type of pain?"

"The kind that hurts. What type of question is that?"

Hannah laughed. "A vague one, I guess. Where was the pain?"

"Right here." Mary rubbed her right side near the upper part of her hip bone.

"How deep inside your body did it feel — just topical, like the skin being stretched, or deeper, like a muscle being pulled, or really deep, like an ache in the bone?"

Hannah listened carefully as Mary answered each question, knowing Dr. Lehman would want a complete report when she called him for his opinion. As the Better Path came into view, there were no signs of Daed and the church leaders. Hannah and Mary went inside with Lissa right beside them.

Maybe the argument with Paul had upset Lissa more than Hannah realized, because she clung to Hannah's dress as they entered the building. Not one to be clingy very often, Lissa would be comfortable with her surroundings in a few minutes, but Hannah lifted the little girl into her arms. The conversation with Mary would just have to remain light until Lissa felt like playing at the tire swing or something.

They stepped inside the open space that included a large foyer, living room, and kitchen, with a lot of office doors off to the sides and a stairway that led to more offices. Five people, including Paul, were sitting in the kitchen. A freshly cut cake sat on the table, and they each had a plate with a slice. The soft chatter and laughs ended as everyone's eyes moved to Mary and Hannah. Obviously they were sharing a special celebration break of some kind, but this wasn't the quiet entrance into the place Hannah had banked on.

Paul excused himself and stood. "Hannah, Mary, right this way." He left his half-eaten piece of cake and walked up the steps, leading them. Once on the landing, he opened a door. "If you use my office, everyone will think Mary's here to read over things for Sarah's release. Since her name's been cleared concerning the fires and everything between her and the community is in good order, she'll be released tomorrow, even though it's a Saturday."

Hannah, Mary, and Lissa stepped inside.

He glanced at his watch. "I won't need my office for at least another hour." He looked to Lissa. "You hungry?"

Lissa shrugged, but Hannah knew she was, even though she'd had a sandwich at Mary's place. The tiny girl could outeat the rest of the family and looked like she never ate anything.

Paul slid one hand into his pant pocket. "I bet you could make us both a peanut butter and jelly sandwich."

Her eyes lit up. "Are you hungry too?"

Paul nodded. "And Halley brought a homemade cake."

Lissa stared up at Hannah, silently begging for Paul's plan to be okay with her. Paul had nailed a way to get Lissa to leave Hannah's side. "Go ahead."

He glanced to Hannah as he was closing the door. She mouthed a "thank you," and he nodded.

Mary checked the door to make sure it was secure and then leaned against it. Tears welled and began running down her face.

"What's going on?"

Wiping her tears, she gazed into Hannah's eyes. "I've made a huge mistake. If you can't help me . . ."

"I'm here to do anything I can." She took Mary by the shoulders, giving a gentle squeeze before lowering her hands to her side. "Tell me what's going on."

"While I was engaged to Luke, the doctor told me not to marry, not to do anything that might cause me to get pregnant. I didn't tell Luke, and . . ." She slid her hand over her protruding stomach. "I didn't want to lose him . . ."

Hannah knew this story all too well, not wanting to lose someone and not telling them the truth. "What did the doctor say was the specific reason for not getting pregnant?"

"He said the baby would be fine but labor and delivery could be really dangerous."

"Mary, how could you do this?"

"At first I thought I was choosing to trust God with the marriage bed." Her shoulders slumped, and she shook her head. "But you have no room to be mad at me. You hid your pregnancy from Paul."

"Good grief, have you looked at my life?"

"But this is different, and I thought everything would work out. Please, we've got to find answers. I'm so scared for the baby, and Luke, and me."

Unwilling to share the fullness of her displeasure, Hannah nodded. "Are you having any other symptoms — spotting or anything?"

"No."

"Any tightening of your stomach

muscles?"

"No."

"Okay, we'll start with a quick exam of your vitals. I need my medical bag out of the car. We've got to find you a local obstetrician, which probably won't be easy at this point in your pregnancy."

"I . . . I won't see just any doctor. That's how I got into this fix in the first place. They're pushy and bossy and look down on the Amish. You know they do."

"Not all of them, only a few." Hannah shook her head. "I don't even have a two-year-degree nursing license. If you think I'm the answer, you're wrong."

"Those doctors can't be trusted now any more than when my mother refused to see them. Why, they just walk in, give orders, and you'll do it their way, or you can take the highway." She shook her head. "I'm really scared, Hannah, but for years I've heard about a slew of bad doctors working with Amish because we don't sue, and it sounds safer to choose the highway every time."

The absolute stubbornness was way too familiar to Hannah. No wonder they had bonded so well as children. They were like two mules in full agreement against all reason. And the fruit of it grieved her for both of them. "Mary, you're tying my hands here, and the safety of you and the baby are at risk."

"I thought . . ." She moved to a chair and took a seat. "Don't you personally know a doctor around here that we could trust?"

"No, but maybe . . ." Hannah knelt in front of her. "Would you trust Dr. Lehman to examine you and then help us find a physician in the area? I think he'd know someone."

"Would he do that?"

"He literally saved my life a few days after I landed in Ohio. He's trustworthy, but it's asking a lot for him to come here."

Mary stood, grabbed the phone on Paul's desk from its cradle, and held it toward Hannah. "Please?"

She took the phone and set it back in place. How long would Mary have hidden this secret if Hannah hadn't come back to Owl's Perch? "After we get some medical facts about what's going on, you have to tell Luke everything."

Mary backed up. "I can't."

"I won't come back here and have a part in dishonesty again."

" 'Dishonesty' is an awful harsh word."

"What you've done is harsh. I'm not sure you get that."

Mary pursed her lips, and Hannah feared if she wasn't careful, Mary would stonewall her too. Wishing she could see the truth of what she'd done, Hannah put her hand against Mary's cheek. "Are you more concerned about falling off that pedestal Luke has you on than doing what's right?"

"He's going to be so mad at me."

"Uh, yeah." Hannah immediately regretted the sarcastic tone. "But you'd be mad at him too if he'd kept such a thing from you. And the longer he kept the secret, the angrier you'd be when you found out."

Her friend stared off to the side before nodding. "Okay, I'll tell him everything after we have word from the doctor."

CHAPTER 19

In the quiet of her hotel room, with Lissa asleep in the bed next to hers, Hannah ended the phone call with Dr. Lehman. Sleep had been impossible, but his opinion was in line with Hannah's thoughts — Mary's pains were due to pressure and stress on the round ligaments. He was off Monday and said it was time for another visit to Lancaster to see his mom anyway, so he didn't mind going the forty miles out of the way to see Mary. He said he was actually glad for the invitation since he'd been wanting to see Hannah's Owl's Perch and meet some of the people from her past.

His willingness to always support her still managed to catch her by surprise. She sat back against the pillows, the Bible in her lap still open. Her damp hair continued to air dry from the shower she'd taken a couple of hours ago. In all the time she'd known him, Dr. Lehman had never let her down.

He constantly trained her to take on more responsibilities at his clinic as a nurse, and sometimes he seemed to expect more from her than from his nurses with four-year degrees, but in many ways he was more like a dad to her than her own father.

Lissa sat up, rubbing her eyes. Without a word spoken, she crawled into the bed with Hannah and snuggled. So grateful for the love Kevin and Lissa brought into her life, Hannah stroked the little girl's hair and kissed her head. "How are you this morning?"

"Hungry."

Hannah rubbed her small back, enjoying the few minutes of having a child in her arms. "Well, then we'll need to take care of that first thing, won't we?" Hannah closed the Bible.

Lissa put her hand on it. "What it'd say this morning?"

"That if someone sins against me and asks for forgiveness, I'm to give it to them."

"Did someone sinned against you?"

Hannah placed her hand on Lissa's head. "I thought they did, and I've not been nice to them, but now I'm not so sure they did what I thought."

"You were mad at somebody who didn't do nothing wrong?"

Hannah slid out of bed, wishing she'd controlled herself rather than screamed at Paul. "Seems so."

"You gotta ask for forgiveness now?"

That uncomfortable idea made Hannah's insides shiver. "Right now I'm going to help you get dressed, and then we'll get you some breakfast."

After Lissa ate fruit, yogurt, half a bagel, and even some cereal at the continental breakfast the hotel provided, they went to the car and headed for Mary's. Sarah should have been released from the Better Path about an hour ago and should be at Luke and Mary's by now. Hannah needed to tell Mary what Dr. Lehman had said, and then she wanted to spend as much time with Sarah this weekend as possible, because when Hannah left this time, she hoped not to return for several months.

The scenery changed from city life to Amish country as Hannah drove out of the Harrisburg area and into Owl's Perch. As she traveled on, Gram's home came into view. She'd once loved this place above all others. Taking note of how beautifully the house and acreage were kept, she spotted Paul mending a fence.

Instead of stopping, she pressed the accelerator.

She didn't owe him an apology. He owed her one.

Her conscience pricked, making her skin tingle like dull pins were poking her. He'd given an apology, several actually, and his words couldn't have seemed more sincere. She'd hidden things from him and then blamed him when he reacted. She clicked her tongue and huffed.

Lissa mimicked her and giggled. Hannah looked in the child-view mirror. Lissa's innocent smile brought a landslide of conviction. What advice would she give to Lissa if she acted as Hannah had — regardless of how justified the reaction may have felt?

Notching the blinker into place, Hannah slowed the vehicle, turned around in a stranger's driveway, and headed back to Gram's. "Lissa, I need to speak to Paul for a minute, okay?"

"Think he needs another sandwich?"

"No, but there's a bridge over a small creek near where he's fixing a fence. You can play on that and toss pebbles into the water while I speak to him for a minute, okay?"

Her little face lit up. "A covered bridge?"

"Well, it's surrounded by trees."

Her head bobbed up and down as if she'd just been given an extravagant new toy.

Hannah pulled into Gram's driveway, hoping Dorcas wasn't here today. In the side yard, not far from the house, Paul wrestled with a fence post.

She got out of the car and helped Lissa unbuckle, and they walked across the yard. With each step, Hannah questioned herself. Memories of their past caught her. Of course they did. What had she been thinking to come here? Except for a few extremely short visits, she'd never seen him anywhere but here. This was where they first met. Where they worked together. Where they became friends. Where she'd fallen in —

Stop it, Hannah.

But the memories didn't stop. A weird feeling crept over her when she caught a glimpse of the bridge through the turning shadows of its surrounding trees. As if in those woods she could again see Paul standing in front of her — broad shoulders, hair the color of ripe hay, blue eyes that used to haunt her dreams.

Unable to dismiss the recollections, she couldn't take another step. Deciding this was a really bad idea and she needed to leave before she was noticed, she reached for Lissa's hand. "Come on, Lis—"

Lissa dodged Hannah's grasp. "Hey," she

hollered in Paul's direction.

Paul looked up.

He stood straight and pulled the rawhide work gloves off his hands before wiping his brow. The early October air had a nip, and Hannah and Lissa had on thick cardigan sweaters, but Paul appeared to have beads of sweat on his face.

Lissa came to a halt right in front of him. "You need some help?"

"Well, good morning, Lissa." Paul lifted his eyes to Hannah, looking quizzical.

She drew a shallow breath, unable to get a deep one. "I . . . we . . . need to talk."

"Sure. We never had a chance to discuss Sarah's progress or some of the suggestions I have that might help her."

Hannah knew professional distancing when she heard it. "This isn't about Sarah. I was hoping to cover some things that . . ." She lowered her eyes to Lissa. "Look right through those trees." Kneeling, Hannah pointed at the bridge. "Do you see it?"

Lissa nodded.

"You can gather some pebbles and drop them into the water, but you can't go down to the water's edge, okay?"

Lissa turned and squeezed her neck, almost knocking her over with her enthusiasm, and took off running into the wooded area.

Hannah's splayed hand against the ground kept her from losing her balance altogether. Paul offered his hand, and she took it.

After helping her stand, he motioned toward the house. "Give me just a minute, and I'll get us a couple of chairs from the backyard."

Hannah stood where she could see Lissa, who was singing joyously to the creek and trees. A minute later Paul put two resin chairs near her. A sense of dishonor covered her, and she was too antsy to sit.

It was time to say her piece and leave. That sounded matter-of-fact enough, but her head spun, and her insides trembled. Worse, she could feel the edge of tears sting her eyes, which really angered her, but she had to get this over with. "It was never my intention to deceive you, Paul. Never. But it did turn out that way. Much of what I'm going to say you've pieced together already, but I need to say it anyway, okay?"

Standing just a few feet from her, he stared across the huge pasture behind Gram's place to the dirt road. "I understand. I'm sure it will help both of us."

Lissa's voice rang through the air, singing. Feeling the weight of the two worlds in which she lived, the one that had reason to sing and the one that continued to cause sadness, Hannah sat.

She tried to swallow but couldn't. "The day you asked me to marry you, while walking home on the dirt road, a man about your age pulled up beside me, stopped his car, and asked for directions. It didn't take long to realize I needed to get out of there, but when I tried to run . . ." She closed her eyes, trying desperately not to relive those few minutes. "That's when I got the scars on the palms of my hands, the ones you noticed the next time we saw each other a couple of months later. Remember?"

"Yes." His gentle voice was barely audible.

"Afterward . . . he tried to run over me with his car, but somehow I avoided it and ran home." Hannah stared at the ground, remembering how arriving home had only added to her trouble. "I wanted to call you, wanted you to make sense of it and say we still had a future . . ." Tears eased down her cheeks. "Even though they didn't know about you, Mamm and Daed said that no one would ever want to marry me if word of the attack got out and that I shouldn't tell anyone — not even my own siblings." She raised her eyes, seeing the grief etched on Paul's face. "And that's when I made the choice to hide the rape. I couldn't even say the word until . . ." She let the sentence drop. "The weeks that followed were all but unbearable. You didn't write. I wasn't allowed to return to Gram's. And I wondered if you'd really asked me to marry you. Now I know I was dealing with shock, then post-traumatic shock, and depression."

As he moved his gaze to hers, she saw his eyes were rimmed with tears as well.

He set the empty chair directly across from her and took a seat. "I know we talked of this before, but I did write. I promise. The letter never arrived at Gram's, and then she began feeling that it was wrong to allow us to communicate through her mailbox when your Daed didn't know about me. There I was at school, longing to be in Owl's Perch with you . . . as if some part of me knew you needed me, but I made myself stay focused on our future."

Understanding that she wasn't the only one with a list of what should have been done, she began to see the person she'd once believed him to be. One who hadn't lied or stolen or even abandoned her, one who'd made a mistake and paid dearly for it. "I held on to one hope. It was the only thing that got me through everything else — that you wouldn't find out and I wouldn't lose you. But then, in late November, I learned I was pregnant."

"Hannah," Lissa called from the edge of the wood, "can I get a leaf and drop it into the water?"

A faint laugh escaped Hannah. "Yes, Lissa, you can."

He intertwined his fingers, propped his forearms on his knees, leaned in, and whispered, "November?"

She nodded. "Between a lack of knowledge, denial, the depression, and then Mary nearly dying in that buggy accident, I just didn't really put it all together. It wasn't until after our last day to catch a visit that I learned I was pregnant."

Paul straightened his interlocked fingers, staring at them. "The day before Thanksgiving."

"Yes. We hadn't seen each other in so long. My parents didn't know why I wanted to go to Gram's, but they knew I wanted it bad enough to do whatever it took to get here. They insisted I take a home pregnancy test. I took it and immediately left to come here. I spent that day with you, so sure I wouldn't be pregnant, so convinced God wouldn't let that happen because it'd ruin everything. You were right. I was naive. I caused a lot of the rumors you heard, but I never meant to flirt with anyone."

Paul's fingertips came within inches of hers before he pulled them back. "I know you were innocent, Hannah. My jealousy and confusion didn't last but a few days. How could my fiancée, who wouldn't even kiss me until months after we'd been engaged, be anything but innocent?"

"I wasn't guiltless. I was selfish, wanting to hide the truth of being pregnant, and it may have cost Rachel her life. The night you came to Mary's to talk to me? I didn't know it then, but later I realized I was already in labor."

Paul's intense gaze tightened. "I thought my running out on you might have caused you to go into premature labor."

Hannah's breath caught. What had she done to him? "No, I'd taken something for pain and was in bed when you arrived at Mammi Annie's. Remember?"

He nodded.

She ran her fingers through the side of her hair, pushing some fallen wisps back into place. For the first time she wondered what he thought of her Englischer look. He was the only one who hadn't shown any disapproval. "I met with the church leaders the next morning. I needed them to believe me about the rape, or I wouldn't be allowed

251

to live with anyone within the community. They doubted me, and the bishop insisted I stay a night alone so I could rethink my story. I gave birth that night." Hannah paused and willed herself to finish. "Matthew built a coffin, and we buried her. Daed wouldn't let me come home. Mary's parents said I couldn't stay with them any longer. I . . . I didn't think anyone would take me." She closed her eyes, taking a moment to gather fresh strength. "When I called the bank, I learned that all the money had been removed from our account. I . . . I thought you'd taken it."

"If we just could have talked . . ."

She shifted. "At that time everything was beyond talking about for me. I couldn't voice to anyone what had happened. Besides, when I did manage to call your apartment, a girl answered, so with all those events combined, I convinced myself all hopes of us were gone, and I boarded the train."

The anguish expressed on his face said more than words. "I roomed with three other guys, who always had girls around, but I never received any message that you'd called. And I never had anything to do with those girls. The night you stayed in Harrisburg with Naomi and Matthew, I came looking for you, even borrowed a friend's cell and had people stationed to receive a call from you here, at my parents', and at my apartment."

Her gaze fixed on Paul, and she was unable to break it. The night before boarding the train she'd called his apartment. A girl answered, promising to give him the message. He never called her back. Nine months after leaving, she'd tried again to reach him by calling here to Gram's home. The same young woman had answered the phone, probably someone from his family or friends. Possibly Dorcas.

Hannah wouldn't point fingers or lay blame. Still, she was getting an uneasy feeling that Paul had never received either message. She forced a smile. Whoever she spoke to may have lied, but Hannah was the one who went into hiding. She was the one who didn't push harder to reach him, only calling twice in nine months and then never calling again.

She inhaled deeply, sensing her burden becoming lighter in spite of the truth she was learning. "The thing is, even if we'd talked before I left, I needed to go. Luke questioned me about leaving, saying I hadn't given you much of a chance to adjust to the shocking news. But, Paul," — she tilted her head, making sure he was looking right at her — "I needed out of Owl's Perch, and even if we'd connected before I boarded that train and you still thought you wanted me, I'd have felt like a charity case, not a cherished fiancée or wife. Can you understand that?"

He nodded. "I knew you needed time. I never wanted to take that from you, but I wanted you to know I believed you and I hadn't taken the money and I was there if you needed me."

But Hannah knew if she'd stayed or even returned soon, she'd have made a mess of his life. His parents and community would not have accepted her, not with the reputation she carried — the scarlet letter she still wore in the eyes of most. And she would never have been able to make herself believe he actually loved her. At that time her self-esteem was gone, her spirit grievously wounded.

She rose. "The good news is that because I left, I met my aunt, a woman I'll always be better for having known. She helped me find myself and a career. She placed seeds in me, assuring me that even a woman has the right to chase her own dream. She modeled forgiveness and hope. I don't regret that time."

Paul straightened his back, clearly relaxing a bit. "I . . . I always thought you'd return healed and successful."

She scoffed. "Instead, I returned outspoken and difficult."

A whispery laugh eased the rest of the concern lines across his forehead. "Well, I'd braced myself for that too."

They shared a laugh, which brought an odd sense of wholeness to her. As if she hadn't fully moved on until she found peace with others whose lives were ripped apart too.

"Hannah." Lissa sang her name.

"Yes?"

"Can I throw a stick in the water?"

"Yes, and you have about five minutes, okay?"

"Okay."

Being at Gram's with Paul and Lissa caused a sense of wonder at life to dance around her, asking to be let inside.

Hannah drew a deep breath, able to finish with more strength than she'd begun with. "At the end I thought I was losing my mind, but with each little town the train stopped at and then left behind, hope began to stir. I seemed to leave behind more of that overwhelming powerlessness, and I could finally breathe again."

"You wrote me the 'nevertheless' letter."

She nodded. "I wanted to lift some of your burden the way leaving freed me, but then . . ." She resented that he seemed to have moved on and found someone else within no time of walking out on her. She swallowed hard. "But later on, I began to harbor resentment, blaming you for things that weren't your fault. I'm sorry."

He put one hand on her shoulder, waiting for her to look at him. "You're forgiven."

She shifted her body weight, wishing she'd covered everything and could just go. "In spite of how I've acted, I'm content and not given to bouts of anger. But one of the reasons I came by today is because I refuse to hide things again."

Paul shook his head. "I . . . I don't understand."

"Within weeks of landing in Ohio, I changed my last name to Lawson."

Lines creased his brow. "That's not your married name?"

She shook her head. "I . . . I'm not married."

He pointed at her left hand. "But you're engaged?"

With her right hand, Hannah wrapped her fingers around the ring on her left hand, feeling the stones — a diamond and ruby

— in her honorary mother's gift. "He's asked, but . . ."

He stood, turning his back to her.

Hannah blinked, feeling a bit startled. "I haven't said yes, but I love him. We have Kevin and Lissa, and we make a good family."

Paul turned, his eyes mirroring things she'd never be privy to. "She's a sweet girl."

"Yeah, she and Kevin seem to be unusually great children." Hannah drew a cleansing breath. It was over. She'd done what she came to do, and now it was time to leave and pick back up with her life. "Lissa, it's time to go."

On the bridge, through the wooded area, Lissa crossed her arms. "Aw, not now."

"Lissa Ann Palmer."

The little girl hurried off the bridge. "I'm coming." She left the edge of the wood, wiping her dirty hands down her sweater. "Don't nobody start talking about taking my desserts away."

Paul glanced at Hannah. "Hannah," he chided teasingly.

She shrugged. "I need leverage. And you know how she responds to food."

Paul agreed and slid his hands into his pockets. "I'm glad Sarah called you home. Wouldn't prevent one outburst you've had to finally get to this point."

Lissa sang while she ran right past them and toward the car.

Paul walked beside Hannah. "How are things with Mary?"

"I talked to her last night. I think she'll be fine, but there are some steps that need to be taken to be certain."

"I'm sure she's better off just having you to talk to."

Hannah leaned against her car, somewhat taken aback at the corner they'd turned. Paul was much the same as he'd been since she'd arrived, but the resentment she'd let simmer for so long was gone, leaving calmness in its place. "I'm thankful to have her in my life again too, but friendship won't be enough for what's going on with her." She paused, trying to gauge how much to share. "Paul, I may need your help."

"Sure. Anytime. What do you need from me?"

Suddenly feeling vulnerable again, Hannah opened her car door. "I . . . I'll let you know later . . . by phone . . . or I may get Dr. Lehman to contact you."

CHAPTER 20

The Saturday afternoon sun extended across Paul's stove as he stared at the boiling water in the pot. The bubbles, big and small, worked their way to the top and burst, releasing steam. He'd forgotten why he put the water on to heat. Macaroni and cheese, maybe? He wasn't hungry anyway. Confusion covered his thoughts like a pounding headache as his heart thumped like mad.

Hannah wasn't married. Or engaged.

By the time she'd returned three weeks ago, he was relieved to realize he was no longer absolutely in love with her. But since then . . . well, he'd come to know her again. She was different, quicker to share her feelings, even her most negative ones. She was harder. Yet, everything that had attracted him to her in the first place — her strength, determination, intelligence — and even her newfound and unshakable confidence drew him.

Until this morning when she said she wasn't married, he'd refused to acknowledge the slightest attraction he still had for her, let alone admit to the growing magnetic pull that seemed powerful enough to drag him to her door. But he'd kept even his most private thoughts in check, honoring the vows he'd thought she'd taken.

Of course, she did say she loved Martin. And Paul was supposed to be committed to seeing only Dorcas, although they hadn't talked about that — exactly.

Hannah knew the truth now about his coming back for her and not taking the money and not having any other girls.

He turned off the stove. No wonder she'd stocked up so many negative emotions against him. They could work through those things now, couldn't they? A vision of Lissa popped into his head. Hannah's new family meant life and joy to her. Any attempt to win her back would be treason to the life she'd built.

Still, his desire packed a hurricane force. She'd finally returned, and she wasn't married. If she loved the guy so much, why hadn't she said yes to his proposal?

Was she here to simply give them both

closure? Maybe that's all they needed and his other emotions were a reaction to the full realization that she was home, unmarried, and now knew things he'd waited years to tell her. Emotions were a tricky thing. Dead on target some of the time and bold-faced liars at other times.

The way she dressed, who she'd become was no longer Plain, not that he had a clue what that did or didn't mean to him. She was here and not married; that's really all he knew. And that desire burned through him like lava, seemingly destroying all other hopes for his future in its path.

The quiet jingle of his phone interrupted his thoughts, and he picked up the receiver. "Paul Waddell."

"Paul, this is Dr. Jeff Lehman. Do you have a few minutes?"

"Sure. What can I do for you?"

"It seems I need a place to see Mary Lapp. Hannah Lawson recommended that I give you a call since the Better Path may have the facilities I need to give an examination."

"I'd need to take the request to the board, but I have to tell you, as a mental health facility, we don't have an exam room. We do have a lab, but the tech only works part-time, and even then a lot of the blood work has to be sent out. We usually get the results within a few days."

"I travel between clinics. Most of what I need I take with me. The real problem is I'm not licensed in Pennsylvania, which doesn't matter as far as dealing with the Amish community, but it might matter for the licensing and rules of your clinic."

"I'll be sure to bring that up at the meeting. The clinic doesn't have a board-certified medical doctor on staff, but we do have one we can use as an umbrella in certain circumstances, so we may be able to avoid any standards issues through that venue. Bob Marvin is the owner and CEO of the place. He'll have the answers you need, but he's out of town this weekend and left word that he's unavailable."

"I'm off Monday and was planning to go to Lancaster to visit relatives. I'd hoped to swing by Owl's Perch on my way. Any chance you can have an answer for me sometime Monday morning?"

"That shouldn't be a problem."

"Unless we don't get the go-ahead, I'll be there that afternoon, because the sooner this is handled, the quicker Hannah can return to her school schedule."

Paul grabbed a pen and paper off the refrigerator. "I'm sure Hannah's very relieved you're able to help."

"She means a lot to me, and I'm glad to do what I can. I'll give you my number, and you let me know as soon as you have an answer."

"I'm ready." He jotted down the info and ended the call, wondering exactly how Hannah came to know the doctor.

He slid the paper into his pocket. Wishing he hadn't canceled hiking plans with Marcus, Ryan, and Taylor, he moved to his aquarium and fed the fish. Diversion with his friends would be nice about now, especially since focusing long enough to read anything seemed impossible.

Couldn't concentrate. Couldn't eat. Couldn't sleep. Yep, the confusion of Hannah was back in his life, sort of. He moved to the couch and stared at the fish tank. The sun went down, and darkness filled the room, except for the light in the aquarium.

A thunderous knock jolted him.

He opened his front door to find his dad and Dorcas on the stoop. She looked frail and upset.

"What's wrong?" He took a step back, inviting them in.

His dad put his hand on Dorcas's back and escorted her in. "I knocked several times. Did you not hear me?"

Paul shook his head. "I wasn't expecting anyone."

His dad studied him quizzically. "I was on my way to visit Mom. Dorcas asked if I'd drop her by your place."

Dorcas's face was pale.

"You okay?"

She shrugged.

His father placed his large hand on Paul's arm and gave it a friendly squeeze. "I need to go. Your Gram's expecting me. You want to take Dorcas home later, or you want me to come back by here?"

"I'll see that she gets home. Thanks, Dad."

He closed the door behind his dad and turned to Dorcas. He figured she'd gotten wind of how much contact he was having with Hannah. Maybe even Gram told her Hannah came by her place to see him yesterday, but he wasn't sure what to tell Dorcas. "What's wrong?"

She held up a white envelope. "I . . . I got this in the mail today." She burst into tears and fell against his chest. "What's wrong with me?"

Paul put his arms around her. After bouts of muscle weakness and severe skin sensitivity for nearly two years, she had gone through a battery of tests a few weeks ago. "You received the results?"

She nodded as the sobs came harder.

He patted her back, hating what she was going through. "It's okay, Dorcas. Whatever is going on, your family and mine will help you find answers."

She cried and talked for hours before sleep took over. He eased from the couch beside her, shifted her legs onto the cushions, and placed a blanket over her. She had spent two and half years waiting for him to get over Hannah. She'd been by him through every step of the ordeal as he pined for Hannah.

Now she needed him — desperately.

From his easy chair Paul stared at the woman asleep on his couch, willing his heart to connect with her. He couldn't stand the idea of leaving someone in overwhelming circumstances again. Hannah had someone. Dorcas had him.

He picked up the crisp, typewritten letter from the coffee table. Unfolding it, he leaned back in the chair. A soft stream of light from the hallway crossed the page. Every result had come back negative, which would be good news except the symptoms she dealt with gave her no relief — the joint pain, the skin sensitivity, the inability to think clearly or remember from one minute to the next.

Needing to be there for her, he tried to put lingering thoughts for Hannah into perspective.

Dorcas opened her eyes.

Paul slid the letter between the cushion and the arm of the chair. "Hi. How are you feeling?"

She sat up. "A bit foolish for coming here and crying in your arms until I fell asleep."

"It's not a problem. You were upset, and you should have come here."

Dorcas's eyes held fast to him. "What time is it?"

"About two a.m."

She winced as she tried to sit up.

Paul went to her and extended his hand. "I called your parents so they wouldn't worry. They wish you'd told them what was going on." He helped her stand. "You steady?" The pain across her face twisted knots inside him.

She nodded and wrapped her hands around his arm.

He patted her hand. "How about if I fix you some food or some hot tea before I take you home?"

She put her arms around him. "I need you, Paul."

He rested his head on hers. "And I'll be

right here for you like you've been for me, okay?"

CHAPTER 21

Matthew turned off the shower, feeling sore, but with more energy than he'd had in a really long time. The ache for David was nonstop, but he was able to grieve and keep moving. That was a welcome improvement. He and Luke had two weeks of hard work ahead of them getting the old buildings torn down. He dreaded facing that, seeing in his mind's eye the day of the fire, the day David died, over and over again as they worked, but it had to be done. They'd begin tomorrow. Today was a church Sunday, and he hoped it'd bring him strength to face the next two weeks.

An aroma of coffee hung in the air as he finished shaving. By the time he slid into his Sunday suit, the smell of scrapple and cinnamon rolls filtered through the upstairs. He stepped into the hallway, almost bumping into his mother as she staggered out of her bedroom.

"Mamm, aren't ya goin' to church today?"

Tears rolled down her cheeks. *"Ich kann net."*

"Mamm, you can." He kissed her forehead. "We need you. Daed's lonely for you. Right now it's like he's lost a son and a wife. Peter still needs his Mamm. He's just a kid, but growing up so fast. And Kathryn shouldn't be tryin' to run the house while helping me rebuild the business."

"I wish I'd been a better Mamm for my sweet David." She brushed tears off her face. "I want another chance."

Guilt. That hopeless, life-choking guilt.

He hated it.

"Kumm." He put his arm around her shoulders. "Please."

She barely nodded, and he escorted her downstairs.

Closing the oven, Kathryn turned. Her gentle eyes surrounded his mother with understanding, but when she looked at Matthew, something else sparked in them. Or maybe he was just hoping he saw something more for him. His Daed thudded through the back door, and Peter slammed the front door as he entered.

"The horses have come inside, ya?" Kathryn looked at his Daed.

He gave a sheepish look, half smiling.

"Sorry, I tripped over the feed bucket."

"In the house?" Kathryn looked at Peter.

"So that's what I did with that thing. Sorry."

"You know, I don't get paid enough for this nonsense." She winked at Mamm and poured her a cup of coffee.

When Kathryn returned to the stove and set the coffeepot on the eye, Matthew sidled up to her. "Mamm's guilt is getting worse, not better." He grabbed the plate of scrapple.

Kathryn looked up at him.

He shrugged. "I was hoping you knew something to say."

Kathryn lifted the pan of cooling cinnamon buns off the back of the stove. "I . . . I have no idea what to say, or I'd have said it already."

"We gotta try something."

She nodded, and they both moved to the table and set the items in place.

Kathryn passed out the cloth napkins and took a seat.

"Mamm, you know Kathryn's dealt with a rough patch of grief too."

Mamm stirred her coffee. "Yes, I know."

Kathryn took a sip of coffee and eased the cup back to the table. "When my brother died, it seemed there was nowhere to put the affection I had just for him. It's like it banked inside me, and I ached to do something for him again. Then I began to constantly relive all the times I fought with him."

Mamm nodded. "Ya, I can see feeling that way."

Daed took a seat and poured himself some coffee. "I'm not short on feeling like I failed him. Over the last few years, I've spent weeks at a time away from home, traveling with the Amish carpenters." His eyes rimmed with tears. "I miss the days when most Amish could make a living farming."

The room was silent, much as it had been since David died, but this time a vapor of hope seemed to swirl, like the unseen aromas of coffee and cinnamon buns.

Peter squirmed in his chair, making it screech against the floor. "I promised him I'd help that day in the shop. If I'd been there, I'd have smelled that gasoline before it could catch fire."

Mamm gasped and grabbed Peter, knocking her coffee over. "No. If you'd been there, I could have lost you too. You have no sense of smell, child. What are you thinking?"

Peter burst into tears mixed with laughter. Kathryn mopped up the spilled coffee. Matthew didn't miss the nod Daed gave Kathryn — a slight movement that carried the weight of his full approval.

When Kathryn took a seat, Matthew slipped his arm around the back of her chair, and she whispered, "Real love — it's the best, most painful thing God ever did for us."

"So really a person should say, 'I'm in pain with you.' " He kept his voice low and tried to hide his laughter.

"Only when they're dealing with you, Matthew Esh."

He laughed out loud, and his Mamm looked at him. He pointed at Kathryn. "It's her fault."

His Mamm's eyes narrowed as she looked from Kathryn to him. He leaned the chair back on two legs so Kathryn couldn't see him as he placed his index finger over his lips and nodded at his mother, answering all the questions she'd never dare to ask. Then he winked at his Mamm.

CHAPTER 22

Inside the Daadi Haus that Luke and Mary shared with Mammi Annie, Hannah rinsed the soapsuds off the last breakfast skillet and stacked it in the dish drainer.

The glow of light from the fall morning danced across the room, turning shadows as fresh air whipped through the barely open window. Luke was like her when it came to open windows. Even in cool weather he wanted a bit of fresh air stirring through a room.

She dried her hands on a dishtowel and grabbed a freshly scrubbed pan to dry it. The kitchen still carried the aroma of a robust breakfast, but the counters were now clean, waiting for the next round of meals. These were the things she remembered most: the steady but calm pace of day-to-day chores, the way daylight filtered through a home void of electric lights, the distinct segments of time — morning, noon, and evening — defined by meals cooked and chores done.

Sarah came into the kitchen, carrying a few glasses. She looked distracted, so Hannah stepped back from the sink. "Did you need to put those in the sink?"

She blinked a few times and then nodded. "I found these upstairs while making beds."

"Okay, thanks." Setting the pan on the counter and grabbing another wet dish, Hannah caught a glimpse of Lissa through the window. The little girl shadowed Mary's every move as they dug up the last of the potatoes for the season. Luke had been ready to go to Matthew's early this morning in hopes that a full day of work would get a portion of the burned-out building torn down today. As he was heading out the door, Mary's Daed and a couple of her brothers had shown up and gone with him.

Sarah's hands shook as she began helping put dishes away. Hannah's time with her over the weekend was something she would carry in her heart for years to come. They'd made cookies, walked the fields, and lazed around while watching Lissa play at the edge of the creek.

Sarah plunked a dish onto the countertop. "I don't want you to go."

"I know. It's been a wonderful visit. I'll be

back after the first of the year." Hannah moved to Sarah's seven-day pillbox, making sure she'd remembered her meds yesterday and this morning. She had, and thankfully, she didn't seem to notice what Hannah was doing. In spite of the telltale signs of nervousness, losing small tracts of time, and being a little scattered, her sister's progress seemed remarkable.

Sarah should thank Paul. He seemed really good at his job, able to work with people from all walks of life. Maybe that's how he'd managed to embrace attending an Englischer college while spending each summer with a Plain Mennonite grandmother and falling for an Old Order Amish girl.

Paul.

She drew a slow breath, trying to control the rogue emotions that hit her concerning him. Aiming to refocus her thoughts, she looked out the window and watched Lissa.

"If you're not married, can't you stay?" Sarah asked.

Hannah had clarified she wasn't married, but that news seemed to make Sarah more determined to hold on to her. "No, I can't." She clutched a handful of flatware from the draining basket and dried each piece before sliding it into place in the drawer. Last night

Luke, Mary, Sarah, Lissa, and Hannah had sat on the floor near the low-burning potbellied stove, playing a game of marbles. Mammi Annie watched from her rocker, saying she was too old to get on the floor to play a game. It was almost as if nothing had ever ripped them apart, but the weekend had carried a heaviness that Hannah bore in silence.

Mary's secret.

If Mary truly understood the seriousness of what was going on, she hid it well. But whatever lay ahead, it had to be dealt with openly. Luke had to be told . . . no matter what the prognosis.

If this Amish district had a medical facility the Plain people trusted going to, like the communities in Alliance had with Dr. Lehman, Mary wouldn't be in this position. Years ago if Hannah would've had somewhere safe to go, her life would be completely different.

Lissa ran inside, chortling. Her cheeks were rosy from the cool morning air. Mary came in the back door, smiling.

"Look!" Lissa held up a funny-shaped rock.

Wondering what Lissa thought she'd found, Hannah glanced to Mary. "What am I looking at?"

Lissa laughed. "It's a rock. Don't you know a rock when you see one?"

Hannah, Mary, and Sarah laughed. It was the kind of thing Hannah and Mary would have pulled on adults when they were kids.

Mary placed her hand on Lissa's head. "Sarah, would you help Lissa wash the rock and then her hands?"

Still laughing at Lissa's joke, Sarah did as asked.

Mary waited for the bathroom door to close. "Any word yet?"

Hannah removed the towel from her shoulder and placed it on a peg. "No. You doing okay?"

Mary shook her hands, as if trying to wake them. "As nervous as a body waiting to be told whether they're gonna live or die."

"How did you manage to push this fear off you for so long?"

"It took us awhile to get pregnant, and I thought God wasn't going to let me have a baby until I told Luke the truth. When I conceived, I soared on the clouds for months, confident nothing could go wrong. When concern tried to creep in, I did a good job of telling it to shut up — until the pains began."

Hannah stifled a sigh. "The part about telling it to shut up — we're just too alike, you know?"

Mary gave a nod. "I'm beginning to see that."

The phone inside Hannah's dress pocket vibrated. She opened it and read an unfamiliar number across the screen. It showed a local Pennsylvania area code, so she pushed the green icon. "Hannah Lawson."

"Hey, it's Paul."

Even if he hadn't identified himself, with one word spoken she'd recognize his temperate, deep voice anywhere, at any time, even after not hearing him speak for more than two years.

Motioning to Mary that she was going outside, Hannah answered, "Any news?"

"The board approved Dr. Lehman coming in. I called to let him know, and he asked me to tell you he's doing all he can to be here by lunchtime."

She had no doubts that Paul had pulled every favor imaginable to get the board to approve this unorthodox visit so quickly, but the news only made Hannah more anxious. What if the prognosis wasn't good? Hannah closed her eyes, praying for Mary.

"Hannah?"

"I . . . I'm here. Just really nervous, but I appreciate this a lot." Why was she telling him how she felt? Was she no longer capable of holding her tongue when talking to Paul?

"I'm uneasy too, but the favor was no problem. I heard from Kathryn Glick last night. She spent most of the weekend planning a community workday. Has lots of people going to the Esh place today to help clear the rubbish off the foundation. She called me last night. Said she'd been trying to keep it a surprise."

"Well, that explains why Luke was so flabbergasted when Mary's Daed and brothers showed up to go with him to Matthew's this morning. I guess Kathryn kept this a secret from Luke and Mary too."

"Are you at the Yoder place?"

Hannah took in the scenery, the hills, pastures, and barns. "Yes."

"I have a client to see first, but then I'm going to Matthew's to lend a hand as soon as I can get there. You know, Sarah should go too and help with lunch."

"You think she's up to seeing something as emotional as tearing down the shops where David died?"

"If it hits her hard, I'll help her deal with it."

"Ah, so you'll be on hand if she wigs out?"

"Wigs out?" Paul laughed. "Is that anything like YoMama from yoTV?"

Laughter escaped her as he quoted bits of

an exchange they'd shared years ago when playing Scrabble. Suddenly uncomfortable for sharing a laugh with Paul, she cleared her throat. "I . . . I better go."

"Just make sure to get only good news about Mary, okay?"

"I'll do my best. Thanks." She closed the phone. Paul loved board games like she did. Maybe one had to grow up Plain to appreciate those types of games, because Martin hated them. He loved computer war games, though, and television and movies, all of which he indulged in regularly while she was at school or work. But when she was home, their lives were so busy she rarely had time to notice something as unimportant as a board game. She slid the phone into her pocket and went to find Sarah.

After telling her about the events at the Esh place, Hannah walked with her across Yoder property to where Esh land began.

Sarah gazed into Hannah's eyes. "When will I see you again?"

"I . . . I'm not sure, but you can use the Yoders' phone shanty and call me anytime."

Could her sister possibly understand how hard it was coming back to Owl's Perch, even for just a visit?

This time had been a bit easier as a few more of her people seemed to be moderately accepting of her. But she figured each one who'd been more open this time knew the same thing Hannah knew; she'd never really fit in anywhere. Not as an Englischer or as an Amish. She was too much like Zabeth, unable to truly become a part of either world. But like her aunt, she'd made her choice. She'd fallen in love with a master of Englischers, Martin Palmer, and she'd live out her days with him. But she couldn't keep going back and forth from one world to another. And that's how it felt, like traveling to different planets with each reentry bumpy and heated.

Thoughts of building a life with Martin pulled on her. They'd make a good couple, and it'd give Lissa and Kevin a steady, loving home.

Sarah slid her arm around Hannah's. "Can you come home over the Christmas holidays for just a day or two?"

She shook her head. "I'll be in Hawaii with Martin and the children. He's flying his top employees and a few friends there for a two-week stay."

"Hawaii?" She stopped walking.

Hannah tugged on her arm, and they began again. "I'll be back after the first of the year."

The frown on Sarah's face was deep, and

Hannah wondered if this news was going to cause a problem for her.

She stopped near where the fields became the Eshes' backyard. "It's best if I go on back now. I don't want to make Matthew's parents uncomfortable by staying, and they aren't the kind to ask me to leave."

"Naomi and Raymond won't mind."

"Maybe not, but I'm not taking that chance."

Sarah hugged her. "I'm sorry you and Paul argued, but I was glad you came barging into that meeting for me." She released Hannah and took a step back. "You really have forgiven me . . . haven't you?"

Hannah knew she had so much to learn about forgiveness that it might help her to go somewhere quiet and stay there until she understood the true nature of it. But clearly, learning didn't come from time alone in prayer. It began there, and then it seemed it became perfected by messing up, digging deeper, and trying again.

Unable to answer her sister, Hannah gave her one last hug. "Go on. You have work to do."

CHAPTER 23

On the front porch of the Better Path, Hannah waited for Dr. Lehman to arrive. He'd called a few minutes ago to let her know he was close. Mary sat inside the waiting room with Lissa, but Hannah was hoping for a minute alone with Dr. Lehman. The rolling hills were ablaze in fall color, and the air carried the aroma of smoke from a fireplace. The peacefulness reminded her clearly that she was among the Amish.

Why had Paul decided to stay this close to Owl's Perch in such a small, out-of-the-way clinic when his grades and abilities could allow for so much more? Martin would rather die than not use every ounce of his ability to increase his influence and standing in life.

Dr. Lehman pulled up to the clinic, and Hannah hurried down the steps to his car.

He turned off the vehicle and opened the door. "Hello."

"Thank you for doing this."

"This is easy, Hannah, especially with my seeing Mom this week anyway." His voice carried more than just an I-don't-mind-doing-this tone. He sounded pleased to do this for her. Passing her his briefcase with one hand, he grabbed his large medical bag off the passenger's seat with the other. He got out of his car, pushed his glasses higher on his nose, and studied her. "How are you?"

The standard three-word greeting meant more than the simple question.

Hannah rubbed her fingertips across her forehead, wishing she had a more appealing answer to give. "It's been pretty good. Better than the first trip."

Dr. Lehman's brows furrowed. "And?"

She dipped her head, sighing. "I still managed to blow up at Paul."

"Mmm-hmm." They began climbing the steps. "Was he innocent again?"

She rolled her eyes and gave a nod.

The gleam in his eye said more than the crooked smile across his lips. "I saw that side of you when we first met in the hospital and you gave me the dickens for wanting to turn you over to social services."

"Was I that bad?" They stopped on the porch, outside the closed front entryway.

"You were pretty bold for a seventeen-year-old Amish girl who'd awakened to find herself in ICU. You thought I was wrong, and you weren't afraid to say so . . . as respectfully as possible, of course."

"So far in this with Paul, I've been far from respectful and the only one wrong."

Dr. Lehman chuckled. "You'll survive. And so will he. The way I see it, you were probably born for something that needs spit and fire once in a while. That's bound to shake things up a bit here and there — nothing wrong with that as long as you're either trying to do what's right or willing to go back and make it right."

She squeezed the handle of his briefcase. "My Daed would totally disagree with you . . . and can quote verses as to why and how your acceptance of my misbehavior is wrong."

"Ah, well, that's a debate I'll never have with him. But we both know you're God's servant, Hannah, not your parents'." He gestured toward the briefcase he'd passed to her. "I spoke with Mary's doctors, but rather than tell you what they said, I'd like you to read the faxes they sent and sum up the diagnoses after her examination. Do you have a vial of blood, a urine sample, and a written report of her emotional state and vitals?"

"Yes. The blood and urine are in the lab, waiting either to be sent out or for you to run the tests yourself."

He moved his medical bag to his other hand. "We won't do anything so elaborate that we'll need it sent out. If she doesn't require immediate hospitalization, which I doubt, we'll see to it that she gets a regular ob-gyn before the week is out."

They went inside. Leaving Lissa in the waiting room playing with toys under Halley's watchful eye, Mary, Hannah, and Dr. Lehman made their way up the steps and into the room provided. The exam didn't take long, and then Hannah and Dr. Lehman went into the adjoining room — Paul's office.

Dr. Lehman sat on the couch, waiting for her to read the chart. "In two sentences or less, summarize what it says, Hannah."

In the overstuffed chair adjacent to him, she shifted. The odd feeling of sitting in the same chair Paul used while with clients made it difficult to concentrate. How had she landed in such a weird place in life? "The concerns are that what was done to stop the hemorrhaging inside Mary's skull when she had a subdural hematoma could blow out upon the increased intracranial pressure during Valsalva."

"Which means?"

"The concerns don't involve any health issues until time for labor and delivery." Tears stung her eyes. "She's in no danger."

"Your medical advice?"

"She has to agree to go to a hospital and have a scheduled C-section a week or so before she could go into labor."

"Exactly. I'll find her an obstetrician who will take her on, but it'll be your responsibility to make sure she follows through." Dr. Lehman removed his glasses, looking at her firmly.

"Yes, absolutely."

He replaced his glasses. "Define Valsalva."

"It's holding the breath and bearing down during labor and delivery."

"Good. Now, in your opinion, why didn't Dr. Hill or one of Mary's other doctors explain this better to her?"

"According to the records, the doctor told her to come in for another CT scan, which she didn't do. He explained that a pregnancy would put the baby in no danger, but labor and delivery would be very dangerous for her. The doctor could've been in a huge hurry and intended to explain more later on, but Mary never went back. Or maybe he didn't think an Amish girl her age would understand anyway. But I think maybe her doctor didn't approve of a teen wanting to get married, so he stayed vague on purpose. Which really irks —"

Mary tapped on the door and then entered. She looked from Dr. Lehman to Hannah, obviously hoping for good news.

Hannah clenched her lips and lowered her eyes to the open chart, trying to restrain herself. It wasn't her place even to hint at the diagnosis. Professionalism at all times meant too much to Dr. Lehman, even today.

Dr. Lehman stood. "I'll go to the lab and run the blood and urine tests myself while you and Hannah talk."

He gave Hannah a nod before leaving the room.

Mary's eyes bored into her. "Well?"

Hannah stood, closed the chart, and laid it in the chair. She took Mary by the hands, smiling so big her face ached. "You and the baby are fine."

Mary engulfed her, clinging to her and crying.

"And you'll be perfectly safe as long as you go to a hospital and have a C-section done." After a long hug, Hannah removed Mary's grasp and stared into her eyes. "You have to tell Luke. You have to be in a hospital a week or more before labor can begin and have a C-section. Do you understand?"

She grabbed Hannah and hugged her again. "I understand . . . the baby and I will be fine. I'll do whatever it takes to stay that way."

And right then Hannah knew every bit of what she'd been through to work under Dr. Lehman, go to school, and reenter Owl's Perch was worth this one thing.

Hannah shifted gears as she entered the Yoders' driveway. "If I leave for Ohio as soon as I drop you off, I can be there in time for class tonight or at least enough of it to get credit for being there."

Mary rubbed her protruding stomach. "I was hoping you'd stay and answer Luke's questions."

"How badly is he going to take this?"

Mary leaned back on the headrest, closing her eyes. "How bad does any man take learning that his wife lied in order to marry him?"

"You lied?" Lissa piped up. "You're not supposed to lie."

Hannah tapped Mary's shoulder. Mary opened her eyes, and Hannah pointed toward the fields behind the outbuildings.

Naomi Esh and Luke walked toward them, coming from the Esh place. Luke's clothes were covered in soot, and he looked almost too tired to walk. Naomi appeared rather worn-out herself.

Mary unfastened her seat belt. "Why is Luke coming back from work in the middle of the day with Naomi?"

"I didn't want to ruin Luke getting to tell you first, but Kathryn organized a surprise workday." Hannah set the emergency brake and turned off the car. "When are you going to tell him?"

"Soon, but not now. Naomi doesn't need the stress of knowing what's going on."

Luke opened Mary's car door. "Where have you guys been?"

"We've been at the Better Path," Lissa offered.

Mary got out of the car. "I heard the good news. How's the workday going?"

"Really good. But Naomi needs to borrow pitchers and sugar and . . . what else?"

Naomi held up a list. "If it's in your pantry, I may need it." She lowered the list and gazed at Hannah. A slow, gentle smile graced her lips, but she appeared speechless. Deep wrinkles now tracked her face.

Hannah forced herself to speak. "I'm so sorry for your loss."

Naomi embraced her. "Denki." She took Hannah by the shoulders and backed her up. "Let's take a look at you, child. I'd heard you'd been here, but they said you were gone already."

Luke shrugged. "I thought you had to leave in time for classes tonight."

"Hannah," Lissa called from the backseat.

"Oh, excuse me for a minute." She opened the back door of the car and unfastened Lissa from the restraint, glad for the interruption. She placed Lissa on her hip.

Naomi stepped closer. "How've you been, Hannah?"

"I . . . I'm good." What could she possibly say to sum up all that'd taken place since the day she'd left Owl's Perch and Naomi had helped take her to the train station?

"I've prayed for you every day since you left."

Hannah scooted Lissa to her other hip. "Thank you. I've needed every one of those prayers."

Naomi tugged on Lissa's shoe. "And who's this?"

"Naomi Esh, this is Lissa Palmer. She's . . . the niece of a dear friend of mine."

With her entire hand, Lissa brushed strands of silky black hair from her face. "She and my uncle kiss."

Hannah's cheeks burned, and she bet her face was now quite pink. "Well, that does make him a good friend, doesn't it?"

"I certainly hope so," Luke added.

Naomi held up the list. "Do you remember Kathryn Glick?"

Wondering what Naomi must think, she managed to hold on to a sense of dignity. "Yes, I think so. I saw her at the annual school sales, right?"

"That's right, along with hundreds of other unfamiliar faces. I think she's a real treasure. On Friday she decided she wanted to surprise Matthew by pulling off a work frolic. She got the word out, but she didn't realize how many supplies it'd take to keep everyone in drinks and food."

Mary took the list and skimmed it. "Luke, maybe it'd be easiest if you hooked a horse to the small cart and used that to tote the items back."

"Good idea." Luke headed for the barn.

Naomi turned to Hannah. "You'll come over too, won't you?"

"I . . . I . . ."

Naomi slid her arm around Hannah's shoulders. "Of course it'll be hard, and some — only some, mind you — will whisper and wag their tongues, but it's my house, and I'm inviting you."

Hundreds of insecurities burned inside her head: her Englischer dress, her Kappless head, the ring on her finger, her hairstyle, Lissa in jeans and a sweater, explaining who Lissa was, finding the right words for each person, totally giving up on going to class this evening.

But how could she say no to Naomi? She'd lost so much, and if a visit from Hannah was what she wanted, Hannah wouldn't deny her. Besides, Mary needed her too.

"Sure I'll come."

She turned to Mary. "By midnight."

Mary nodded. "By midnight."

Luke came up behind her. "What happens then?"

She jolted. "I thought you were getting the cart."

Luke pointed to where the horse and cart waited to be loaded. "Are you two up to something?"

"These two?" Naomi smiled. "Never."

Luke looked doubtful and glanced from Mary to Hannah.

Mary motioned toward the house. "Let's get the stuff on the list."

They loaded the items into the cart, and while Luke walked beside the horse, Lissa held the reins and drove the wooden rig across the bumpy fields. Hannah's mouth was dry, and her insides felt far colder than the nippy October air, but this seemed to be the right thing to do. She sat on the bench between Lissa and Mary, not at all sure riding in this jarring rig was a bit easier than walking. It was easy to understand why Naomi had insisted on walking. They crossed the knoll and soon were entering the Eshes' backyard.

Dozens of men in straw hats, broadcloth pants, suspenders, and work gloves knocked down beams with sledgehammers and hauled burned timbers to the back of a large wagon. There were a few Englischers among the mix: Russ Braden and Nate McDaniel, drivers for the Amish, and Hank Carlisle, the milk pickup man. All of them knew her and her past.

Long tables covered in sheets were set up end to end across the flattest part of the yard, and there the large gathering ate their lunch and supper. The women served the men first and waited on them. After the men left the tables, the women would serve the children and then themselves. Staring straight ahead, she tried to brace herself for the afternoon. It wasn't that anyone would physically lay a hand on her, certainly not. They probably wouldn't even question her directly or share their opinions. But she'd get looks and whispers, and when the work was through, they'd get into their buggies or cars and not hold back sharing their thoughts. She'd like to know why something that toothless took so much strength to face.

Hannah viewed the burned shops again. Matthew had added several new ones during the time she'd been gone. Through a rickety, half-standing wall of an almost dismantled shop, she caught a glimpse of a broad-shouldered man helping carry a load-bearing beam.

Paul.

A dreamlike feeling engulfed her again. Luke led the rig around to the front yard, and Sarah came into view, dumping trays of ice into a cooler. Hannah stepped out of the cart and helped Lissa down while Luke did the same for Mary.

Mary beamed up at her husband, placing her palm on his cheek. "I love you." She whispered the words, but Hannah heard the joy in her voice that Mary couldn't yet explain to her husband.

Luke squared his shoulders, clearly teasing. "Of course you do."

Mary lowered her hand. "You'd better get back at it with the men. We're fine from here."

Luke walked toward the shops, but he

kept turning back, catching a glimpse of Mary. Hannah believed him to be more in love today than when he married her dear friend, and it warmed her. Mary lifted a casserole from the seat of the cart and headed for the steps to the Esh home.

Naomi passed Hannah an armful of items: pitchers, ladles, and sugar. She then passed a few wooden spoons and cloth napkins to Lissa before grabbing as much as she could carry. "Come on." Naomi nodded toward her home.

Hannah followed, and they entered Naomi's kitchen. Food lined several worktables that were covered with fabric. More than two dozen women were scurrying about to have the next meal ready by suppertime. Hannah remembered well that when dealing with this many mouths to feed, there wasn't enough time, supplies, or energy between dinner and supper.

Naomi cleared a space on the table. "We need however many loaves of bread you can bake, Hannah."

There would be no introduction, no fanfare concerning her return. If some of the women chose to talk to her, they would. If they didn't, they'd pretend she wasn't there. When she looked across the room, a few halfhearted smiles greeted her. The blank stares of others were far from warm or accepting, but no one spoke.

Kathryn Glick, someone she barely remembered, passed her a sack of bread flour. "Hi, Hannah. I'm really glad you're here."

From somewhere across the room, Hannah's mother emerged. Mamm's eyes told Hannah she loved her. Her mother moved forward and hugged her. "I'm glad you came. You do know that, right?"

"I do now." Hannah squeezed her, letting years of ache melt away. When she opened her eyes, she saw several women crowded around. Edna reached for Hannah, and soon tears blurred her eyes as she received hugs from more than half the women in the room.

Her mother wiped tears from her face. "If you'll do the bread, we'll handle everything else, including setting the tables and serving the men."

Lissa gazed up at her, nodding her head. "I'll help."

Hannah placed her hand on Lissa's head. The girl seemed to live in perpetual excitement for life, although her attention span for anything in the kitchen wouldn't last like her love of creeks and water. She'd be by Hannah's side for maybe ten minutes, probably less.

Thankful for a set job, Hannah nodded.

Now, was she still capable of making bread like she used to? It'd been a long time since she'd made a batch of dough in a kitchen without electricity. Determined to give it her all, she walked to the pantry.

CHAPTER 24

Afternoon shadows began to creep across the yard as the sun moved westward. Luke stood still for a moment, trying to catch a glimpse of Mary. She was setting pitchers of water on the table. He hoped she wasn't doing too much. In spite of the workday and all the hope and socializing it brought, the weight of losing David Esh was heavy on everyone, especially the womenfolk. He'd seen Mary's fears over their unborn child increase since the funeral. Hannah's return gave Mary someone she could talk to. That was good. He was glad. Really. But he got the feeling they were hiding secrets again.

By midnight.

What did that mean, anyway? He hadn't had any reservations about the day Hannah helped Mary dig potatoes. But then today they'd gone out by themselves, ignoring any reservations the bishop might have if he found out. His wife and sister sure did a lot of private talking, didn't they? Then again, it was only Hannah's second visit to Owl's Perch in over two years. Mary spotted him and waved. He trotted to her.

"Hey." The word came out breathless. "Maybe you should get off your feet for a spell."

"I'm doing great. Why, Hannah was telling me that women who stay busy and even those who have some extra stress in their lives are more likely to give birth to healthy babies than the women who live too soft and easy. She said the baby comes out ready to fight for life."

"You want us to have a fighter?" Luke laughed.

Mary ran her hand over her stomach. "Not if you put it that way."

A deep male voice called Luke's name.

"I need to get back. You take it easy, okay?"

She nodded, but there was something in her eyes, something he'd asked her about a dozen times over the last few months.

"Mary?"

She gazed up at him.

"Something wrong?"

She shook her head. "Everything's great, but I . . . got some things I want to tell you. Good things, really."

300

"Can't you just say them right now?"

"No, and not at home either, not with Sarah and Mammi Annie listening."

Luke tried to read his wife. Their bedroom was private enough, but Mary wouldn't let any disagreements be aired out there. That had to be done elsewhere, usually outside when they went for a walk, sometimes at the supper table, in front of Mammi Annie, but never in the bedroom. "I . . . I thought you said it was good news?"

"It is, but —"

Several more men called Luke's name. He looked up, and four or five of them were watching him, waiting. As an owner of E and L, he was supposed to be supervising. "You hold those thoughts, and as soon as things settle down for the day, I'll come find you."

Hannah turned the last loaf of cooling bread out of its pan and then wiped her hands on the towel that lay across her shoulder. The report Naomi had given about thirty minutes ago was that most of the men had eaten and some had gone on home. Only the younger men were still at it, with sledgehammers and wheelbarrows.

Shouts from several men filled the air, and the few remaining women in the room ran outside. Hannah took a peek through the kitchen window, wanting to spot Lissa. The girl stood near the tire swing with several other children, waiting her turn. Hannah looked out farther, trying to see what'd caused the ruckus. She couldn't see the shop area for the sprawling leaf-covered branches of oak trees, but Luke was walking toward the house. When he spotted her in the window, he motioned for her. She ran outside.

He pointed at the shops . . . or where the shops used to be. The men had removed almost all the charred debris from the concrete foundation in one day. Impressive.

Luke shook his head. "We were too tired and shoulda quit earlier. Paul's hurt, but he says it's not bad enough to be seen. Will you do me a favor and take a look?"

"If he says he's not hurt . . ."

"Hannah." Luke lowered his voice, giving an entire lecture in her name.

"Fine. Where is he?"

"There." Luke pointed across the yard to a group of men near a wagon. A pile of charred wood lay on the ground around the men's feet.

They picked up their pace. "What happened?"

"A couple of men were trying to get a load

of heavy beams on top of what was already in the wagon. When the load began to slide, Paul caught it with his shoulder, slowing the landslide long enough to give Jacob time to get mostly out of the way before the load came crashing down."

Luke and Hannah closed the gap. Paul's shirt was covered in soot and tattered from the day's work. In spite of the black stains, Hannah saw blood soaking his shirt, starting above his elbow and dripping off the end of his finger.

"Paul," — Luke motioned to her — "let Hannah take a look."

Paul glanced at her. "I'm fine. Really."

Was he afraid her scarlet letter would once again be shared with him? That any contact with her would break whatever threads of goodwill he'd sewn between himself and the Amish community in her absence?

"Then let me look." She stepped closer and pulled at the edges of the ripped sleeve, trying to see the source of the blood.

Ignoring his stiff reaction to her presence, she tore the sleeve of his shirt where it was already tattered and took a look at the injury. "We need to irrigate it, disinfecting it. And you might need stitches." Like changing gears while driving, she let her nursing skills take over. Someone needed to get her medical bag for her. "Where's Matthew?"

Luke tugged at his straw hat, tightening it onto his head. "He went to the Bylers' to use their phone. Since we're getting so much done, he's gone to check prices and delivery for timber."

"Oh, okay. This isn't an emergency, but, Peter, could you bridle a rested horse for Luke so he can go to the Yoders and get my medical bag quicker and easier than walking?"

"Sure thing." Peter hurried toward the stables.

Paul angled his body away from the others, clearly wishing to convey something only to her. "I'd be more concerned about Jacob if I were you."

Hannah looked at the young man, Mary's brother and Sarah's one-time beau. He'd grown half a foot since the last time she saw him, but more important, he was pale and shaking, his breathing shallow.

She removed the kitchen towel from her shoulder and placed it over Paul's wound. "Hold this tight and try to hold the sides of the gash together to slow the bleeding." Stepping over to the young man, she asked, "Jacob, how are you feeling?"

"I . . . I . . ."

Hannah took his chin and directed his face so she could look in his eyes. His pupils were dilated. She took his wrist. His pulse was racing, his breathing irregular, and his skin cold.

Was this a reaction to seeing blood flow freely from Paul? Or maybe it was a combination of being startled by the incident and seeing the blood. It seemed an extreme reaction to those things, so maybe he was hurt more than it appeared.

The crowd around them grew larger. Hannah turned and saw Kathryn. "I need several blankets, please."

She nodded and headed quickly for the house.

Hannah placed her hand under his arm. "Jacob, I want you to lie down."

He started easing to the ground, and then his legs apparently lost their power, because he landed on his backside with a thud.

Hannah glanced at the women. "Could someone keep an eye on Lissa for me?"

Mary spoke up, saying she would.

Hannah placed her hand on Jacob's neck and head, easing him to a lying position. "All the way on your back, please."

He complied.

"That's it." She stood and moved to his feet and lifted them. "Just relax." Glancing at the group, she saw Jacob's mom, Becky, at the back of the crowd, trying to see. "Becky?"

She threaded her way through quickly, looking worried, but the more involved Hannah could keep her, the calmer she'd remain.

"If you'll hold his feet about a foot off the ground, that'd be very helpful."

Becky knelt, doing as instructed.

Hannah reached into her pocket and grabbed her car keys. "Luke, my medical bag is in the trunk of my car. It's a brown leather tote bag." Showing him the keyless remote, she pointed to the unlock icon.

Luke stared at her, much like during her first visit to Owl's Perch. "You have a medical bag?"

"It was a Christmas gift from Dr. Lehman, and I always keep it with me."

She showed him the right icon on the keyless remote again. "When you're beside the car, push that twice. Then push the trunk icon, and it'll open."

Luke took the keys and studied the keyless remote. "You sure?"

"Yeah, if it doesn't, you can use this key." She pointed to the right one. "But it doesn't work well on the trunk and has been known to set off the alarm. If it does, ignore it and bring me the bag. Okay?"

Peter arrived with a bareback horse, and Luke pulled himself onto it and galloped off.

Hannah checked Jacob's pulse. It was already a little more even. "We'll have some blankets for you in just a minute." She ran her hands over his chest. "Did you get hit when the accident happened?"

"J-just a bit."

"Where?"

He pointed to the top of his shoulder.

Knowing that couldn't cause any bruising to an organ, she pressed on his sides, kneading his flesh under her hands. "Did any other part of you get hit with the boards?"

He shook his head. Kathryn came back with the blankets, and Hannah spread them over him.

Matthew's Daed walked up with a drink and held it out. "Here, this will help."

She shook her head. "A drink right now isn't a good idea, but thank you. He needs to stay lying down. But I could use a knife to cut his shirt. I need to see the injury."

Someone passed her a knife. The sun hung low in the sky, making it a little harder to see, but he had no cuts or gashes, only a good-sized bruise on his shoulder. She ran her fingers over his shoulder, feeling for any signs of a dislocation or break.

Becky held on to Jacob's feet, stroking his pant-covered legs. "What's wrong with him?"

"I think his sympathetic nervous system is reacting to the situation, which is similar to experiencing mild shock. He seems fine except for the bruise on his shoulder. But I can't tell if anything is torn or broken. He may need an x-ray."

Becky studied her son. "Do you think he needs one?"

"I can't be sure."

"But you know what you think," Jacob's Daed added firmly.

Hannah glanced to Paul. They didn't want the Englischer nurse's version — go let an expert see you, even if you think you're fine. They wanted a trust-your-gut Amish answer — if he's likely to be fine without seeing a doctor, then give that a chance first.

She shrugged. "It's too early to tell. I'd like to give his body a few minutes and see how he reacts. I'll check his vitals as soon as Luke returns. Right now we're going to make a thick pallet beside him and get him off the cold ground, and someone's going to get a chair for Paul."

Several women helped Jacob shift onto the pallet and covered him with a blanket. Both his pulse and color were returning to normal. When Luke returned, Hannah checked Jacob's blood pressure and the reaction of his pupils to the light of her ophthalmoscope. All of his autonomic systems were coming back into normal range.

Jacob tugged at the blood pressure cuff. "Can you remove this thing and let me up now? I feel fine."

Hannah shook her head. "You can sit up, but that's all. If that works, we'll go from there."

His mother released his feet, letting him sit upright. She shooed everyone back. "Go on and eat or clean up or rest or whatever. We're fine. If Hannah needs anything, we'll holler."

The group slowly dispersed, walking back to the Esh home. Paul sat in a chair about five feet away. Someone had brought two extra lawn chairs, and a washbowl filled with clean water sat in one of them.

Hannah paused, insisting her legs keep moving. The oddity of Paul patiently waiting mocked her. She took a deep breath, trying to repel feelings that were a betrayal to Martin. Sitting next to Paul, she pointed at his shoulder. "Let's take a look."

As he eased his hand away, she placed hers over the towel.

Ignoring the strangeness of being so close to him, she focused on her duties. "Are you on any type of medication?" She spoke softly, trying to honor his right to privacy even though Jacob and Becky were just a few feet away.

"No."

"When is the last time you had a tetanus shot?"

"About two years ago."

"Good. You won't need to get another. Do you take baby aspirin or ibuprofen regularly?"

"Baby aspirin?" He laughed. "If you have something to say, Hannah, don't beat around the bush."

She suppressed a smile. "I take it the answer is no?"

"Yes . . . I mean, correct. The answer is no."

Closing her eyes, she shook her head quickly, as if he were driving her nuts. He laughed.

She slowly peeled the towel off his gash. "Your blood clots fast. For cuts like this, that's generally good, except I have to open the wound back up to clean it out, and it'll start bleeding again. I'm really sorry."

"You sure you're sorry?" he teased.

Willing herself to be painfully honest, she

310

realized humility didn't come easily for her. "Sometimes the words just don't cover it," she whispered, refusing to look him in the eye.

"It's behind us, Hannah. Forgiveness has happened. And now we move forward."

Feeling her mouth go dry and her heart palpitate, she looked up. In that brief moment a piece of her soul seemed to become his. Shifting her focus, she pulled prepackaged items out of her medical bag. "I've been horrid and mean. Is forgiving that effortless for you?" She laid the items in her lap.

Paul held out his arm to her. "Forgiving you is easy. You weren't culpable. Forgiving myself takes a good bit more faith, daily."

She pulled a pair of scissors out of her bag and slid the opened shears up the sleeve of his shirt and then around his bicep, removing the fabric completely. Desperate to turn the subject elsewhere, she thought of a topic. "I . . . I can't believe how much better Sarah is." Hannah reached into her bag and grabbed a bottle of cleanser. She poured the povidone-iodine solution into the bowl of water and stirred it with her finger.

"Hey," Jacob complained, "can't I get up now?"

"Yes, but stand slowly." She watched to see if he wavered any. He appeared steady. "Are you feeling the least bit sick to your stomach?"

"No, just hungry."

Hannah dried her wet finger on a piece of gauze. "Becky, why don't you see that he eats and drinks a small portion . . . slowly, of course. And just as a precaution, he should take it easy for twenty-four hours. I'll check the range of motion in his shoulder later, and then we'll discuss getting x-rays."

Becky squeezed Hannah's shoulder. "Thank you."

"Glad to do what I can." Hannah ripped open a package holding a sterilized bulb syringe, filled it with the disinfectant solution, and began cleaning Paul's gash.

He tilted his head, looking at the cleaned-out, slightly bleeding gash. "Can I ask how things went with Mary?"

Hannah filled the syringe again and squeezed its contents onto the gash. "Beautifully. If ever a bad decision turned out well, it's happened for Mary. I just wish Owl's Perch had a better situation for the medical issues that come up."

"The Plain community is in need around here. I agree."

"Every specific group requires targeted medical help they trust — moms of newborns and preschoolers, teens, elderly, athletes, cancer patients. The list is endless and includes the Amish, which is a subgroup all its own, in my opinion."

"And where your heart lands in spite of not wanting it to?"

She cleared her throat, uncomfortable with just how easily he saw some things. "Yes." She paused, trying to find some piece of emotional ground between betraying Martin and being near Paul. "This situation with Luke and Mary will be expensive, but fixing the actual issue is so simple. Time and time again issues that can take someone's life have a relatively simple answer, as long as the patient is informed and willing."

"That's probably why you were drawn to becoming a nurse."

She refused to look at him, but she couldn't stop the smile crossing her lips. "I used to drive you crazy wanting to study your science books each summer."

"It was fun for both of us. Do you still have that anatomy book Luke's doctor gave you?"

She glanced up from his shoulder. "I'm never without it." She pointed to her medical bag. "It's in there."

"The desire to be a nurse was always deep inside you, wasn't it?"

"It sure looks that way."

"Tell me about the expenses you mentioned."

After laying the syringe to the side of the bowl, she dipped a wad of gauze into the solution and cleaned the area surrounding the wound. "She'll have to check into the hospital before she goes into labor and have a C-section, but she's in no danger." She pulled a fresh piece of gauze out of its package and dried his skin. Showing him the container of butterfly bandages, she pulled out several. "These will probably do the trick, but stitches would do a better job of preventing scarring." After laying the strips in her lap, she opened the tube of antibiotic cream and applied it.

"A scar makes no difference to me." He stretched out his fingers several times. "Without insurance, the hospital and surgery will be really expensive for Luke to cover."

She nodded as she wiped the cream off her fingers. "Still, after what they could have been facing, it's a small price to pay. Mary gave her word she'd tell him everything before midnight tonight." Hannah removed the backing from one side of the Band-Aid.

"Is your hand asleep?"

"Barely." He flexed his hand, opening and closing it.

She squeezed together the skin at the top of the gash and placed one thin-stripped bandage over it. "If there's any redness or swelling, you need to be seen. If the tingling in your hand or arm continues for even a few hours, you need to be seen. If —"

Paul held up his hand. "I got it, Hannah."

A quick glimpse into his eyes revealed a straightforward openness that startled her. Undemanding. Honest. And steady as the ticking of time. In spite of years of convincing herself otherwise, those things did define him.

How she wished they didn't.

She looked away, gathering items into her medical bag. Being next to the man she'd once loved and intended to marry had every nerve in her body on edge. In his ways she saw why she'd carried feelings for him so long. The force of guilt over Martin ran through her, screaming warnings.

"You're cold," Paul said.

The evening air didn't match the warmth of the kitchen she'd been in most of the day. She shrugged, and while she removed the backing to another butterfly bandage, Paul went to where Jacob had been lying and grabbed a fleece throw blanket. He folded it in a triangle, like a shawl, and placed it over Hannah's shoulders, his warm hands resting there longer than necessary.

"Hannah," Lissa called from across the yard. Sarah was beside her, holding her hand, standing rigid and staring at the ground.

Paul took a seat.

Hannah swallowed, reeling her emotions back in. "Yes?" She ignored the bit of trembling in her fingers and placed another butterfly bandage next to the first one, squeezing the skin together as a stitch would.

"Can I comed over there?"

Hannah glanced up. Her sister stood firm, as if an invisible line lay in front of her and she didn't dare step over it without permission, but her eyes were on the palm of one hand as if she was confused by it. The young woman either still had a long way to go to find freedom, or she'd always have odd ways about her — or both. "Sure."

Sarah released Lissa's hand, and the little girl sprinted to Paul. "Did you cut yourself?"

"A little," Paul answered.

"On what?"

"A nail sticking out of a board."

"Maybe you need some cookies. I cut my

leg a few weeks ago." She sat on the ground and rolled up her pant leg. "See?"

Hannah continued putting on the bandages, eager to be done.

"Wow, that's quite a battle scar."

Sarah joined them, and Paul smiled a silent welcome.

Lissa beamed. "I broke my uncle's glass shelves, and he didn't even care. He said I was tougher than nails about the stitches too. On the way back from the hospital, he bought me some cookies 'cause Hannah weren't home to bake them. She was here. He tooked really good care of me."

A wrinkle creased Paul's brows as he looked up at Hannah, but whatever was on his mind, he didn't voice it.

Hannah smoothed Lissa's hair back from her face. "I think someone is missing her uncle about now."

Lissa nodded, the truth of Hannah's words reflected in her eyes. "We goin' home soon?"

"Tomorrow. First thing."

Lissa stood and pulled a broken, lint-covered cookie out of her pocket. "You need a cookie?"

Paul chuckled. "Thank you."

She dusted off her hands. "You're welcome. Can I play on the tire swing, Hannah?"

Spotting Mary near the same area, Hannah nodded. "Yes." She dumped the bowl of solution onto the grass and placed all the old gauze and wrappers in it.

Paul leaned back in his chair. "Martin is her uncle?"

"Yes, but he's raising . . . we're raising both her and Kevin."

Silently Paul stared at the disfigured cookie.

Sarah took the bowl, her eyes darting from Hannah to Paul. She looked addled. "I . . . I . . ." She ducked her head. "Never mind."

Paul rose and slid the cookie into his pocket. "She's leaving tomorrow, Sarah. If this is important to you, ask."

The tautness across Sarah's face made her appear unbalanced. "I . . . know . . . but it'd help me . . ." Sarah stopped talking midsentence and stared off into the distance.

"Sarah." Paul spoke firmly.

She slowly pulled her eyes from the distance and looked at him.

He focused on her as if willing her to hear him. "Find your thought and express it. Don't let fear steal your ability to live in the here and now."

Sarah's blank face slowly seemed to gain a more normal look, and she nodded. "If we could walk to where Rachel is buried . . ."

Hannah froze. She had a right to several things, all of which her sister was intruding upon. Privacy. An undisturbed burial place for Rachel. And her past left alone. Sarah hadn't even known Hannah was pregnant until after the baby had been buried. Why did she need to see the grave?

Hannah rubbed her forehead. "It's not marked at all. It'll look like any other ground under a beech tree in the field."

Sarah stared at one palm while rubbing invisible smudges off. "Paul wouldn't even try going without your permission, and he didn't think I should ask one of the few who know."

His loyalty was disconcerting. She pulled the blanket tighter around her shoulders. "Okay, I'll take you."

Sarah's eyes grew large. "I . . . I want Paul to go."

Of course she did. Pulling Paul into Hannah's life seemed to be Sarah's gift. Glad to be going back to Ohio first thing in the morning, Hannah gave a nod.

Wearing the small blanket draped like a shawl, Hannah walked in silence as Paul

319

and Sarah talked about putting the past to rest. Paul's words to Sarah wrapped around Hannah's heart, and she recalled the various conversations she'd had with Paul since her first trip back to Owl's Perch three weeks ago. In spite of her resolve to ignore his rock-steady and gentle ways, they fought for attention.

Dusk settled over the fields, and the birds had grown quiet. As they topped the ridge, golden-bronze leaves of the beech that hovered over Rachel's grave came into sight. Hannah swallowed, no longer hearing the words that passed between Paul and Sarah.

But she could hear Paul's voice, see him in yesteryear as clearly as she could turn and see him now.

He'd stood in front of her during one of their rare times together, turned her hand palm up, and kissed it. *"Conversations make a relationship strong. Unfortunately, they won't be a part of our relationship for a while. But we can clear away whatever weeds grow during this time if we hang tough and faithful"* — he'd winked — *"until May."* He'd squeezed her hand lovingly. *"Eight months, Hannah. No problem for us, right?"*

No problem.

Had they been given one small break in any area, it wouldn't have been a problem, not for them. Unwilling for Paul to catch a glimpse of what was happening inside her, she kept her gaze steady on the ground as the three of them continued walking. Her heart suddenly felt too large for her chest as an epiphany hit. Paul had believed in them.

In her.

And he'd waited.

No longer able to resist, she lifted her eyes — tattered shirt, injured arm, blond hair, broad shoulders, and none too weary for the day's work he'd just performed. His energetic steps defied the gentleness with which he spoke to Sarah.

How long had he waited?

It didn't matter. He had Dorcas. And Hannah loved Martin. When she thought of how rare it was to find a quality man, it seemed pretty incredible that she'd managed to find two. Maybe good men weren't as scarce as she'd thought.

Paul's eyes moved to hers and lingered. A hint of a smile crossed his lips. She knew that smile, the one that wasn't born so much from the joy of easy living as from the small pleasures life brought his way.

Edged with a fresh sense of betrayal of Martin, she turned her head without smiling. Scanning the fields, she remembered the whispers she'd heard the day Rachel was buried, calling Hannah's name and whispering, *"Kumm raus"* — to come out.

In the midst of heartbreak, the voice had beckoned and hopelessness gave way. The next day she set out to find a woman she wasn't sure existed. Even today she remained unsure if the vaguely familiar voice had been her inner self begging for freedom, or her imagination, or God's own whispers, or something else. But at the time, it'd kept her from being swallowed in brokenness and had helped her find the courage to leave.

Sarah grabbed her arm, shaking all over. "Look."

Less than fifteen feet ahead of them there appeared to be a grave marker, a headstone.

Sarah tightened her grip and dug her heels into the ground, stopping both of them. "I . . . I changed my mind. I want to go home."

Paul placed his hand on Sarah's shoulder. "We can't believe our emotions over sound reason. Your emotions are terrified. Reason says there is nothing to fear."

Sarah tugged on Hannah's arm. "Let's go home. I don't like it. Maybe some ghost from the past —"

Paul cupped Sarah's hand, making her ease up on her grip. "You're hurting your sister."

Sarah stopped squeezing but held on. "But who . . . who would have done such a thing?"

Hannah stared at the grave, goose flesh crawling over her whole body. The perimeter of the tiny grave was edged in white marble the size of bricks and the area surrounding the spot was meticulous, almost like a lawn.

"Someone who cares," Paul offered.

Hannah wrapped her blanket-shawl tighter and moved forward. Sarah balked, and Hannah freed herself of her sister's grip and took a step forward, a thousand memories and emotions ripping at her.

"I . . . I'm not ready. I can't!" Sarah's scream echoed over the field.

Ignoring her sister, Hannah went to the grave, stunned at what she saw. Thoughts of the many seasons — snowy winters, rainy springs, sweltering summers, and glorious falls — ran through her mind. Yet someone had been faithful. Behind her she could hear Paul talking in muted tones to Sarah.

The sense of loss seemed to be without end, but even so she could feel the trust she had in God to find a way to make up for it. That was part of who He was, wasn't it? Thieves came in and stole, and God redeemed. But standing here right now, she didn't feel redeemed, not when it came to certain things. She was redeemed by Him in a thousand ways — Martin, Lissa, Kevin, school, Dr. Lehman, the Tuesday quiltings, and her Amish friends. Still, the loss of a thousand hopes she'd had before the attack stood firm.

Paul eased up beside her, hands folded and reverent. He stared at the ground. "I'm sorry you dealt with this alone."

If the idea that someone had been taking care of the grave wasn't enough, his reaction made her heart stir. She'd thought all these years that he was . . . incapable of understanding. Yet as surely as she knew he'd once loved her as she had him, she understood the violence she'd experienced hadn't happened just to her. It had happened to them.

Seems like I should have recognized this long before now.

With her heart beating wildly and her eyes misting, she held her hand out for his. "Nevertheless," she whispered.

He placed his warm, rough hand inside hers, and there in the quiet fields ablaze in fall colors, an unexpected healing soothed her heart. The quiet between them left only the sounds of leaves rustling.

She knelt, releasing Paul's hand. It seemed this odd journey back to Owl's Perch had made her more ready to let go of the past than she'd ever been. She wasn't running from it anymore. She had it in her to rise and move on. And the difference brought a sense of well-being she'd never known existed for anyone, and certainly not for someone who'd been assaulted.

Sarah approached the grave and knelt. "All this time I wanted the baby to be alive . . ."

Hannah put her arm around her sister's shoulders. "Choose reality, Sarah. It's the only place where strength and faith can begin to work."

Sarah placed the palm of her hand over the grave.

Hannah squeezed her sister's shoulder. "It's time to let go and live."

"You ever gonna do anything to hunt that guy down?" Sarah's voice trembled.

Hannah closed her eyes, asking herself the same question. Cool air whipped through the trees, making the leaves sound like rain as they swirled across the ground. "No," she whispered. "What was done happened over three years ago. I can't identify him. I have no idea what type of car, nothing. The only way the police could start to track him down would be to take Rachel from her resting place so DNA testing could be done, but that would only help if he's already been caught for another crime. I won't do that to Rachel . . . or to me." She rubbed her sister's back. "Right or wrong, I choose to let go and move on. It's the way we were taught, ya?"

Sarah nodded. "Ya."

Hannah removed her arm. When she and Sarah began to shift in order to stand, Paul held one hand out for each of them. Sarah took his hand, and he helped her get to her feet. Hannah stood up on her own.

"I bet Daed's been doing this, keeping the grave tended to."

"Sarah . . ."

"No," she interrupted, "you don't know what he's like when nobody's looking. He wrote in a diary about watching for you to return. Pages of stuff, but when I found his secret stash, he burned everything, as if he could think it and feel it but he couldn't stand anyone knowing."

Unwilling to argue, Hannah began walking. The trip back toward the Esh home was done in silence. An odd sense of peace surrounded her more than the darkness of the night. She pulled the blanket tighter around her shoulders. Sarah seemed to have found some resolution about life too.

But somebody had put time and money

into edging the perimeter of the tiny grave in white marble.

Someone cared. It couldn't be Daed, could it?

CHAPTER 25

The sounds of hoofbeats made all three of them look up.

Jacob stopped the cart beside them, looking directly at Hannah. "Mamm said I needed to see you first and then give you and Sarah a ride back to Luke and Mary's. Mammi Annie said to tell you that Lissa wanted to go on home with her."

Hannah removed the blanket and passed it to Paul. "I'm not heading back right now, but hop down, and let's check out that shoulder." She had Jacob do several slow range-of-motion moves. "On a scale of one to ten, with ten being the worst, how does it feel?"

"About a three, maybe less."

"I think you're fine without an x-ray for now, but if the pain increases or your range of motion decreases, go in to be checked out. And all those things I just had you do with your arm, do them four times a day, slowly. Okay?"

"Sure. Thanks, Hannah. I guess being a nurse comes in handy, especially out here in the sticks, huh?"

Unsure if he'd understand that she wasn't even a registered LPN yet, she opted not to try to explain it. "It did today."

Sarah gave Hannah a hug. "I'm really tired." She said nothing to Jacob, her old beau, as she climbed into the work cart. "You'll wake me in the morning before you pull out?"

Hannah nodded. "Sure. Good night, Sarah."

In the Esh yard, Matthew's parents, along with a few other men and women, stood chatting in small groups. Kathryn was next to a driver's car, saying good-bye to several men from her community, including a man Hannah recognized as Kathryn's Daed. And the way one of the young men hovered near her, he was either Kathryn's boyfriend or wanted to be.

Closer to the house, Hannah's father glanced up from the men he was chatting with but then acted like he didn't see her. She and Paul walked toward the side yard, where a kerosene heater shed light on a circle of chairs. The tables looked barren and well-worn without the fabric or food covering them. Mary, Luke, and Matthew sat around the heater, talking. Three empty chairs sat in the circle, probably an invitation for her and Paul. If Hannah had her intuition going right, the other chair was for Kathryn.

Of all the day-to-day events that'd taken place while she'd been gone, Matthew and Elle's breakup was probably the most surprising. But Matthew seemed at peace with it, maybe even relieved about it.

More than ready for a few quiet moments alone, Hannah turned to Paul. "I'm going inside. I'm sure there's more I can help with in the kitchen."

"Thank you for doing that for Sarah."

The distant whispers of just how in step she and Paul could be circled inside her. She didn't respond to him, as guilt concerning Martin nibbled at her.

The house appeared empty as she entered it. Void of earlier voices, the kitchen felt secure in ways it couldn't before. The lowing of cows waiting to be fed drifted through the slightly open window and across the room. A kerosene lamp on the windowsill above the sink added a glow not much brighter than two electric night-lights. She moved to the faucet and turned it on, letting the water get warm before she filled the sink and squirted dishwashing liquid into it. As she continued washing the pans, women occasionally came in and gathered their clean dishes. Most of them spoke a reserved farewell on their way out, and she returned it. If they didn't speak, she respected their silence and held her tongue.

The lantern sputtered as it began to run out of fuel. Through the window, she saw several families climb into their buggies and head out, leaving only one more buggy waiting for its owner — her Daed's. But her mother was sitting inside it.

"Hannah."

Her muscles tightened at the sound of her father's voice. Turning her head to face him, she held her sudsy hands over the edge of the sink. "Yes?"

Shadows angled this way and that as the flames of the lamp wavered. Her father stood there, looking as if he had something to say but couldn't. She grabbed a towel off the peg beside the sink and dried her hands.

He eased into the room, crunching the brim of his hat in his hands. "You're leaving tomorrow?"

"Yes." She stepped away from the sink.

"You . . . you'll write to your mother more this time, ya?"

How could so much lie between two

people that they couldn't manage to say anything worthwhile? "Yes."

"Good." He started to leave, but with his head ducked and his shoulders stooped, he didn't appear to have said what he came to say.

"Daed?"

He turned, staring at her as if he still wasn't sure who she was.

"I was innocent."

He wiped his forehead with the back of his thumb. "None of us are ever innocent. I thought you'd understand that much by now."

She fought to keep her shoulders back and chin up. His words were both true and a lie. But he'd never see his part, only hers. Is that what he came in to tell her, that regardless of all he'd accused her of that she hadn't done, she still bore the mark of a sinner?

And with his words spoken, her father turned to leave the house.

"Daed?"

He faced her again.

"The grave site . . . it . . . it's been taken care of . . ."

He clenched his jaw. "I'm not as disloyal as you seem to think."

"We're all disloyal. I thought you'd understand that by now."

He stood firm, staring at her. "You win, Hannah. I haven't been able to stay a step ahead of you since you turned fifteen. I haven't done anything right. But as God is my witness, I tried."

"I wasn't up-front about Paul, and maybe I was wrong about that, but you knew the truth of what'd happened the night of the attack, yet somehow later on you completely justified abandoning me. No, worse, you turned on me and brought the church leaders with you."

He opened his mouth to speak, but then, without another word, he walked out, pulling the door closed behind him.

The door eased open again, and Paul stepped inside. "You okay?"

Her eyes filled with tears. "Always." She cleared her throat, gaining control of her emotions.

"Everyone's gone but Luke, Mary, Matthew, Kathryn, and us. Matthew's parents walked to the Yoder place to look at some lumber John has stored that could be used for rebuilding. I guess Mary will talk to Luke soon, and we'll call it a night." He walked to the table and grabbed a slice of homemade bread from the cutting board. "Since you're leaving tomorrow and we may never meet up again under relaxed and friendly circumstances, I was hoping you'd join us outside." He breathed in the aroma from the slice of bread and gazed up at her. He'd always said he could tell whether homemade bread was made by her hands or not, because he could smell the heat, like the fires from her soul.

Turning her back to him, she reached for a clean pan and then began drying it. They'd walked to the grave and shared something she could never share with another human; he understood things about her no one else ever would. And he forgave her in ways she hadn't known she needed until it was given to her, freely. But now she needed distance.

"I think it would do Sarah a lot of good if you could return and help her find a passion of some sort. She's too old not to have a job that brings her a sense of self-esteem and satisfaction — something she can look at and feel good about."

Hannah faced him. "Like I told Sarah, I can't."

He sat on the edge of the table and propped one foot on a chair. "Yeah, I know, you're too busy until after the first of the year. But maybe after the snows are gone? I think it's important. It'd be better if it could be done before winter sets in, but if you can't, you can't."

"What exactly did you have in mind?"

"I wish I had a clue, but I'm confident you can think of something."

She leaned against the sink. "Sarah should have met Zabeth and lived in that cabin with her."

"Ah, she smiles at the thought of it." Paul's lopsided grin made her remember a hundred others. "What was she like?"

A male voice startled her. Thinking the voice came from the front of the house, she went to the dark foyer and peered out the open front door. Paul followed her.

Luke stood at the foot of the steps. "What were you thinking?"

Mary smoothed her hands over her protruding tummy, her eyes locked on the ground. "I was afraid you'd leave if we couldn't marry right away. Your father left his roots, and Hannah too, and you were angry with your Daed and the church leaders for how they treated your sister, and antsy and talking about going into Lancaster to work and —"

"Those are your excuses for lying to me?" Luke interrupted her. "Telling me the doctor gave you a clean bill of health? You told me —"

She held up her hand, stopping him from saying more. "I know, but I lied to myself. I thought I was trusting God when I was using that as an excuse to get what I wanted. I . . . I didn't want to lose you."

Hannah eased the door shut, stopping it just short of clicking. From inside the house, she could still hear their voices, but she tried not to listen. "Those words are a red flag, too often spoken right before lies and cover-ups."

"Look at me, Hannah."

"What?"

"If you're talking about yourself, it's time to let it go," Paul whispered. "Just let it go."

The weight of everything seemed to close in — the dark, the empty house, the closeness, the whispers between them. Unable to find her voice and void of knowing what to say if she could, she just stood there, staring at him. Did he feel it too?

He motioned toward the kitchen. "I . . . I think I'll go out the side door and meet up with Matthew."

He turned, leaving her alone.

Guilt hounding her, Hannah moved back to the kitchen, now completely dark since the lamp was out of fuel, and sat in a ladder-back chair. She couldn't return to the Yoders just yet. She'd told Mary she'd stay close to answer questions Luke might have. Otherwise she'd have returned to Ohio earlier. She hoped he'd have questions and not just anger.

Hannah rested her forehead against her fingertips. That's where she should be, in Ohio with Martin, not here building bridges with Paul.

Matthew came in the side door and motioned for her. "Luke's asking for ya."

She willed the confusion to slide into its hidden place, assured it'd find its way free to be wrestled with later. "Okay." She rose and silently walked out the back door, thoughts of both Martin and Paul lingering.

Kathryn, Paul, Luke, and Mary were sitting around the kerosene heater, stark silence reigning. No one else remained on Esh property. Hannah took a seat in one of the empty chairs, and Matthew followed suit.

"So this is why you stayed?" Luke's sharp tone interrupted her thoughts.

She sat up, clearing her throat. "Yes."

Her brother's face was rigid, jaw set as he stared at the ground. The concern in Mary's eyes was deep, fear of losing his love and respect, of bearing his anger in various measures and ways for years to come.

Kathryn stood. "I . . . I thought we were

going to talk business. I think I'll call it a day. Good night." She walked toward the house, and Matthew jumped to his feet and went with her.

Hannah leaned in, catching Luke's eyes. "You have a right to be angry, but please don't hold on to this."

"Mary should have trusted me to make the right decision based on truth and trusted God with her future." Luke slumped, brooding.

Hannah warmed her hands near the red-faced heater, unable to sit still and unwilling to look at Paul.

Luke gestured in the air, exasperation evident. "So now what?"

Without her permission, Hannah's eyes moved to Paul and stayed. His blue eyes focused on hers as if Luke's question hung between them rather than between Mary and him.

Shifting, Hannah turned her attention to Luke. "Dr. Lehman will find a good obstetrician willing to take her in spite of her impending due date and lack of insurance."

"Explain to me everything, starting with why her doctor didn't want her to get married."

Hannah explained all of it, careful to interject assurances as often as possible.

Luke studied his wife, seemingly torn between anger and complete terror for her safety. "How can he be so sure this plan will work?"

"Because Dr. Lehman is incredibly intelligent and spent hours tracking down every test and every doctor's report concerning Mary's health after the accident."

Luke narrowed his eyes at Mary. He gestured toward Hannah. "Swear to me you two are hiding nothing else."

Hannah held out her hands, palms up. "Nothing. I promise."

"And she and the baby are completely safe?"

She lowered her hands. "As safe as any healthy woman giving birth using modern technology and a skilled surgeon."

Luke slid back in his chair, anger radiating off of him. "I can't just let this go. We should have waited to marry."

Mary broke into tears. "You can't regret marrying me. You just can't. It will taint . . ." She stood and hurried across the yard toward the back fields where her parents' property met Esh land. And Luke let her go.

Paul shifted in his chair. "Luke."

He looked at Paul, and the two men seemed to hold a silent conversation. Her brother finally nodded, stood, and took off after his wife. "Mary, wait."

Hannah fidgeted with a button on her skirt. "Your silence seems more powerful than most people's words. I'd like to know that trick."

"No trick. We just share enough history from my own mistakes."

Hannah looked up. "And you couldn't have said *nothing* earlier and spared Mary some of this?"

"Luke wasn't ready to hear it earlier."

"Hear what? You didn't say anything."

"Hannah?"

"Yes?"

"You're giving me a headache."

They shared a laugh before Hannah leaned back on the chair, noticing for the first time how clear the evening sky was. Thousands of stars sparkled as if the Susquehanna's surface that gleamed under the sun's rays had been broken up and spewed into the sky. The harvest moon, in all its golden orange glory, was a clear sign that fall was far more than just a chill in the air. In spite of the heater, she shivered.

Paul tossed her one of the blankets from earlier. "This would be our first real time to be together after dusk."

Without sitting up or taking her eyes off

the sky, she spread the blanket over her. "Maybe it's not so amazing that we didn't make it . . . as it is that we forged a relationship around all the constraints."

Paul didn't respond, and she wasn't about to look at him. They'd shared something special earlier today, and clearly they'd been ripped apart years ago against both their wishes, but she loved Martin. She could list his qualities endlessly and felt privileged that he wanted to share his life with her — an ex–Old Order Amish girl who didn't dress or act anything like the hundreds of women he'd dated before her.

Hundreds? Had there been that many? Well, he was eight years older than she was and considered dating a sport he was good at, even up to a year and a half after meeting her.

She shuddered, suddenly wishing she hadn't thought about this. Martin wasn't an outdoor guy for the most part, but when the weather was nice and time permitted, he'd leave his television, computer, game systems, and phones and sit with her. "Some of my favorite times are when Martin and I sit together outside and talk."

Paul reached across the chair that separated them and tugged at her blanket. "I'm guessing that's mostly a summertime event."

She waved her hand at him, shooing his teasing away. Besides, she really shouldn't be here talking with him, and it'd suit her overloaded guilt wagon just as well if they waited out the rest of this Mary and Luke saga in complete silence.

To their left, a hundred feet away, stood Luke and Mary. She had Luke's hand pressed against her stomach. Hannah cleared her throat, trying to dismiss the lump. Love wasn't all that touched their lives on this planet, but it made everything else endurable.

The movement under Luke's hand made his heart thud like a wild man inside his chest trying to get out. His child was inside her, responding to his voice. He held his tongue, and the infant stayed still. He spoke, and the baby shifted. Feeling like a true head of the household, a man with the responsibility to take great care with his words and even his tone, he looked at Mary. "You were wrong," he said softly.

She nodded, fresh tears splashing down her cheeks. "I know, but if you regret marrying me, you'll taint what we've shared . . . our marriage bed. Remember our first night?"

Luke nodded, recalling many treasured nights.

His eyes stung with tears. He'd trusted her completely. Always had. And now he felt shaken and used. "All those months of crying when you didn't conceive, you should have been rejoicing. I . . . I don't understand."

"I took my vows before the church, knowing I was hiding the truth from you. I feared God might not ever let me conceive, especially if I didn't tell you the truth. But more than that, I feared you'd never love me the same if you knew the real me."

Luke studied his wife. She wasn't who he'd thought, no doubt. She had flaws and weaknesses he'd not known about until tonight. Now he knew her failing — she feared losing him more than she feared answering to God for a lie. If he wanted power over his wife, something he could use at will for the rest of his life, it'd been given to him tonight.

Mary caressed his cheeks. "I've repented a million times, but it doesn't undo what I've done."

He'd had his own repenting to do since they'd known each other. The reality of their weaknesses ran a long list through his mind. When the doctor had told her to wait about getting married, she was devastated, afraid he'd find someone else. But there was no one else to find, not for him. And the truth was, he would have waited for her, but he'd jumped at the chance to marry her at the very next wedding season. He didn't ask to speak to the doctor; he just married her as quickly as he could.

The list had silly things on it too: the time he'd left the gas-powered refrigerator open all night, the times she made them late for church because she couldn't find her hairpins, and the times he ignored her when she called him to supper, because he wanted to read the newspaper. He guessed this was what being married meant: having someone who knew both the best and worst about you.

With her hands still on his face, he gently took hold of her wrists. "I guess I can only hope you feel as strongly about marrying me today as you did two years ago."

Mary smiled. "You know I do, Luke." She shifted, moving his hand to her stomach again. "We both do. But I shouldn't have loved you or myself more than God, and when I covered truth to get my way, I did just that."

Luke wrapped his arms around her, hoping his wife was as safe as Hannah thought.

CHAPTER 26

Matthew filled the kerosene lamp with fuel and set it on the kitchen table. He struck a match and lit it. Kathryn pulled a calculator from the desk drawer, along with the cost of building supplies. He studied her face. Did she believe their relationship was only business?

She folded her arms in a relaxed manner and stared at the papers. "Do you really think you can start making money on orders before the shop is completed?" Her soft voice soothed his nervousness.

He adjusted his hat. "Completely sure. The storage at Luke's has most of what we need already. After getting a few more supplies, all we need is a place to work that has a roof."

"E and L can't work out of Luke's shop?"

"We could, but it's a distance to get back and forth. That'd cut way down on my time to work on rebuilding for the most part of the day and filling orders during only a few hours."

"I see what you mean."

"You're the only one who understands the orders since the fire. Ya did the work, made hours of calls to make sense of them, even reorganized the storage shop while I was gone. You can line everythin' up — the customer orders, the supplies, the restocking of parts we don't have in the storage at Luke's old shop — while me and Luke use that time to construct the new buildings. If you're willin' to stay and keep everything lined up, we can stop construction for a few hours each day and begin pecking away at filling orders. If we don't have you doin' that part of the job for us, we can't fill any orders until the buildings are completed."

Kathryn folded her arms and leaned back in the chair. "I set up this workday to help you get ahead, and now you come up with this plan?"

"Today was great, Kathryn." And it was, even if Joseph did show up and cause Matthew to turn green a few times. "We got a lot done. My whole family needed this — the distraction, the fellowship, the hope. But . . . what was your goal?"

"I wanted to make the tearing-down process easier and quicker. Are you disappointed in my plan?"

"No, no, not at all." Matthew rubbed the back of his neck. "Well, a little."

"What's going on?" Her voice was as peaceful as when she was bidding him good morning or good night. This type of calm, reasonable reaction was one of the many things that drew him to her.

He took a seat beside her. "Tonight, as ya told your Joseph good-bye, it dawned on me what all our hard work today meant. That you'd go home for several weeks, maybe all winter, while we got the sides and roof up. I . . . I don't want that to happen." He brushed the back of her hand with the tip of his index finger. "Surely you know that."

"Matthew, you're barely broken up with Elle. You can't possibly think you're remotely interested in me."

"That's not an exact account. I'd sent her a letter endin' things before you ever came to work for me. Your first day here she showed up to object to me breaking up with her. Then a month later, the day of the fire, she returned again, asking me to reconsider. After the devastation of losing David, I thought I felt a spark of interest."

"So you run off to Baltimore with anyone you think you have a spark of interest for?"

"I went because I was willing to consider and reconsider anything that might help me find my way. What I learned while there is" — Matthew moved in closer and took Kathryn's hand — "it's your friendship, your ways that speak to me."

"Well, okay, friends, yes, but I . . . I'm seeing Joseph."

"If he means all that much to ya, then tell me so. All I'm askin' is for some time for me to court you."

She wound one string of her prayer Kapp around her index finger. "That's not all you're asking. Us seeing each other is a gamble, one that, if we lose, will end this friendship, and please don't try to tell me it won't."

"And you'll take that gamble with Joseph but not with me?"

"That's different."

"Different how?"

"For one thing it isn't a working relationship with him. You and I work well together. I don't want to mess that up."

"And . . ."

She pursed her lips, looking really aggravated. "That's plenty for you to know."

Maybe he wasn't being fair to her. The grief over David was still thick, and maybe he was mistaken to think Kathryn cared more for him than for Joseph, but he'd seen her around Joseph today. She was a little cool and distant, wasn't she?

Matthew played with the corners of the papers spread out in front of them. "If ya really care for Joseph, that's one thing. But you don't owe stickin' with him because your Daed wants you to live close to home and Joseph is available."

"Matthew Esh, you're out of line." She pushed the papers and calculator away from her. "And what about the bishop? He's overlooked a lot where you've been concerned, but going off with someone who's not even a church member . . ."

Matthew sighed. It sounded so much worse when she put it that way. "I've made my share of mistakes, and I'll deal with them with the bishop."

Kathryn played with the strings of her prayer Kapp again, something she did when thinking and deciding. "I . . . I don't know what to think, Matthew. Fact is, I'm not likely to sort through it until I go home."

"Will you at least come spend some time with everyone tonight?"

"Luke and Mary are arguing. I'd rather not."

"Whatever they're arguin' about, they'll get over it soon. I'm sure of it." He stood.

"Okay?"

She rose and put the papers and calculator away. "Okay."

Hannah remained in her seat, watching as Luke and Mary entered the tiny circle of chairs. They walked side by side, glowing.

Wondering if she and Martin ever glowed, Hannah pulled the blanket off her body. "Does this mean I can get some sleep now? And return to Ohio tomorrow?"

Before she finished her sentence, Matthew and Kathryn came out the side door. Luke gestured for Paul to move over one chair. Paul then took the empty spot next to Hannah.

Luke took a seat. "Ohio." He looked about the group. "Does anyone else here think it's odd that she never calls it home?"

Matthew propped his foot on the rough-sawed coffee table. "I noticed that. Paul?"

Paul shrugged. "I'd rather talk about the price of tea in China."

"Knock it off, Luke. You too, Matthew. Zabeth's cabin has been home since I first saw it, but I had to move out of there, and . . . and Martin's place isn't quite comfortable yet."

Luke's brows knit. "You're living with him?"

"No, of course not. I didn't mean it to sound like that. I live in the cottage behind his home. It makes taking care of Lissa and Kevin easier."

Luke studied her. "Yeah, for him."

Her ire grew, and she leaned forward. "I know how this must look, and I appreciate that you're concerned for me, but Martin and I have needed and helped each other from the first day we met. When Lissa and Kevin's mother abandoned them on my doorstep, Martin and I formed an even tighter team. If anyone has a problem with that, they need to keep it to themselves."

Matthew pulled a well-used deck of Dutch Blitz cards out of his pant pocket.

He ruffled the cards while looking at Hannah. "Ya go to church?"

"Yes, when I'm not on call and helping deliver babies."

Luke shifted. "Martin goes too?"

Hannah reminded herself that they were asking because they cared, but she wasn't used to people prying. In her world no one asked. "He's more faithful about it than I am."

Matthew continued shuffling the cards. "That's because he can tolerate it better. I attended one of those Englischer churches. Give me a hard, backless pew and a three-hour service in someone's living room or a barn any day over the loud music, squealing microphones, and messages on the walls."

A light chortle went through the group.

Kathryn rose and tugged on Matthew's collar. "Before you deal, let's fix some hot chocolate and popcorn for everyone."

Matthew shoved the cards into his pocket. "We'll be back."

Hannah placed her folded forearms on her legs, leaning closer to the heater. "A few unexpected things happened today, so Paul and I made some good progress with Sarah."

"I can't tell you how glad I am to hear it." Luke folded his hands. "She became such a mess after you left, but if we could have gotten her some help then . . ."

Hannah shivered. "I knew she was dishing out grief to me — spreading rumors and lies about me everywhere — but I never recognized her behavior as a red flag that she needed help. You probably can't imagine how muddled that time was for me. Some parts of it were too vivid, and other parts were so vague it's like I wasn't even there for the events."

Paul turned up the heater. "Yeah, I guess that's a pretty accurate description, isn't it?"

Luke grabbed a blanket off a nearby chair and passed it to Mary. "I know it took Paul days, maybe weeks, to decide whether to hire a private investigator to help find you."

Hannah turned to Paul, not at all sure she could calmly handle hearing about this.

"I wavered in what to do, and I'll never know if I was right or not, but it seemed inherently wrong to track you down when you had good reasons for leaving and equal reasons for not wanting to return. And you knew how to reach me . . . if you'd wanted to."

Without any lingering doubts, she knew Paul had never received the messages when she'd called. She had to let Paul know about that, didn't she?

She finally understood all, or nearly all, of what had taken place. "You weren't wrong to let me decide for myself. Besides, finding me would have been impossible. With or without a name change, I almost couldn't find myself."

Paul laid his hand over hers. "I'm proud of you, always have been."

Her eyes misted. "I needed that freedom so I could make totally new stupid mistakes all over again."

Paul laughed softly with her. "You and me both."

Hannah was confident that throughout the years to come they'd remain friends rather than merely tolerate the presence of each other. With him so firmly rooted in Sarah's life, respecting each other was a real perk. Still, shouldn't she tell him the truth about his not receiving her calls? What if it was Dorcas who hadn't passed him the messages? Didn't he need to know that? Or had she handled things in the only way she knew to protect Paul?

Knowing she needed time to think this through, Hannah leaned back. "I'm curious, Paul. My shortcomings are easily seen by those around me, but yours?"

He laughed softly. "Are you asking me to spill all my weaknesses?"

"Come on, no one gets off scot-free."

His grin faded. "You've had to survive a few of them, you know."

Hannah tried to piece things together in her mind. "I'm drawing a blank here."

He slumped in mock resignation. "And you just have to talk about this now?"

She nodded. "Yep."

"Women," he muttered, a half smile making him look mischievous. "I have . . . hopefully it's I *had* a strong tendency to jump to conclusions and then act on them as if they were facts — like when I left without hearing you out or when I assumed you were married because your last name was different."

Luke scoffed. "Well, horse neck, Waddell, weren't you justified?"

"To follow the clues and be mistaken in my conclusions, yes. To act on my assumption without asking questions, digging deeper, and listening, no."

Hannah kept her focus on the gas heater, but she wanted to offer some encouragement to Paul. "Zabeth once said when you figure out where you're messing up and you hate that behavior bad enough, that's where all the good parts of you begin."

"Guys," Kathryn called from the door of the house, "can I have a head count of who does and does not like whipped cream in their cocoa?"

Mary stood. "I should probably just give her a hand."

Luke rose and caught her by the hand. "I'll go with you, just to make sure you don't lift anything too heavy."

"Whipped cream?" Mary paused midstep. Paul and Hannah nodded.

She snuggled under the blanket. "So, what do you do for fun?"

"Ah, a much easier question to deal with." Paul stretched out his legs in front of him.

"I hang out with some of my college buddies. We hike, fish, camp out, play some tag football, shoot some pool. You?"

"I work, go to school, and study. Around those things I try to find time for Martin, Lissa, and Kevin."

"It sounds like you're doing your college years a lot like I did mine — all work, no play. I don't recommend it."

"Martin does the event planning for us — band gatherings and stuff — but if he didn't, I wouldn't miss it."

"Don't you have something you do that's just fun, something you'd really miss if you didn't do it?"

"Sure, Kevin and Lissa."

He chuckled. "I meant something indulgent. For me it's ball games, major or minor league. Baseball is my favorite, but football ranks up there too."

"But that's . . ." She dropped the sentence, not wanting to make him defend himself.

"Not allowed in the Plain life? Uh, if it was, I probably never would have struggled with whether to remain Plain or not."

"But how do you keep up with it — radio, television, newspaper?"

"Yes."

She laughed. "Paul Waddell, you're not allowed television and radios."

"If during a game I just happen to go to a restaurant that has those televisions hanging from the ceiling, or if there's a game on the radio while I'm riding in my car . . ."

"Isn't that cheating?"

He shrugged. "Sure, but overall I believe in the Plain ways. I can't see giving up the Plain Mennonite faith just because I enjoy an occasional spectator sport."

"I guess having an area like that might help build a rapport with clients who aren't Plain."

"You know, that's a really good excuse." His smile spoke of jest, and she knew his quiet, respectful, noncooperation ways were showing again. He interlaced his fingers, staring at his hands. "I would have told you about this secret love, but I didn't want to scare you away by telling you too soon."

"Uh-huh. And does Dorcas know about this vice?"

"She thinks I've given it up."

"I see. Afraid you'll scare her off too?"

"Nah, she —"

"Women's work." Luke rounded the side of the house, carrying a tray of mugs with steam rising from them. "How do I always get roped into doing women's work?"

Matthew followed, carrying a huge bowl of popcorn, while Kathryn toted the napkins and paper plates. Mary was last, carrying spoons.

The most genuine smile Hannah had seen yet revealed itself in Paul's eyes and slowly edged his lips. Freedom to embrace life anew had taken place for him too. Closure between them mattered to him, and she knew it always would. She lifted a mug of hot chocolate from the tray.

She'd stay as long tonight as her brother wanted her to. They'd all play cards, and she'd probably end up laughing until her sides hurt, but she longed to return to her life in Ohio: the birthing clinic, nursing school and clinical rotations, and the two children who needed the home life she craved to give them.

And Martin. Her heart skipped a beat, and she could see him in her mind's eye and feel inside her the warmth of who they were. Always. Always. Martin.

CHAPTER 27

Mist rose from the valley where the creek ran, and the new day's sunlight skimmed the tops of the trees. Pulling her sweater around her a little tighter, Hannah leaned against her car, sipping a cup of coffee and waiting for Sarah to grab something from inside the house.

The trees swayed in the morning air, bearing leaves from light yellows to deep golds, from bright reds to sharp maroons. The movement seemed to beg Hannah to linger and watch. She loved Owl's Perch, always had. And now, with healing running through most of the relationships she'd once left behind, the beauty of the place strengthened her. Zabeth would be so pleased for her, and that brought even more comfort.

In jeans and a sweater, Lissa played in the soft dirt near the edge of the garden. She seemed to love the feel and aroma of tilled soil as much as Hannah.

Sarah tapped on an upstairs window, signaling that she'd be down in a minute. She barely looked like the young adult who less than a month ago had poured gasoline around her and threatened to strike a match. She'd needed medication to help, but it seemed to Hannah that, more than meds, she'd needed to find forgiveness and have a sense of power over her life.

Without any doubt, Paul had done a great job of helping her find much of what she needed. His ability to help Sarah seemed more connected to who he was than to his degree. Hannah knew little of psychologists as a whole, but this one used his education as a tool for offering insights and wisdom for living.

Sarah still easily lapsed into talking like a baby and continued with some very odd behaviors, but she was making good progress.

She bounded out the back door, carrying a package wrapped in brown paper with an arrangement of fall leaves on the top for a bow. "Here." She held the gift toward Hannah.

Tears welling in her eyes, Hannah accepted it. They'd come such a long way, and like a garden in spring, Sarah's heart was being cultivated, making all they'd been through worthwhile. She removed the wrapping to find the "Past and Future" quilt. "Sarah, this was on loan to you. It can't be given to me."

Sarah pouted. "He gave it to me." It was a few seconds before she seemed to regain her thoughts. "Besides, I asked Mary. So listen up and hush up." She cleared her throat. "You saw to it that the quilt was made from patches of cloth from family and friends as well as every Amish household in our community. We are a part of your past, and we'll always be a part of your future. I want you to have it so you'll always remember who you are."

In spite of the childlike voice her sister spoke with, it seemed to Hannah that she saw deeply. There were many days Hannah wasn't at all sure who she was. Memories of her Amish childhood swirled like falling leaves. She slid her hand across the quilt. "Thank you. I'll cherish it always." She drew a sharp breath, trying not to cry.

"Mary gave this to Paul to keep him warm while he waited for you to return." She picked imaginary lint off the quilt.

Wishing Sarah hadn't reminded her about Paul waiting, Hannah simply nodded. It was frustrating and embarrassing that part of her wanted to know how long he'd waited.

"I'm grateful you're better, and it means a lot to know you're doing well enough to want to give this to me."

Sarah gazed at the sky, growing distracted. "Before we started having trouble getting along, we used to lie in bed each night and talk. Remember?"

"Yes."

"You used to say the hardest thing in life was that no one understood you or helped you find yourself."

Hannah cupped her sister's cold cheek against her palm, causing Sarah to look at her. "Those were childish thoughts. Life is about doing what's right and moving on." But even as she said the words, she knew lives were shaped by kindred spirits and support . . . or the lack of them. How different would her life be if her father had understood her rather than tried to dictate who she was to become?

Sarah leaned her cheek into Hannah's hand, looking more like a child than an eighteen-year-old. "Paul sees you, Hannah."

The words hit so hard, Hannah fought against tears. It was true. She knew it was, but it didn't matter. Couldn't matter. Surely even Sarah could understand that. Hannah tried to keep that truth from sinking in, but it burned through her, and her heart marched against her chest as if it wanted to get free and run to Paul on its own.

Martin tried to see her. The fact that he didn't sometimes was not his fault. He tried, and that should be enough. No, it had to be enough. What was wrong with her? Was she so weak that her heart wanted the freedom to long for one man when she was committed to another?

She stood straighter. "I have a new family now, dear sister." She pulled Sarah into a hug and held her. "Thank you for the quilt." Hannah kept her in her arms, savoring their newfound victories. Finally she took a step back. "I need to go."

After a few last hugs with Luke and Mary, Hannah and Lissa climbed into the car and headed for Ohio. Fastened into her car seat, Lissa used her CD player and earphones, snacked a little, and slept soundly throughout the trip, leaving Hannah to ponder fairly uninterrupted. Her mind took more twists and turns than the back roads. Soon enough they were on the turnpike, putting mile after mile between them and Owl's Perch.

She rapped her palms against the steering wheel. It'd happened. She'd faced the worst of herself — the horrid, ugly truth — and found peace. Even faced things that couldn't be covered in explanations of events or expressed in a multitude of words, yet Paul seemed to understand every nuance. But that bothered her for reasons she refused to think about.

Martin's two-story stone home came into view, making the drive here feel about two minutes long even though she'd been in the car for hours and it was now past lunchtime.

"Lissa, honey, it's time to wake up."

She began stirring. Hannah reached across to the passenger's seat and stroked the fabric of the "Past and Future" quilt, ready to begin life again, only this time with a serene connectedness to the missing parts of herself. Regrets, yes. They were inevitable, but there wasn't one part of her that was running or hiding or afraid to look in the mirror concerning her past.

She studied the stately house. The immense windows, arched entryway, stacked-stone siding, and meticulous lawns were astoundingly different from the life she'd left behind hours ago.

If it hadn't been for Martin's willingness to barter with her, she wouldn't own a car. But he had done more than help her carry the load of her new life. He became her friend. After parking and cutting off the engine, she got out and opened the door beside Lissa.

She raised her arms, waiting to be unbuckled. "What're you smiling about?"

Hannah lifted the slight kindergartener from the seat, giving her a kiss on the cheek, and settled Lissa on her hip. She then headed for the back door. "I was thinking about your uncle Martin. I have so many things I want to tell him, things he'll want to hear." She closed the car door. "But first I'm sure we need to do damage control to the house. Then we'll unpack, go by your school and pick up any work you've missed, spend at least an hour at the Tuesday quilting, and get groceries. Next we'll cook a meal, and after dinner we'll get your makeup work all squared away for school tomorrow."

She opened the storm door and twisted the knob to the back door, but the door remained shut. Martin always left the door unlocked and then set the alarm. That way Hannah could get in easily and then turn the alarm off.

"I've got to go potty," Lissa whispered.

"Okay, sweetie, just a minute."

Keeping the storm door open with her backside, she set Lissa's feet on the patio and began digging for her keys. After shoving the house key into the lock, she turned the key. The bolt clicked open. She turned the handle and pushed. The door didn't open.

"Hannah." Lissa sounded desperate. "I need to go."

"Just one more second." Hannah leaned her shoulder into the door. "I know it unlocked. Why isn't it opening?"

"Now." Lissa elongated the word while dancing around, holding her jeans.

Hannah released the storm door and held out her hand. "Let's go to the cottage instead."

While they hurried across the yard, she located the correct key on the ring. After unlocking the deadbolt, she tried turning the doorknob. Someone had flipped the handle lock, and she didn't have a key to that. No one had a key to that. Exasperated, she kept her voice as cheerful as possible. "Lissa, honey, I think you're going to have to use an outhouse like Mammi Annie has, minus the actual house."

Lissa laughed. "I don't think Uncle Martin will like that. He said me and Kevin weren't allowed to do that no more."

Their mother had trained them that when they were outside playing, they weren't to bother her by coming inside to use a bathroom. It was one of many lazy sides to Faye's child-rearing methods that, thankfully, Martin didn't allow. "He'll understand this one time."

While Lissa hid behind the bushes, Hannah called Martin. He didn't answer his cell phone, so she called his private line at his office. He didn't answer there either. It made no sense for the doors to be locked. She sat on the steps of her cottage, and Lissa soon joined her.

"Hannah?"

"Hmm?"

"I'm hungry."

Suppressing a sigh, Hannah smiled. "Well then, we'll just change plans. How about if we go by the grocery store and get some yogurt and fruit for lunch and then go to your school and get your makeup work? Surely by then we can reach your uncle."

"Can I have an ice cream on a stick?"

"We'll see."

They were halfway out of the subdivision when Hannah's cell phone rang.

"Hi."

"Hey, sweetheart. Sorry I missed your call. I was in the middle of something. So are you home yet?"

"I was, but I couldn't get in."

"Was it locked?"

"From the inside, like someone had latched the keyless deadbolt. And someone had twisted the little lock on the door handle to the cottage too, and we both know no one has a key to that."

The phone line was quiet. "Oh." His voice sounded stilted, and the line went silent again. "It's just a mix-up and no big deal."

"Okay. Did I tax your patience by staying an extra night, and now you've locked me out, or what?"

"No, nothing like that."

"Martin." She crooned his name. "You're acting odd, which is outside of your usual aim to be charming, so what gives?"

"I renegotiated with Laura, and she now works full-time as a nanny and housekeeper. She moved in over the weekend and has a thing about keeping the place locked up." He blurted out the info quickly.

"Oh." She wanted to say more, but the words didn't form. Agreeing to hire Laura part-time had been a concession on her part, not a step plan. He'd been right that they needed her. Hannah would readily admit she'd been wrong to avoid getting help, but to move into having full-time, live-in help and not even talk to her about it?

Phones were ringing in the background at Martin's office, and she could hear him being paged. "She's not there?" he asked.

"Her car isn't. I didn't knock or anything."

"Did you try the front door? She couldn't have used the keyless deadbolt on the front and back doors unless she's inside the house."

Trying to process this from his viewpoint, she still couldn't dispel the disappointment. "No, I didn't think about trying the front door. It didn't occur to me that someone would be in the house." She steered the car to the curb so she wasn't trying to talk on the phone while shifting gears.

"You're upset?"

"I . . . I'm not sure. If you feel we need her . . . but to not even talk to me . . ."

"But you agreed to her being there part-time, and we've both come to like and trust her, so I figured what possible harm could be done? Something came up, and I needed to go in to work on Saturday. When I called to see if she could come over, she'd been out trying to find a more affordable apartment than the one she was living in. Since we have the guest-room suite off of the kitchen . . . I went for it and asked her spur of the moment. I should've told you."

"Yep." Despite feeling hurt, she kept her tone light and easy. They needed to talk about this, but he meant no harm, and it was his house, his niece and nephew, and his girl who was juggling the typical life of a twenty-year-old — college, work, and family. Still, something about this nagged at her, but she couldn't put her finger on it.

"So you're not going to be angry?"

"Depends. Is that a request or a demand?" she teased. "Just so you know, the answer is request. And because of this, you owe me."

"Yeah?" He sounded more like himself again. "Every time I try to give you anything, you balk, so what could I possibly owe you?"

"Um, I'm off tonight, and there's some peace and quiet for all four of us at a little place up a winding, dirt driveway. Has a wood stove . . ."

He moaned his disapproval. "I'm going to put that place up for sale if you keep this up."

"Watch it, Palmer. I know where you live . . . although I can't manage to get in, even with a key."

He chuckled. "Let's not all go tonight, okay? Laura can do everything for Kevin and Lissa — meals, homework, and getting them into bed. That frees us to go somewhere really nice and quiet."

The niggling feeling returned, making her wonder just what it was about Laura's living in the house and taking over full-time that bothered her. Was it her own ego? Did she want to be everything for Martin and this shifted things? At sixty-two years old, Laura wasn't exactly a threat in the attraction department.

"I'm sure Ol' Gert is in need of people attention."

"I contacted the Sawyer family, the ones who live up the road from the cabin. Their oldest boy and his sister are feeding her and riding her regularly. It'll make tending to her during the winter easier now that you're living in the cottage."

Hannah wondered when he'd hired the Sawyer teens to take care of the horse. "But even if we don't go to the cabin, I haven't had any time with Kevin yet."

"Your guilt is working overtime again. He's fine. We had a great weekend, and he didn't miss you anymore than when you pull weekends helping deliver babies."

Torn between what Martin wanted and what she wanted, she said nothing.

"Come on, phone girl," he spoke up. "I deserve a night out with just us. I have the state engineering exams next weekend. I've been studying like crazy, and I want a real date, okay?"

"I did miss being here for your birthday and even for the makeup date for your birthday. We'll go wherever you'd like."

"Well, then I'll make reservations for us and surprise you. I'll also call a locksmith and have him replace the doorknob on the cottage. Hopefully he'll be able to get to it soon." Someone paged him over the intercom again. "I'm looking forward to tonight, but I'm late for a meeting that can't start without me."

"Not a problem. See you tonight."

After grabbing a bite to eat, Hannah and Lissa ran a few errands before returning to Martin's with Lissa's schoolwork in hand. Laura was unloading groceries when they arrived. Martin had been right. Laura had gone out the front door, and Hannah could have entered that way. While Lissa prattled to Laura about the trip, Hannah went into Martin's home office and called the nursing school. She explained to the director of nursing about her family needing her, but she didn't go into detail. Hannah waited while Kim looked up her records. In encouraging tones, Kim told her she had to make up any tests and clinical rotations she'd missed, but she wasn't in danger of not graduating.

The good news coursed through Hannah, bringing her fresh energy. Leaving Lissa to get her makeup work done with Laura's help, she headed to the birthing clinic, ready to see her ever-faithful Tuesday afternoon quilters. She might not get time at Zabeth's cabin tonight, but she'd sneak in a few hours with her Old Order Amish quilting friends.

Hannah turned onto the gravel driveway of the birthing clinic. To her right was the health center. Past that, farther to the right, was the quilting house. The sight of the shop awakened something odd inside her. Horses and buggies were hitched in various places near the quilting house. Smoke rose from the chimney, assuring her the Amish women hoped she would arrive this afternoon. This community of Amish seemed more open to learn and less likely to judge quickly. If there was one thing she would like to take back to her Amish community in Pennsylvania, it'd be the grace she'd found here — with Zabeth, Dr. Lehman, and these Amish women.

The sprawling branches of the oaks were carrying full-peak colors: gold, orange, yellow, and brick. In a few weeks the leaves would turn brown and fall off, and the subtle beauty of barren branches would replace the intense color.

Hannah entered the small room. A chorus of welcomes hit her so hard her eyes misted.

Sadie rose from the table and engulfed her in a hug, whispering a welcome in Pennsylvania Dutch. *"Kumm, saag uns wege dei Bsuch do yetz."*

Is this what Hannah came for, to tell them about her latest visit with her Amish family? She was here to answer medical questions while they worked on another quilt for charity, wasn't she?

She gazed at the group. Over a dozen women were here. Verna pointed to a metal plate sitting on the wood stove. "Fresh-baked chocolate-chip cookies."

The mist in Hannah's eyes turned to full, brimming tears, but why?

Lois offered a wobbly smile. "They aren't that bad. We promise."

Sadie squeezed Hannah's hand as the room broke into laughter. These women knew what it took to live Old Order Amish, and they understood the pain of breaking away. They'd had loved ones who'd left.

Today she wanted more than just to leave with a sense of peace about her future. None of them would ever prod her to talk, but they were willing to listen, and she wanted to tell them of her past — all of it. And she wanted to share her present, in hopes of never forgetting to carry into her future some part of who she'd once been.

By the time she left the quilting house, it was clear that her emotions had been more raw from her visit back home than she'd realized, but the women's love and acceptance wrapped her in warmth. She hurried to Martin's place, determined to get as much time with Kevin as possible before leaving for the evening. Guilt was already weighing on her, but she and Martin did need an evening to talk. As she climbed out of her car, Kevin barreled out the back door and ran into her arms.

She went to her knees, feeling a thousand hopes and dreams for this child as he held her tight. "Hey, how are you?"

His little face beamed as he released her. "I got something new. Want to see it?"

"Absolutely."

Kevin pulled her into the house.

"Hannah," Laura called.

Almost to the stairway, Hannah and Kevin stopped midstep. "Yes?"

Laura appeared in the doorway of the kitchen. "Martin's secretary called. The locksmith won't be here until after eight."

"Okay. Thanks."

Kevin tugged on her hand, and they went up the stairs and to his room, where he talked nonstop for more than an hour. At some point the doorbell rang, and Laura answered it, apparently receiving a delivery. After Kevin finished talking and was ready to do something besides chat with Hannah, she grabbed her overnight bag out of her car and went to Martin's room to shower and get ready for her date. When she stepped into his bedroom, on his bed was a box with a bright red bow and her name in bold letters across it. This had to be what was delivered.

She opened the card.

Since you're locked out of the cottage, I thought you might need a dress for tonight.

Love you, Martin

The note was personal enough, but it wasn't in his handwriting. She opened the box and lifted out a red, formfitting, silk dress covered with a loose layer of matching chiffon. The dress had ruched cap sleeves, which would show more skin than she was comfortable with. Not at all sure what to think, she held the dress against her body. It was gorgeous, but . . .

Something inside the box caught her eye, and she moved a layer of tissue to reveal a black silk jacket. She couldn't help but smile. Martin thought of everything all the time. It wasn't the least bit practical, and there was no telling what he'd paid for it, but for his birthday dinner he'd bought her a dress, and she intended to wear it.

Leaving the jacket on the bed, she took the dress and her overnight bag into Martin's bathroom. After a soothing shower and drying her hair for a few minutes, she slid into the red dress.

Red.

She gazed at herself, her long, curly hair draped about her. She didn't look anything like the women she'd grown up with, the ones she'd spent time with over the weekend, or the ones she'd been with this afternoon. But Martin would definitely be pleased. She paused, looking into her eyes. Yet she had to admit that being Plain was more than just a part of who she'd once been, as hidden as that seemed while wearing a red silk and chiffon dress.

She grabbed the pins and began winding her hair into a bun. A rap at the bedroom door caused her to peer out of the bathroom.

Martin leaned against the doorframe, smiling and looking as confident as ever. "I think I like your being locked out of the cottage and forced to wear something different."

She slid the last hairpin into place and stepped across the threshold before turning a complete circle.

"Oh yeah." He nodded his approval, his eyes fixed. "Definitely. Amy clearly has great taste."

"You hadn't seen it before now?"

"Too swamped. Amy Clarke picked it out and then called me with a description. I made sure she bought a jacket, just in case it showed too much skin for your liking."

"Well, according to the look in your eye, you're pleased with the outcome of your joint effort with Amy."

"We've teamed up on projects for years, but we've never yet produced anything near this gorgeous."

She crossed the room. When Martin opened his arms, thoughts of Paul popped into her mind, as if he had his arms open for her. Suddenly a bit shaken and weak-kneed, she snuggled into Martin's embrace.

He held her for a moment before shifting and planting a kiss on her lips. Then he put a bit of space between them, keeping her face inches from his. "How's Paul?"

Slipping from his embrace, she stared at him. "What?"

"Lissa was just telling me that he was injured and you helped him."

"Oh . . . yeah . . ." She adjusted the sleeve of her dress, unsure how to explain what'd taken place, really taken place. "A lot of good things happened for me, and I'd planned on our talking about the whole trip later tonight."

"I'm not interested in the whole trip, just the parts that go down memory lane with an ex-fiancé." His eyes and his tone held the intensity of an owner of a thriving engineering firm.

She knew right then that trying to explain what she and Paul had experienced this past weekend was a really bad plan. Martin had been her closest ally since she'd landed here, broken and friendless. But she'd become the woman he was in love with, the one he intended to marry. And maybe, inside of that relationship, full disclosure of every feeling wasn't a wise move, at least until she understood them herself.

Placing her hand in the center of his chest, she studied his handsome face, remembering dozens of parts of the journey that had bonded them in ways no one else could understand. "Paul and I found some closure, and now I own parts of myself that were stolen from me years ago. I came home ready to tell you what went on, feeling like I can begin life anew and having a peace with my ghosts that I never expected. And I don't deserve the tone in your voice."

Do I?

The sensation of Paul opening his arms and her slipping into them had been an unwelcome thought, one that had to be more symbolic than evidence of hidden desires. Her love for and connection to Martin completely outweighed all else. He and the children were her future, her freedom, her strength.

Martin eased his arms around her. "I didn't mean to have a tone."

She dipped her chin, allowing him to kiss her forehead. "You're honest and to the point about whatever is on your mind. I love that about you, even if you ruined a good moment."

He took her left hand and cradled it in his, running his finger over the ring he'd given her. Turning her hand over, palm up, he eased her fingers open. "My heart is right here." He lifted her hand and kissed the center of her palm. "Have I ruined this greeting completely, or can I get it back?"

"Wow," she whispered. "I'd say it's definitely not ruined."

CHAPTER 28

From the roof of the building, Matthew anchored his foot on the top of the ladder as Luke passed him another heavy piece of decking. *"An drei. Eens. Zwee. Drei."*

On *three*, Luke hoisted the wood upward, and Matthew heaved it toward himself at the same time. They moved the last piece of decking into place and hammered it down before taking a seat. His back was completely healed, and except for scarring, he had no signs of ever having been injured.

Luke removed his work gloves and looked at his aching hands. *"Die Arewet iss net zu hatt."*

Matthew chuckled. Both of them were worn out and beat up. "Ya, not *too* difficult." They sat in silence for a bit, resting, the cold air making every breath visible. "Phase two of getting the roof on is complete. Do we have the energy for phase three?"

"Not at this very minute, no." Luke

cleared his throat. "So you wanna tell me what the bishop said when he came to visit yesterday?"

"At the next communion, I may not be allowed to participate. He's frownin' really hard about me goin' to the city to stay with a woman." Matthew shrugged. "And he said I had no right to be engaged to an Englischer. Of course I reminded him that it wasn't an official engagement and that her own bishop had been convinced she intended to join the church. He then began talking about the sin of being with a woman before marriage, like going to Baltimore for those two weeks meant I shared a bed with Elle. It wasn't like that."

"I believe you. Never doubted it. But what does Kathryn think happened between you and Elle?"

"I haven't talked to her since she left for home two weeks ago, but she never spoke of it. You think she may be holdin' on to that quietlike?"

"Seems to me women are hard to figure. What might make one as difficult as a stinging nettle barely seems annoying to another."

The bell rang, signaling lunch was ready.

Luke motioned. "Come on. Let's eat and rest for a spell, then we'll get back at it. I'd like to get the felt laid and half the roofing on by sundown.

"Sure." Matthew wasn't really all that hungry, but he'd go inside and eat. It was easier than seeing the lines of concern across his mother's face.

Once they were on the ground, Luke placed his hand on Matthew's shoulder. "Two weeks and no word from Kathryn, right?"

Matthew nodded.

"Well, for better or worse, I do believe you're about to get a word." Luke pointed at a car pulling into the driveway.

Kathryn sat in the front passenger's seat, her head tilted down as the car pulled to a stop.

Luke smacked him on the back. "I'll tell your Mamm you're busy."

"Thanks." Matthew went to the driver's side of the car, pulling his billfold out of his pocket. How had he managed to only have two girls in his life and both lived far enough away they had to travel by driver in order to see him?

The woman driver rolled down the window, told him the price, and took the money.

"If you'll pop the trunk, I'll grab her bags."

"She doesn't have bags in the trunk."

Matthew glanced up, trying to catch Kathryn's eye, but she was looking at the shop. No bags wasn't good news. The driver left, and Matthew wasn't sure how to begin the conversation.

Kathryn walked toward the shop. "It's coming right along, ya?"

"Ya." Matthew followed her.

The young woman had a head for business, a heart for people, and moods as steady as the passing of time. He only hoped she saw half as much in him as he saw in her.

She stepped through the framing and into the shop area. "I didn't think you'd have the decking on already."

"The aim was to have the roof up by the first of November. In spite of two days of rain when we could do nothin', we're still a couple of days ahead of schedule."

"If I'd stayed and had things organized like you wanted, you could have worked in the barn, filling an order during those rain days."

"I wanted you to stay. That part's true enough. But I'm not all that interested in what buggy-building work could've been done." He grabbed one suspender. "I take it you're not stayin'."

She tightened her black shawl around her

shoulders. "I didn't tell Joseph about you wanting us to see each other."

"And you didn't bring any luggage, so I guess I've hit the top prize, messing up our working relationship too." He hadn't really banked on the complications that could come out of this, but he was far more disappointed in losing her than losing a worker, albeit a really fantastic one. He figured she must care for Joseph a whole lot more than it appeared when he saw them together, but the truth was, none of it was his business.

She placed her hands on the framing, as if testing its strength. He studied the delicate lines across the backs of her hands, wondering what all she'd accomplish over the coming years. Like him, she was goal minded. Unlike him, she brought a sense of order to the chaos of each workday. He'd probably not even have the burned-out building removed by now if it wasn't for her skill at organizing.

Kathryn turned to face him. "I didn't tell Joseph because my reasons for not seeing him anymore aren't because of us. He's . . . safe, and as much as part of me wants that, it's not good enough anymore."

"But you're not staying?"

"Your Mamm's up to running her own household now. We dropped my luggage off at the Bylers' before coming here."

"This is sounding much better as we go along."

"You're not safe, and I find that scary."

Matthew chuckled. "Joseph is, and it seems that's not what you're lookin' for either — whatever 'safe' means." He stepped in closer. "Explain this safe thing."

She shrugged. "I can't, not really. I just know Joseph is and you're not. You want to be. I believe that, but I'm not sure wanting to be is enough."

"Safe." Matthew gazed into her eyes, seeing a beautiful, steady woman, one whose friendship gave him strength. Elle used to drive him crazy with her passionate decisions that she put no thought into. Then when the emotion faded, she had no reason to follow through. "Does this feeling that I'm not safe have anything to do with me going to Baltimore with Elle?"

Her brown eyes studied him. "Should it?" The question wasn't an accusation and didn't hint of jealousy or insecurity.

"No. But the bishop's got me on probation over it. If you're willing for us to court, it'll have to be kept private, real private."

Her brows knit. "I don't understand."

"He'd forget the trip thing if he thought I was seeing a baptized member, and I'll not use you to get out of trouble with the bishop. And I'll not drag your name through the gossip that will take place if he doesn't allow me to take communion."

The lines of concern faded, and a beautiful smile moved clear up to her eyes. "A few years back, when the rumors about Hannah started, it wasn't long before you became a part of them too. You and she were friends. She was pretty far along being pregnant, and you stuck by her — disobeyed the bishop about going to see her. You even stayed overnight with her when you took her to the train depot. That about right?"

"Yes."

"When I heard the rumors, I hurt for Hannah — whether it was her doing for being pregnant or not. But as to your part . . ." Clearly hesitant, she paused. "It won't make any sense. I mean, it's just strange."

"Strange? That can't be the right word when talkin' about me."

She laughed softly. "My opinions are the strange thing, not you. See, I thought you *had* to be worth getting to know if you disobeyed the bishop to help her and yet were willing to return and take whatever correction he was gonna give."

He stopped all movement, waiting to be able to breathe again.

"The idea of who you were had me curious." She shrugged. "This current problem with the bishop is because you needed time away. You came back with your head on straight. I won't hold going to Baltimore against you."

She made him feel as if what they had could not ever belong to anyone else, and he wanted a name for her that no one else used. "Katie." He said it softly, and the slow, warm smile that crossed her face said she liked it. Matthew lifted the strings to her Kapp and gave them a little tug. "Just where were you when I was going to every singing lookin' for . . . for you?"

"In Snow Shoe, staying safe."

The back door to the house slammed, and Matthew took a step back. "Are you willing for us to court?"

She nodded. "I am."

Matthew glanced up, seeing Peter walking toward them. He moved his body slightly, brushing his fingers along Kathryn's hand. "Then we keep it a secret for now, ya?"

She lifted her hand that he'd just stroked and stared at it. "Ya."

He'd had no words to express his grief. Now he lacked them to convey his hope.

CHAPTER 29

Hoping Mary would return her call before time to leave for school, Hannah patiently pointed to an equation at the top of Kevin's math sheet. He sat at the kitchen table, pencil in hand, frown in place, and she stood beside him.

She had an idea to share with Mary about what Sarah could do as a job — rescuing dogs or maybe training them. Her sister seemed to have a lot of misdirected feelings of affection. Maybe working with animals would harness those emotions in a positive way, but Hannah needed feedback from Mary and Luke. If Luke thought it was reasonable, he could talk to Paul about it.

Hannah placed her thumb near the equation Kevin had just worked. "If you have no apples, can you take five apples away?"

He pointed to the paper. "But if you have five and you take zero away . . ."

"You have zero and need to take five away.

You subtract the bottom numbers from the top numbers."

"Oh yeah, I forgot." He studied the paper for a second. "Wait. I think I got it." He lowered his head, writing on his paper.

Hannah ruffled his hair and kissed the top of his head before glancing at the work in front of Lissa. Mary should have received her message by now. It'd been two days, but it was possible no one had checked the answering machine in the phone shanty, and since the cold November weather had set in, they probably hadn't heard it ring.

Laura was out running a few errands, picking up items Kevin needed for a science project he'd forgotten to mention was due tomorrow. After three weeks of Laura's working full-time, the edge of impatience in Martin's voice had faded.

Hannah grabbed the potholders and opened the oven. The back door swung open, and a cold blast of early November air swept through the room as Martin walked inside, looking every bit the executive. Like rockets taking off, Kevin and Lissa jumped up from their seats. Martin lifted Lissa into his arms and kissed her cheek before she wrapped her arms around his neck and stayed there.

Kevin leaned in and hugged Martin

around the waist. "I saw a Porsche today on the way to school."

"You did?" Martin gave him a one-arm hug, patting his back while his gaze met Hannah's.

The image of the children clinging to him warmed her. When Faye first left, Kevin and Lissa were most comforted by Hannah's presence, but over the months they'd grown to love him, and he'd gone from tolerating them to loving them as if they were his own, which said a lot since he'd never wanted children.

Kevin nodded. "And on the way home I saw a convertible, a Corvette."

Hannah took the lasagna out of the oven. "How does he know that stuff?" Closing the oven door with her hip, she glanced his way before setting the hot dish on the stove.

"It's guy stuff." Martin raised his eyebrows, teasing her. He put Lissa's feet on the floor and came up behind Hannah, resting his chin on her shoulder. "Smells good."

From his college years on, Martin had avoided eating at home, but with a new family underfoot, he conceded to the routine without complaint.

Hannah glanced at the clock. "Laura ran to the store. I need to leave for class in forty minutes. Let's clear the homework off the table and eat. Kevin, you get each of us a bottle of water and set it on the table."

Martin slid out of his winter coat and hung it on a peg just inside the back door before he grabbed Lissa's papers and backpack off the table. "Only six more weeks of nursing school left, not that I'm counting or anything."

Hannah laughed softly while passing four plates to Lissa. The way he said it, mixed with the look in his eyes, made her realize he'd been counting for a long time. "Yep, I graduate on the Friday before we leave for . . ." She stopped herself. Just the mention of the two-week Hawaiian trip over the Christmas holidays made Kevin and Lissa spiral out of control with excitement.

He caught her eye, assuring her he knew what she meant. He'd been right that all of them flying to Hawaii, along with his top employees and a couple of friends, would distract Kevin and Lissa from missing their mother over the holidays. He continued clearing off the table while she placed rolls in a basket. The kids were eager, but Martin seemed to long for this trip more than anyone.

"Oh, Dr. Lehman asked if I'd join him full-time at the clinic after the first of the year."

His face twisted with displeasure.

Holding a handful of flatware, Hannah stopped directly in front of him. "Actually, I'm thinking about it."

"Come on, Hannah. Working more hours for him means being on call more. We can't schedule a life around on-call hours." Martin took the utensils from her.

"I would only be on call eight days a month. Four of those days would be every other weekend, and four would be on Tuesdays and Wednesdays, and I'm there every Tuesday anyway. It's quite doable."

He placed the flatware in the wrong spots near the plates. "You make nearly nothing there."

Lissa went behind him, straightening them.

Hannah grabbed a spatula and began cutting the lasagna. "But this is really important to me."

The phone rang, and Hannah glanced at the caller ID. *Mary. Or maybe Luke.*

"Sorry, but I've been waiting two days to hear back from Mary."

He shrugged. "As long as no one expects you to drop everything and blast off to Owl's Perch, Pennsylvania."

She grabbed the phone. "Hello?"

"Hannah." Mary sounded a little breath-less.

"Hey, Mary, it's about time you returned my call."

"Your call? I didn't know you called. How . . . how are you?" Mary's voice sounded hollow.

Trying to hear over the clatter of plates and the conversation between Martin and the children, Hannah motioned for them to begin without her, and she took the cord-less into the other room. "I'm fine. We're about to eat dinner, and then I'm off to school. A better question is how are you? Did you like the obstetrician Dr. Lehman found for you?"

"She seems okay. I had an ultrasound yesterday, and I'm scheduled for the C-section on Monday."

Where is the excitement at having seen the baby?

"Monday? Your doctor must think you're a few weeks further along than you figured."

"Ya, that's sort of what she said."

Sort of?

"You okay?" The silence that followed answered Hannah's question. "Mary, what's on your mind?"

"Nothing . . ."

Searching for the right words, she took

into account all she knew of Mary, being Amish, and what Dr. Lehman had taught her, before she started talking in Pennsylvania Dutch. It wasn't long before Mary was telling her what truly was on her mind — the odd sensations in her body, the fears about Monday, and the fact that Luke wasn't home.

Every symptom Mary was hem-hawing about indicated she might be in labor. "Mary, is there someone within sight? Someone you could holler for to come to the phone?"

"No, but I think Jacob and Mammi Annie are on the property somewhere."

Unwilling for Mary to tread up and down hills looking for someone, Hannah's mind jammed with a dozen possible ways to handle this. "Mary, listen to me." She kept control of her voice, trying to sound authoritative and reassuring at the same time. "I need you to hang up and dial 911. Tell them you need an ambulance. Then slowly make your way inside and lie down until it arrives."

"That's silly. I'm going in for a C-section on Monday. I . . . I'm fine until then."

"Everything you just described means you could be in early labor."

Mary began sobbing. "I can't . . . Luke's

not here, and —"

"I'll get hold of Paul and send him to find Luke for you. They'll meet you at the hospital."

"No . . . please. I . . . I don't want to do this."

"But you *can* do it, and you will for both the baby's sake and yours."

"Will the lady doctor be there?"

"I don't know, and I don't want you staying on your feet long enough to find out. I'll call Dr. Lehman and get him to do what he can, but if she's not there, another surgeon will be."

"I'm so scared."

Hannah's insides quaked. "It'll be fine. Just do as I'm telling you."

"What if you're wrong? What if I'm not in labor or anything?" Mary echoed Hannah's own thoughts.

She could be overreacting, and the ambulance trip and Mary being admitted into the hospital would not only cost Luke a fortune but would cause a lot of distrust and anger against Hannah. Again. But she couldn't take a chance. "I'm not wrong." What else could she say? If she left Mary with any doubts, her friend would ignore the symptoms, maybe until it was too late.

Mary broke into sobs.

In spite of wanting to join her, Hannah remained outwardly calm. "You're going to be fine, and you'll have that baby in your arms even sooner than Monday."

"This is so scary."

Hearing the desperation in Mary's voice and the giggles of the children as they talked to Martin over dinner, she felt the knot in her stomach tighten. The pull to go to Owl's Perch and the desire to be here weighed on her. "You do what needs to be done. I'll come visit as soon as I can and hold this niece or nephew, okay?"

"Ya, okay." Mary sounded calmer now. "You'll find Luke?"

"He's never far, and Paul will find him. Depending on how much time has passed, he'll either bring Luke to the house or take him straight to the hospital. Now do as I said and get off your feet. I'll see you soon." Hannah disconnected the call and phoned Dr. Lehman.

He agreed to try to reach the doctor and at least see if she was on call tonight and, if she wasn't, to explain the circumstances to whoever was on call. He then relayed all the numbers the clinic had given him for reaching Paul. If Paul wasn't on call, he wouldn't have one of two cells provided by the clinic. Wondering if that was part of his decision to stick to the Plain lifestyle or if money was the issue, Hannah said her good-byes.

She pressed the numbers for each cell, but no one answered.

Martin ambled out of the kitchen. "What's up this time?"

"I think Mary's in labor." She held up her index finger for him to give her a minute. After dialing the Better Path, she listened to a message about the office being closed and reopening in the morning. Before it finished telling her how to reach someone in case of an emergency, she hung up. "I told her to call for an ambulance, and now I'm trying to locate Paul so he can find Luke and get him to the hospital."

She had the number for two other places he could be, Gram's and his apartment. She called his apartment first.

Martin's eyes narrowed, and he stepped closer. "You're shaking. You okay?"

"This isn't good news, Martin. Could be really bad news. I won't know for a while." After twenty rings and no one picking up, she disconnected the call and dialed Gram's. "I don't know how long she's been in labor . . ." Someone answered at Gram's house.

"Hello."

Great. She'd finally reached someone, and

it sounded like the same young woman who'd answered the phone the two times Hannah had tried to reach Paul years ago. "This is Hannah Lawson. I need to speak with Paul."

"I, uh . . . he's . . . he's . . . not here . . . At least . . . I, uh —"

It was definitely the same person, and she had no doubt it was Dorcas. Hannah's blood turned hot. "Let me interrupt this little spell of confusion for you, Dorcas." She began pacing the floors. "I want to speak to Paul. Now." She measured each word distinctly, softly demanding respect. "And if you don't want him to know about any other times I've called and not gotten through, I highly recommend you find him ASAP."

"Hold on." Dorcas's voice wavered more than Mary's had.

Hannah turned to find Martin studying her.

"What?"

He shook his head. "Nothing." But his eyes were glued to her, perplexed.

"Hannah, what's up?" Paul's voice held that steady calmness she'd come to expect over the last six weeks.

"I received a call from Mary. I think she's in labor, and I told her to call for an ambulance. Luke's not at home, and she's not sure where he is. Can you find him for her?"

"I'll certainly try, but would you rather me get Mary and take her to the hospital?"

"I thought of that and decided against it. If she's in labor, her best option is to be in an ambulance with medical assistance."

"Okay, I trust your judgment. You stick to trusting it. I'll find Luke and call you as soon as I know something. Are you on your way?"

"I'm not sure. I have class. Do you have my cell?"

"I have it. Bye."

She closed her phone and her eyes, praying silently.

Martin slid his arms around her. "Can't they take care of themselves?"

Clueless as to how to share the complexities of her roots, she said nothing.

He held her tighter. "Can I do something for you?"

With her head against his chest, she took a deep breath. "I want to be there."

"It's more than four hours away. Whatever is going to take place will be over before you could arrive."

"I know."

He placed his hands on her shoulders,

backing her up and gazing into her eyes. "You can't miss another class."

"I'm not going to be able to concentrate anyway."

"Hannah," he snapped, "the answer is no. I'm not budging on this one." He pulled her back into his arms. "Just wait, and I'll drive you there myself on Saturday as soon as your clinical rotation shift is over. That's just the day after tomorrow. She'll probably still be in the hospital, right?"

"Since she's having a C-section, yes."

CHAPTER 30

The teacher scribbled some type of equation on the board, but Hannah kept fiddling with her cell phone lying on her desk.

When her phone vibrated, she jerked it up, opened it, and pressed the green icon while walking out of the room. "Hannah Lawson." She spoke softly as she stepped into the hallway of North Lincoln Educational Center. Then she tried again, louder. "Hello?"

"I found Luke," Paul stated calmly. "And we're at the Holy Spirit Hospital in Camp Hill. Mary's in —"

Paul's voice stopped.

"Hello?" Hannah thundered into the phone but heard nothing back. "Hello? No!" She slammed the phone shut, reopened it, and punched the call-back button. "Come on."

A rapid busy signal meant something was keeping her from getting a connection. She hurried down the hall to the office. No one was inside, but the door was unlocked. She went behind the desk, tapped a letter on the keyboard to wake the computer, and then connected to the Internet. Within seconds she had a phone number to the maternity division of the hospital.

Using the landline phone on the desk, she made the call. All her hours of working for different hospitals during clinical rotations were paying off in a way she'd never expected. She knew whom to talk to and how to word her request so they'd be willing to locate Paul and give him the landline number where she could be reached.

She sat by the phone, holding a silent prayer vigil. One thing about being raised Amish — faith in silent prayers was as much a part of each day as chores, sweat, and laughter.

The office phone rang, and Hannah jerked it up. "Hannah Lawson."

"Hey, I tried calling you back on your cell. There's no news yet. The nurse said they wheeled Mary into surgery the minute she arrived. We've been here about ten minutes."

"C-sections are fast. You should hear something soon. Just stay on the line with me, okay?"

"Yeah, sure. But don't you need to be in

class or something?"

"I'm here. Technically that's all that matters. I'll get the notes off the board and see the teacher before I leave."

"Did you take a course out there in Englischer land on how to track down people via phone or what?"

"I have a little savvy, but mostly I don't take no for an answer anymore, especially when it comes to reaching people. Oh, I thought of an idea about Sarah. It has all sorts of issues for you to work through."

Paul laughed. "And you just happen to tell me that on the heels of saying you don't take no for an answer. What's the idea?"

She began telling him, and within twenty minutes they'd plotted a half-dozen ways Sarah could work with a dog-rescue-and-placement group, maybe even learn how to train dogs for specific jobs.

"This is really good, Hannah. I never would've thought of it."

"Hey." Luke's muffled voice sounded like he was beside Paul. "Is that my sister?"

"Yeah. Hannah, Luke wants to talk to you."

"Perfect. Thanks."

"Mary's in recovery, waking up." Luke sounded thrilled. "The doctor said she did beautifully and that getting to the hospital that quick may've saved her life."

Hannah drew several deep breaths. "Oh, Luke, I'm so grateful."

His boisterous laugh made chills run through her. "I told him my sister's a nurse and knew what to do. We have a girl! Mary's going to want to see you soon. The doc's gonna keep her a few days, maybe run a CT scan before letting her go home." Her brother's fast-paced, excited speech was a bit hard to decipher, but she caught it all.

"I'll be in Saturday evening, around eight or so."

"Around eight?"

"It's the earliest I can make it. I have a work shift first."

"Okay, we'll be here. You and Paul make a good team. You know that?"

Hannah didn't answer. She'd seen inklings of it long ago. "I'll see you on Saturday. Congratulations, Luke."

"Thanks, Hannah. Bye."

She hung up the phone and went back to her classroom, but she was too thrilled and relieved to concentrate.

Hannah rode with her eyes closed and her head against the backrest, glad Martin was driving. His sports car handled the curves and bumps more fluidly than her Honda.

He kept a variety of music playing while Hannah rested. Between school, studying, clinical rotations, working for Dr. Lehman, and juggling her ready-made family, she needed the rest.

The night Mary gave birth Hannah didn't sleep. Adrenaline had pumped through her for hours. Memories of her childhood with Mary filtered through her mind as if she were reliving them.

Martin scrolled through the song list on his iPod. "I really don't get why this trip is necessary. I mean, you lived without talking to Mary, without sending much in the way of letters for more than two years, and now you act as if your world will fall apart if you don't get time with her."

"I didn't have contact with her for that time, but then her life was in danger, and now we have a baby to celebrate."

He shrugged. "Seems like a phone call should have been plenty."

"Maybe we should do the band gathering by phone next time, okay?"

"Totally different." He turned up the music.

She settled back and closed her eyes again. From nowhere, thoughts of Paul demanded her attention. Refusing to indulge them, she shifted in her seat and opened her eyes.

"How's work?"

"We never talk about my work."

"Maybe we should."

He glanced from the road to her several times. "Nah, if I do that, then I have to hear about babies being born and about events in the lives of those women who come for the Tuesday quiltings."

When silence fell between them, recent snapshot images of Paul ran through her mind. The first glimpse she caught of him at Gram's — his honesty and patience in the face of her anger. Hours later — his gentleness and wisdom with Sarah. In the barn as they talked afterward — his calm but unyielding insistence that she speak to him with civility. Later that same day in the kitchen at the Better Path preparing food. He could have eaten at Gram's, but he'd fixed omelets at the clinic. Had he done that for her?

She turned off the music. "Talk to me. Find something and talk."

"Would you relax?" Martin grabbed his leather CD wallet and pulled out a fresh disc. "I haven't loaded this onto my iPod yet, but I've been wanting you to listen to a couple of songs on my newest album so we can talk about which ones to add to the band's list."

"Meaning some of the words are controversial."

"Not by most people's standards, but, yes, that's what I mean."

Hannah nodded and tried to focus on the songs. Against her will, thoughts of Paul pushed forward again, recounting conversations that had passed between them since she'd returned. As the memories circled, she picked up on nuances of who he was that she hadn't noticed before. More than ever she understood that it hadn't been his apathy that had let her go. It was his patience. When he was hurt at Matthew's, he'd seemed standoffish for a bit, and she thought he was trying to avoid being affected by her proverbial scarlet letter. Clearly there were times when she misunderstood his quiet demeanor.

"Hello?" Martin's sarcastic tone catapulted her back to the present.

She turned toward him. "Yeah?"

Under the glow of streetlights, she saw a lopsided smile ease across his lips. He moved his hand to the back of her neck, rubbing it gently. "I'm going to assume you heard none of the songs."

"Sorry."

He gestured out the window. "It's spitting sleet, and we're pulling into the parking lot.

I'll drop you off and then park the car."

"Okay."

She went into the hospital. Paul was in a seat some twenty feet away. She started to go to him but decided maybe she should keep her distance and wait for Martin. It'd be rude to be with Paul when Martin came in. She glanced in the direction he was looking.

Television.

Deciding she couldn't pass up harassing him, she smiled and walked over to him. "Sports-bar restaurants and hospitals?"

Paul rose to his feet. "Hi, Hannah. Someone needed a lift to the hospital, so while I was here . . ."

"If I had a picture phone, I'd send a snapshot of this to your bishop."

"You think he has a picture phone to receive it?"

She laughed and he joined her.

"Besides, it's Penn State and Michigan. His disapproval would fall on deaf ears."

"I get the distinct impression you'd not repent one bit, Paul Waddell."

"In the words of Hannah Lawson, 'You think?' " His eyes sparkled with mischief. "You handled this with Mary right. There is only good news to celebrate."

He motioned to the chair beside him, and

they both took a seat. "Your Daed's in the waiting room. Luke told him you were coming in, and he asked me to bring him here so he could see you."

She quirked an eyebrow. "Didn't you just say there was only good news?"

Paul looked at his folded hands, focused on them while a smile covered his face. "I never pegged you for a legalist, Hannah." Slowly his eyes moved to hers, looking at her the same way he did years ago when he walked so lightly, so carefully with a young girl's heart, never asking for even a kiss though he was in the midst of the lure of college life.

But they did kiss . . .

Bombarded with memories, Hannah couldn't seem to breathe. She remembered standing in the November rain, wishing all of life were different and their love wasn't forbidden. Through the misting night, she spotted his old truck. He'd come to Owl's Perch, trying to catch a few minutes with her after being separated for months with no contact. The door opened, and Paul jumped out. Ignoring all sense of protocol, she ran down the hill and embraced him. He nuzzled against her neck, even daring to plant a kiss on her cold, damp skin. Her arms tightened, and she remembered fearing it might be just a dream. But his warm, caring hands moved to her face, cradling it, and slowly a smile eased his tense features as he lowered his face until his lips touched hers. Warmth and power swept through her. Her first kiss. So powerful —

"Hannah." Martin's voice drew her back.

She jumped to her feet. "Hi." She slid her hand into his, dismissing romantic thoughts of Paul. Her life, her family, her dreams were with the man beside her.

Paul rose.

Martin's eyes flicked over him before he focused on Hannah. "Problem?" Smoothly he pulled his hand free from hers and ran his arm behind her, placing his palm on the small of her back. A reminder of her real life. The one she'd built despite everything. The one he'd helped her attain.

"No, not at all." She smiled, offering an unspoken apology.

His professional demeanor seemed to be in place, and his features didn't return an ounce of warmth.

Trying to dispel the tension, she motioned toward Paul. "Paul, I'd like you to meet Martin Palmer. Martin, this is Paul Waddell."

Martin's green eyes flashed with annoyance for a moment before he gave a nod.

411

"Paul." With his left hand still on Hannah's back, he held out the other.

Paul shook his hand. "Have any trouble finding the place?"

"No, but I get the feeling it'll be hard finding a topnotch hotel." Martin's features edged with tautness as he checked his watch. "Why don't we go upstairs so you can see Mary before it gets too late?"

Paul gestured down the hallway. On their way to the elevator, they passed a few groups of people, their voices hushed as they headed for the exit.

Keeping one hand on Hannah's back, Martin punched the elevator button. "It's nearly nine. I'm sure visiting hours are over, so we need to wrap this up quickly." He spoke softly, and she knew he expected a nod.

She didn't respond.

Her dearest childhood friend and her closest sibling had a baby girl. Hannah wanted to celebrate, to watch the joy on their faces as they held this little girl. It meant so much more than the fact they were her family and she'd known what to do to help them. It meant finding strength and tucking it away for days that carried no hope. And she didn't want to be rushed through it.

Only the three of them stepped onto the

elevator. Paul pushed the button with the number four on it and the doors closed.

Martin leaned against the wall, eying Paul with disdain. "So, how's the shoulder?"

Paul's expression seemed rigid. "Healed."

Martin rolled his eyes. "I'm sure."

Hannah looked from one man to the other. The gentlemanly welcomes had faded. Martin's thinly veiled manners didn't fool her. He could not care any less about Paul's arm. He wanted Paul to know he knew — everything. And Paul's one-word answer drew a distinct boundary — around what she wasn't sure — but she was becoming familiar with this in-your-face, unmovable side of him.

She knit her brows slightly, trying to pass Martin a silent message to be nice, but he acted indifferent to her subtle messages. "Paul said that my Daed is here."

Martin gave half a nod. The doors opened, and she stepped off with Martin right behind her. While Paul went on ahead, Martin tugged on her hand, and she stopped.

"Do you think maybe you could not flirt with him while I'm here?" His words were but a whisper, his anger deep.

She shook her head. "I . . . I . . ."

"I know what I saw in the lobby, Hannah — your eyes locked on his."

What was she going to say to him? Tell him the truth, that sometimes being near Paul was just too much?

Martin started walking in the same direction Paul had, but he was not within sight. They'd only gone a short way when she realized she didn't have a room number for Mary. Turning to go back to the nurses' station, she spotted her father walking toward her.

"Daed . . ." She pressed her hand down the front of her dress. "I'd like you to meet Martin Palmer. Martin, this is my father, Zeb Lapp."

"Hi." Martin's tone was neither warm nor cold. He had little respect, if any, for her father, the man who'd given Zabeth a difficult time when she chose to leave the church after becoming a baptized member.

Without any appearance of anger or resentment, her father studied Martin before he shook his hand. "Hello." He had no idea who Martin was, no clue that his sister, Zabeth, had spent her adult life helping raise him.

A grin caused lines to crease around her father's mouth. "It's been a couple of days, and Luke's still about to burst he's so excited about being a Daed, but he says no one but him and Mary can hold the baby until you and that Mennonite . . ." He let the sentence drop, dipped his head apologetically, before looking her in the eye again. "Until you and Paul do."

"What? I had no idea."

"Since most don't come to the hospital for such things anyway, it doesn't matter much. They'll wait until Luke and Mary are home to go by and see the baby." He tilted his head, studying his daughter. "You told Mary to call an ambulance and come here?"

Hannah froze, her mind running a thousand miles a second. He seemed to be asking sincerely and was clearly confused by the contradictions of what'd taken place two nights ago — the ambulance, the surgery, Luke and Mary not allowing anyone in until Hannah and Paul went in. Yet in spite of the confusion and mystery, he didn't seem to be accusing her of any misdeed.

"I did."

Daed adjusted his black winter hat. "You have no more to say than that?"

She shook her head. "No."

Her father's eyes stayed hard on her. "You're a tough one to figure, child. When you were a little girl," — he held his hand two feet off the ground — "just a tiny thing, you were more independent than half the men I knew. And smart." He scoffed. "You scared me. You should have seen yourself. It was something to behold. I wavered during your whole childhood between being proud of you and fearing you'd turn against God." He rubbed his rough, dry hands together. " 'Do by self.' That was one of the first things you ever learned to say, and say it you did, all the time." He paused, pain reflected in his eyes. "I never once intended to be a cause for you to turn against Him. I thought I was holding you in place, keeping you submissive to a higher calling."

"There is no higher calling than freedom in Christ."

"But I'm your father. I had the right to decide where you should be, how you should dress and act." He lowered his eyes. "And who you should be with."

Determined to share her mind without sounding harsh, Hannah set her will to speaking softly. "Then when is it a parent's responsibility to let go and let their offspring find the path God has for them?"

Her father sighed and removed his hat. "I got some things to say, and I don't mind saying them right now, unless you got a problem with that."

"Go ahead."

"When I insisted on you talking to the church leaders before I'd let you move back home from Mary's, I thought I was helping clear your name. I was sure they'd hear you out and say you were innocent of any real wrongdoing, but then during the meeting I learned that you'd been sneaking around behind my back with Paul and that you'd been keeping all sorts of secrets from me. I got so mad when I learned that, I was convinced you'd lied to me about everything, including the night of the unmentionable. It made sense to think you'd had a fight with him that night and while running home you'd fallen headlong, cutting your palms. And I figured all those tears and rough times you went through were because you was pining over him. Those sorts of conclusions happen when a parent learns a child's been lying." He drew a long breath, twisting the hat in his hand around and around. "But bringing you before the church leaders turned out to be unjust. I just wanted you to tell the truth so we didn't look like heathens with you needing a place to raise your child outside of wedlock, but I never once thought you'd up and leave before we worked everything out."

There she stood, needing to forgive a man whose hand in dishing out misery to her was every bit as real as her attacker's. The second hand on the wall clock made its little *tick, tick, tick.* Words didn't form in her mind. Among the Plain, withholding forgiveness was cause for losing all chance of salvation. The words *I forgive* had to be spoken, and then the person could wrestle with any lingering resentments on their own.

Still, she said nothing.

She could feel Martin's hand on her back, nudging her. He wanted her to speak. Flashing him a look to stop, she sidestepped him.

"That's all I needed to say. Maybe you can think on it a spell, and we'll talk later."

Her father wasn't going to lecture her that her salvation was at stake?

"I . . . I'd like that." As wobbly as a new calf, she gave him a kiss on the cheek.

His eyes misted. "Go on, now." He pointed down the hall.

She glanced to Martin.

"I'm fine. Go do whatever it is Luke wants. I'll sit with your dad."

Her Daed took a seat.

Martin pulled change from his pocket and moved to the vending machine. "Care for a drink, Mr. Lapp?"

Their voices faded as Hannah entered the hallway. Farther down the corridor, she spotted Paul outside one of the rooms, waiting on her. When she came close, he put his hand on the door as if he was going to open it, but then he paused. "Hannah, in spite of any problems this caused you, Luke and Mary are very grateful you came."

She understood. He was giving assurance that whatever price he thought she was paying with Martin was worth it because of Luke and Mary's gratefulness. But Martin wasn't who he appeared to be to Paul. He was deep and wonderful, but if she defended him right now, Paul wouldn't believe her anyway.

Without answering him, she pushed the door open herself. Mary was propped up in bed, her prayer Kapp in place and a tiny infant in her arms. She smiled broadly, radiating joy so strong Hannah basked in the strength of it.

Luke crossed the room and hugged Hannah, almost stealing her breath. "How can I thank you?"

She held on to him. "Oh, I'll have to think that over and come up with a way here or there, regularly for decades."

Luke chuckled. "You do that."

"Look." Mary's raspy voice was barely recognizable. She fidgeted with the blankets surrounding the tiny bundle in her arms.

Hannah moved to one side of the bed and Paul to the other, each looking at the new life in Mary's arms. She lifted her daughter toward Hannah, which made the baby start crying.

Hannah eased the infant from her mother's arms. *"Shh, Liewi, Ich denk nix iss letz. Ya?"* She bounced her gently, assuring her that nothing was wrong, and the newborn became quiet.

Looking like his shirt was entirely too small for his swollen chest, Luke smiled. "We thought about naming her Hannah."

Hannah froze. "What? No. Don't —"

"But we decided to name her after someone easier to raise than you," Mary teased.

"Than me?" Hannah quipped. "What about you?"

Mary giggled and then grabbed her stomach and moaned. "Oh, don't make me laugh. It hurts."

Luke moved to Hannah's side and placed his finger against the palm of his daughter's hand. "We'll do our best to guide her, but as far as who she is or becomes — what will be, will be. And she'll be my daughter the same as she's His daughter, no matter what she chooses. We named her Amanda. It means 'worthy to be loved.' "

"Perfect," Hannah whispered, marveling at the little girl in her arms. An ache tugged at her for all the babies she'd never have and even for the lifetime of holidays and birthdays of her nieces and nephews that she'd miss. Mary and she gushed over the baby for quite a spell before she walked around the bed and gently laid the tiny infant in Paul's arms.

Paul held the girl as if he'd held newborns many times before, and Hannah was sure he had. His sister had children, and no telling how many other relatives and friends had babies. His tall, muscular body appeared gigantic next to the tiny newborn.

She turned to Luke. "If you want to do something nice for me, I'd like for you and Mary to meet Martin."

The newborn started fussing again, and Paul eased her back into her mother's arms.

Luke glanced to Paul before nodding. "Sure, go get him."

When she stepped into the hallway, she spotted Martin leaning against a wall. She motioned for him. When he was toe to toe with her, she stayed put, looking him in the eye. "About Paul in the lobby, I should've been more aware, more careful. I'm really sorry."

He started to brush the backs of his fingers down her arm but lowered his hand.

What had she done to them?

Martin sighed. "I know." Unlike other arguments, this time she received no understanding smile or kiss on the forehead. "Can we get out of here now?"

"Soon. I want you to meet Luke and Mary first." She wrapped one arm through his and kissed his cheek. He remained unmoved, staring at her. Then he slowly turned her hand palm up and eased his finger across the center of it, telling her his heart was hers. Closing her hand around his, she returned his message. She didn't want his heart anywhere else.

He finally drew a deep breath, and she saw a hint of a smile.

Hannah held his hand as they began walking. "They named the baby Amanda, and she's absolutely perfect."

CHAPTER 31

Inside Dr. Lehman's office with the door closed, Hannah bolted to her feet and began pacing. "I don't want to know this."

Dr. Lehman pressed the ends of his fingers together. "That's not the reaction I expected."

"You told me when I woke from that coma that I couldn't have babies."

"No, I said you were unlikely to, and I had no idea you thought 'unlikely' meant no chance. Although looking back at how young and confused you were, I guess I should've clarified it long before now." He tapped the latest edition of a medical journal that lay open in front of him. "There's an article in here that says after a few years of healing, women who were in your situation and your age bracket conceived again without medical intervention."

"Why are you telling me this now?"

"Because I thought you'd be glad to know,

and if you're not, then you definitely need to know, don't you?"

His reasoning was sound, but this information would only complicate things between her and Martin. She plunked into a chair.

Dr. Lehman propped his elbows on his desk. "Want to talk about why you're reacting like this?"

Hannah shook her head, wishing the news meant life and love and joy. Instead it meant confusion and . . . probably arguments and compromises.

"Hannah, I really thought you'd be encouraged by the news."

"One would think." She ran her fingers across her forehead. "Martin's asked me to marry him, and he doesn't want children. I'll have to agree to use birth control when the time comes. Do you know how difficult that is for someone who's been raised Amish?"

"As a delivery doc for the Plain community, I've got a strong idea. It crosses a moral line for most, and in spite of being such a practical group, their love of family outweighs all else."

"I didn't want to know this." Her eyes met his.

He closed the journal. "I can tell. Need to

go for a walk or something?"

She wanted to go spend time with Martin and hope he had something wise to say that could make this news work for both of them. He had his usual pre-Thanksgiving entourage at his house right now, playing music and enjoying the day without her.

Hannah glanced at her watch. "How close do you think Elsie is to delivering?"

"With it being her first, a while yet. I suspect at least five hours."

"Can I go to Martin's and you call me when her time is closer?"

"You've been with her, answering her questions, since before she was married. She'll be upset if you're not here."

"I know. I'll be back." She needed to sort through this, and seeing Martin always helped.

"Be back here in two hours."

With her head spinning, Hannah drove to Martin's house, wondering how she'd tell him. He'd probably tell her not to worry about it, that he'd have a vasectomy or she could have her tubes tied or something. Not being able to conceive was one thing, but trying to prevent it? That was an issue she hadn't worked through. The idea of birth control was disconcerting to the very center of who she was. And if she could possibly conceive, she'd need birth control for decades, not just a few years.

Deciding that after their trip to Hawaii was probably a better time to share her new-found info, Hannah felt a little peace wash over her. It seemed that in nothing flat she was parking at the front curb of Martin's house. One glimpse of the place made her wonder just how many extra people he'd invited for this year's pre-Thanksgiving blowout. The driveway and turnaround were packed with cars, and she couldn't afford to get blocked in.

When she opened the front door, she heard Martin singing with the band. Newly hung Christmas lights surrounded door-frames, wound up the staircase, and out-lined the windows. Unfamiliar voices echoed throughout as loud laughter greeted her. Hannah slid out of her coat and hung it in the hall closet. She spoke to various people she knew as she went to check on Lissa and Kevin. The children were surrounded by other kids, all of whom barely glanced up from their video games. She refused to go look at the cover of the game. Her vote was to limit their watching television or playing video games to G-rated ones and only once a week, but she stayed out of Martin's decisions on such matters.

Content that things were running smoothly, albeit not in a manner she would have chosen, Hannah went to the kitchen to check on Laura and found her restocking a platter of food. "Hey, you're back. How was it?"

Hannah popped a grape into her mouth. "A young woman I've worked with for a long time is in the early stages of labor in her first pregnancy."

Laura threw an empty plastic platter in the trash. "Don't you usually stay when you're on call and someone's in labor?"

Feeling the familiar pull of her many worlds, she aimed not to let her voice share too much. "Yeah, but Martin forgot I was on call, so I hated to be gone the whole evening." The music came to a stop, and she nodded to the other room. "Speaking of which, it sounds like they're taking a break, so I'm going to let him know I'm here." Hannah weaved her way through the crowd of mostly strangers until she met up with Martin. "Hi."

He smiled. "Well, hello. Fancy meeting you here."

"Uh, yeah, it's fancy all right."

He held up his hands in surrender. "Laura's doing. She put up the lights before anyone arrived today." Placing his hand on her back, he directed her toward the kitchen. "But it does look good."

Hannah noticed a petite woman with shoulder-length blond hair watching them. The woman stepped forward, wearing shiny high heels, a gently molded, knee-length skirt, and matching cashmere sweater. It was the type of outfit Martin would like to see Hannah wearing, modest with a twist of alluring. But it wasn't modest by Plain standards, and she didn't think she could ever dress in that manner on a regular basis. Wearing fancy clothes was hard enough on very special occasions, although she'd have no problem wearing something alluring in the privacy of their home once they were married and the children were down for the night.

Martin paused and gestured toward the blond woman. "Hannah, I'd like you to meet Amy Clarke. Amy, this is Hannah Lawson."

Hannah shook her hand. "Hi, Amy, it's nice to finally meet you. You own the landscape architect business in the same building as Martin, right?"

"Yes, my mom owned it originally, but after I graduated from college, she trained me and then took an early retirement. Martin and I have worked together for a lot of years." She tilted her head and looked at Martin with obvious admiration. "I've been interested in meeting you. Since you've been on the scene, he's easier to convince when he's wrong and he refuses to work too much."

"Don't give her too much credit, Aim. She's known to bring out the worst in me too."

Amy shifted her stance. "So, Hannah, are you counting the days until vacation?"

Martin ran his hand up and down Hannah's back. "She graduates the Friday night before we leave. She can't help but tally each day."

Amy laughed.

Martin opened his mouth to say something else, but the phone in Hannah's pocket rang loudly.

She slid it from her pocket. "Excuse me."

Martin rolled his eyes. "Speaking of bringing out the worst in me . . ."

She smiled at him before she pressed the green button. She listened as Dr. Lehman's answering service told her to come in right away. She said she'd be there as soon as possible and then ended the call. "I'm sorry. I have to go."

Martin sighed. "Of course you have to leave, because working for no money while disrupting our lives is just right up your ever-altruistic alley."

The sting of embarrassment was complete. If his aim was to make her pay for having to work today, he'd accomplished it.

"Amy, it was nice to meet you, but I think Martin's right. I just brought out the worst in him. If you'll excuse us for a minute, please."

She took Martin by the hand. They stopped by the closet, and she grabbed her coat before they went out the front door. She closed the door behind them, confident her cheeks were still red with anger. "I'm not the one who forgot I was on call. It's only reasonable for me to work this holiday weekend if I'm off during Christmas. And if you'd shared your *extravagant* plans concerning today with me, I'd have reminded you about my schedule." She jerked her coat on.

"You say the word 'extravagant' like this party is something to endure." He shoved his hands into his pockets and moved to stand at the top of the porch steps. "You know, it'd be really nice if just once you did more than tolerate what I have to offer. Just once, Hannah."

"And could that be followed up by you

not making plans first and telling me second?"

Martin said nothing, and she hated that they'd had so much trouble communicating lately. They'd once shared everything, and when they first started dating . . . well, actually, they argued and almost broke up before the very first date, but then they talked things out, and she saw a deeper part of who he was. They became closer that night. That's what they needed — to talk like they used to.

She forced a smile, aching with the things that tore at them. Since the night he'd gone to the hospital with her three weeks ago and had seen her being more than civil with Paul, there had been more stress between them. She'd blown it and done damage, but she would not accept defeat. They'd get past this as well as the news Dr. Lehman had shared, but it wasn't the right time to tell Martin about that.

He kissed her forehead. "Look, we've stumbled on a gap that needs a bridge. You're right. I am guilty of making decisions first and telling you second. It's a habit that needs breaking now that I'm part of being a couple. But if I didn't push, you'd still be living in that cabin, avoiding the lifestyle of the professional and modern world around you. Are you ever going to be ready to let go of the Plain ways and enjoy what's right in front of you?" He kissed her cheek. "Come on, phone girl, make a choice for us."

Hannah slid her arms around him, remembering their first kiss. With one connection of their lips, he'd swept loneliness from her, an isolation that was colder than the Arctic and just as secluded. She loved him more than he probably realized, but was the next great movie, blowout party, gaming station, or extravagant vacation so very important?

She kissed his cheek before taking a step back. "Look, I've gotta run — should have left fifteen minutes ago. Let's talk about this later." She didn't wait for another kiss as she hurried down the steps. "Bye."

"Drive safe." He waited until she was sliding behind the wheel to wave, and then he went inside.

CHAPTER 32

Restless beyond his own tolerance, Paul stood in the backyard of his parents' home, splitting firewood. The day before Thanksgiving was always difficult. The sky hung low with gray clouds, matching his mood. Regardless of how much life had separated Hannah and him, each year they'd had this one day to visit from early morn to almost sunset. The day had demanded little but provided time for talking and playing games while baking foods at Gram's in preparation for Thanksgiving.

With the Better Path closed, and in need of a diversion, he'd come to Maryland to spend time with his family. It wasn't helping. He grabbed a two-foot-long, unsplit log. After setting the round upright on the tree stump, he took the ax in hand and slammed it into the wood, splitting the log from end to end. It seemed that a distraction from Hannah didn't exist. Anywhere.

Over and over again he chopped, tossed, and grabbed another piece. When she'd first arrived back in Owl's Perch and he'd thought she was married, he convinced himself that he had waited for her out of guilt. Even if that'd been true, after being around her for just a few days, he was captivated again. Now everything about Hannah beckoned him, and he felt miserably cantankerous. With everything they'd resolved between them, only one thing kept them apart — her being in love with someone else.

He slung another piece of split wood onto the growing pile, and a thought of Dorcas pushed its way forward in his mind. He felt so bad for her. Not only was he falling deeper in love with Hannah every time he saw her, but his tolerance for Dorcas was becoming thinner. In an effort to be reasonably up-front with her, he told her Hannah wasn't married, and for his effort, Dorcas's health took a turn for the worse.

Mutilating another piece of wood with the ax gave no release from the turmoil inside him. He'd wanted to tell Dorcas there was no way he could court her. Ever. For both their sakes, he wished he was at least attracted to her. After two and a half years, he'd come close to having a few feelings for her, but that was before Hannah drove back into his life. Because of Dorcas's health, he didn't dare tell her how he really felt, so she continued to wait in hopes of a true courtship.

"Paul?" His sister spoke loudly.

He glanced up, surprised Carol was standing near him, looking perplexed.

She stomped the ground and wrapped her black wool coat tighter around her. "You don't even have on sleeves."

"I'm fine."

"Only because you've been out for hours working like a sled dog. What gives?"

"Nothing."

She didn't budge.

Paul motioned toward the house. "Space would be really nice, okay?"

She shook her head. "I don't understand. Dorcas is finally diagnosed. Lyme disease isn't easy to cure, but she's not dying and stands a good chance of eventually having a full recovery."

Guilt smothered him. "How's she feeling today?"

"She's inside, arrived about an hour ago. Why don't you come sit with her?"

He shook his head. "Not now."

Looking resigned, Carol folded her arms tightly across her waist. "She's relieved to have a diagnosis that isn't terminal. Scared at how difficult it's going to be to recover. In pain from what the illness has done to her body."

He set an unsplit round on the stump. "I'll come in and see her after a while." If Dorcas felt decent enough today, she'd have come outside to be with him. Regardless of the reason, the space was welcome. It wasn't her fault that his attraction to her barely registered on any scale during their best days together.

"If I guess at what's eating you, will you nod if I hit it?"

Swinging the ax, he landed the cutting edge on the top of the round, splitting it partially. "Leave it alone, Carol. Just go inside and pretend that if you ignore how I really feel, it'll all go away. That's what you and Mom and Dad have done for years, isn't it?"

Carol stared at the ground. "Yes, we have, but it hasn't changed the truth, and I'm ready to admit that." She lifted her eyes to him. "Tell me what to do."

Paul set the ax to the side. "It's too late. There's nothing to do. Hasn't been since the night I left Hannah."

"Oh, Paul." She sat on the huge stump he'd been using to split the wood. "Is that what's eating you? Are you still in love with her after all this time?"

Hearing the sincerity in her voice, he sensed his restlessness ease a notch. "Sounds crazy, I know."

"Dorcas said Hannah's been in and out of Owl's Perch and that she's not married. So now what?"

"Nothing. She's in love with someone else. The man has a young niece and nephew they're raising. Life keeps moving."

"Paul, maybe you're better —"

"Don't." He pointed at her. "Don't say that maybe I'm better off. It's not true, and if you knew her, you'd know that too."

She shook her head. "I can't believe this is happening to our family again. First, Uncle Samuel living all his days unmarried because of one girl, and now you. Why do you have to care for someone outside your reach?"

"But Hannah wasn't out of reach for me, and I wasn't for her. We had family things to work through, and we could have, if only . . ."

If only.

The list that could finish that phrase was so long he couldn't make himself admit even half of it. If only he'd followed her home in his truck each time, the attack would never have happened. If only he'd listened to her that night, she'd never have left Owl's Perch without him. If only he'd received a call from her, he'd have left everything and gone to her. If only . . . she wasn't in love with another man.

It was enough to make him think he might spontaneously combust.

Carol touched his shoulder. "I'm sorry. Sorry I ever argued with you about her. Sorry Dorcas is sick and you can't get free to look for someone better suited to you."

His sister's empathy surprised him completely.

He decided to tell her some of his quieter thoughts. "I'm considering doing volunteer work with our service this coming summer, maybe even something overseas. I just need to make things right with Dorcas first."

"Maybe you'll find someone through missions and service, although when Dorcas can tolerate hearing such a plan is anybody's guess."

He nodded. "I know, but it's also wrong not to tell her."

She sighed. "It's my fault that Dorcas has been invited to hang around all the time. Between my inviting her and her being the daughter of Mom's best friend, we've thrown you two together. I was just sure

438

you'd come to care for her if given time. I never realized it might take a millennium."

"I won't spend my life pining for what could have been with Hannah. It's just that being with her again and seeing her with Martin will take awhile to shake free of. I . . . I'm . . ." He shook his head, deciding not to tell her he had concerns whether Martin was the best person for Hannah. His snippet view of the man did nothing to boost his confidence in Martin Palmer. "Anyway, after Dorcas is better, I'll make my plans clear, and then I'll . . . I'll move on."

That was the only thing that made sense. His phone rang, startling his sister.

"Sorry." He dusted off his hands. "I started carrying one of the clinic's phones . . ." Since the night Hannah had to call too many places trying to reach him.

"Hello?"

"Listen, I'm on my way back to you."

Warm goose bumps ran up and down his body as Hannah spoke the words.

She drew a breath. "I got caught at Martin's, and now I'm hung up in traffic, some sort of horrific, heart-wrenching mess that I have to break free of before I can get moving, but I'll be there. Assure Elsie of that, even if she delivers before I arrive. How far apart are her contractions now?"

"Hannah?" He knew who it was and wondered why he'd made it sound like a question.

The line went completely silent. "Paul?" She laughed, a warm, beautiful, robust laugh — the kind that haunted his dreams and woke him with a longing to hold her. "You're not in labor, are you?"

"I've chopped over a half cord of wood so far today. That's definitely labor."

"Well, I'm not catching each piece of wood, bathing it, and wrapping it in a blanket. You can bank on that one, bud."

"Bud?" he teased.

"It's a word."

Realizing they'd said the phrase 'it's a word' to each other while playing Scrabble on numerous occasions over the years, he ached anew for the friendship they'd lost. He decided to keep this conversation going as long as possible, much as he had all those board games they used to play. "Yeah, but it's not worth any points since it's a name."

"Wouldn't matter. You'd find a way to rip off any points I came up with anyway."

She'd answered him without hesitating, as if the memories were never far from her either. Was he imagining that? "I never cheated."

"Ah, but did you play fair?"

The cool air whipped through his short-sleeved shirt, and he felt the coldness for the first time today. "Define 'fair.' "

"Ewww, I tend to forget how good you are at wordplay," she scoffed mockingly. "You win this round. I only have four numbers stored in my cell phone, and I was only half watching while scrolling for Dr. Lehman's number."

With emotions pouring into him at the speed of Niagara Falls, he sat down on the stump Carol had abandoned. "Only half watching what: the phone or the road while driving?"

"Yes." She paused. "I'm now a regular statistic — young women in their cars on their cell phones while driving — but I did not cause the accident."

"Says the girl who's on her cell phone, laughing and chatting feverishly."

She broke into laughter again. "Shut up, Waddell."

"You don't sound the least bit displeased about being an Englischer statistic."

"There are things I like about the Englischer life."

Wanting more time, Paul challenged her. "Name them, all of them."

His sister held up a coat for him that she'd

apparently retrieved from the house. Holding it out so he could slide one arm in, she offered a concerned smile. He shifted the phone to his other hand and finished putting on the jacket.

"Thanks." He mouthed the word to her. "Hellooooo?" he called to Hannah.

"Paul?"

His name came out broken, and he knew they were losing the connection. Then the line went silent. He closed the phone and paced the yard, thoughts coming at him faster than he could process. *Listen, I'm on my way back to you.*

Carol cocked her head. "She called you?"

"By accident. She was trying to reach Dr. Lehman at the birthing clinic where she works."

"But you immediately began a really friendly conversation with her." Carol sighed, looking unsure of what was taking place. "How are you ever going to move on if you keep having contact?"

"Well, so much for deciding to support me."

"Just don't set yourself up for another hard fall, okay?"

His phone rang, and he jerked it open, taking a second to glance at the caller ID. Her name wasn't logged in this phone's memory, but he knew her number by heart. "We lost the connection."

"Alliance is hilly with dips. Plus we have the Allegheny Mountains between us."

That wasn't all they had between them, but he didn't want to think about that right now. In spite of a niggling sensation that he was involved in something closer to an affair than a friendship, he wanted more. "So, can you tell me that list now?"

He had no intention of asking why she'd called him again or of turning the conversation into something that would make her back off. It was their day, the day before Thanksgiving, and she'd called — by accident — but still his Lion-heart was on the other end of the phone.

"Paul, I didn't mean to call you the first time, and I . . . I called back because . . . well, follow-through is important, but I should let you go."

Follow-through?

If she'd had some of that a few years ago, they wouldn't be in this fix. "Come on, Hannah. How great can your relationship with Martin be if it can't handle your talking to me for ten minutes?" He regretted the jab at their relationship the second he said it. "I'm sorry. I shouldn't have said that."

"It's okay. I understand. I'm sure Martin looked like a jerk the other night, but you don't know him. What you and I do know is there's too much between us sometimes. Martin saw proof of it the last time I was there, and he lost his temper." She paused. "Not one second of this is right or fair to him."

More clearly than ever, Paul heard just how completely forthright she'd become while living in Ohio. Unfortunately, a little less frankness would give them some cover to act like their feelings didn't run so deep, to behave like all they had was friendship and no threat to Martin. "Maybe I'm wrong, but I'm not all that concerned about what's fair for Martin. You landed there devastated, and I bet he's stuck like superglue. But because of him, you can't give us a few minutes to just chat?"

"Paul." She spoke softly, as if she understood all too well the truth of his words. "I won't do anything to hurt Martin. Ever. And if he knew I called you by accident, he'd be fine. If he knew I called you back and we chatted about fun things, it'd undermine who we've become. I won't do that. And we have Kevin and Lissa too. But . . ."

"Well, don't stop now."

"Can you deal with me saying something

completely honest?"

"More honest than you've already been? Will I survive it?"

She didn't respond to his jesting. Whatever was on her mind was more serious than the information on Martin.

"Go ahead, Hannah."

"There's something I've wanted to share since the workday at Matthew's. Something I knew I would eventually have to say, okay?"

"Sure."

"I'm not sure Dorcas is . . . Well, I think you need to be careful, make sure you really know her."

Wondering what would make her say that, he answered, "There's nothing between Dorcas and me. It'd make my life easier if there were."

"You're not courting her, not engaged, not anything?"

"Nothing."

"I'm really relieved to know that. You can trust me that caring for her would not make your life easier. Not ever."

She sounded so sure of knowing Dorcas and seemed deeply relieved he wasn't involved with her. Why?

"Okay, but isn't that the same as my deciding what Martin's like based on seeing him once for a few minutes?"

"No, it's not. Martin's a truly great guy who sometimes has a short fuse. Dorcas is . . ." She cleared her throat. "As much as I'm tempted to say more, I've said plenty. Look, I need to go. You have a good Thanksgiving and no fudging at Scrabble."

"Bye, Hannah." Paul closed his phone, with armies of thoughts marching through him.

Her words reverberated through him over and over again — *Listen, I'm on my way back to you.* He looked to the heavens, wanting to believe what had just happened was some type of message and all he needed to do was hold on.

And she was worth years of waiting if he could have her love. But why was she so relieved he wasn't involved with Dorcas?

He tumbled that thought around, but then another one came front and center, screaming in his face, making all others disappear. Had she just admitted to caring for him and Martin knew it? Hope rocketed through him. Whatever she carried for him was strong enough for Martin to see it and be angry with her at the hospital. But even if she cared, she'd just said that they'd ruined their chance and she was with Martin now. The blast of hope faded some but far from completely.

Too many things about their past and present just didn't add up. Like how did Hannah return knowing about certain areas of his life? Had Gram told her during their short visit before Paul and Dorcas arrived — the day Hannah had the flat tire in Gram's driveway? It wasn't like Gram to be so open. She was awful tight-lipped about family stuff. But no one outside his immediate family knew about the disapproval he'd been under with his church leaders after Hannah first left.

Except Dorcas.

At the thought the muscles down Paul's back stiffened, and the view around him became invisible. The dark roller coaster his mind had been on came to a screeching halt.

When Hannah called him just now and the call dropped, she called him back just to say a proper good-bye. Yet when she left Owl's Perch for good, she didn't call? She said she'd called at some point, but when?

Suspicion clung to him, begging to be explored.

Until this moment he thought the intensity of her anger with him when she returned to Owl's Perch was to be expected, but that day in Gram's driveway, she'd made a sarcastic remark about how little effort he'd put into talking with her, as if he'd had chances somewhere along the line that he never pursued.

But how?

When she left over two years ago, she had three phone numbers to reach him: Gram's, his on-campus apartment's, and his parents'. He knew for sure now what he thought he knew then — that Hannah had a deeper sense of justness than to hold everything against him for his reaction the night he discovered she was round with pregnancy and he left.

But then why had she not called him?

Paul grabbed the ax and slammed the blade of it into a round. The sound of splitting wood echoed against the silence. He continued working, hoping for a revelation.

Mostly I don't take no for an answer anymore, especially when it comes to reaching people.

The words she'd spoken to him only weeks ago echoed inside him. She said when she'd called his apartment, a girl answered. He'd assumed she'd called on one of the many nights between their last good visit and when he left her, but did she? As he worked, thoughts fell into place that turned his stomach. His suspicions grew like billows of smoke and were just as impossible to pin down.

But one word kept coming to him over and over again.

Deceit.

CHAPTER 33

In the middle of another song, Martin saw Lissa come to the door, tears streaming down her face. He moved out from behind the keyboard, and she ran to him.

He lifted her. "What's wrong?"

"I hurt my knee, and the other kids laughed."

"Oh, so it's a double whammy, eh? So, which hurts worse, your knee or your feelings?"

Lissa wiped at her tears and hugged him tight. "My knee."

"Well, let's go take a look." He carried her down the steps into the kitchen and set her on the island near the refrigerator. "Let's see if we can roll your pant leg up, okay?"

She nodded while rubbing her eyes. More than anything she looked tired, and he might need Laura to take her out to the cottage to sleep before the party ended. He managed to get the corduroy pant leg up high enough to see her knee. "It's only red. I thought maybe it'd be green or orange polka-dotted."

Lissa giggled. He kissed the top of her head before grabbing a bag of green peas out of the freezer. "Let's use these." He lowered her pant leg and placed the frozen bag over her knee.

"I love you, Uncle Martin."

"Yeah, you're not so bad yourself, kiddo." He winked. The thing was, he had a love for Lissa and Kevin he hadn't known existed inside of people. As frustrated as he'd been with Hannah of late, Amy was right, she had opened his eyes and heart to life beyond work and to these children. It'd taken an Old Order Amish girl to make him reach deep inside and connect with God in a way that'd changed everything about him. And now they were griping and snapping at each other regularly. There was no way he could really tell Hannah what he was thinking. He loved her, which meant a lot since he'd never been in love before, but sometimes he was torn between wanting to direct her steps and accepting that their ideals for how to live rammed against each other.

"Uncle Martin." Lissa patted his face. He looked up. Amy had entered the room. Doug walked in right behind her.

He removed the bag of peas from Lissa's knee. "All better?"

"Yep."

He helped her down. "Hey, Aim, Doug. Care for something to eat or drink?" He motioned to the other island where the food was spread out.

Doug took a paper plate and began putting a variety of snacks on it. "Great gathering."

"Glad you like it."

Amy grabbed a bottle of water out of the open cooler. "Are you and Hannah taking Laura with you to Hawaii?"

He tossed the peas back into the freezer. "No, she wasn't hired full-time when we planned the trip, and it's impossible now to get her a ticket to fly out that close to Christmas." He slid onto the island. "I shouldn't have talked to Hannah the way I did."

Amy leaned against the bar. "You were pretty bad, Martin, but the one you need to apologize to is her."

"I will. The pressure we've been under will melt once she graduates and we go on vacation. We both know that. This year's been too long with too many things to adjust to."

"Hey, does Hannah golf?" Amy asked.

"No, but while we're in Hawaii, that's not

a bad idea. It's got all the right earmarks of something she might just enjoy — games and being outside are definitely high on her list of fun things. How long has it been since the three of us and Alex have been part of a foursome?"

"It's been a couple of years, I think."

Doug licked barbecue sauce from his fingers. "News update. I gave up golfing. It's expensive, and I'm horrible at it."

Martin's and Amy's eyes met for a moment as they suppressed a laugh. How poorly Doug played golf was not news, but he was a lot of fun on the course anyway, so no one cared.

Amy took a sip of water. "My dad's a great golfer, and he's my *significant other* for the trip."

"Maybe the four of us can play a few rounds — you, me, Hannah, and your dad."

"Sounds great. I bet you have no clue how much I'm looking forward to this trip. I haven't been in over a decade. I'm doing every luau I can manage."

"I've never been." And he wondered if Hannah would go to a luau. She might not, with girls in skimpy outfits dancing around, but they'd have fun anyway.

"Really? You did such a fantastic job of planning this trip. I just assumed you knew what you were doing."

And for the first time in a very long time, he felt something other than the need to compromise. He felt respected for decisions he'd made.

With the word *deceit* rolling through his head, Paul strode across the yard and went inside.

The aromas for tomorrow's Thanksgiving feast filled the air as Gram and his mother baked a lot of things ahead of time. He wasn't sure where Carol and her husband, William, were, or Dorcas, but his dad was at the kitchen table reading a newspaper.

"Hey, Gram, something's nagging at me."

"I'm listening," Gram called over her shoulder as she loaded the sink with several messy pans.

"I was wondering about the day Hannah came to visit you. Did you tell her about my change of careers or that after she left, I was in trouble with the church leaders over some of my decisions?"

"Of course not." Gram flicked the hot water on and poured dishwashing liquid into the sink. "That's personal family happenings. Besides, I was afraid if I mentioned anything personal about you, she'd up and leave before we had a chance to visit."

Paul figured Gram was right about that. Hannah had returned wanting nothing to do with him, and he was reminded just how far they'd come since then.

"Well, she knows."

"Maybe that friend of yours, her brother, told her," Dad offered.

Paul shook his head. "I don't think he knows."

Piling mounds of baked cornbread into a huge bowl, his mother arched an eyebrow. "I trust we can find a better topic than that girl during our holiday."

Paul straightened, looking directly at his mother. No one seemed more set against Hannah and him than his mother. "Mom, have you ever talked to Hannah?"

"What?" The lines across her face revealed her shock. "Never. And I thought you were over this."

"Dad?"

Glancing to his wife, he looked a bit uncomfortable. Gray colored most of his once-blond hair, but he still managed to look more than a decade younger than his wife. "Your mother and I don't agree on this subject. As badly as you needed to see that girl again, I'd have given about anything to see it work out."

His always faithful and calm dad said what

Paul already knew. He'd never betray his son. Paul looked up to see Carol and William now standing in the threshold of the double-wide doorway. "Carol?"

She shook her head. "No. I thought she was a huge mistake on your part, but I'd not withhold that from you."

He nodded, catching a glimpse of the hem of Dorcas's dress around the corner, near the entryway of the makeshift nursery for his sister's baby. Was she eavesdropping?

Dorcas's behavior pricked him.

Something Hannah had said about two months ago returned to him: *"When I did manage to call your apartment, a girl answered."* He'd assumed Hannah was talking about calling him any night but the one, the only one, when he'd asked his sister and Dorcas to man the phones while he looked for Hannah.

"Dorcas, come on out."

She eased out from behind the wall, facing him, looking too frail to be questioned.

Guilt defined her features. Surely it couldn't be true. She'd been his ally, giving him advice, helping him cope. He wasn't in love with her, but he counted her as a friend. "Did you ever answer a call from Hannah?"

"Paul!" his mother called. "Stop this. That

456

Amish girl nearly ripped us apart when we found out about her, and you're going to help her do it again?"

He pointed at his mother. "That 'Amish girl' did no such thing. Your own anger that I'd have a girl you hadn't approved did that. Nothing else." He returned his focus to Dorcas.

She stepped out of the hallway and toward the kitchen, shaking her head. "I wouldn't . . . I wouldn't do anything to hurt you."

Paul wasn't sure she'd actually answered his question. "Hannah called me a little bit ago by mistake. The call was dropped, and she called me back to say a proper good-bye. She didn't want to say anything else but bye. Now why would someone like that not call after leaving Owl's Perch in such a rush?"

"Maybe she changed over the last few years," his brother-in-law offered. "She was a teen and returned as an adult. That makes a difference, you know."

Paul didn't move his gaze from Dorcas, who was avoiding looking at him. "Or maybe she called and someone's not telling me."

Dorcas stared at a group of photos on the

wall that showed Paul at various stages of his life.

Paul's fist came down hard on the countertop. "Answer me, Dorcas."

Her chin quivered. "She told you." The words were barely audible.

Hannah knew?

Tempted to lie, he stayed the course. "I want to hear it from you."

She shook her head, tears trailing her face.

"What, you can bulldoze my life, but you can't admit to it?"

Dorcas looked to each person, as if searching for support. "She was pregnant. We all knew it wasn't Paul's because he never once hesitated to consider that it might be his. Every one of us thought the same thing about her."

Carol stepped forward. "We *thought* a lot of things. What did you do?"

"I . . . She called. Only twice, Paul. I swear it."

"Only twice? Do you have any idea what you've done?" Paul measured his tone, refusing to yield to the rage inside him. "Tell me when, Dorcas."

Tears ran down her cheeks. "The first time she called, we all thought she was guilty of cheating on you. All of us. Even you thought that for a few days. Then the next time you were beginning to get over her, and . . ."

Carol looked horrified. "Oh, please say that she didn't call Paul while he had us at his apartment waiting to hear from her."

Dorcas covered her face with her hands, sobbing. "I'm sorry."

Paul couldn't budge, afraid if he did, he might hurt her. "The night she was staying at a hotel, waiting for her train to leave? It didn't leave until early afternoon the next day! I could have gone to her and stopped her from going!" Paul clenched his fists. "Are you crazy? Or just flat-out mean?"

Dorcas lowered her hands, her eyes begging him to understand. "I . . . I thought she'd been lying to you."

"And the next time, what did you think then?"

"You were beginning to care for me . . . I could tell, and everyone wanted us to be together."

Paul looked at his mother and gestured at Dorcas. "This is your choice over Hannah?" He clutched his head, total disbelief rocking his world. "How could you, Dorcas? I trusted you. You encouraged me to let her make the first move, to return on her own, but you kept her from reaching me." He took several deep breaths, trying desperately to see the room around him as his vision went red. "It's your fault she's with someone else. And the truth is we'll never know all the hurt and damage you've caused to Hannah . . . all the lives you've altered along the way, but as long as you got what you wanted, right?"

Needing to get some air, he turned to leave, but then a thought hit, and he turned to face her. "Did you remove the money from our account?"

Dorcas gaped at him, and she looked as if she might keel over. His dad went to her side, and William grabbed a kitchen chair and ran it over to her.

Paul took a step closer. "The bank showed me photos of someone wearing Amish clothing — someone pretending to be Hannah. The bank officials and I figured her rapist stole her bankbook and emptied the account. But you could have taken my bankbook. You have Amish relatives and knew enough to pull that off. Did you take our money?"

She dropped into the chair. "No, I'd never steal from you. I'll put my hand on the Bible if you need me to."

"Never steal from me? What do you think you've done?"

Dorcas broke into fresh sobs, and his dad passed her a box of tissues. While Paul stood there watching her, a memory hooked on to something inside him, and he tugged at it, like reeling in a fishing line.

The day after he'd asked Hannah to marry him, he was here in his parents' home, writing her a letter, when his sister and Dorcas came into his room and interrupted him. He'd penned the fullness of his heart in those pages, and receiving it would have meant so much to Hannah. Those days had been unbelievably trying, nearly impossible to make contact and keep up with each other's life. What were the odds of the only letter his sister and Dorcas knew about being the one that disappeared?

"Did you steal the letter?"

Dorcas's hands fell limp to her side, and her head remained bowed. "Yes."

His sister stepped forward. "Paul, you know enough of the truth. Please stop."

Disgusted with Dorcas, he turned and walked out of the house. He got in his car and started driving. He hadn't started out trusting Dorcas. The whole time they went to middle and high school together, he thought she was selfish and manipulative, but when she was receptive about Hannah, he convinced himself she was a decent and honest person. He should have trusted his gut.

The years of betrayal played through his mind; the ache over all he'd lost by trusting Dorcas seemed to circle endlessly inside him. More than two hours later he pulled into Gram's driveway. He walked across the dark yard, through the pasture, and into the patch of woods. He didn't stop until he was at the footbridge that crossed the creek. This was where he'd asked Hannah to marry him. The place where everything he'd ever wanted seemed to become possible. As clearly as if it'd happened yesterday, he remembered Hannah whispering yes to his proposal. It'd taken a few minutes to convince her that he was serious, that he had no one else on campus, and that they would find a way to win her father's approval.

He'd lost everything he'd ever hoped for due to a violent man, his own knee-jerk reaction, and Dorcas's manipulation. What Dorcas had done under the guise of friendship and warmth was unbelievable.

The price he'd paid — incomprehensible.

Even now, hours later, his hands shook. Looking down at the creek bed, watching the dark water ripple along its winding, twisting path, his thoughts turned to all the things this liquid would do before most of it flowed into the ocean: provide nutrition for the tiny creatures that lived in it, supply water for nearby trees, cattle, and wildlife. It'd smooth stones and bear life. Some of it would evaporate and sprinkle down no telling where in the world.

God had ways that couldn't be seen or calculated from a small bridge while watching the beauty of dark waters pass under his feet. Everything in life carried more, accomplished more than could be seen with the naked eye or even imagined.

He prayed that both Hannah and he would accomplish more than either of them could see or imagine. But their courses had been altered. His was still free enough he would welcome — no, he'd be ecstatic to have her back every second of every day for as long as they lived. But she would have to have her heart ripped out again to return to him.

CHAPTER 34

Inside Alliance Community Hospital, Hannah shoved her timecard into the slot and punched out, ending her last round of clinical rotations for nursing school. The Saturday shift ended two hours earlier than usual for the students, and ideas of trying to squeeze in a visit to Mary pulled on her. Hannah needed to talk to someone who would understand her feelings about Martin and babies and birth control. Mary would get it.

Hannah wanted perspective before mentioning the *news* to Martin. It'd been ten days since Dr. Lehman told her she might not be as infertile as she'd thought. Martin had to know, but first, Hannah needed to figure out her own thoughts and feelings about it. She and Martin were having enough trouble communicating of late. The last thing she needed to do was start a difficult conversation without knowing her own mind and heart.

Talking to Mary was the answer. Hannah was sure of it, but she couldn't do it over the phone. The girl would freeze to death in the phone shanty before Hannah finished explaining the mess. Besides, Mary had a baby to tend to. But what about Martin? She'd been at work or school so much lately that they'd had no time together. Still, she needed to find some answers to help strengthen their relationship. Finding peace on this birth-control topic was more important for Martin and her than having a date night.

Confident of what she needed to do, Hannah unlocked her car door and called Martin.

"Hey, sweetheart, I'm on the other line. Can you hang on a minute?"

"Sure." Hannah turned the engine, warming the car while waiting. About the time warm air started to flow, Martin came back on the line.

"Hey, I'm back. What are you doing calling at this time of day?"

"I got off early."

"Good. That works even better. Vance Clarke . . . I don't think you've met him yet. He's Amy's dad, and he's passed us four TobyMac and Jeremy Camp concert tickets.

Kevin and Lissa are psyched. It's at the Canton Civic Center tomorrow, and I was on the other line making reservations at a hotel, so —"

"At a hotel?" Hannah interrupted him. "Canton is what, thirty to forty minutes from your place?" She laughed, trying not to sound like a wet blanket.

"It's an adventure, Hannah. The kids get it. Try to keep up," Martin teased.

"Am I familiar with TobyMac's and Jeremy Camp's music?"

"Sure you are. We sing a couple of their songs. Remember the —" His voice cut out, letting her know he had another incoming call. "Hey, Amy's dad is on the other line. He probably wants to know if we're able to use the tickets."

"Martin, you guys go, but I want to slip to Owl's Perch and see Mary. I'll be back to your place before you are tomorrow."

"What? No," he snapped. "Hold on."

The line went silent for a minute or two.

"You still there?" Martin's voice said it all. She'd ruined the fun.

"Yeah, I'm here."

"Since when did you decide traveling four hours one way is *slipping* to your friend's house? And why are you letting all these visits come ahead of us?"

"It's not like that. I just need to talk to her about some things."

"Then call her. Come on, Hannah. The concert will be fun."

She'd never been to a concert. She imagined booming music, multi-colored electric lights flashing everywhere, and people center stage enjoying the limelight, like the concerts Martin had on DVD that he liked to watch. It was so far removed from the Plain life that she wouldn't be able to enjoy it. Besides she really wanted time with Mary.

"Fun for who?"

"For whom," he corrected, "and obviously not for you."

"You have four tickets. Let Laura use mine. And I'll see you as soon as you get home tomorrow."

"Laura's over sixty. She wouldn't want to go."

"She's a well-paid nanny, and she'll help with the children."

"This stinks. I've already told the kids and made reservations. I can't back out."

"And you shouldn't. You want to go to the concert, and I want to see Mary."

"Hannah." He said her name like he was scolding a dog. "For once, could you —"

"You know," she interrupted him, "it's not my fault you made the plans and told the children *before* talking to me. But if you had, I'd say the same thing: go, have fun. I'll go to Mary's, and we'll meet back at your place before sundown. What time is the concert?"

"Six."

"Oh, well then, I'll meet you back at your place *after* the kids' bedtime on a school night."

"There's no need for that tone. They'll be fine. Laura can take them to school an hour or so late if need be."

"And you'll be fine going without me, okay?"

The phone was silent again.

"It was my last clinical rotation. I only have one more full week of school and then one day of finals the following week. Then I'm through. Yay! I'm even thinking of breaking out the pompoms for this."

"You don't own any pompoms." The frustration in his voice faded into jesting. "But I'll buy you some . . . and maybe a cheerleading outfit to boot."

She laughed. "I'd really like to see Mary before we leave for Hawaii, and making a quick trip this weekend is my only chance."

"Yeah, okay." He sighed. "I figured you'd balk at going."

Which probably explained why he made

so many plans first and then told her. She wondered how often that worked in his favor without her realizing what he'd done.

"Are we good?" she asked.

"As good as we get, I suppose. I'll see you tomorrow night."

"Martin, wait." She couldn't stand the idea of them arguing like this. "I know it seems like I'm being unfair, but just give me this last spur-of-the-moment trip, okay? I'll do better. We'll start everything fresh beginning the night I graduate."

"Seeing her is that important?"

"Yeah, we'll talk about why in a few weeks. It's sort of prewedding planning stuff."

"As in our wedding, the one you haven't said yes to yet?"

"That'd be the one."

He chuckled. "Suddenly I like this conversation. Try saying the good stuff up-front next time."

"Sorry, I'm still new to this argue-as-you-go plan."

"Yeah, we've got a few things to work out."

"But you know we'll work them out, right?"

"Yeah, I know. Bye, sweetheart."

"Make sure Lissa and Kevin wear hats so they don't get an earache, okay?"

"Will do. See you tomorrow night."

"Yes you will. Bye."

The night skies threatened snow as Hannah pulled out of Mary's driveway. Without being asked, Mammi Annie had given them privacy to talk all morning. She had left the Daadi Haus where she, Luke, and Mary resided and had gone to the main house with Mary's mother.

Mary had listened and understood in ways no one else could. Unfortunately, she didn't have much in the way of advice — except to keep it honest between Martin and her and to think in terms of what her decisions would mean over the long haul of life.

Mary and Luke didn't know what they'd do from here on out, but no matter what they decided, it wasn't going to be easy. If Mary conceived often, she'd end up needing a C-section every year or two, possibly causing other health-related issues over the course of years. If they chose to avoid that, Luke would be unable to share the marriage bed with her. Neither would ever consider using birth control.

The electric lights shone bright from Gram's kitchen, tempting Hannah to pull into her driveway and visit for a few minutes. She checked the clock. Five thirty. Hannah had plenty of time to visit and still get home before Martin and the children.

She rapped on Gram's door and waited. The thump of her cane against the floor grew louder. The porch light came on.

With the chain lock in place, Gram opened the door to peer out. "Hannah." She slammed the door, unhooked the chain, and swung the door open wide, motioning Hannah inside. "Why, I've done near wore the phone plain out picking it up to call you. I asked God to give me a sign if I was to tell you, and here you are."

"Tell me what?"

Gram hesitated, looking like she might cry. "Dorcas has been sick for some time, and maybe because of this extra stress and maybe not, she's in the hospital, not doing well at all. They can't get her heartbeat regular, and she's in and out of consciousness." Gram clutched her chest.

"Gram, let's get you to a chair." Hannah supported Gram by her free arm and helped her to the couch.

After sitting, she shooed Hannah back. "I'm fine. My chest aches when I get all nervous, has since I was a young woman. Don't worry none about me."

"Gram." Hannah sat on the edge of the couch beside her. "What's wrong with Dorcas?"

471

"Lyme disease. She had it nearly three years without being diagnosed."

"Why would you want to call me about Dorcas being sick? I know nothing as a nursing student that could help her."

Gram placed her knobby hand over Hannah's and patted it. "I wasn't going to call about Dorcas." She sighed. "I thought I was doing the right thing when I stopped letting you and Paul use my mailbox to write each other."

A little concerned as to why Gram's conversation was rambling all over the place, Hannah decided she would stay awhile. "It's okay, Gram. You were doing what you thought was right. I'll not put blame on anyone for that."

"But what Dorcas has done to Paul by pretending to be his friend when she didn't tell him about your calls . . ."

Hannah's breath caught. "He knows?"

Gram's eyes misted. "I can't stand watching what's happening with Paul, and I don't know how much more he can take."

"Paul's tough. I see a power and strength in his eyes that can't be damaged even by what Dorcas has done."

Gram squeezed the handle of her cane. "Right now that power and strength Paul has is dead set against Dorcas. Go, look him in the eye, and see if Dorcas's deceit isn't eating him into bitterness. He doesn't care if she dies, and she just might."

"She's that bad?"

Gram nodded.

"I . . . I didn't know Lyme disease could do that, but I'm not sure I can help anybody deal with forgiveness."

"He'll listen to you . . . Please, Hannah."

She knew so little about forgiveness it scared her. Every time she thought she had it covered, anger seemed to blindside her. She checked her watch. Almost six o'clock. If she went an hour out of the way to see Paul, she might not arrive at the house before Martin and the children. Guilt nibbled at her. Even if she was able to get there before him, she wouldn't like Martin going to see an old girlfriend like this.

But part of this mess was her fault. She knew the same girl took both messages she left for Paul. She could've tried to reach him again or called Gram and left a message with her, but she didn't. And he needed to know and understand why.

"Do you have his street address?"

Gram wrote the directions to Paul's place, and Hannah went to her car. Concern for Paul weighed on her as she drove mile after mile. Snow flurries swirled through the dark skies. An hour after leaving Owl's Perch, she was pulling into the parking lot of his apartment. She stopped at the curb of what she hoped was Paul's building. Once at the door that matched the info Gram gave her, she heard the muffled voices of several men. She knocked.

"Enter," a male voice boomed.

She knocked again.

"Yeah, yeah, yeah, come in already!"

Whoever said the words, it wasn't Paul. She eased the door open and stepped inside, seeing no one.

"Just leave the pizza on the counter and take the money."

In spite of the one voice that was doing all the talking, in the background the voices of several men vibrated the room — Paul's being one of them. She closed the door and walked in that direction. He was at a table with three other guys, playing cards.

He slapped a card faceup on the table. "If you can't win . . ."

"You lose." Two men repeated the words loudly, making the third guy throw his cards onto the table. A round of laughter pealed from all of them.

Gram was mistaken. Paul was fine, and he looked good too, tilted back on two legs of his chair, smiling.

"Excuse me."

Paul jolted, losing his balance. He jumped to his feet as the chair fell over backward. The men broke into laughter. "Man, Waddell, with half the decent single women chasing you, one would think you wouldn't lose it over one saying 'excuse me.' " A man with jet-black hair and a five o'clock shadow spoke the words and then turned to look at her. "Then again . . ." He slapped a card onto the table, staring at her.

Paul's eyes didn't move from her. The hardwood floor was covered in chunks of mud and debris. Every one of the men still had on the messy boots.

Bachelors all of them. Probably. Hannah suppressed a smile.

The guy with the five o'clock shadow looked from Paul to Hannah, while the other two kept talking. "Whoa, idiots."

Movement stopped.

The guy moved toward her. "I'm Marcus King."

She knew his name well. He'd been best friends with Paul since they were kids and one of Paul's college roommates. She guessed the other two were Ryan and Taylor.

"I'm Hannah."

He smiled, shaking her hand as if he

already knew her and liked her. "It's good to finally meet you." He turned back to the table. "Guys, we're leaving. Now."

The doorbell rang.

"That'd be the pizza." Marcus went to the door.

Each of the other two men dipped his head as a silent hello while heading for the door. Shock faded from Paul's face. He picked up his chair and ran his hands through his disheveled hair.

"Hey, Paul," Marcus called, stepping back into view. He held up one of three pizza boxes. "I'll leave this one on the counter."

Marcus closed the front door behind him, and the only sounds left were the ticking of a clock and the bubbling of water. Hannah looked around, spotting the source of the trickling sound. An aquarium, every bit as large as Martin's fifty-something-inch, HD, flat-screen TV. Colorful, graceful fish swam about, giving the whole room a peaceful feel. Five feet away, a recliner with a reading lamp behind it faced the tank. Lines of twine ran a foot above her, running from one end of the room to the other, with dozens of Christmas cards straddling the cords.

She closed her eyes, feeling the . . . quiet of the Plain traditions. No television, gaming stations, or blasting stereos. No Christmas trees or lights or fancy decorations. Opening her eyes, she saw a stack of Christmas presents in the corner, some already wrapped, some not. Christmas celebration was certainly looked forward to, but keeping life simple all year long was the Plain way.

Not better. Not worse. Just one of the many ways believers honored God. A way she understood and respected, even if it wasn't what she had ended up choosing.

She went closer to the aquarium, trying to think of something to say to break the sudden awkwardness. "I like your place."

He came up behind her. "It serves its purpose."

She shifted, looking straight at him, and suddenly the current between them seemed as powerful and tumultuous as the Susquehanna during the spring thaw. Feeling naive for not realizing the upheaval coming here would cause her, she cleared her throat and moved to the strings of cards. "You must have a lot of friends."

"I have a lot of people who send Christmas cards. Whether they're friends or not, there's no real way to know, is there?"

The taint in his voice was distressing. Unable to face him, she continued looking at the cards.

"Hannah." Paul's voice was barely above a whisper.

She turned.

His eyes searched hers, clearly looking for answers. "What are you doing here?"

"I heard about . . . Well, Dorcas was wrong, and you have every right to be angry."

"Thanks, I'll keep that in mind."

His tone held the quiet anger of a man lied to by too many women, and she hated herself for her part in it.

"Gram said . . ." She ran her fingers through fallen wisps of hair, trying to push them back into place. "Here's the thing, Paul. I'm the one who chose to only call twice. I could've called again and made sure to leave a message with Gram. But like I told you before, I really didn't believe you wanted me, and even if you'd told me otherwise, I never would have believed you. Never. I would've spent the rest of my life feeling like a charity case, and as badly as I wanted you to make everything better, I knew my lack of self-esteem would grow to rock-hard self-hatred if I didn't start fresh. Those things aren't Dorcas's fault."

"So you're here to set me straight so Dorcas doesn't pay any penalty for her wrong?"

"I'm here because we're friends, because no one understands the frustration, the deep-seated anger, the complications of all we've been through more than we do. Your other friends will try to get it. Martin tries, Dr. Lehman tries, Zabeth tried." She shook her head and sighed. "I get it, Paul, and I guess I thought maybe you needed that."

"What I needed passed me by long ago. The thanks for that go to Dorcas. I know that our Plain ways say we have to forgive immediately, right then, but she carried out her deceit for years. I may pay the price forever for what she's done. Do you honestly think I'm wrong in this?"

The heaviness of his words settled on her like a cloak, and she took a seat on the couch, unable to respond for a while. "Is it possible faith in God over our future must outweigh our feelings in the things of today? And maybe there are lots of types of forgiveness just like there are lots of kinds of love."

"There is no way to forgive what she's done. None. She used her free will to remove mine in a sneaky, underhanded way. Don't talk to me about reaching out to offer her *any* type of forgiveness. Even if you needed that time in Ohio, all of it, I had the right to receive your calls — a God-given right. Of course you were feeling unworthy and having second thoughts after you made those calls, but you reached out. I'll bet you had a ton of conflicting emotions and plans, right?"

Remembering one of her reasons for changing her last name, she nodded. "Yes." She knew she would always hope he'd come looking for her if she kept her last name. Oh, she'd also wanted to keep Daed from finding her, but more than that, she needed to free herself of always hoping Paul might show up for her one day.

"My Daed wants forgiveness."

Paul's stiff-legged stance slowly relaxed, and he sat on the edge of his recliner near her. The arm of her couch and the arm of his chair sat at a right angle, mere inches apart.

"He asked me for it the night we all went to the hospital for Mary. I just stood there, Martin's hand on my back, nudging me to say what should be said. And I couldn't. I didn't come here because I think I have answers to offer. I guess there are times when it's easier to forgive strangers than our own."

Paul placed his forearms on his legs, leaning in.

The aroma of fresh outdoors clung to him, reminding her of when she used to consider the scent of him equal to what integrity would smell like if it carried a fragrance, and in spite of herself, she took a deep breath. "I can't figure out how to connect with forgiveness sometimes. I understand that when we forgive, we're saying what was done to us is not more powerful than God's ability to redeem us from it, and sometimes I'm able, and sometimes I just wish no one asked, no one made me face what's inside."

With his elbows on his knees, Paul cupped his hands together and rested his chin on them. "I hate . . . this."

"I find it comforting that God hates things too."

"Yeah, I guess He does." He paused, and they remained silent for over a minute before he placed one hand over hers. "She doesn't deserve forgiveness."

Hannah nodded. "Nevertheless."

He rubbed his hand back and forth over hers, and she wished the pull to him would give her a break.

"My fiancée once wrote a letter to me, and I have every word memorized. It got me through . . . a lot. One of my favorite parts reads, 'Someone did not place his desires under God's authority — nevertheless, God's power over my life is stronger than that event.' " He paused, gently holding her hands in his. "Come back to me, Hannah."

Tears filled her eyes. "You know I can't."

His eyes bored into her, and she was sure he knew much more about her heart than he should.

She slid her hands from his and wiped tears from her cheeks. "He's a good man, and we have Kevin and Lissa."

Paul stood, rubbing the back of his neck while he walked to the far side of the room. He turned. "So that settles it?"

"Yes."

After holding her gaze, Paul gave one nod of his head. "Dorcas is in a hospital less than ten miles from here. I'll go see her tonight. But I will not let her back in my life. She's proven who she is."

"I'm not sure, but I don't think forgiveness means you have to open your life up to them again."

"Maybe you should rethink taking care of things with your dad as soon as you can."

Fighting to stay composed, she stood. "Okay." She glanced at her watch. "I . . . I need to go."

Paul walked her out to her car and opened the door. "You drive safe and take care of yourself."

"I will." Trembling, she turned the key, waved, and left the parking lot, unable to look back. She began the drive back to Ohio, hoping the pain would ease.

CHAPTER 35

Matthew slid the hand plane across what would eventually be the dash of a buggy, shaving off enough wood to make it fit in its designated spot. Across the room Luke pulled, tucked, and fitted the last corner of black leather over the frame of a buggy's bench seat.

At the sound of the clanging bell, he glanced out the window. Kathryn stood on the front porch of his home, sliding the striker onto the triangle dinner bell. With only one shop built and no room designed just for painting, the windows had to stay open for cross ventilation. December's freezing temperatures had forced Kathryn to move into a makeshift office inside his home.

Matthew laid the plane and dashboard on the workbench and removed his tool belt. He stepped outside for a moment, catching Kathryn's eye and motioning for her to come to the shop.

Luke tapped the nail in place before looking up. "I think I'll go home for lunch today."

"You do that." Matthew headed out the side door to the spot where he and Kathryn met when they wanted a minute of privacy.

She'd returned six weeks ago, and they'd been secretly going places together since. Grief over the loss of his brother still clung to him, but Kathryn's presence brought him a deep, satisfying peace with life. He did, however, wish he knew a little better what her feelings were toward him. They had fun, no doubt. Talked often and about everything. Laughed and played even during work-hours. For him, the bond grew deeper each day. But for her? He wasn't sure.

The deal with the bishop hadn't rattled her, even though he was checking up on Matthew regularly. The more he knew her, the more he enjoyed life. He believed with Elle he *could* have enjoyed life if . . . if she were different, if she had a clue about keeping her word, if she understood any aspect of balancing desires with reality.

She walked toward him and stopped in the yard for a moment to scoop up a mewling kitten. With Kathryn, he *did* enjoy life, even in the midst of grief, because of who she was and what she brought with her naturally as she went throughout her day.

They came toe to toe. Matthew's eyes met hers as he scratched the kitten's head. "How's it goin'?"

She snuggled the kitten deeper in her arms. "It's even colder out here than in the shop, you know?"

He laughed. "Didn't we discuss this once?"

"I'm allowed in the house, but the kitten isn't."

Matthew mocked a sigh. "Fine. Put the cat's bed near the wood stove in the shop, but if she gets stepped on . . ."

Kathryn giggled. "She won't. She'll stay right up under the bench until she's old enough to climb up high on the rafters." She stroked the kitten. "Oh, I forgot to tell you that I got a letter from my Daed yesterday, and I'm expected to spend Christmas Eve and Day there."

"I guess there's no excuse we could give that would allow me to show up at your house on Christmas without people realizing what was going on." He'd long ago adjusted to not having someone special near him on a holiday, so although this was disappointing, being alone for only a day or two was a nice change.

He tugged on one string of her prayer Kapp. "I guess it's reasonable enough since we did get Thanksgiving together . . . in a house full of umpteen relatives. Can you be back the day after Christmas? I'll take off."

Her eyes danced. "Oh." She stretched out the word, letting him know she had ideas about that. "With last weekend's snow, if we get another layer in the next two and a half weeks, it'll be perfect for sledding."

Aching to kiss her, Matthew continued playing with the string of her Kapp. "I could enjoy sledding."

"Maybe we could race."

"Two sleds instead of sharing one? Not what I had in mind."

She shook her finger at him, teasing before her expression changed. "The bishop came by earlier."

"Yeah, he came into the shop and spoke with me before he left. Didn't ask too many questions though. Maybe he's decided to give me a break."

She smiled, petting the kitten. "Soon you'll be in his good graces again, then I can quit being just hired help. Ya?"

"Does playing the part of just employee make you uncomfortable?"

She leaned her back against the outer wall of the shop. "Nah, I'm enjoying it. A bit of sneaking around is good for the soul."

"Is it now? Your preacher at home must teach somethin' awful different from mine."

Standing up straight, Kathryn chuckled. "I better go."

Matthew placed his hand on the wall in front of her, stopping her from leaving. She dipped her chin, scratching the kitten's head. "You know how I feel about . . ."

She let the sentence drop, but he knew the rest of her thought. She'd made herself clear on this subject before their first outing. She was convinced every relationship should be a no-handholding deal unless the couple intended to marry.

He moved in closer. "I do."

She lowered her eyes, and the set of her stare said she was thinking. When she raised her head, he was sure he saw a hint of invitation inside the sparkle.

"Katie, ya know" — Matthew tried to sound casual — "there's nothing wrong with giving me an early Christmas present."

She pursed her lips, mocking frustration as she stared into his eyes. "Are you taking advantage of my pleasure in this secret-keeping thing, Matthew Esh?"

"Trying to, yes."

With an adorable smile in place, she shook her head and went to step around him. He moved directly in front of her. Since he was convinced she was the one for him, all this courting and no kissing was simply too much, but until today she'd not given any signal that he should press the matter. She stopped, seemingly waiting on him to step aside. He leaned in, and she backed up.

"I don't intend to be an Amish house-wife."

Matthew's heart skipped. "You don't? Do you want to be an Amish husband instead?"

She laughed. "I'm trying to be serious."

"Then try makin' sense."

"I don't want to give up working beside you in order to have your babies."

"Mmm." Matthew nodded. He had the sneaking suspicion that Kathryn Glick was ready for the first kiss of her life. "You gonna set up baby beds and playpens in the shops?"

"And under the trees in warm weather. Near the garden during planting. And . . ."

Matthew wrapped the strings to her prayer Kapp around his fingers. "Your need for plannin' and organizin' is steppin' all over my spontaneous moment."

"If you want a housewife, I need to know now. That's not who I am, but your Mamm would be willing to help and love every minute of it."

"Glad you have it all planned out," Matthew whispered. "I got no objections to your plans." He mumbled the words and brushed his lips across hers.

Taking several steps back, she bumped against the wall, staring at him. Reeling from the connection, Matthew drew a breath. She'd just talked about marrying him without his even asking. He was fully satisfied in this moment.

She ran her fingers over her lips before pouting. "Is that all the present I get to give?"

Taking his cue, he wrapped his arms around her. "I didn't want to be greedy."

"I could tolerate a little selfishness now and then."

"That's good to know." He kissed her, feeling confident that nothing would ever come between them.

Mamm called their names, and Kathryn slowly pulled away.

Matthew put a few inches between them, noticing the cat was still sleeping undisturbed in the crook of her arm.

Kathryn smiled up at him. "I like this secret-keeping thing."

"Not too much, I hope. I want to tell everyone when the dust settles with the bishop."

She squared her shoulders, mocking smugness. "Oh, we'll tell *everyone,* all right."

It was her first hint that she wanted Elle to know. He didn't blame her.

Kathryn passed him the kitten and slipped out from between him and the wall. "But until then" — she pointed for him to stay — "we'll enjoy this little mandate of yours."

Enjoy it? It was something he insisted on, and now she was making the boundaries of his decision not only comfortable, but fun.

"Put her somewhere cozy, count to forty, and then come inside, okay?"

She started to walk away, and he pulled her back to him, kissing her again. She wiggled free, her laughter filling the air as she took off running, turning twice to glance back at him, a flirtatious smile across her face.

So Kathryn had a romantic side to her well-rounded way of dealing with life. He should have figured on that. He could still feel her lips on his. Catching one of her glances, he winked, realizing anew that everything he'd ever wanted was right here on the land that'd belonged to his great-grandfather and with a woman whose roots were as true to the Old Ways as his were.

CHAPTER 36

Hannah unlocked the cabin door and shoved it open. The December cold inside Zabeth's cabin was as unyielding as the loneliness inside her. Silvery moonbeams stretched across the floor, and she moved to the piano without turning on the light. She plunked a few keys. It needed tuning, but she remembered the wonderful songs Zabeth played while Hannah sat beside her, watching.

As a baptized member of the Amish faith, Zabeth had broken ties with every relative to pursue her love of music. Martin carried that kind of passion for music. Hannah enjoyed it, but it didn't reside in her like it did in them.

She walked to the window and looked out back. It was there on the bench she'd first met Martin.

Inside this cabin they formed a friendship and fell in love.

If he'd just come to the cabin . . .

But he wouldn't. He wanted to sell it. Worse, she'd given in.

Everything between them began to change once this was no longer their haven. This is who she was, and he'd come here over and over again and embraced that part of her.

One lone light bulb hung from the ceiling. She went to the light switch and flipped it on and then off and then on. It was the first place she lived that had electricity . . . and freedom. Zabeth had supported her every dream, and she'd loved and accepted everything about Hannah.

Still wearing her coat, Hannah flicked the light off and lay on the couch. She needed to leave in just a minute. It was Tuesday, her night off, and Martin was expecting her.

His words beckoned to her — *"Come on, phone girl, make a choice for us."*

She had chosen. The decision was made.

Her future was with him.

After the children were in bed Sunday night, she'd told Martin about seeing Paul earlier that evening. The anger he'd expressed still made her shudder. She rushed through her explanation for going to Owl's Perch — that she needed to talk to Mary because Dr. Lehman had said Hannah might be able to have children. Anger drained from his face, and the conversation shifted. By the time she went to the cottage, she'd agreed to his having a vasectomy.

Lying on her back staring at the ceiling, warm tears trickled down the sides of her face, and she closed her eyes.

Her phone rang, and she jerked. Fishing it out of her coat pocket, she sat up. "Hi."

"Hey, where are you?"

Hannah blinked. "I . . . I must have fallen asleep."

"You're at the clinic then, and someone is in labor? I thought you were off tonight."

"I am. I . . . I'm at the cabin."

Silence.

It seemed to define their relationship more than anything else of late.

"I'm leaving right now."

"It's ten thirty, and you're there while I'm here waiting. Didn't you hear your phone ring half a dozen times tonight?"

"This is the first time it's rung."

"It is so time for you to get a new phone."

"I just wanted to see the place, Martin. You used to like it, remember?"

"You used to live there, and what I liked about it was you."

He'd never understand why she didn't fully appreciate his guiding her toward change for the better. And she'd never

494

understand why he couldn't enjoy and appreciate the simplicity of a single light bulb hanging from a ceiling or the pleasure of warm soil under her bare feet as she tended her garden.

But he'd taught her how to navigate the Englischer world. They'd laughed and bonded and fallen in love. He'd healed her broken heart and made it possible for her to slip into a new life. And she loved him. They'd get through this transition. He was right; the cabin needed to be sold, and she needed to move on.

"I'm leaving right now."

She went to her car, barely paying attention to the roads as she drove to Martin's. It was after eleven when she pulled into his driveway. Carrying an armload of books and dry cleaning, Hannah pushed her hip against the car door, closing it. Streams of yellow gold light shone through the huge arched window of the main house onto the sparse layer of snow across the backyard. Martin stood at the second-story window, looking down.

The constant ache that'd taken up residence inside her increased. If they could just talk about what was happening to them, maybe they'd find their way back to each other again.

They'd tried. Both of them.

He'd told her that she needed to finish letting go of the Plain life. They'd sell the cabin, but she could take the on-call hours Dr. Lehman offered. Martin would have a vasectomy, but she could continue with her nursing school.

The concessions he wanted were great.

With the eyes of two young children staring at her even in her sleep, she would become whatever he needed her to be. If she thought about it the right way, the compromises were rational. He was asking her to adjust better to the Englischer life. He wasn't wrong in wanting that.

In spite of her full arms, she managed a wave. Martin raised his hand slowly, returning the gesture. Hoping desperately that the trip to Hawaii would be all they needed it to be, she went to the cottage.

If she could just get Paul out of her mind, many of their other issues would fall to the wayside. Wouldn't they? Balancing all the stuff in her arms, she struggled to open the unlocked door to her cottage. Without flipping on a light, she walked through the dark room and plunked everything onto the small, round kitchen table.

Her cell phone rang, and she dug through her coat pocket to locate it. "Hi."

"Hey, phone girl." Martin sounded sleepy or maybe just tired.

"Hey, yourself." She wrestled to find words and not to sound as empty as she felt. "How was your day?"

"Usual. Yours?"

"Normal stuff, except we delivered a set of twins. The Fishers now have two sets of twins in their brood of nine children."

"Fascinating I'm sure. Can you imagine what the day is like for those parents?"

She flicked on a light. "How one feels about that depends on what their goals in life are." Taking her dry-cleaned uniform with her, she walked into the bedroom and hung it in the closet before returning to the kitchen.

"Yeah, I guess so. I've been meaning to ask about Friday night's graduation. Did you need to do something about a cap and gown?"

Spotting a large envelope on the table under the books she'd piled there, she slid it free. "No, all I need is my nurse's uniform. I actually sent it to the dry cleaner so it'd look its best. I picked it up earlier today."

It was addressed to Hannah Lapp Lawson, but it had no return address. It must have come in the mail today and Laura brought it to the cottage and left it on the table. Maybe her Daed had responded to the letter she sent him. It'd been a very short note — *Dear Daed, all is forgiven. I love you, Hannah.*

It'd taken her hours to write those simple words, but by the time she wrote them, she meant every one. She opened the envelope and shook the contents onto the table. A letter on green stationery and one very thick white envelope slid onto the table. She flipped the white envelope over and stopped cold.

Her first name was written across it in Paul's handwriting.

"Helloooooo?" Martin called.

"I . . . I need to tend to some things. How about if we talk tomorrow?"

Martin said something she didn't really hear before she said good-bye and disconnected the call.

She unfolded the green stationery first and glanced to the end.

From Dorcas?

She returned to the top of the page and began reading.

Hannah,
You cannot imagine how much I do not want to write this letter. I've wished you weren't in Paul's life since the day I

498

learned of you. I wanted Paul to feel toward me the things he wrote in this letter to you. But if love never fails, it seems self-interest is doomed to fail — and now I hold less of his heart than I thought possible.

When you left, he debated over what to do and decided to give you time to return on your own. Whenever he wavered in that decision, I encouraged him to stay the course. He waited for you. And I never told him you called. He waited until he saw you in Ohio with a man he thought to be your husband. And a week later you returned, and he began falling for you again. Perhaps you've truly moved on and I'm only making things worse, but I felt I had to make sure you knew everything, which is what I should have done for both of you to begin with.

Please forgive me,
Dorcas

With temptation to read his letter pounding, she felt guilt close in around her. Reading Paul's letter would do nothing but cause her mayhem. In the tumultuous quiet, an image of Kevin and Lissa filled her, and she was absolutely confident what had to be done. She put Dorcas's letter with Paul's and slid them back into the larger envelope. With her voice screaming inside her, she ignored the desire to read his letter and walked to the trash can. But her fingers wouldn't let it go.

He'd written to her in love and waited more than two years for her to return. Was she really going to throw all the sincerity he'd poured onto paper into the garbage?

"God, help me."

But He didn't. She felt no added strength to release the letter and no freedom to read it. Paul's words from two weeks ago rang inside her head: *Come on, Hannah. How great can your relationship with Martin be if . . .*

Her need to protect herself from Paul wasn't just about Martin and her. It was about Kevin and Lissa. She wouldn't abandon them. Couldn't. Their dad had, and a few months later their mother had too. Hannah wouldn't add to that rejection. Besides, Martin wasn't likely even to have Kevin and Lissa if she hadn't pushed and prodded him. She couldn't ever turn her back on any of them and still be able to find any part of herself. Dropping the letter into the trash can, she felt her chest constrict. Ignoring the feeling, she went into the bedroom. The mirror that hung on the back of the door caught her eye, and she gazed at herself. The only thing she'd ever wanted was a life with Paul Waddell. That's all. Tears stung her eyes, and without changing clothes, she flicked off the light and crawled into bed.

All Dorcas had managed to do was make the hurt worse. Willing herself to sleep, Hannah closed her eyes. Hours passed, and her desire to read the letter only grew. The temptation to feel some part of what she would have felt then embarrassed her. Disgusted with herself, she eased her legs over the side of the bed and sat up.

She could tear it up or burn it, but she figured that would only cause the longing to mutate into a regret she could never undo. She swallowed hard. This was ridiculous. There was no way she could ignore the letter. If it lay in the trash for a thousand years, she'd still know he'd written it and waited for her.

Wasn't her fear of facing the truth most of what had destroyed them to begin with?

She'd feared what he'd think of her if he learned she'd been raped and later was pregnant, so she tried to hide both. She'd feared watching him fall in love with someone else and have children with her, so she ran. She'd feared if she stood before him vulnerable, he'd reach out to her in pity, so she didn't give him the chance. She'd feared if they worked through everything else, she'd tear him from his family, and his life would never be healed again.

Darkness cloaked the room, and she longed for rays of the new day to come, but there were still two hours of nighttime ahead. Sick of how she'd let fear rule her, she went to the kitchen, flicked on the light, and moved to the trash can. She lifted the envelope from the trash bag, noticing it was wet from sharing space with a used coffee filter. She pulled the white envelope from the manila one. It was slightly damp, and the color of the wet coffee grounds had seeped through. Dorcas had kept it pristine for more than three years, but Hannah had already managed to stain it.

Feeling as if she messed up everything she touched, she sat down, slid the letter out, and opened it.

Dear Hannah,
I've waited so long to get to share how I really feel. My heart is so full now that you've agreed to be my wife. Tonight my family had a party, and I could only dream of having you by my side. Sharing your love and laughter is my deepest

desire, and I can't wait for the many gatherings of friends and family in the future when we can be together as man and wife.

I know you are worried about your family and what will happen, but I'm convinced we can work through any struggle and overcome anything or anyone that would separate us. I will do everything I can to win them over.

There are so many unique parts to you, my Lion-heart. I know you can't see it and don't even want me saying it, but I realized it the first day I saw you at Gram's, tending to all the meals for the workers. Just a thought of you brings back a dozen memories of who you are and who we are together. And I don't want you to bury your gifts and talents to be only a helpmate to me. My dream is that we both aim to be exactly who God called us to be. I don't think He stocked you with talents so they would rust or get buried while you play a dutiful wife.

We can't know what life will hold, but I have no preset desires of who I want us to be or what I want, except I want you, Lion-heart, just you, wherever that may lead us.

Unable to read any further through her tears, she lowered the letter and folded it.

Reading it was a mistake. Knowing he'd waited for her and was still in love with her was too much. Now she'd hear his voice inside her all the rest of her days.

She'd fought so hard to let him go because of reasons that now were as lifeless as last year's garden. Nauseous and tired, she went to take a shower.

It was just as over today as it was six months or two years ago, only now her heart was too vested in Paul to be fair to Martin, and she had no idea how to untie her heart from Paul's. She soaked under a hot shower until it started running cool. Longing pulled at her, and there was no ignoring it.

She dried off and slid into her thick cotton bathrobe.

The feelings tore at her. How had Paul handled waiting for her all that time?

The sun was rising, dispelling the darkness. Funny how the smallest light could dispel darkness, but light was never dismissed that easily.

She went into the kitchen and fixed a pot of coffee.

There was a tap at her front door. Closing her eyes for a moment, she drew a deep breath and hoped Martin didn't notice how stressed she was. It wasn't like him to stop in before work.

She opened the door and stepped back. "Hi."

He came inside and closed the door. "I saw the light on."

"Care for some coffee?" She lifted the decanter.

"No thanks."

He sounded different, milder and not agitated at all.

Pouring herself another cup, she tried not to respond to the stare she could feel coming from him. "What's on your agenda for today?"

"The usual. Yours?"

Feeling tears sting, she took a seat, staying focused on the counter, the mug, anything but looking at him. "Not as much to do with school over. I thought about going shopping for clothes for the trip. Maybe begin packing for Lissa and Kevin."

He pulled out a chair and sat. "Before I met your Daed and heard what he had to say, I would have told you to wash your hands of them and *never* look back."

She plunked sugar into her cup and watched the black liquid swirl as she stirred it. "But we both know that somewhere between being done wrong and *never*, people change."

The hum of the furnace and the various soft noises of the electric coffeepot hung in the air, but neither Martin nor she spoke for more than five minutes.

He finally reached across the table and took her hand in his. "Hannah, sweetheart, could you look at me, please?"

She slowly looked up, surprised not to see anger in his eyes.

Martin let out a long, slow breath. "There she is. That's the girl I used to see when we first met, only then she was in love with *what's his name.*" Martin kissed the back of her hand. "He didn't turn his back on you like you thought, did he?"

Hannah swallowed and shook her head. "How . . ." She choked back a sob and couldn't finish her sentence.

"When Mary was in labor and you were trying to find Paul, you said something to Dorcas about the times you'd called and she hadn't told him." Martin rubbed her hand gently. "When did you find out?"

"The second time I went back." Tears worked their way free. "I've not handled this with Paul right. I'm so sorry."

"I promised Zabeth I'd let you go, help you go, if you ever seemed interested in returning to your community — unless we

506

were married by then." Martin shook his head. "I know you love me, and I know you don't want to leave Kevin and Lissa, but the problems go deep into who we are. We want to be right for each other." He cursed softly. "We tried to be and almost convinced ourselves we could do it, but I don't think we can. Not in all the ways that make a marriage good most of the time."

Through blurry vision she watched him.

"I want someone who wants me, phone girl. I deserve that, and Zabeth would want — no, she'd demand that for me too, just as she'd demand it for you. I haven't waited this long to settle for someone who is in love with me and someone else at the same time. You don't even love anything about my lifestyle — not my house, my hobbies, or my dreams for the future."

"But Kevin and Lissa — they are our dreams and future too. They need us. Please, Martin."

He held up his hand, trying to make her hush.

Hannah searched his face. "They need both of us. I'll try hard —"

He smacked the tabletop, stopping her midsentence. "No more, Hannah. The decision is made." His booming voice made the room vibrate. He closed his eyes and sucked in a ragged breath. "Do you hear yourself? Everything about staying with me is based on Kevin and Lissa!"

Her hands were shaking as he spoke a truth she didn't want him to know.

"You're twenty years old, and they aren't yours. You do know Faye could return, right? I won't give them to her unless she spends time here and goes through drug testing to prove herself, but I will make room for her in their lives and on my property."

Hannah withdrew her hands, placing her palms over her moist eyes.

Martin tugged at her wrist, waiting on her to look at him again. "Could you just think about something for a minute? If you stayed because of Kevin and Lissa, you'd be saying you don't believe God can provide anyone else for them. Or for me." Martin gave a confident smile. "Trust me, there are other women out there who would love to step into your shoes. Some of them are even worth having."

"This can't be happening."

"I always knew there was a chance I'd lose you to the Plain ways and maybe even to what's his name. The moment you got that call from Sarah . . . from home, I think I knew I had begun to lose you. I just didn't want to admit it."

A sob broke from her, and she covered her face.

"Look, we'll do graduation with Kevin and Lissa, and afterward we'll do a going-away party with the band so the kids get closure. You can invite . . ."

He let the sentence trail. She didn't have any friends, not in Ohio. She had Dr. Lehman, maybe the Plain women from the Tuesday quiltings, but they'd never come here for a party. She only had Martin, Kevin, and Lissa. All the people who kept Martin's home a buzz of activity were his friends, ones she never managed to truly connect to. Maybe if she'd tried harder . . .

"I'll transfer your ticket to Hawaii into Laura's name, and we'll explain to the kids that you've decided to move home. I don't want to wait until after Christmas. Between school, work, and returning to Owl's Perch, they've adjusted to you being gone a lot already. The trip to Hawaii will be a good transition time for them." His speech was slow and methodical, as if he'd memorized what he'd say and the tone he'd keep while saying it, but the hurt and anger behind his well-behaved exterior was deep.

Breathing seemed almost impossible as she fought against the tears. In spite of crying, she lowered her hands and looked him in the face. "I'm so, so sorry. This is all my fault."

"Your fault?"

"I pushed you to stop dating others and date me."

"Get real, Hannah. I've never been pushed by any girl into anything I didn't want to begin with. And that includes you."

His words came out as arrogant and condescending as the first time they'd met, and he must have realized it, because he sighed, and then his countenance became more gentle.

"You've changed me, Hannah. Without you, Kevin and Lissa would be in foster care, and I'd be a scrooge in the making, torn between wanting my own way and feeling guilty for abandoning the two most precious things I could imagine. You were here for Zabeth when I was so overwhelmed I was beginning to hate life."

"You never told me that."

He took her hand and turned it palm up. "My heart landed right here because you earned it, but maybe we tried to turn the love we have for each other into something it wasn't supposed to be. As just a friend and the niece of Zabeth — that's a relationship we could've made work for a lifetime. I want someone who can't live without music. Someone who takes pleasure in the same things I do, including my kind of church, the band, friends, movies, fine restaurants, vacations, and swimming, and golfing —"

She held her hand up to stop him. "I get the idea. Thanks."

"We tried, phone girl. We really did. But I don't like who I'd turned into lately in order to try to hold on to you. I didn't sleep last night, trying to think this through. You don't look like you slept much either."

She shook her head.

He stood. "I need to go."

She gazed into his eyes, clueless how to express all she was feeling. "You're a remarkable man, Martin Palmer."

His green eyes held a hardness she knew he was capable of, but Zabeth would be proud of the gentlemanly way in which he was handling himself.

"We'll finish this out amicably, Hannah. I promise." And with that he left.

She went to the door and closed it, then slumped against the frame and sobbed.

CHAPTER 37

The December chill went right through Hannah as she knelt in front of Lissa and Kevin. Since this was the meeting place for everyone who was going to Hawaii, Martin's driveway was a bustle of activity as luggage was moved into the vehicles that would caravan to Cleveland. Christmas was in three days, and the whole gang would be on the island before bedtime tonight by Hawaii's time zone.

Hannah buttoned Lissa's coat. "You have lots of fun and eat fruits and vegetables, okay?" She tugged at Kevin's winter cap, making sure it covered his ears better. "And don't forget to use that digital camera to take photos. Laura said she'll help you e-mail them to me."

They each held a carry-on that Hannah had loaded with things to help keep them busy during the fourteen-hour flight.

Kevin held up the new camera Martin had

given him for the trip. "It's gonna be so much fun! You'll be sorry you let Laura take your ticket and didn't wait to move back home until after the vacation."

"I'll be with my brother and niece over the holidays while you're with your uncle and sister. It just makes sense."

"I get it." Kevin shrugged. "Uncle Martin said you're moving, not leaving. We'll see you some, right?"

She nodded, unsure how much contact Martin would allow. He wasn't willing to discuss it.

Lissa hugged her. "Laura said I can have a meal and a Coke and choose my own snack when we're on the plane."

"Oh that'll be fun." Hannah held the little girl close, memorizing the warmth of her. When Hannah and Martin had explained to them she was moving back home, they'd accepted it with only a few tears. Martin was really good at knowing how to divert the children's attention while they adjusted to new facts in their lives.

He clapped his hands. "Okay, guys, you're in the vehicle with me and three other adults. Go."

They took off running, squealing with laughter. The heavy silence between her and Martin bore the weight of shattered hopes.

Graduation had come and gone. Dr. Lehman and the nurses from the clinic had attended, each carrying a carload of Plain women from the Tuesday quiltings. Laura and the children came. Martin said he needed to work, but they both knew that work had nothing to do with why he hadn't come. Hannah even wondered if he was already dating again. But true to his word, he'd been amicable to the very end.

Since graduation Hannah had logged a lot of work hours, getting the clinic as ready for her departure as she could. Dr. Lehman hadn't come to the going-away party, saying he wanted her to come see him at least once every two months. Whether she did or didn't, he'd come see her every time he went to Lancaster to visit his mother. So they'd made a pact.

Martin pulled his gaze from the van to her. "So, this is it." He paused, looking as if he felt sorry for her. "I'll let Laura help Kevin and Lissa call you whenever they want to, but other than that I could use some distance."

"I understand."

"You're all packed?"

"Almost."

"If you need anything . . ."

"Thank you."

He pulled some papers from his pocket and held them out to her. "The cabin, as well as about thirty thousand dollars, are yours on your twenty-first birthday — a gift from Zabeth that she wanted you to have when the time came. She had a small life-insurance policy, and you were the beneficiary. Just contact the lawyer who's listed."

She eased it from him, wishing this wasn't happening and yet knowing they had no choice. Tears burned her skin, and she tried to swallow the ache in her throat.

He shrugged. "I sold Ol' Gert to the Sawyer family a few days ago. It's going to be a Christmas present for their children. I didn't figure you'd mind."

She shook her head. "That's fine." Except as things dragged on, this felt more like a divorce than a breakup of two people who'd dated for nine months. But she hadn't run out in spite of how painful the last two weeks had been. The adjustment Kevin and Lissa had made during that time was surprising, like she was a sibling going off to college.

"Take care, phone girl." He wrapped his arms around her, the first truly kind gesture he'd made since he'd ended things between them. She broke into tears. "Sh." He kissed the top of her head before taking a step back. "Don't work too hard."

Laura was in the front passenger's seat but facing the back as she spoke to the other adults in the rented van. She acted more like a grandmother than a nanny, and that seemed to fit both Martin's and her needs. Amy Clarke was in the backseat, helping Lissa get buckled in.

After Martin left, Hannah would leave. That's what they'd agreed to, for the children's sake. They'd also agreed she'd keep the ring, because it'd become clear during this lengthy departure time that wearing Kevin's and Lissa's birthstones was a heart connection for them.

The van backed out. Kevin and Lissa were smiling and waving. Hannah put a smile on her face as she waved until they were out of sight. Martin never glanced back. She slowly walked to the cottage. After crying for quite a while, she took a long, hot shower and finished packing. It was past lunchtime when she left her house keys on the table of the cottage and locked the door behind her.

Barely able to see for the tears, she slid behind the wheel. The pain of leaving seemed just as horrid as the pain she'd carried when she'd arrived in Ohio. But in spite of her heartache and guilt, she didn't regret her time with Martin. Still, he was right; he deserved someone to love and enjoy all of who he was and what he had to offer.

The tears eased some, and she began to pray for him. As the hours passed and darkness took over the winter skies, a bit of hope replaced her anguish, and she began to sense that he'd eventually be happier without her than with her. That meant the children would be too.

As peace began to warm her, thoughts of Paul seeped in again. It was too soon to contact him, to even hint at what was going on in her life, so she drove toward Luke's place. There would be time for her and Paul to talk later. He'd waited for her for nearly three years. Surely she could wait a few more weeks to finish giving her relationship with Martin a decent grieving time. No one knew she was coming, but she figured she could stay with Naomi Esh or Luke and Mary until she found a place of her own.

She reached over to the seat next to hers and ran her fingers across the gift-wrapped present for Paul. In spite of her sense of disloyalty toward Martin, she'd reopened Paul's letter before daylight today and read all of it for the first time. Paul's ability to understand and accept her just as she was had washed over her anew as she read the words he'd written so long ago. Afterward, she wrapped the "Past and Future" quilt for him. She wasn't sure when she'd give it to him, but she knew it'd be soon enough — sometime next month, for his birthday this summer? When was soon enough too soon?

The pastures on each side of her were covered by a blanket of snow, and the clear skies had a purple hue under the quarter moon. From the opposite side of the road, a horse and buggy came toward her. As they passed each other, the rhythmic clopping of the horse's hoofs unleashed dozens of emotions within her. Unlike witnessing horses and buggies in Ohio, Hannah felt she was home. The snow glittered like shards of glass under the moon's glow, enveloping her with an odd yet familiar sense that she couldn't define. She pulled her car off the side of the road and got out. White fields spread out before her with barren trees lining the horizon.

"Hannah."

A whisper swooshed across the field with the winter wind, rustling a few dead leaves with it. Eeriness ran over her, reminding her of the whisper that had called her from Owl's Perch years ago. Now it returned? Just as familiar, just as indefinable.

"Kumm raus."

Almost overwhelmed, her legs wobbled.

She knew that voice. Didn't she? Chills ran wild, and she felt so strange. Years ago she couldn't place the voice.

Today she could.

"Oh, Father, was it Paul all along?" Inside her coat pocket, she clutched the letter he'd written to her. She backed against the car for support as epiphanies poured into her. He'd not just come back for *her.* He'd returned willing to marry her and take on the child she carried. Barely able to remain on her feet, she drew cold air into her lungs.

The first time she'd heard the voice to *Kumm raus* — to come out — she'd stood by her infant's grave, yet it came with a multitude of sentiments: hope, longing, freedom . . . and love so deep she'd thought maybe it was God Himself. And part of it had to have been God. He'd certainly stayed with her through her journey, giving her all the things she sensed inside that whisper — hope and a future.

"God?"

Knowing more pieces to the puzzle than ever before, she sensed that leaving to find Zabeth had not been a mistake. And she could never regret knowing Martin — even if dating him should not have been part of their relationship.

Unable to let go of the whisper, she

stayed, but the desire to see Paul grew with every minute. He'd waited so long, so patiently, as if "Kumm raus" didn't mean coming to him — not immediately. If it had been Paul's voice beckoning to her, he'd called her to come out from under her father's rule, her community's gossip, and the brokenness that was heaped upon her. But he'd been willing to wait until she was also free from the pain.

Because she couldn't reach him, she became entangled in new things that kept her in Ohio.

The need to see Paul intensified. Surely if she handled herself right and kept a careful watch over her actions, it wouldn't be dishonorable to go to him, to give him the quilt and let him know she was . . . home.

She got into her car and headed for the clinic. If he wasn't there, she'd go to Luke's. Maybe. She glanced at the clock. It was almost seven. She drew close to the four-way stop near the Better Path. The parking lot was empty except for Paul's car.

She shifted gears, pulling into the parking lot. Through a second-story window of the Better Path, she saw Paul in a room that wasn't his office. He appeared to be reading something in his hand. She flipped open her phone and scrolled to the number she'd logged as Paul's — the number she'd accidentally called four weeks ago.

"Hannah," Paul answered, "what's up?"

She tried to find her voice.

"Hannah?"

"Yeah." She managed a whisper.

"Are you okay?"

"Could you look out the window?"

He walked closer and peered down. The surprise on his face made her smile.

"What are you doing here?"

"I . . . I brought you something."

Through the window he held her gaze for a few seconds. "I'll be right there."

She closed her phone and got out of the car. By the time she'd walked to the passenger's side and lifted the gift from the seat, he was on the front porch, wearing only short sleeves. His gorgeous eyes spoke of love so deep she almost couldn't bear to look. Physical strength radiated from him. She moved to the foot of the steps with the gift.

"Making a quick visit home before flying out, eh?"

That was Paul. Unassuming. Upbeat. And careful in his tone and words to honor the decision she'd given him concerning Martin.

She held the gift toward him, and he lifted

it from her. It was wrapped, but it wasn't inside a box.

He removed the gold wrapping paper easily, letting it fall to the ground. "The 'Past and Future' quilt."

"It seems it came full circle back to me, and now . . ." She choked back the tears.

"Hannah, what's going on?"

She pulled the letter he'd written three years ago out of her coat pocket and held it up to him.

He'd barely looked at it when recognition registered on his face. "Dorcas shouldn't have sent that."

"It was the right thing to do." She slid it back into her pocket. "Paul, I was a part of your past, and I want to always be a part of your future."

"Hannah?"

"I . . . I'm not sure I should have stopped by here. It's too soon."

He stepped closer, and the rush of power she felt from being near him was something she experienced nowhere else.

"Martin and I . . . aren't together anymore."

With the gentle movements that so defined him, Paul caressed her cheek with one hand and held her gaze, saying so many things neither of them could voice — not yet, not for a while. "I'm not going anywhere."

"I . . . I may not be able to have children."

He shifted the blanket to her arms and cradled her face, his hands trembling. "I want you. That's all. Surely you know that by now." He eased his arms around her, holding her tight while resting his head on hers. "You're home," he whispered, his voice hoarse.

Hannah had ached for a moment like this for so long, dreamed of it even before he'd asked her to marry him and oh so long after she thought she'd lost his love completely. With the quilt between them, she wrapped her arms around him.

After long minutes of holding her, he took her by the hand. "I have something I want to show you." They went inside and up the stairs to the room he'd been in when she arrived. Documents were scattered everywhere, and a set of plans were spread out on the table.

Paul held up a finger. "While you look at that and figure out what I'm working on, I need to get something from my office." He stopped at the door and then returned to her. Lifting her face toward his, he studied her. "You're here."

She nodded, choking on fresh tears.

"You're really here."

Tears spilled down her cheeks. He placed his hands on her shoulders, his eyes glistening and a gentle smile covering his face. "I'll be back . . ."

She looked over the papers, chills covering her as she realized what he was up to. He came back into the office with a shirt box and set it to the side.

Had he been expecting her?

He couldn't have, so how did he have a gift for her?

She studied the info spread out in front of her.

"Do you know what you're looking at?"

"Plans for a clinic."

"Not just a clinic. One that will be designed and staffed as an Amish and Plain facility."

Her heart was pounding so hard she could hear it echoing against her eardrums.

Paul pulled out a chair for her. "It'll take a couple of years, but the board has already voted to turn the guesthouse into an Amish clinic. We have few patients who need to stay there, so allocating that building for housing isn't the best use of it. When you returned in September, my eyes began to be opened to the difference a medical facility for the Plain community would make, more so for the local Amish than Mennonite. I'm not sure how we'll staff it with a doctor and all, but we have plenty of time to work on filling each position."

Remembering years back, before Paul or anyone but her parents knew her secret, she'd felt as if she'd become an empty kerosene lamp, the outward part of no use without its fuel. Oh, how she'd longed for Paul to know everything about her and still love her. How she'd desperately needed to find one thing she was good at and hold on to it. And now all those things were hers. Was this really happening?

"I want to get a bachelor's of science degree in nursing. I just need to know all I can in that field and mix it with all we know of being Plain."

"The board will want you to become a member and use your knowledge and influence, if you will."

"Of course I will."

"Then we'll begin raising money. By the time the clinic is ready to open with all the equipment and supplies purchased, staff hired, and licenses acquired, you'll have your degree."

Paul shifted the box he'd brought in, placing it in front of her, but she couldn't move. He lifted the lid off the box. "Remember House of Grace?"

Powerless to answer, she watched as he picked up photos of a little girl.

"We've been her sponsor for nearly three years now. Look." Paul took out a couple of handmade cloth pouches with cross-stitching around the border.

After running her fingers across the fabric in his hand, she reached into the box and pulled out a large stack of drawings on colored paper.

"She creates pictures from the markers, crayons, watercolors, and stacks of paper we send."

"We?" Hannah choked.

Paul sifted through some of the items in the box until he pulled out one beige paper, a letter from Global Servants. It had Paul Waddell and Hannah Lapp listed as the sponsors.

Hannah closed her eyes, trying to absorb it all. He'd not only waited, but he'd remained faithful to the things they'd begun. Speechless, she returned to looking at the girl's handiwork. The young girl had amazing talent for drawing and painting. Absolute giftedness. Hannah laid one aside and looked at another until she came to a card the girl had made. She'd drawn a beautiful picture of a home with yellow light streaming from the windows. It said:

I love you.

A-Yom

"We'll have children, Hannah. Maybe never our own, but this earth isn't lacking for those who need someone to love them."

Hannah stood. "Am I dreaming?"

Paul moved in close, staring into her eyes as if he was unsure too. "I keep thinking the same thing. It may take years of waking to find you near to convince me it's all real." He wound around his fingers the wisps of her curls that had broken free of their confines. "You're here. It's a gift that came with a high price. I'll never forget that."

She couldn't tell him she loved him, not yet, probably not until Martin was past being so angry with her and had moved on. But she didn't have to. He got it. Just as Sarah had said, Paul saw her.

He studied her. "When you said 'too soon,' you meant we can spend time together as friends but nothing too serious for now, right?"

In every way he understood her. "Yes."

"Good. This will be a holiday like no other."

Removing a loaf of bread from the oven, Hannah could feel Paul's eyes on her.

Laughter and voices gently roamed through Gram's kitchen from the living room, where the group played board games. Friday nights seemed to bring a new tradition for Paul and her — dinner and games with friends.

Luke and Mary were here with Amanda. Sarah had come with them. Matthew and Kathryn wandered in an hour ago. Unlike the gatherings with the band, Hannah connected here — even when the guests were Paul's friends whom she barely knew. She glanced his way. With his shoulder resting against the doorframe, he watched her, saying everything she wanted to hear.

Since Hannah had arrived two months ago, she'd fallen so deep for Paul her mind couldn't comprehend it. The first few nights she was back, they'd stayed near the roaring fire here at Gram's, talking until Hannah fell asleep on the couch. More than once she'd awakened to find Paul sitting in a chair, sipping coffee and watching her.

She had hundreds of memories packed inside these past two months. She'd taken and passed her state board exams. But she'd missed the application deadline for entering nursing school this winter, so she and Paul were putting their free time to good use.

In spite of the cold weather, they'd gone

to the beach, and for the first time in her life she saw the ocean. They'd gone sledding with Matthew and Kathryn, spent time with their friends and family, and shared quiet evenings talking. They'd driven to what had once been his college campus and might become hers too. She'd enjoyed the state museum in Harrisburg so much they'd been three times already, and they'd also gone to City Island. They took a trip to Alliance's train depot, her beloved cabin, and Dr. Lehman's clinic. Paul had met all the women from the Tuesday quiltings. The women were beside themselves to learn she'd returned to the Plain sect, even if it wasn't Old Order Amish. They'd spent time in old town Alliance, hoping to find Kendrick, the young man who'd kept her from freezing to death when she'd landed in Ohio nearly three years ago in the dead of winter. She'd been so busy trying to survive and to put the past behind her that she'd given little thought to Kendrick over the years. But Paul wanted to find him, to thank him and to see if there was anything they could do for him.

Each outing caused the gaping hole of their time apart to close a little more, and now it seemed as thin as a hairline fracture. Paul had asked nothing of her emotionally

— not for commitments, or plans, or words of love. But no one read her heart more than Paul, and he had to know she loved him completely. Out of respect for Martin, she'd kept herself in check and not kissed Paul, but her desire to marry him grew by the day.

The first visit to his parents' home started out awkwardly, but clearly she was welcomed by his dad, sister, and brother-in-law. His uncle Samuel came by just to meet her, and he'd more than made up for the hint of standoffishness that Paul's mother, Hazel, gave off. By the end of the evening, his mother was warming up a bit, and Hannah was fairly confident they would eventually become friends on some level. Whatever vibes Hazel gave off, they were friendlier than what Paul was likely to ever receive from her Daed. But Paul and she were together, and aside from the ache harbored in her heart concerning Kevin and Lissa and the regret she held for the hurt she'd caused Martin, no one else's likes or dislikes regarding this relationship mattered.

As amazing and healing as the last two months with Paul had been, she wanted to know how Martin was doing. Kevin and Lissa called her from Laura's or Martin's cell regularly, and she shared in a few minutes of their lives each time. With Laura's help, they e-mailed her photos and called to talk to her about them.

Paul strolled into the kitchen. "What do you think about getting a rescued pup from Sarah after she's done some training and she's ready to put the first ones up for adoption?"

Her cell phone rang, and she pulled it from her dress pocket. The caller ID said it was Martin's phone. "It's Kevin or Lissa."

Paul nodded. "Absolutely. Answer it."

"Hello?"

"Hey, it's me. Got a minute?"

Martin sounded upbeat, and hope that he'd weathered the worst spread throughout her. "Sure. Give me a few seconds." She hit the Mute button. "It's Martin."

"You'll want somewhere quiet." Paul motioned to the back door and helped her slip into her coat.

Walking across the back porch, she took the phone off mute and put it to her ear. Solid white lay across the fields, the night silent as new snow fell from the black sky. "I'm here." Snow crunched under her feet as she went into the yard. She waited for him to speak, praying he'd forgiven her and was ready to embrace happiness again.

"We're gearing up here for a musical

blowout. It's a celebration because I received notice earlier today that I passed my engineering exams."

"Congratulations! Although I never doubted you would. Was Hawaii every bit as glorious as you'd hoped?"

"It was even better."

"I'm glad you weren't disappointed. Kevin and Lissa haven't stopped talking about it yet."

Silence hung, and she waited.

"I, uh, I get it, Hannah. I mean, I'm the one who ended things, and I understood even before that, but now all of it makes sense. I'd always banked that with enough time and gentle pressure, you'd become a perfect fit. When I talked you into moving out of the cabin or the dozens of other things I was always pushing you to do, my hope was to get you comfortable in my world."

She figured this was his way of telling her she was right to return to Paul and he was ready to move on. Relief eased its way through her, and tears blurred her vision.

A knock on a door filtered through the line.

"It's open," Martin said.

Hannah couldn't hear all the words being spoken to him, but it sounded like Amy

Clarke's voice, telling him where she'd be when he was off the phone.

"Okay, I'll be there in a minute. Listen, Hannah, Kevin and Lissa are asking a lot about seeing you. They're off next Thursday and Friday. You could take them through the weekend too, unless you're schedule isn't free."

"Really?" Her resolve broke, and she sobbed.

He had to be doing a lot better. Before he left for Hawaii, he wouldn't even hint that he might let her see Kevin and Lissa again, but now, if they wanted to see her, he'd allow it. The plan would need to fit around his schedule, which seemed more than fair, and exhilaration danced within her.

"You know, if you could stop crying . . ."

She wiped her tears, trying to contain her excitement and relief. "Sorry. Go ahead."

"I just figured you needed to know I'm fine." He paused. "No, I'm better than fine now. I know we're both right where we're supposed to be."

As if boulders were being removed, guilt lifted, and she couldn't find her voice.

"Nothing meant more to Zabeth than keeping the Palmer family together as much as possible. She grew too weak and died before that happened, but you came in, and . . . well, you finished what she began, and now Kevin, Lissa, and I are a family. If it took falling for you for that to happen, I'd do it again."

"Thank you, Martin."

"Just give Laura a call next week, and she'll meet you with the children at the cabin or the clinic or wherever. Okay?"

"I'll be grateful for this forever."

"Back at you. Bye."

Closing her eyes, she shut her phone. Like the snowfall around her, memories seemed to swirl and land gently in random places. As much as she grieved for the pain she'd caused Martin, she could never regret the privilege of being by Zabeth's side — a dying, shunned woman, desperate to hold together whatever could be salvaged in the Palmer family.

Maybe Martin was right; she'd helped change him, and because of that, he was firmly rooted in Kevin's and Lissa's lives.

God was able to bring good out of tragedy, missteps, and even stupid mistakes. Gazing into the snowy dark sky, she trusted God more than ever. "Nevertheless."

Wanting to see Paul alone for a minute before joining the others, she opened her cell phone and called him.

"Hey, you can't win if you're not in here

to play."

"Meaning you're losing for the both of us."

The back door opened, and Paul walked across the porch and into the yard. "Something like that, yeah." With one look at her, a smile crossed his handsome face. He tucked his phone back into his pocket. "That was a good call."

She stretched her arms out and twirled around before she ran to him and threw her arms around his neck, laughing.

He held her so very gently with her feet dangling off the ground. "I love you, Hannah. Always have. Always will."

He set her feet on the ground, staring into her eyes. Leaning down, he brought his lips to hers, and the power of every once-forbidden hope and dream danced as a reality within her. He kissed across her cheek and down her neck.

Her knees gave way a bit, and she backed away.

"Hannah?"

"I just need to sit." She sank onto the cold snow. Tilting her head, she looked into his eyes. "Talk about sweeping a girl off her feet."

Clearly the reason for her needing to sit began to dawn on him, and he chuckled.

"You had me worried for a minute. Are you sure —"

"I'm sure."

Paul offered her a hand, but the gesture was more than a moment of help. Everything she had ever wanted or would ever want stood with open arms — just waiting for her. She slid into his embrace, wrapping her arms around him and resting the side of her face against his chest. "I love you, Paul." Her voice cracked, and tears threatened. "I love you."

EPILOGUE

The warmth of waking with Paul's arms around her caused gratefulness to work through her. The first rays of light waited just below the horizon to stretch across the land, dispelling the dark that filled every corner of the room. Enjoying the rumble of the attic fan as it drew in mixed fragrances through the opened window — fresh-cut hay, their vegetable garden, and hints of the patch of woods surrounding the creek — Hannah relished the start of a new day. Life itself stirred her, making her feel as if she were soaring over fields like an eagle. The feeling had become a permanent part of her as she watched Paul build this home during their engagement. The house sat on the ten acres of land that Gram gave them, but the porch, with its ceiling fan for summer and outdoor fireplace for winter, was their favorite spot. It overlooked the footbridge where he had proposed.

The "Past and Future" quilt lay across the foot of their bed, waiting patiently for cold weather to arrive. Her Mennonite prayer Kapp rested on the nightstand beside her. Next to it sat the hand-carved box Paul had made for her, one that held years of letters from people she loved — Paul, Daed, Mamm, Lissa, and Kevin, even a rare note from Martin or Amy, telling her when and where they were traveling so she or Paul could make plans to pick the children up from Laura.

The letters were a reminder that love didn't have to be perfect when forgiveness was applied. That truth guided her through each part of life — even though her father had not yet allowed her in his home. Accepting her Daed for who he was kept hurt from stealing from her when he hadn't attended her wedding. She found that same understanding was able to strengthen her when it came to dealing with difficult people from all walks of life.

Her mother came to visit her on at least one nonchurch Sunday a month. Although Hannah saw her Daed here and there when moving about the community and he always spoke to her, she was more grateful that he wrote to her a few times each year and came by her clinic on occasion just to see her. He had come to their home to eat with Paul and her once, but the idea of his daughter having electrical and phone lines coming into her house worried him. In spite of his unbending beliefs, he tried to open his mind and heart to her. And she, in turn, tried to identify with him. The reality of forgiveness planted and growing in her daily life amazed her. She couldn't claim to understand how it worked, but the freedom it brought was undeniable. And when she got it wrong — overreacted, underreacted, or flared with an incorrect response — forgiveness waited to be embraced.

Running her fingers over the honorary mother's ring that now hung on a necklace she hid under her Plain clothing during the day, Hannah could hardly believe the children were on the brink of becoming teens and that Martin and Amy would soon celebrate five years of marriage. The former Amy Clarke not only filled everything Martin had been looking for in Hannah, but she adored and respected him deeply, bringing a sense of well-being to him that he richly deserved. As much as it grieved Hannah, Faye had never returned, and Hannah doubted that she was still alive. Thankfully, Kevin and Lissa seemed to be doing well, gleaning life lessons from the two households — Palmer and Waddell — that loved them unconditionally.

Zabeth's cabin was a second home to Paul and her. During the school year Hannah worked for Dr. Lehman's clinic one weekend a month, leading a quilting Q and A on Saturday. In the summer she worked at the clinic twice a month. Each time, Paul and she stayed at the cabin. Kevin and Lissa would often stay with them, and in the spring of each year, Paul helped them plant a garden. Kevin chose to grow only watermelons that he sold door to door in Martin's neighborhood. Lissa never wanted to sell anything from her garden. She wanted her produce used for their meals, or she'd have Paul drive her to the local mission, where she could give the food away.

Hannah arched her back ever so slightly, stretching just a little, but she felt Paul stir.

He planted a kiss on her shoulder and rubbed across her rounded stomach. "Sleep, Lion-heart, it's still dark."

But she couldn't will herself back to sleep. Didn't want to, really. The love that ran between them and the love they gave away to others kept life renewed and exciting. For six years Paul and she had contentedly accepted being without children, enjoying every part of the life they'd been blessed with. Always proud of her work and school accomplishments, Paul took satisfaction in their busy schedules, and they continually grew in finding pleasure in each other's arms — unlike anything they'd expected. And now . . . she could feel their child moving within her.

After attending the deliveries of so many babies, she was even more amazed by the miracle of what was taking place inside her. At twenty-seven years old and with her master's in nursing, she was expecting their first child in mid-December.

Although she worked at the Plain Ways clinic just behind the Better Path, she spent much of her time going to Amish homes and visiting. She met resistance from some, especially the men, but she applied respect and forgiveness and continued to make headway talking with the families about women's health issues.

When it suited Paul, he'd come to the birthing clinic during the long nights and stay in the sleeping room with her. When they were off, they had treasured friends to enjoy — some Amish, some Plain Mennonite, and some Englischers.

Hannah's thoughts continued to roam. Thankfully for Mary's health, she didn't conceive too often. She and Luke had one more child thus far, a son. In the years since Matthew and Kathryn had married, they'd had three children. Kathryn loved organizing her household and working beside Matthew. They'd built a small home near the shops, and Kathryn brought more joy to Matthew than could be measured in a lifetime.

Hannah believed Dorcas's regret for what she'd done was real and her repentance complete, but the heartache of losing Paul still seemed to cling to her. The battle to keep Lyme disease from ravaging her body was a long one, taking years of medicine and physical therapy to regain her health. She was now overseas, doing missions.

Gracie, Paul and Hannah's Australian Shepherd, came to the side of the bed. Hannah scratched her head, thinking of all the dogs Sarah had trained and sold over the years. Sarah was still single, not yet trusting her stability enough to marry and have children. She remained on her medicine and in counseling. Moreover she trusted Paul's and Hannah's word against any lies her emotions or mind conjured up. In spite of her times of struggling with mental health issues, she continued on, being as productive as possible, sheltering rescued Australian Shepherds. The community had helped fence three acres surrounding Luke's old place for her dogs, and she trained Aussies for all kinds of jobs — from herding sheep to herding Canada geese to helping farmers guard their crops from deer. She also trained dogs to become working companions for several physically handicapped children. Giving Gracie a final pat, Hannah said a quick prayer of thanks for Sarah. God continued to bring healing in her sister's life and ways for Sarah to use her gifts to help others.

Paul brushed locks of hair off Hannah's neck and kissed it, causing goose flesh to run down her. He drew a sleepy breath. "I love you, Hannah." He planted another kiss on her neck. "Are we up for the day?"

"The joys and victories and challenges of the day are calling. Can you hear them?" She put his hand over the left side of her stomach. "And your son seems to be up for a while too. You don't have to be." But she knew he would. They seemed unable to take the other one's presence for granted.

"It's not even daylight . . . again. He's taking after his mother already?" he teased.

She sat up, smacking him in the face with a pillow.

He laughed, deflecting the bombardment before he pulled her into his arms, and she snuggled against his bare chest. Throughout their years together, the laughter that rang through their small home as they juggled work with play continued to bring healing to both of them.

They worked with healthy people to keep them healthy and with the unhealthy of mind or body to help them find or regain their health. Life didn't always go the way the suffering ones wanted, but Hannah and Paul drew their strength and peace from things they could never fully understand, that inside the God of *nevertheless,* abundant life could always be found — even on a fallen planet.

"Nevertheless," she whispered.

Paul's warm hand gently moved to hers, and he interlaced their fingers. "Nevertheless."

ACKNOWLEDGMENTS

To those who believed, helped, and encouraged — your faithfulness made this novel, as well as this series, possible. Thank you!

Shannon Hill, my editor and mentor at WaterBrook Multnomah. Marci Burke, my critique partner and dear friend. You two are amazing.

Miriam Flaud, my Old Order Amish friend. Your companionship alone has made this journey worthwhile.

Steve Laube, my agent. I stand amazed — from handling stress for me to helping me get a handle on a new project.

Eldo and Dorcas Miller, whose expertise and insights about the Plain Mennonite kept my course steady throughout this journey. Your prayers have sustained me over and over again.

Joan Kunaniec, whose wisdom in the ways of the Plain Mennonite life has been a blessing beyond words. Your knowledge, deep.

Your willingness to share, complete.

Jeffry J. Bizon, MD, OB/GYN, whose medical knowledge and energy for this three-book project have been greater than my gratitude can cover. Kathy Bizon, whose friendship, encouragement, and brainstorming help keep me focused.

Vicki Cato, RN, outpatient surgery Northeast Georgia Health System, who's always willing to answer medical questions.

Terry Stucky, whose time and insights into the story and character arc of this three-book series were very beneficial.

Rhonda Shonk, Office Manager, Alliance City Schools Career Centre and the Robert T. White School of Practical Nursing, whose knowledge continued to keep Hannah's schooling experiences accurate.

Carol Bartley, my line editor, whose gentle but thorough edits are trustworthy and absolute as we turn each final manuscript into as seamless a story as possible. I would not have wanted to do this without you!

And a special thank-you to everyone on the WaterBrook team — sales, marketing, publicity, and cover art. I'll never know how I managed to get to work with such a gifted group, but I'm deeply grateful.

GLOSSARY

aa — also, too

an — on

Arewet — word

bin — am

bin kumme — have come

bis — until

bischt — are

Bobbeli — baby

Bsuch — visit

bsuche — to visit

da — the

Daadi Haus — grandfather's house. Generally this refers to a house that is attached to or is near the main house and belongs to a grandparent. Many times the main house belonged to the grandparents when they were raising their family. The main house is usually passed down to a son, who takes over the responsibilities his parents once had. The grandparents then move into the smaller place and usually have fewer responsibilities.

Daed — dad or father

dei — your

denk — think

denki — thank you

die — the

do — here

do yetz — recently

draus — out

drei — three

du — you [singular]

eens — one

Englischer — a non-Amish person. Mennonite sects whose women wear the prayer Kapps are not considered Englischers and are often referred to as Plain Mennonites.

es — it

ganz — quite

genunk — enough

glei — soon

Grossmammi — grandmother

gut — good

hab — have

hatt — difficult or hard

Hatzer — hearts

helfe — help

ich — I

in — in

iss — is

kann — can

Kapp — a prayer covering or cap

kumm — come

letz — wrong

Liewer — dear (used when addressing males past preschool age)

Liewi — dear (used when addressing females and young children)

loss uns blaudere — let's talk

Mamm — mom or mother

Mammi — shortened term of endearment for grandmother

mei — my

mitgebrocht — brought

net — not

nix — nothing

Pennsylvania Dutch — Pennsylvania German. The word *Dutch* in this phrase has nothing to do with the Netherlands. The original word was *Deutsch,* which means "German." The Amish speak some High German (used in church services) and Pennsylvania German (Pennsylvania Dutch), and after a certain age, they are taught English.

raus — out

rumschpringe — running around

saag — tell

uns — us

unsrer — our

verbinne — unite

viel — much
was — what
wege — about
Welt — world
wunderbaar — wonderful
ya — yes (pronounced *jah*)
zu — too
zwee — two

* Glossary taken from Eugene S. Stine, *Pennsylvania German Dictionary* (Birdsboro, PA: Pennsylvania German Society, 1996), and the usage confirmed by an instructor of the Pennsylvania Dutch language.

ABOUT THE AUTHOR

Cindy Woodsmall is the author of the best-selling novels *When the Heart Cries* and *When the Morning Comes.* Her real-life connections with the Plain Mennonite and Old Order Amish families enrich her novels with authenticity. Cindy lives in Georgia with her husband, three sons, and one daughter-in-law.